A Death In The Making

A tale of the 25th Century

A Death In The Making

INGE MELDGAARD

A Novel

Published by Inge Meldgaard
18 Colby Drive, Belgrave Heights
Victoria, Australia 3160

Australian distributor:

Digital Print Australia
135 Gilles Street, Adelaide
South Australia, Australia 5000
www.digitalprintaustralia.com
books@digitalprintaustralia.com

Revised Edition: June 2013

National Library of Australia Cataloguing-in-Publication entry:

Author: Inge Meldgaard
Title: A Death In The Making
ISBN: 978-0-646-55445-7
Dewey Number: A823.4

Cover design and artwork by Inge Meldgaard
Website: redmatilda.artworkfolio.com

Cover photograph of Norwegian Forest Cat:
Copyright ataglier-Fotolia.com

To Harry

'We must, between periods of digging in the dark, endeavour always to transform our tears into knowledge.'

Alain de Botton
The Consolations of Philosophy
2001

Thanks are due to my sister Tove for her generous assistance with editing this manuscript and to author Liz Davies for proofreading the first edition. This revised edition owes a great deal to the expertise of author Kathryn Deering, whose help has been invaluable.

MAIN CHARACTERS

The Peacekeepers

Freddi	Jamaican, based in Brisbane, Australia.
Nyneve	Stanthorpe, Queensland, Australia.
Smithson	Stanthorpe, Queensland, Australia.
Chiu Liow Jones	Based in Melbourne, Australia. Half-brother to Freddi.
Morag MacIain	Coordinator, Federation Special Investigation Unit, Luzern, Switzerland.

Former and Current Residents of Stanthorpe, Queensland

Rhianna O'Connor	Born 2414 in Stanthorpe. Travel consultant in Brisbane.
Leihana	Rhianna's mother.
Robert	Lives near Stanthorpe. Rhianna's cousin.
Agathea	Rhianna's aunt. Lives with Robert.
Eirann	Robert's father. Brother to Leihana's bondmate.
Marietta Ross	Attended school in Stanthorpe. Now lives in Melbourne.
Ruth Baillieu	Attended school in Stanthorpe. Now lives in Brisbane.
Edric	Attended school in Stanthorpe. Now lives in Brisbane.
Stefano Salvarez	Attended school in Stanthorpe. Now lives in Brisbane and is a friend to both Rhianna and Edric.
Margrethe	Former Stanthorpe Preceptor specialising in mathematics. Now ninety years of age and living in Stanthorpe.

Others

Meng Jarrah	Australian Palaeontologist and Forensics expert. Bondmate to Freddi.
Gwenllian	Works with the Werribee Breeding Centre for Cats in Melbourne.
Michiko Yamada	Silversmith by profession. Former bondmate to Kenjiro Kakura (see *The Cicada*). Cultural and Artistic Director of Wyvern Meridian.

Felicity   Michiko's adopted daughter.

The Cats

Shela   Companion to Freddi.
Sylvie   Companion to Rhianna.
Harriet   Companion to Margrethe.
Peri   Companion to Stefano Salvarez.
Zarifa   Companion to Edric.

PART I

CHAPTER ONE

Lying warm and snug between the sleeping bodies of her two companions, Shela yawned, rolled over, and idly stretched out a paw to pat Freddi's hair. When Freddi murmured and twitched, resisting being woken from her delicious dream, Shela stood and carefully walked up the bed until she could brush Freddi's face with her whiskers. A hand came from under the covers to push her away, but the huge black cat was insistent.

Blinking, and rubbing her nose where it had been tickled, Freddi propped herself up on one elbow to stroke Shela's head. The cat began purring, so loudly that Meng Jarrah woke up as well and put an arm around Freddi's waist in an attempt to draw her back down into the cosy comfort of their bed. It was too late. Their hungry feline was demanding breakfast!

Freddi kissed Meng Jarrah on the forehead, then lightly on her lips, saying, 'She won't let up until I get her something to eat, my love.' Meng Jarrah held her close, passionately returning the kiss, but when Shela wailed in protest, reluctantly released her. 'I give up!' she exclaimed, laughing. 'So, what will you get *us* for breakfast?'

Freddi grinned, got out of bed, stretched, then reached for her robe. 'You'll see. Come on Shela, and stop being such a nuisance!' The cat jumped onto the floor with a loud thump and bounded along the corridor towards the kitchen, tail in the air.

Meng Jarrah stayed in bed a few minutes longer, idly watching a large huntsman spider move slowly along the wall opposite. When it crawled down low enough to be caught, she got up, neatly captured the creature and carried it outside, then had her shower and dressed. Yawning, and contemplating how best to spend her day, Meng Jarrah had just finished brushing her thick, dark brown curls when Freddi called out from the kitchen for her to come and have breakfast, which she had placed on the verandah table so they could enjoy the view while they ate. Despite being the middle of winter, the sun shone brightly in the clear sky, and the air was fresh with the wonderful tang of eucalyptus.

The view was impressive, for the house lay close to the foot of Mount Cootha and was surrounded on all sides by well-established, centuries-old gardens. As an added bonus, the nearby Brisbane River provided a delightful destination when they wanted to use up some of their own, and Shela's, excess energy with a good long run. In overall appearance, their home was a replica of an early nineteenth-century style known as 'the Queenslander', with an extensive verandah and ornate latticework to enhance its appeal. However, as was now customary throughout Australia, the building had self-sufficient energy, water and waste-disposal systems, and was modern in all its functional aspects.

After gobbling down her substantial meal of oat porridge and soymilk, Shela stretched in satisfaction, then found a patch of sunlight to sit in while she cleaned her face. Once finished, she rolled lazily onto her back, trying to entice someone into stroking her stomach. However, much to her disgust, they ignored her for the time being – Freddi and Meng Jarrah were too intent on enjoying their own breakfast of strong, freshly brewed coffee, savoury pancakes with melted cheese, and fresh peaches.

When Freddi at long last gave Shela the attention she had begged for, the cat caught at her hands in delight, although with long claws carefully sheathed. Meng Jarrah turned from the last of her food to watch, chuckling at the sight of her two friends, who had taken to rolling around on the floor together, pretending to wrestle. They were a beautiful pair. Freddi's black hair, long and dressed in ringlets, hung down over her face as she played, hiding her unusual light golden eyes.

Just as Freddi finally stood up to take a shower, her comlink chimed. To her dismay, it was the Coordinator of the Brisbane Peacekeeping Force.

'So sorry to interrupt your morning, Freddi, but there's been a suspicious death and we want everyone who's part of the criminal investigation squad on hand. I know you were looking forward to an uninterrupted day off, but it appears to be an ugly case. You'd better pack your bags – you'll probably have to stay in the area for a while.'

'Where am I going?' asked Freddi, suppressing her shock at the news. Murder, if it *was* murder, was a relatively rare occurrence, although Freddi had had more than the usual peacekeeper's experience with it when, six years ago, a rogue corporation used it as one of their weapons in an attempt to compete with the Federation for control of the world's highly lucrative market in forest products.

'Stanthorpe,' replied the Coordinator. 'It's a couple of hundred kilometres from Brisbane – on the New England Highway, not far from the New South Wales border. It's fairly high above sea level, in case you haven't heard of it, so take some warm clothing. Apparently it's cold there at this time of year. One of the locals told me the birdbaths froze last night!' He gave a brief smile at the notion, quite foreign to the usual Queensland climate. 'When can you get there?'

'I should be able to leave in about thirty minutes. Send me what you have in the meantime and I'll read it on the way. Do you want me to bring Meng Jarrah, if she has time?'

'Yes, that's a good thought. We don't yet know how long the body's been there, or the time of death, which means a pollen analysis would be helpful, as well as any other details she can provide, botanical or otherwise. I've already sent our own entomologist and the Stanthorpe pathologist will be there as well. I'll let them know Meng Jarrah might be coming with you. Anyway, if you give me a call once you've arrived and have had an initial look-see, we can take it from there. The local peacekeepers have secured the site and begun some preliminary work, but they're waiting for us before they do much more... Oh, and your transport should arrive soon, so good luck,' he added, before closing the connection.

Meng Jarrah had been listening and nodded when Freddi turned to her with a brief explanation. 'Of course I'll come with you. If you're planning to be away for a while, I'd prefer to come along and help. Our forest regeneration trials at Lamington are doing extremely well, as you know, and there's nothing urgent about any of my other research to prevent me from going with you.'

Delighted at the idea of a long trip, as well as the chance to explore somewhere new, Shela purred and padded over to the walk-in closet where her leash was kept. She pulled it down from its hook and carried it to the front door, then sat down to wait. Before long, Freddi and Meng Jarrah had packed the few things they needed and were ready to leave. As promised, an airjet was humming quietly on the trafficway a short distance from the house. Once they were all comfortably settled, it lifted and sped off, with Shela gazing out the windows, ears twitching and nose pressed to the plastiglass window.

Stanthorpe was first settled by Europeans after the discovery of tin at Quartpot Creek in 1872. Over time, it grew into a thriving agricultural community, and its wineries, flower farms and orchards were still famous throughout Australia. As they flew over the distinctive granite outcrops surrounding the small town, the two women stared at each other in astonishment. The whole district was spectacular!

The airjet finally landed in a clearing several kilometres south of the town, in a region that was part of the former Girraween National Park, now part of a wider conservation area. The pilot climbed out and watched in amusement as Shela leapt to the ground, gleefully sniffing the air, as well as everything else within reach, tail waving high. Meanwhile, Meng Jarrah and Freddi gazed in awe at the area's angular granite tors and massive boulders, which sometimes gave the illusion of teetering on the point of falling.

They didn't need to be shown where to find the body of the person whose death had defiled this beautiful place; Shela led the way to where a small group of local peacekeepers and the two forensics experts were patiently probing and then recording what they saw. Approaching with caution, Freddi called out, and one of the peacekeepers turned and walked slowly towards them. The woman hesitated before introducing herself, somewhat taken aback by the sight of Shela and her unusually tall and striking companions. At two hundred and fifteen centimetres, Freddi was some thirty-five centimetres above average height, while Meng Jarrah was only a little shorter.

Understanding her expression, Freddi smiled and said, 'I was hoping our Coordinator would tell you about Shela. She goes everywhere with me, and often helps solve our cases.'

The peacekeeper, whose name was Nyneve, met Shela's inquisitive gaze and shook hands with them. 'Well, any additional help will always be useful, I'm sure,' she replied, then indicated they should all walk back to where the body lay.

A cold wind had sprung up and Meng Jarrah ran a slim, dark hand through her hair, brushing it from her eyes and shivering, despite the warm clothing. When they reached the vicinity of the body, she stared at it, frowning. Having worked on a part-time basis for over two years as a forensics consultant to the Brisbane Peacekeeping Force, this was still the first suspected murder victim Meng Jarrah had seen, although not the first violent death. What she saw appeared to have been a relatively young woman of about forty years of age, slender, although well built, with long, wavy black hair and what might once have been a beautiful face. Now, some of it had been eaten away. She was not wearing any clothing, only a pair of simple silver ear circlets.

The person who was evidently the entomologist was carefully collecting specimens of maggots and insects from the body, as well as taking small pieces of the tissue from which they came. The other forensics specialist was taking samples of earth, while meticulously searching for any foreign objects that could have belonged to the dead woman, or to whoever was with her.

Freddi shook her head, saddened by the sight. Turning to Nyneve, she said, 'I think Meng Jarrah had better start gathering information about the local flora. It looks as if the weather might change soon, don't you think? Also, who discovered the body?'

Nyneve was studying the sky, a worried expression on her face. 'Yes, I think we're in for quite a storm. We probably have only a couple of hours at the most before it starts. Fortunately, our trackers have already worked out that two people carried the woman here and they've marked the likely route taken. Also, no signs of a struggle have been found, so it's possible she was either dead already, unconscious, or sedated. Now, before I answer your question, I'll just have a quick word with my colleagues...won't be a tick,' and she headed off.

As they waited, Meng Jarrah donned protective clothing and unpacked her kit. The entire local flora would already be on file, so her main objective would be to catalogue all the vegetation in the immediate area and to take sets of soil and other samples along the path identified by the trackers.

Before long, Nyneve returned with the peacekeeper who recorded the apparent route and who had meticulously compiled a report containing the evidence that led to his conclusions. He shook Meng Jarrah's hand and introduced himself as Smithson, offering to show her the way. She quickly accepted, but before setting off, waited to hear what Nyneve had to say.

'It was a pair of Italian bushwalkers and their cat who found the body,' Nyneve told them. 'Beautiful creature,' she added, remembering the animal's deep blue eyes and silky, chocolate-coloured fur. 'Their names are Pietro and Elena. Naturally, they're deeply distressed, so we took them to the medcentre in Stanthorpe. We haven't pressed them for much information...just let them talk for as long as they wanted. They obviously *needed* to talk, because with a few simple promptings they gave us a fairly complete picture anyway. It seems that when they rounded that huge teetering boulder up there,' and Nyneve pointed to a spot about three hundred metres away, 'their cat screamed and bolted back the way they'd come. Pietro ran after her, but Elena could see an unusual mound of rocks down here and decided to investigate. She could smell something off by the time she came close, but very bravely in my opinion, covered her nose and mouth and then removed some of the rocks to see what was in there.'

Hunching her shoulders slightly against the cold wind, Nyneve held up an evidence bag she had brought with her. 'This red blanket covered the entire body before Elena moved it aside a little. When she saw a hand, she cried out and vomited, yet had the wits to call us once she'd calmed down. By that time, Pietro had caught their cat and was struggling to bring her down here. However, she wouldn't come any closer. In the end, he left her tied to a small tree and ran down to join Elena. He removed a few more rocks from where he thought the body's head should be, and then they both moved away from the smell to sit with their cat and wait for us to arrive.'

'It must have been hard for them, with their cat in hysterics,' said Freddi, looking back to where the body still lay.

'Yes,' agreed Nyneve. 'Just finding a dead body would have been bad enough, but the state they were in by the time we arrived had a lot to do with the effect their cat was having on them. We decided to call the Breeding Centre in Brisbane to get some advice on how to calm her down; nothing our local medcentre or animal healer could do helped. She was trembling and panting so much, we all thought she was about to collapse.'

'What did the Breeding Centre suggest?' asked Meng Jarrah.

'We were to give her a strong sedative to put her into a deep sleep while we waited for someone from Melbourne to arrive. Apparently there's a woman from the Breeding Centre there by the name of Gwenllian who has an unusually strong bond with cats.' Nyneve glanced at her comlink to see what the time was, so didn't at first notice the astonishment on the faces of both her listeners. Looking up again, the peacekeeper said, 'She should be in Stanthorpe in less than an hour... Do you know her? You both seem incredibly surprised.'

Freddi and Meng Jarrah nodded. 'Oh yes,' replied Meng Jarrah, 'we know her very well indeed.'

They arrived in Stanthorpe as the first drops of rain fell. The old town was quiet, orderly and pretty, with very few people walking along the brightly coloured trafficway. Meng Jarrah absent-mindedly noted that the flowers covering its surface were quite different from those commonly used in Brisbane, or for that matter, anywhere else she'd seen in Australia. 'Ah well,' she thought, 'no time to dwell upon things like that now,' amazed, under the circumstances, she had even noticed.

When their airjet landed, they all concentrated on unloading the body and their specimens. The morgue formed a rear annexe to the medcentre, where the practitioner on duty was waiting for them. She had never encountered a death quite like this one before, and beyond making the facilities available, had no wish to be involved, particularly if it turned out to be a murder. After one reluctant, sideways glance at the covered form on the hoverbed, she led them to the examination room.

'All the door and storage locks are ready for your security details to be entered, and so is our building's knowledge base. You can code in your voice patterns and handprints whenever you want. This main door will respond to your retina scans and no one else's...other than mine and those of the other staff when they're on duty, of course. Do you think this will be enough, Nyneve?' asked the practitioner, gazing at them all with a somewhat frozen expression.

Nyneve said it was ample and thanked her warmly for the help, at which point the practitioner left, appearing immensely relieved.

The facilities were excellent, thought Freddi, as she surveyed the large room, with its shiny equipment and plastiglass-fronted cabinets and drawers. Meng Jarrah had already spotted a suitable workstation where she could examine the material she had collected, so began unpacking then setting up her equipment. The entomologist hummed to himself as he did likewise, while the pathologist was busy laying out the body on one of the examination benches. Fortunately for everyone else, the bench was located in its own screened containment field to ensure no one other than the pathologist had to either view or smell the corpse unless they needed to.

After putting on sterile coveralls, Freddi and Nyneve entered the containment field, gave their names and Federation identity numbers to the pathology computer and pressed their thumbs onto its keypad. The pathologist then made a formal statement giving the current location of the deceased, where the body was found, who found it, and the names of the people who were to undertake the initial investigation. He also confirmed the time and date: fourteen hundred hours, sixteen minutes, on Saturday the fifteenth of July 2456.

Meanwhile, Shela lay quietly outside the morgue in an inconspicuous spot, tail moving gently from side to side, her eyes narrowed, sniffing the new and intriguing scents. She knew better than to interrupt anyone during these proceedings with her own views on the matter. The cat stretched out her front legs and rested her chin on them, content to listen and to watch the little she could see.

Pietro and Elena gazed at Gwenllian in wonder as the slender, pale-skinned woman cradled their cat, Bella, in her arms, touching her forehead to the cat's and crooning softly. A strange rainbow-coloured aura surrounded them both, shimmering in the winter sunlight coming into the room through a break in the dark clouds outside. The rain had stopped, and except for Gwenllian's hypnotic voice, the silence in the room was profound. The plaintive cries of fear, which had sounded in their heads since Bella first detected the aroma of death and again when she woke from her induced sleep, began to subside, to be replaced with a surge of pleasurable excitement as the cat recognised Gwenllian as one of her own kind.

When Gwenllian finally gave Bella a hug and stood up, the aura disappeared as suddenly as it had formed. 'She'll be fine now,' she said, 'and might even be fairly mischievous for a few days. I'm a little unusual, you see, and tend to have that effect on cats. I have telepathic powers too, just as they do.' Gwenllian inclined her head and smiled at Bella's companions, her hazel eyes seeming almost too large for her thin, oval face.

Both Pietro and Elena continued to stare at her in astonishment. Pietro was the first to recover. 'This really is too much for one day, you realise. How are we to comprehend this?' he said, taking Elena's hand in his and holding out the other to Gwenllian, who grasped it firmly in her own. 'You have our profound thanks for bringing our dear Bella back to her senses, however you did it. But, telepathy in humans? We have never come across such a thing before!'

'Have you always had this power, if you don't mind my asking?' added Elena softly, studying Gwenllian as she might a new species from another planet, although with respect as well as awe.

'No, it developed without warning almost six years ago. At first I didn't want to believe it was happening, but events overtook me and I was forced to accept it. I've worked with the Breeding Centre in Melbourne for about five years now. It's one of the places where Australian cats are bred and trained. The gentechs there, as well as the feline nursing mothers, helped me develop my mental abilities and learn to control them. My range is now greater than that of most cats, although the skills are practically the same. The only differences I've noticed so far are the creation of the aura under certain circumstances and, not surprisingly, I can deal with more abstract concepts than they can. I *am* human and *they* are still cats, so of course this fundamental difference in our minds allows me to understand things they can't.'

Gwenllian smiled again, and this time they returned the smile, while Bella rubbed herself against Gwenllian's legs, purring contentedly.

'The nursing mothers,' asked Pietro, 'did they accept you as one of their own, or were they alarmed by you, to begin with?'

'No,' answered Gwenllian, remembering her first encounter with the cats at the Breeding Centre, 'they immediately recognised me as one of their own and treated me as if I was one of their kittens.' She laughed. 'They told me off if I didn't do as they wanted. Evidently, I was a bit slow to learn.'

There was a quiet knock at the door and the practitioner entered, raised an eyebrow, and cast a questioning look at Gwenllian, who nodded and smiled. Turning to the others, the practitioner said, 'I gather everyone is feeling a great deal better? Good. I'd like to do a final check, and afterwards you can go back to your lodgings, if you like.'

Pietro and Elena waited patiently while they were examined, and then, when they began to collect their coats and other belongings, the practitioner said, 'The peacekeepers will want to speak with you tomorrow, or so they've asked me to tell you. Gwenllian, they'd like you to be present, if you don't mind, just in case your help is required. Shock sometimes returns in cases like this.'

Gwenllian immediately agreed. 'Perhaps I can stay at the same communal house as you?' she asked the two Italians. 'Do you think they have any spare rooms?'

'Well, let us call and find out,' replied Pietro, sounding practical and level-headed. Before long, he nodded to Gwenllian and handed her his comlink so she could speak with the house supervisor.

Having made their arrangements, they were about to take advantage of the break in the storm to make their way to the communal house when another knock at the door sounded. Gwenllian smiled to herself as she turned around; she had wondered how long it would take before Meng Jarrah left the morgue to find her. It hadn't been a surprise to sense her friend's presence, as well as Freddi and Shela's, when she arrived in Stanthorpe. There were very few crimes this serious, and very few peacekeepers with sufficient experience to be chosen to help with the investigation. It was therefore only logical Freddi would be here, and equally logical that Meng Jarrah would accompany her to assist.

Meng Jarrah came in and swept Gwenllian into her arms, lifting her off the floor in a ferocious hug before kissing her soundly on each cheek. 'Gwen, it's wonderful to see you again!' she exclaimed. 'It's been over a year. How are all your cats?'

Gwenllian laughed. 'They're all marvellous. More and more of them are becoming official members of the Melbourne Peacekeeping Force. They seem to thrive on accompanying the peacekeepers, once they understand they have to refrain from taking matters into their own hands, so to speak.'

'Yes, they can be a tad underhanded if they're allowed to be,' quipped Meng Jarrah, grinning broadly. Turning to Pietro and Elena, she shook hands with them and said, 'Hi, I'm with the investigation team from Brisbane. I'm glad to see you're both beginning to feel better after finding the body this morning and that your cat is as well.' Crouching down, she held out a hand for the cat to sniff, which Bella did, very delicately, before licking one of the offered fingers. They made an attractive sight, thought Pietro. The woman's skin was almost the same colour as their cat's fur.

Meng Jarrah gently stroked Bella's head, then stood up, saying, 'Freddi's here as well, Gwen, but you probably know that already.'

'Yes, and I'm delighted. It means we should be able to clear all this up fairly quickly, don't you think?'

'Are you staying on, too?' asked Meng Jarrah.

'It might be a good idea. Nyneve knows about my work with the Melbourne Peacekeepers, so thought that since I had the time, I could be of use here, at least to begin with. Naturally, it's up to Freddi to agree as well, but I don't think she'd mind some extra help, do you?'

'I'm fairly certain she'd be very pleased, but you can ask her yourself. She should be finished soon. Where are you staying?'

'In the same communal house as Pietro and Elena. What about you?'

'Nyneve has offered us her spare room – at least for the time being. I guess it depends upon how long we're here. However, enough chat for now. I'd better get back to work... Do you want to join us for dinner tonight?'

Bella sent a silent cry of protest to Gwenllian; she wanted to spend more time with this strange grimalkin.

'Would you mind if I stayed with these good people instead?' replied Gwenllian. 'There'll be plenty of time to catch up tomorrow.' She briefly touched Meng Jarrah's hand. 'Tell Freddi and Shela I look forward to seeing them. I'll be here at 09:00, if that would suit?'

Meng Jarrah agreed, and before returning to her work, gave Gwenllian one last hug.

CHAPTER TWO

With the assistance of the entomologist, they were able to estimate that the woman had been dead five days. The pathologist now combed her hair more tenderly than any hairdresser might have done, while her skin had already been closely examined before being washed. Anything unusual found on its surface would be used to trace where she came from before being buried at Girraween. The fingernails contained their little secrets too. They added to the story of who she once was, as did the semen found by the swab, routinely performed for all unexplained deaths. Satisfied, the pathologist set aside all the small containers for analysis. Very little could be hidden from them now.

Meanwhile, Meng Jarrah had begun searching through the stomach and gut contents for remaining plant and animal material. Based on the available DNA fragments, a list was soon compiled of the woman's last meal. She had evidently dined well. There were traces of kangaroo, as well as rock oysters, leeks, potatoes, shitake mushrooms, chicken pâté, raspberries, wheat and rye.

Freddi raised an eyebrow when Meng Jarrah showed her the list. In an era when eating meat, especially red meat, was fairly unusual, kangaroo was only to be found in the few restaurants serving meals made from the annual cull. This meant there was every likelihood of tracking down the venue where she last ate. As to her identity, this was far more straightforward since her DNA was registered in the Federation database, as was everyone's. Her name was Rhianna O'Connor, born here in Stanthorpe forty-two years ago, although normally a resident of Brisbane.

'The phoenix tattooed on her thigh is unusual,' the pathologist remarked. 'Tattoos aren't particularly common in Australia.' Pursing his lips, he considered for a moment, his head tilted to one side. As he did, he bore an extraordinary resemblance to a wise owl, with his round face, thin, hooked nose, and enormous eyebrows that tweaked up at their outer ends. 'Her general health was extremely good,' he continued, 'but this bruise on the side of her neck, immediately below the jawbone, is odd. I can't say I've ever seen anything quite like it before, have you?'

'Well, yes, I have actually,' replied Freddi, leaning over for a better view. 'I'd say it's possible she's been in a fight — one involving someone with advanced martial arts skills, for example. It could explain the slight bruising on her breasts. Didn't you say those marks might pre-date the event that caused her death?'

'It's not entirely certain. There's a margin of error of several hours, but yes, they might. Well, we'll keep searching, given we haven't found the definite cause of death yet, which in itself is remarkable. Still, if she was struck, I'd have thought that type of blow would have killed her immediately. If so, and judging by the state of the food in her stomach and gut, it would have happened approximately three hours after she finished her last meal. At any rate, hopefully we'll know more once we have a complete toxicological analysis of her liver, as well as some detailed studies of her lungs and kidneys.'

The pathologist glanced at the nearest laboratory computer, which displayed the time in large numerals. Being already a few minutes past 19:00, he was ready to finish up for the evening. 'I think I'll take the remaining specimens I want for tomorrow then tidy her away. Would that suit you?'

Freddi nodded, looking over to where Meng Jarrah was still peering at their samples. Turning back to the pathologist, she said, 'Would 09:00 tomorrow be convenient for me to come back? I don't know when Meng Jarrah wants to finish up tonight or start again tomorrow, but I don't imagine you'd mind her staying on if she needs to?'

'Yes to the first question, and no to the second,' replied the pathologist, with a brief smile. 'It's an honour to work with Meng Jarrah, being the foremost expert in her field.' He paused, then in a low voice added, 'If you don't mind my asking, what brings her here? I would have imagined she'd still be concentrating on her research.'

Freddi returned his smile, almost as briefly. 'Forensic work is an interesting sideline that suits her,' she explained. 'It means she can sometimes keep me company while I'm working. We met five years ago, when I was part of a team unravelling an unusually complex case, which, amongst other things, involved sabotage of her research centres, as well as various Federation sites. I was the investigating peacekeeper in Myanmar, where one of her centres is located. We developed our bond through working together and have lived with each other ever since.'

The pathologist felt the two suited each other immensely, in personality as well as in appearance, with Freddi's ebony skin and strong build perfectly complementing Meng Jarrah's warm, brown features and wiry strength. 'She's Australian, isn't she?'

'Yes, her people, the Yugambeh, originally came from the Lamington region, but that was a long time ago. She still feels the strength of her ancestry though, particularly in her love of the land. She's passionate about her work, and since we met has been helping with the restoration of the Lamington region's soils and forests.'

'I see,' answered the pathologist, nodding thoughtfully. He turned away and silently placed Rhianna O'Connor's body into its cool-storage cabinet, then cleaned and tidied his worktable, all the while humming softly. Looking up at Freddi, who had watched him, fascinated by the fastidious care he had taken of the dead woman, he said, 'And what about you? Where did you originally come from?'

'Jamaica,' she replied, 'and I have a half-brother here in Australia, who was also involved in the case I mentioned. He's a peacekeeper in Melbourne and headed the investigation for a time. He was part of the reason I decided to move to Brisbane. We work well together, and sometimes share cases and information. Anyway, I'd better see how Meng Jarrah's doing then find my cat. I expect Shela's thoroughly bored by now. I'll see you tomorrow.'

Freddi walked slowly over to Meng Jarrah and lightly put an arm around her shoulders. Meng Jarrah absentmindedly took Freddi's hand in hers, pressing it to one cheek and briefly looking up before turning back to her specimens.

'Do you mind if I keep working a bit longer?' she asked, her head still bent over her work.

'No, of course not. I'm about to fetch Shela, then find something to eat before bothering Nyneve. Do you want me to bring you anything, or would you prefer to take care of yourself?'

'Umm...you could bring me something in about an hour, if you like. I'm sure I'll be ravenous by then, and with a bit of luck, I may have worked out what's puzzling me.'

At this point, Freddi heard a distinct, cat-like wail in her mind. Shela was evidently hungry, and with all this talk of food, had finally chosen to make her presence felt. Freddi gave Meng Jarrah a quick kiss, then left her to concentrate.

Shela had, in fact, been unusually bored. Normally there were so many emotional colours in the minds of the people around her that she could amuse herself by surreptitiously listening in and, very occasionally, gently nudging them in a direction she felt to be more suitable – though had never confessed to Freddi she did such things. Of course, Shela knew better than to interfere with anyone connected with one of her companion's cases. That would have meant crossing a boundary her nursing mother at the Breeding Centre in Jamaica would have totally disapproved of. She would even have given her a cuff on the ear for daring to contemplate such a thing! Today, however, Shela had been constrained to wait as patiently as possible in the anteroom to the morgue, it being out of the question for her to have wandered at large throughout the medcentre. Since her fur could cause contamination, she certainly wasn't allowed into the morgue itself; it was simply not feasible for a cat to be properly draped in protective clothing. Grimacing at the picture she conjured up in her mind, Shela sent another small wail of hunger in Freddi's direction.

As the doors finally slid open, she bounded over to her companion, stretched up, and placed her enormous paws on her midriff, purring loudly. Freddi stroked the cat's head, took hold of her paws and set her down. Crouching, she gave her an enthusiastic hug and a kiss on the forehead. Satisfied, Shela sat still while Freddi picked up her leash from a side-table and attached it to her collar.

The small anteroom held facilities for making fresh coffee, as well as a variety of good teas, a selection of fresh fruit, and a thermolyte full of enticing sweets, together with a healthy variety of snack-sized, pre-prepared meals. Freddi could easily have helped herself instead of hunting for a nearby restaurant, but she felt like a walk and change of scenery. Meng Jarrah could just as easily have helped herself, although Freddi knew she would keep working and forget about food unless she brought her something and prompted her to eat it. The communal dining room, where Gwenllian was no doubt sharing a meal with Pietro and Elena, was also an option, but she was not in the mood for company. At the moment, a restaurant seemed more to her liking.

The corridors were quiet and deserted as they walked side-by-side to the front entrance. Outside, the temperature had dropped dramatically and Freddi shivered, having forgotten to wear her warm coat. It must still be inside, she thought, and considered going back for it, but decided the cold wasn't too unbearable after all. There was no wind, and the sky was clear and full of stars. She gazed up at the incredible panorama, a display only ever seen in its full splendour in the countryside, far from city lights. Shela sat down to stare upwards as well, fascinated by the sweep of starlight and by the silence. Her attention was diverted by the call of a strange bird she had never encountered before. Perched on a nearby fencepost, it resembled a piece of wood. She sent a silent inquiry to Freddi, the tip of her tail twitching ever so slightly.

'It's a tawny frogmouth, Shela,' her companion answered. 'They fly around at night with their mouth open, waiting for some insect to fly into it, and then they just swallow. Wonderful, aren't they?'

Shela thought it a strange way of obtaining food and said as much, having no taste for insects herself. Freddi laughed softly, peering at the bird more closely. They were fairly rare, so this was only the fourth she had ever seen. After a while, it left its perch to disappear into the night and they resumed their walk in search of somewhere to eat.

The main street of the town was relatively short, but she could see lights on in at least five places, so hoped one of them might have food for sale. They covered the remaining few hundred metres and were soon standing before an attractive venue that, going by the menu on display in the doorway, seemed to offer a reasonable variety of dishes at fair prices.

The beautifully warm interior of the restaurant smelled of good cooking and cleanliness. Each small table of highly polished antique wood was decorated with a pot of fresh flowers, while the floor, also of antique wood and lovingly maintained, gleamed in the soft light. The walls were liberally decorated with beautifully preserved photographs dating back to the time when such things were created with what Freddi seemed to recall were termed 'film cameras', then painstakingly printed by hand on special paper. Each print was slightly faded, yet she marvelled at how well they had been preserved behind their glass covers. The images appeared to record the early history of Stanthorpe, portraying men and women in clothing of the time against a backdrop of buildings from this street. One was of a structure called a post office, quite lovely, and another showed a building called a bank. There were old petroleum driven vehicles in the dusty street, and even one picture of a horse-drawn cart, which seemed to belong to someone who grew crops since it was full of crates holding fruit of some type.

As Freddi walked slowly alongside one wall examining the photographs, still with Shela on her leash, the proprietor of the restaurant entered and studied them curiously. As well as being an exceptionally beautiful woman, Freddi was an unusual sight in this small town, with her above-average height and in her black Brisbane Peacekeeper's uniform. Shela was also an interesting 'customer'. Cats weren't rare in Stanthorpe, although very few were brought onto the premises.

'May I help you?' the proprietor asked courteously.

Freddi turned around, but her answer was forestalled by Shela, who sent the proprietor an image of a large bowl of cheese and mushroom omelette, accompanied by some water.

The woman laughed good-naturedly. 'And what can I get you, Peacekeeper? Your cat has already told me what she wants!'

Freddi smiled and picked up the menupad from the nearest table. 'I'll have some of your pumpkin soup, followed by the lasagne, with a glass of your best local shiraz. I'd also like to have some of the lasagne in a self-heating container, if possible, as well as the cucumber and celery salad, and a pear juice, to take to a friend of mine once I've finished.'

When the proprietor nodded and bustled out into her kitchen, Freddi sat down at the table, letting Shela off her leash. The cat immediately began investigating each and every corner, peering and sniffing under the tables, while mentally developing an olfactory picture of recent customers, which included what they had eaten. She was still fully absorbed in this fascinating activity when her investigations were interrupted by the smell of food as her meal arrived and was placed on the floor near where Freddi was seated. Shela ran gleefully over to the bowls, devouring her omelette at

15

such a rate that Freddi was sure she'd be sick. It was, apparently, extremely tasty. Freddi's own meal was just as good and the wine even better. She was enjoying the last mouthful when her comlink chimed. Sighing at the interruption, Freddi answered, to be greeted by Meng Jarrah's broadly grinning face.

'I've worked it out!' she said.

When she returned to the medcentre, Freddi found Meng Jarrah, as predicted, still peering at the results in front of her. She stretched and yawned, then stood up to give Freddi a brief hug, before pointing at the complex model on the computer screen.

'You really ought to eat before you explain all this to me,' said Freddi, stroking Meng Jarrah's hair and smiling. 'Your dinner is ready in the anteroom. If you don't have it now, I'm not sure how long Shela will be able to resist stealing and eating it for you!' She put an arm around her bondmate's waist and gently pulled her towards the door.

Shela had stared longingly at the lasagne for the last few minutes, and it was her projections that at long last persuaded the reluctant diner to eat. Meng Jarrah meekly followed Freddi and sat down to taste the food. It was excellent, so she ate in silence for some time while Freddi made coffee and watched. Eventually, Meng Jarrah leaned back, sipping the remainder of her pear juice and regarding Freddi with satisfaction. Their relationship had developed a strength and mutual understanding she had never experienced with anyone before. Whether Shela was a factor, she didn't know and didn't really care. She loved the big cat and saw her as an important part of Freddi's own identity, finding it hard to imagine one without the other.

Sensing these thoughts, Shela sent her a quick emotional image of love in return. Smiling, Meng Jarrah glanced over to where she lay, with her head resting on folded paws, then turned to Freddi and said, 'Am I allowed to talk about the results now?'

Freddi grinned and nodded, so Meng Jarrah described what she had found. 'There's an organic substance in the vaginal smear that contains a compound I couldn't initially identify, together with faint traces of others that I could. They're common herbs, used for centuries to enhance sexual pleasure. I ran a probability model based on the DNA I found. Fortunately, the substance wasn't only pure herbal extract, which meant DNA *was* present.'

Freddi compressed her lips and nodded again, but without interrupting with either questions or comments. Meng Jarrah studied Freddi's face more intently before saying, 'The compound appears to be a previously unknown amatoxin, commonly found in a group of fungi often referred to as destroying angels. They're most often a species of amanita, including *Amanita phalloides*, though there are also various other genera. This one isn't a currently known species. Mind you, that doesn't surprise me, as even after all this time, there are probably still many fungi we haven't identified, particularly in Australia.'

'Do you think it killed her?' asked Freddi pointedly.

'Possibly, but not necessarily immediately. It often takes a number of days to die. The liver, and most likely the kidney, analysis should confirm whether it behaves anything like the known amatoxins. They're taken up by the liver, secreted into the blood, then taken up again to repeatedly circulate throughout the body. However, it's the liver that ultimately becomes irreparably damaged; the RNA-polymerase is inactivated, causing gradual cell death. Nasty...' added Meng Jarrah thoughtfully.

'So, if this particular amatoxin is similar to the known ones, and if the substance that was used to introduce it into her system was applied some days beforehand, then we may have found the cause of death. But then how did she manage to feel well enough to indulge in an expensive gourmet meal before she died?'

'Typically, she would have begun to feel sick half a day, or thereabouts, after being poisoned, would have started vomiting and experiencing violent gut pains, with diarrhoea, then may have felt better for a few days before finally becoming extremely ill and dying.'

'Assuming she wasn't being held captive, why wouldn't she have sought medical treatment at the outset, when she first felt ill?'

'Who knows! We don't have much to go on yet, but it does seem strange. Can't say I've heard of this particular method of poisoning before, either. Usually people eat the fungus by mistake, though even that's fairly rare.' Meng Jarrah hunched her shoulders, caught herself doing it, and consciously relaxed, then stared at Freddi for a long moment before saying, 'As a matter of fact, that's quite possibly why she ended up dying. She could have gone to a medcentre and been misdiagnosed, treated for the symptoms they saw, then sent home after beginning to feel better.'

Freddi suddenly recalled the most recent case of amanita poisoning that she was aware of. Five years ago, Kenjiro Kakura, the director of the international corporation Wyvern Meridian, died from eating something contaminated with the fungus. Kakura had been central to the series of crimes being investigated at the time she and Meng Jarrah first met. 'What an odd coincidence,' she remarked.

'What is?' asked Meng Jarrah.

'Don't you remember? I met you during the investigation that ended when Kenjiro Kakura was poisoned by *Amanita phalloides*, and now we're working together on yet another case where someone has been poisoned by an amatoxin.'

'Oh yes! I do remember now. Odd, I'd forgotten how he died. It seemed such an anticlimax. He should have lived and been brought to trial. It would have been much more satisfying, don't you think?'

'Not really, Meng. I don't think he ever *would* have stood trial. There was very little direct evidence against either him or his corporation.'

Freddi stood up and held out her hand to Meng Jarrah, saying, 'Time to take ourselves to our temporary home, I expect. I'm sure Nyneve will need to be up early tomorrow, and so will we. Besides, I wouldn't mind an early night. What about you?'

In reply, Meng Jarrah stood up and kissed her. Shela purred, winding herself around their legs.

CHAPTER THREE

Here in the country, houses were usually built above ground, unlike in some of the larger cities such as Melbourne, where they were built below ground for aesthetic reasons, as well as for energy efficiency and safety. Nyneve's house was made from red brick, with double-glazed windows and wide eaves, which were a pale gumleaf green in colour. Its design was based on late nineteenth-century architectural ideas and featured a steeply pitched roof, as well as a beautiful casement window beneath the tented eaves. The ground beneath the eaves, at least at the front, was neatly tiled in an intricate, multicoloured pattern. The oddest feature, however, was a chimney, something which Freddi and Meng Jarrah had never before seen, and out of it came a plume of smoke, gently curling upwards into the still night air. Altogether, the effect was enchanting.

As they approached, the door automatically opened for them, and inside, Nyneve was waiting, smiling and looking quite unlike her earlier self, with her black hair cascading around shoulders encased in a dark green angora shawl, despite the cosy warmth of the entrance hall. She shook hands with them then led the way to her dining room, asking if they had eaten their evening meal.

'Yes, we have,' replied Freddi, wondering whether she should apologise. 'I hope you didn't keep anything for us?'

'No, I guessed your work would keep you late, but I do have something you might like for supper, if you can fit it in?'

When they entered the dining room, they could see the reason for the chimney: a blue enamelled stove containing a cheerfully burning fire. The stove was of a plain but elegant design, sitting on four short, curved legs. The flames could be seen through a small window in its front. A big basket of wood sat nearby on the hearth.

Nyneve noticed their expressions and laughed. 'We do actually have wood to burn out here in the country! The gumtrees drop so many twigs and branches that if we didn't burn them, we wouldn't be able to move for all the litter. The stove is an old Scandinavian design and highly efficient; it only takes a few pieces of wood every few hours. I usually keep it for the evening, particularly when I have guests. Cosy, isn't it? The weather gets so cold here in winter that the stove is a luxury I thoroughly enjoy, although I have solar energy as well, of course.'

Meng Jarrah moved closer to the stove and tentatively opened the small front door to see the burning wood. 'May I?' she asked, turning around.

'Please do!' replied Nyneve, grinning broadly. Meng Jarrah picked up the fire tongs and placed a piece of wood from the basket into the stove, then straightened up to enjoy the effect, before closing the door again and holding out her hands to the heat.

'Let's sit down and I'll make you some tea, if you'd like?' offered Nyneve.

When both her guests gladly accepted, she conducted them into her little kitchen, which was as charming as the outside of the house, with pale cream walls and dark red furnishings. Brightly coloured, handmade plates decorated the walls, while a large Hoya hung from a beam in the ceiling. The plant was in full flower, which Meng Jarrah thought was late in the season. Its waxen clusters of star-shaped blooms were sweetly scented, and the leaves, a dark, glossy green. A brightly polished antique brass kettle hung from the same beam, as did an old kerosene lamp that must surely date from the early twentieth century. The lamp was battered and worn, yet still had character, matching the charm of the house. It seemed a travesty to come here to investigate a death, and quite possibly, a murder.

Sighing, Meng Jarrah sat down at the old wooden table. 'Silky oak,' she decided, and fondly stroked its smooth surface. It must have cost Nyneve a great deal, but it loosely matched the other furniture in the room, which indicated she might be a collector. Accurately guessing what she was thinking, Freddi smiled and held out her hand to Meng Jarrah. She stood up and they went back into the dining room. Nyneve soon followed, carrying a tray laden with deep-blue teacups, a matching teapot, small plates, and a magnificent chocolate cake studded with halved walnuts and pieces of marzipan fashioned into leaf-like shapes.

Freddi offered to help lay out the teacups, then with a smile of anticipation, offered to slice the cake as well. As she did, the household security system chimed. Nyneve looked up in surprise. 'I wasn't expecting anyone,' she said. 'I hope they're not about to ask us to go out again!' However, Nyneve was relieved to see Gwenllian's face on the security system's screen, so let her in.

Gwenllian entered the room, shaking herself and going straight over to the stove to warm up. She was not at all surprised by the sight of the fire, and surveying the table, laughed. 'I've arrived in time!'

'I didn't think we'd see you tonight,' replied Meng Jarrah, standing up to give her a hug.

'Pietro, Elena and Bella were all exhausted and went early to bed. They're fine... I made sure of that, but they've decided to return to Italy. The shock was too much for them after all. Still, they were due to return in a few days anyway. I don't blame them. Bella and I had a good 'talk', so she now realises there's no need to be afraid of the dead body, although she

20

couldn't understand why anyone would want to kill another wight...which is what cats call *us*,' she explained to Nyneve. 'But I don't want to talk about all that any longer.' Gwenllian sat down at the table and looked longingly at the teapot. 'Let's just have a lovely evening of gossip. We can return to the outside world tomorrow. What do you think? One thing though, Freddi... I'd like to stay on to help. Would you mind?'

'Not at all... I'd be glad if you did, Gwennie. It's an odd case. I'm sure your particular talents will be useful.' Freddi smiled, though a little grimly.

The others murmured their agreement and Nyneve picked up the heavy teapot to fill each cup, then handed around generous slices of the cake. They each ate and drank in silence for a while, enjoying the peace of the country house, only interrupted occasionally by the call of a possum or the other night creatures that had come out from their hollows and nests to eat and to hunt.

'I like your stove, Nyneve,' said Gwenllian at last. 'I've seen them before, in Norway, and they have one over at the communal house. It's quite a luxury, isn't it?'

'Oh yes... I was saying before you came that we have enough wood here for the occasional fire, unlike you poor city dwellers! Now, would you like a small brandy with your tea?'

They all nodded, so Nyneve fetched a set of crystal glasses and a matching decanter from her sideboard, also made from silky oak, and poured the golden liquid. Everyone sipped slowly to savour its fine flavour.

'It's made locally, from our own grapes,' explained Nyneve. 'We're very proud of the brandies here, as well as our wines and other distilled spirits.'

'Have you lived here all your life?' asked Freddi, before drinking more of her deliciously hot and fragrant green tea.

'Yes, I have. This was my parents' house. They died five years ago, I'm sorry to say, in an accident. It should never have happened.'

Her three guests stared at her in surprise.

'What *did* happen?' asked Gwenllian, sending a delicately soothing thought to her host's mind.

'Oh, they were swimming in a part of the river that's not often used because of the strong current and my father's foot was caught in a submerged tree. They liked swimming, even in autumn when the water's extremely cold. This time, I think he developed hypothermia. Apparently my mother tried to rescue him, but he was almost twice her size and she wasn't as strong a swimmer as him. It seems she drowned in the attempt, and so he drowned with her. At least, that's what the Coroner concluded.'

'That's terrible!' exclaimed Gwenllian, placing a hand on her shoulder. She saw the grief in Nyneve's mind and withdrew.

Nyneve sipped her brandy, then said, 'Yes, it is, but they had a good life and died together. They would have found it hard to live if one died first, leaving the other alone. I find comfort in that.'

'Were they getting on in years?' asked Freddi.

'They weren't old, only seventy-five. They didn't often think about either of them dying, yet strangely enough, my maternal grandmother died relatively young, at eighty-five. Sometimes my mother wondered if she might die much younger than usual too. Naturally, this upset my father, whose parents are still living and well over a hundred.'

Meng Jarrah reached across to take Nyneve's hand in hers for a moment, then settled back in her chair, gazing sympathetically at the peacekeeper. 'Have you lived alone since then?'

'Yes, I enjoy being alone. I spend so much time with other people when I'm working that I feel the need for solitude when I'm at home. My spare time seems to fly past all too quickly, too. There's the garden to see to, as well as the orchard. I grow stone-fruits for the local market.'

The others nodded, impressed by this self-contained woman. Shela sent an inquiry to Nyneve, who blinked, startled by the directness of the cat's question. 'Your cat just asked me why I don't have someone like her in the house,' she said, looking at Freddi, slightly bemused. 'I didn't know cats spoke to anyone other than their companions.'

Freddi glanced over to where Shela lay, dozing comfortably in front of the stove, stretched out to her full length, exposing her furry stomach and absorbed in enjoying this novel source of heat. 'They don't very often, but Shela's an unusual cat. Wouldn't you agree, Gwennie?'

Gwenllian swallowed a mouthful of tea. 'Yes,' she replied, after considering the question for a few seconds. 'She *is* much more confident than most in dealing with strangers, probably because you take her to such peculiar places and expose her to all manner of weird situations and dastardly people!' Gwenllian laughed when Shela silently agreed with her. 'Which reminds me... Karla, Mik and Tamara send their love, as do all the cats. They're friends of ours, Nyneve. Karla has one cat, and Mik and Tamara have three, which is rather amazing. They all work at the Willsmere Research Centre in Melbourne on soil and forest regeneration, though Karla specialises in genetic engineering of food crops as well. I met them while I was being investigated as a possible suspect in a case Freddi's brother was leading. Do you know him, Nyneve?'

'Yes, I do. Chiu Liow Jones is well known, at least throughout Australia, and possibly even in other countries. Even more so since the Wyvern Meridian affair was made public, although I hadn't realised you were once a suspect, Gwenllian. What were you suspected of?'

'Oh, engineering the initial security breach at Willsmere...the one in which Mik was injured. I used to work at the Melbourne Central Computer Site as an information technologist, but resigned once the case was closed. I wanted to concentrate on my research, and on the work I was doing with the Breeding Centre.'

'Which reminds *me*, Gwennie, did you ever find out what happened to Marika's son?' asked Freddi. 'Oddly enough, no one's ever told me, and this is the first time I've remembered him. Your mentioning the Computer Site reminded me. Did he continue living with his father?'

'Marika was one of the murdered suspects, wasn't she?' asked Nyneve, remembering the details she had read.

'Yes, and a friend of mine, sadly,' replied Gwenllian, running a slim hand through her recently cropped hair. 'It took a long time to get over her death and also her likely involvement in the Willsmere, and possibly even the Lamington, security breach – although we never obtained irrefutable proof she was the one behind it. Her son has done very well though, which is good. He did stay with his father, and inherited all Marika's work on holographics. He was already involved in her project, helping with the designs and doing most of the routine programming, in spite of being so young. He's had several public performances of his work. You might have heard of them, even though they were held in Bendigo, in Victoria. They're the first true holographic creations in the world. His name's Zarik.'

Everyone looked at her blankly. Apparently they didn't follow the world of art and theatre. Gwenllian grimaced and shook her head in mock despair. She had made a point of being present at Zarik's first opening, and afterwards, of congratulating him on his superb effort. Despite not having maintained any personal relationship with him after Marika's death, Gwenllian occasionally contacted his father to hear if the boy was doing as well as she hoped.

'Did he have a sponsor?' asked Freddi. 'Presumably the Bendigo Theatre Company maintained their interest in the work, even after the death of Mervyn Bradshaw?'

'Yes, they did, but they never had enough money to sponsor it. That was the reason we think Marika was tempted when Bradshaw made the Willsmere offer. He was extraordinarily wealthy and a patron of the theatre company. Now, this is where life becomes rather strange.' Gwenllian paused for dramatic effect. 'You will of course remember Michiko Yamada, Kenjiro Kakura's bondmate?'

Her audience all indicated their agreement, regarding Gwenllian intently – although Meng Jarrah was still savouring the chocolate cake, carefully cutting it into small pieces with a delicate silver cake fork while she listened.

'Michiko was herself an artist of great ability, specialising in silver jewellery and household ornaments, as well as decorative pieces for ceremonial weapons used by martial artists... Freddi, you might remember the items found in their home after Kakura's death? Well, for some time, Michiko went through a period of extreme grief, even though she had her three children for company. Mind you, they were probably heartbroken by their father's death too and may not have been able to comfort their mother. However, she quite suddenly took up her life again and stood for election to the Board of Wyvern Meridian. This was when the Federation opened it to the public for the second time and withdrew their supervision of the company. That was almost one and a half years ago now. She succeeded, and is now their Cultural and Artistic Director, a new position I gather, though in her case, voluntary, and only for up to fifteen hours a week, because one of her children is still under the age of ten.' Gwenllian was referring to Federation requirements that parents take care of their children on a fulltime basis for their first ten years of life, although how Kenjiro Kakura himself avoided this duty, no one entirely understood.

'Cultural and Artistic Director!' exclaimed Freddi, staring at Gwenllian in disbelief. 'Wyvern Meridian *has* changed! What does she actually do?'

'It appears they are now major sponsors of new and groundbreaking artistic endeavours, and Zarik is one of their investments. I'd call that justice, wouldn't you?'

Meng Jarrah shook her head, finding it difficult to comprehend how Wyvern Meridian could have become something as benign as a benefactor to struggling young artists, even if the intervening years and strict Federation supervision were taken into account. 'Wasn't Michiko completely under Kakura's control? How did she manage to change from being invisible, other than through her silverwork, into someone as high profile as that?'

Gwenllian ate a little more of her cake before replying. 'Impossible to say, really; I've never met her. But she's not the first woman to find a direction of her own once a controlling man has gone from her life.'

A piece of wood in the stove cracked and sent out sparks against the glass door, but Shela paid little attention, other than to lazily raise her head for a few seconds, yawning widely and luxuriously stretching out her legs. For several minutes there was no other sound in the room as they each thought about the past, while still enjoying the warmth and peace of the present.

Finally, Gwenllian stood up to announce it was time for her to leave. 'I want to be up early tomorrow to take a walk before we start work. I'll see you then.'

Freddi and Meng Jarrah stood up as well, to give her a hug. Nyneve kept back a little, smiling her farewell. Meanwhile, Shela purred softly and rolled over to look at Gwenllian, too lazy to leave the delightfully warm place she had found. Her golden eyes were almost closed in contentment. Gwenllian, fully understanding, dipped into the contentment for a few moments before putting on her warm, dark red coat and venturing out into the night. The sky was still clear and the temperature had dropped to almost freezing. There would almost certainly be a heavy frost. She didn't mind, taking time to raise her face to the stars, revelling in their bright remoteness, just as Freddi and Shela had done earlier in the evening.

The red blanket used to cover the dead woman before she was buried had very quickly been identified as having belonged to her, being of exceptionally fine quality and of a very expensive type and therefore easily traced. The small pieces of dust and other debris the blanket contained were collected for analysis. Their last task would be to reconstruct Rhianna O'Connor's face in order to allow formal identification by her nearest relative without them having to actually view the body. That would have been asking far too much of anyone who might have loved her.

While Meng Jarrah and the pathologist did their work, Freddi, Nyneve and Gwenllian put together a list of people to interview. They wanted to reconstruct Rhianna's life as well as her face, so given she was born in this small, peaceful country town, they needed to speak with anyone who knew her before she left Stanthorpe at the age of twenty-two to attend university, as well as any who might have remained in contact with her.

'I think we'll start with her cousin, who seems to be one of only two direct family members still living, other than a grandparent in Wales,' announced Nyneve, once they had completed their initial search of the Federation's population database. 'Afterwards, depending upon what he can tell us, we should speak with these three, who went to the local school with her.'

'There aren't many left from her school days,' remarked Freddi, moving closer to better see the list on Nyneve's screen. 'Don't people tend to stay in Stanthorpe after they've finished their first level of education?'

'Oh, most do. We have a few new ones come to live here now and then, but on the whole, the population is fairly stable. This is actually a bit odd. The school is quite small, so there were only fourteen others who went through with her at some point, of whom just these three stayed... Well, we can keep that in mind as peculiar, although it may not be relevant.'

'What about preceptors?' asked Gwenllian.

'Yes, there's one... Margrethe. She taught me, at one point. Her speciality was mathematics. Her house is over near the lake and has an unusual garden. She's taken up the old-fashioned fascination with roses and grows around one hundred and twenty varieties!' Nyneve's eyes widened in remembered amazement at the extraordinary display of blooms during her last visit.

Strangely enough, although soils and plants comprised a major portion of her research, Gwenllian had never felt the urge to own any 'tame' ones, as she considered those growing in gardens, being content instead to study and enjoy wild plants and their habitats. Still, it might be interesting to speak with someone who had rather a mania for collecting a single plant type, although they most likely wouldn't be in flower at the moment. 'Perhaps we could begin with her, instead of the cousin?' she suggested.

'Margrethe sounds interesting, and probably knows a great deal about what went on in Stanthorpe when Rhianna lived here.'

'You just want to see her garden,' said Freddi, laughing, 'but it's a good idea. She may even know something about the cousin. It doesn't hurt to have some background information before we speak with him. What do you say, Nyneve?'

'I don't mind at all. I only know him by name and reputation. He keeps to himself and lives rather a long way out of town on the Whiskey Gully Road, making a living from lavender farming. I can't stand the smell myself...don't know how people can work with it all day. Still, as we can see from the records, he's quite a few years older than Rhianna. Margrethe could probably tell us a little about their relationship.'

'Well, I guess there's no time like the present,' she added, standing up. Nyneve spoke to her comlink, which confirmed that, according to Margrethe's household computer, she appeared to be home. Her house was less than a kilometre away, so they walked, arriving to find the elderly woman they were seeking hard at work in the garden.

'Margrethe!' Nyneve called out as they approached. 'How are you? I've brought some visitors. Do you mind if we take up a bit of your time?'

Margrethe slowly straightened her back. She had grey hair, but appeared much younger than her ninety years. Laughter lines spread across her face, which was a healthy brown from working outdoors. Small, bright blue eyes studied them with interest as they walked towards her and held out their hands in greeting. She shook each one in turn with a firm grasp, not bothering to apologise for the soil on her own hands. It was, after all, good, healthy earth!

Freddi and Gwenllian introduced themselves, while Shela pressed herself against Margrethe's legs, tail in the air and purring. They left it to Nyneve to explain the purpose of their visit.

'We have, sadly to say, found a body in Girraween which appears to be that of Rhianna O'Connor,' she began, peering carefully into Margrethe's face for signs of distress, ready to give support. Thankfully, she saw only the normal sense of shock and sorrow that any good person feels for the death of someone they knew.

Margrethe wiped her hands on her trousers before replying. 'How did she die? Are you able to tell me?'

'We only know it may have been something poisonous, and that it was unlikely to be a natural death, but we don't yet know how it happened, or how her body came to be in Girraween. You're the first person here in Stanthorpe we've spoken to, so for the time being we'd prefer you didn't tell anyone else about it.'

Margrethe nodded, waiting patiently for Nyneve to continue. The mid-morning sun shone warmly on her back and the peaceful garden seemed a strange place to discuss someone's death, yet she fully accepted that death was also part of life.

'Is there somewhere we could sit down?' asked Gwenllian.

'Yes, of course, come this way,' replied Margrethe, smiling kindly, her eyes meeting Gwenllian's. 'Would you like some tea? I have the feeling there is a great deal to discuss.'

CHAPTER FOUR

Gwenllian and Freddi had never seen anything quite like the extraordinary, apricot-pink rose now in bloom. The flowers were large, of a delicate shape, and as they soon discovered, sweetly scented. The plant climbed over an arbour situated near the rear door of the small, dark green house, its leaves shining in the winter sunlight.

'I expect you're not used to seeing a rose flowering at this time of year,' said Margrethe, smiling. 'It's not the only one I have. There are several others, but this is my favourite. It's a slightly modified variety of 'Lorraine Lee', an old Alistair Clark tea rose. Have you heard of him?' When her audience all shook their heads, she explained: 'He was a great Australian rose breeder, who developed the original in 1924. The climber was a mutation discovered in northern America some years later, and this particular variety came along in 2123. It's strong and healthy, although the originals were rather prone to mildew... There's a different one in flower just over here.'

Margrethe led them to a warm, red-brick wall at the side of her house, where a pale yellow rose clambered happily along its length, enjoying the warmth of the sun and flowering profusely. 'It has a wonderful scent,' she told them, her face crinkling in amusement at their astonished expressions. 'Have a good, long sniff. It's called 'Lady Hillingdon'. The original bush was a tea rose from England, bred in 1910, and the climber was another mutation that popped up in 1917. Don't you think they're wonderful, the way they bring out something new for us without any interference at all?'

Agreeing, her three visitors smiled, then walked onwards a short way. The garden was serene, without being particularly orderly, and not only were these two roses flowering in midwinter, there were at least a dozen others doing the same.

As if she had read their minds, Margrethe said, 'I don't like pruning things. It's much nicer if the plants can find their natural shape. I grow roses that only want the dead bits taken off now and then. Did you know, there are around twenty-five thousand different types? There were some fifteen thousand at the end of the twentieth century. Quite extraordinary when one thinks about it, but roses have the most peculiar genes — all muddled. They mutate very, very easily. However,' and she broke off, almost abruptly, 'I'm sure you've had enough of me nattering on. Come back to the arbour and we'll talk about Rhianna.'

They obediently followed her, each taking a seat around a small outdoor table. Margrethe brought out a cloth from one of her deep pockets to wipe its surface, even though it wasn't particularly dusty, then sat down as well. Shela immediately sat next to her, resting her chin on the closest knee and gazing adoringly at her. Freddi said nothing, but sent a question to the cat, which was studiously ignored. 'Well,' she thought, 'no doubt I'll find out one of these days why Shela has suddenly become her devoted friend!'

'Rhianna was an unusual child,' began their host, this being the manner in which Margrethe conducted herself. 'She was exceptionally pretty, highly intelligent, and very independent. Consequently, she was unpopular. The usual jealousy, I'm sure. She joined in with some of the other children but never followed anyone else's lead unless she chose to. *We* were all very fond of Rhianna, and you won't find it strange to hear *that* didn't help her become any more popular. Sometimes the older children tried to hurt her – physically – but Rhianna could be very fierce and soon worked out how to defend herself. She was fairly tall, but not strongly built, although she didn't let that worry her. I remember Rhianna once bit one of her tormenters until she drew blood...' Margrethe paused as she remembered the incident, absentmindedly patting Shela's head until the cat purred in contentment.

'Margrethe,' Gwenllian said softly, 'would you mind if I tried to see her? I have the ability to look into people's minds, almost in the same way as a cat does. You may think that's strange, but it's true. It's easiest if I can touch you.'

The older woman looked closely at her, then placed her fingertips on Gwenllian's face, saying, 'By all means, though you might be surprised by what you *do* see.'

Gwenllian started as the soft brown fingers touched her cheek. 'You're the same as me!' she exclaimed. 'A grimalkin!'

'Yes, but not as powerful. I can sense that.' Margrethe withdrew her hand from Gwenllian's face and instead, took her pale, slender hand in her own. 'There are a number of us, though as far as I know, not many. Of course, there may be some who never reveal themselves. Most people aren't yet fully aware of what cats can do. Very few would feel happy with the notion of people having these abilities.'

Freddi and Nyneve stared at Margrethe as if hypnotised. Nyneve had only just come to terms with Gwenllian having cat-like powers, yet here was another woman who was apparently part of the feline tribe as well! She wondered just how many "a number of us" represented. As if reading her mind – had she? – Gwenllian asked Margrethe this very question.

'I've met eleven during my long life and extensive travels, which isn't many amongst all the thousands of people with whom I've come into contact, is it? Now I've met twelve.' Margrethe smiled and gently pressed Gwenllian's hand. As she did, a fat, shorthaired, short-bodied, black and white cat waddled out towards them from the open rear door of the house. She was the plainest cat any of them had ever seen. Her tail was thin and stumpy, while one ragged ear was definitely crooked. One eye was yellow, the other blue. Her head, on its thick, strong neck, was rather large for her body, yet despite her physical shortcomings, the cat beamed at them, then rubbed herself against their legs, each in turn, purring loudly and snuffling a little. Shela stood up to sniff her, towering above the other cat as she did.

'Meet Harriet,' said Margrethe, bending over to pat the cat's head as she licked Shela's nose. 'She's thirty-six years old and somewhat worse for wear, but I've had her since I visited the Breeding Centre in Melbourne – which was the only one at the time – and decided this was the pussycat for me. She's beautiful, isn't she!'

Margrethe obviously meant what she said. As each of her guests stared at Harriet, they were intrigued by the sense of utter calm and supreme contentment the old cat projected. Gwenllian suddenly had a fit of the giggles. 'Harriet's told me she knows she's not as handsome as Shela, but says she has a wonderful personality instead!'

'Does that mean she thinks Shela doesn't have a wonderful personality?' asked Freddi, laughing. Harriet promptly reassured her, curling up next to the huge black cat, who, it seemed, felt her new friend needed a good clean.

'Did you develop your powers without any warning, Margrethe, or did you always have them?' asked Nyneve, still astounded at finding someone like her in the town, and at not having found out before.

'I've always had them. To begin with, I thought everyone did, and it took a while to realise this wasn't the case. I only began to meet others of our kind after I retired from working at the school, when I started to do some travelling. I was seventy-five by that time, and to be honest, even once I discovered I wasn't the only 'grimalkin', it still wasn't clear what I should do with my powers – for the benefit of others, that is. Naturally, I did use them while I was a preceptor – very discreetly, of course. I must admit, they helped me work out what my charges were up to!'

Margrethe laughed as she remembered some of the incidents of her younger years. 'They behaved well with me because they were never able to fool me, and I could help them sort out their differences with each other too, which was useful. Sometimes, when they were having trouble with their parents, I could even do some much-needed counselling. I often wondered at how well the other preceptors did their jobs without my special abilities! I was very lucky. Now, I'm sure you're feeling bewildered, Nyneve, but if I'd told anyone, they would have thought I was simply a dotty old woman, wouldn't they, or a silly fool who had too high an opinion of her own abilities.'

'I gather you didn't fancy doing any work with us, or even formal counselling?' remarked Nyneve, wryly.

'No, I could perhaps have volunteered for that type of thing, but at times it's quite difficult having this ability to see inside other people's minds. I *feel* what they feel, and that can be painful in the type of situation you're referring to. I didn't want to take on such a heavy burden, particularly as it would have meant revealing myself to the entire town. No, I enjoy my solitude here and my garden, and Harriet's company is mostly enough for me. I get quite a few visitors though: my former charges sometimes come to see me. That's what I still do to help... I listen to them and help sort out their troubles.'

Margrethe leaned towards Nyneve, softly saying, 'I know so many people's private thoughts that I need to be very careful. If I had offered to help you in your work, how could I have kept all the town's secrets? How could I have remained someone they could come to and trust? No, it's better this way. Rhianna is different. Now that she's dead, her secrets won't hurt her any longer, and we must find out how she died and if someone killed her.' When Margrethe's features assumed a sudden fierceness, Harriet raised her head and meowed. 'It's alright, my dear,' Margrethe told her. 'I'm not upset, just angry her life has ended like this.'

Having 'watched' the images running through Margrethe's mind while she spoke, which the older woman had no objection to, being fully aware this was so, Gwenllian could fully understand how she felt about her powers. People were still suspicious of those who were different from themselves, although not to the extent of centuries past, thank the Sun. 'Margrethe,' she said, 'I think you did the right thing, if that's any help. Nyneve, would you have believed her if she'd come to you offering to assist in solving your cases through some sort of 'psychic' ability?'

Nyneve smiled. 'Probably not, I must admit. Still, I'm glad to know now, Margrethe, and I promise not to tell anyone unless you want me to.'

'Thank you. Let's keep this to ourselves. I have quite a few more years to live in this small town, I hope, so would like to enjoy them.'

Harriet added her agreement, projecting it loudly to all three visitors. Shela purred and licked her on the forehead.

'Would you like some tea before I tell you more about Rhianna?' offered Margrethe.

While their host went inside to fetch the tea, they admired the roses in the arbour, then walked around the garden to enjoy seeing the others in flower. One was a riotous pink, with a neat, metal label placed clearly for all to see: "Nancy Hayward, 1937". By the great size and gnarled trunk of the plant, it could almost have been that old, though none of them knew if roses could live to such an age.

Margrethe soon returned, carrying a heavy tray laden with small cakes and fine china. It being mid-morning, they were all more than happy to enjoy a short break and the excellent tea. Small finches flitted in and out of a large wisteria growing around the rear verandah of the house, no doubt eating the small insects living in its crevices. Twittering loudly, they busily flitted from twig to twig. Neither cat took the slightest notice.

'Now,' said Margrethe eventually, and after they had all started on their second cup of tea, 'I'll tell you more about Rhianna.'

They all looked at her expectantly. Even Shela raised her head from her paws to gaze upwards, as if she too wanted to know about the girl Rhianna had once been.

The pathologist was satisfied with his work. He had managed to reconstruct Rhianna's face without any difficulty. The bones were undamaged and there was enough skin tissue left to determine its appearance prior to death. The hair was still in good condition too, but the eye colour, a deep blue, could only be determined from her genetic profile. The result was a woman of extraordinary beauty. High, well-defined cheekbones and a well-formed chin framed a straight, finely moulded nose. The broad forehead and shapely ears balanced a wide, full mouth with almost perfect teeth, which were enhanced rather than detracted from by somewhat longer than usual incisors. With her long, slender neck, she was altogether an elegant and memorable person.

He unveiled the reconstruction with a slightly dramatic flourish. Meng Jarrah sighed and shook her head, at a loss as to how someone once so alive could now be a corpse in a morgue, being pored over in minute detail.

'Can we contact her cousin now for a formal identification?' she asked. 'When he's done that for us, we'll need to keep him for questioning; I've found his DNA in amongst the cells you combed from her hair. Do you want to contact Nyneve to arrange the interview?'

The pathologist appeared vaguely put out. 'Her cousin?' he repeated. 'But as far as I know, she hasn't returned to Stanthorpe in more than seven years, and I gather he rarely leaves. That's most peculiar. Yes, I'll call the peacekeepers, but before we get him in, we'd better have a complete record of her travels, at least as far possible.'

He immediately went over to his laboratory computer and asked it to contact the peacekeeper whose job it was to check Rhianna's movements. Before long, the cheerful, sun-browned face of Smithson appeared on the screen.

'Good timing,' said the peacekeeper, grinning. 'I've just completed a listing of all her movements using the public transport system for the last two years. I can't account for everywhere she's gone because it appears she owned a private landjet, but the public system's been used often enough to give a reasonable picture of where she habitually went, including her trips overseas and interstate.' The ease with which Smithson had tracked Rhianna's movements was due to everyone having a Federation identity number, which, together with various other forms of physical identification, was used to access a wide variety of services, including the public transport system.

He paused to consult his computer. 'I'll send you the results and you can see for yourself. I've summarised them into a picture of both her typical movements and the more unusual events, the most important of which are fairly regular trips to Argentina. The most recent was on the third of July, twelve days before we found her. That is, she returned from Argentina on the third, but left Brisbane on the fifth of June. She didn't use public transport while she was in Argentina, which means we don't know where she went while she was there, other than her initial destination, which was Córdoba. She didn't pay for anything either and didn't stay anywhere requiring payment. Therefore, we don't know who she visited or why she went there. The same pattern turns up every three to four months for the period I checked.' Smithson scratched the tip of his nose. 'I think I should do a trace going back further, don't you? Yes, I'll do that when we finish,' he said, answering his own question.

'Beginning with the end, so to speak,' he continued, 'her movements during the last five days of her life can't be traced. She didn't use public transport and, again, didn't pay for anything or stay somewhere that recorded her name – which is odd, given she must have *eaten* something.' Smithson absentmindedly scratched his chin and wrinkled his brow in thought. 'Perhaps she had an incredibly well-stocked larder that lasted the whole time she was away, though nothing *fresh* would've remained. Oh well, maybe some people don't mind doing without fresh food... Or, of course, she could have eaten with friends. We'll know eventually.'

'Then she didn't pay for that last meal of hers?' asked Meng Jarrah. She had sent the results of her analysis through to the peacekeepers, which meant they were aware of what Rhianna had eaten before she died.

'No, but we've located the restaurant serving it, which wasn't difficult,' replied Smithson, beaming at them. 'It's in Brisbane... The Hotel Grand Chancellor in Petrie Terrace. The one near the Roma Street Parkland. Do you know it?'

'Yes, it's extremely old and very fancy indeed. She must have had some good friends, or perhaps the meal was associated with her work. We haven't put together a full personal profile yet. Have you?' Meng Jarrah had concentrated so hard on the minutiae of the death that she hadn't had time until now to wonder who Rhianna O'Connor had been as a person.

'Yes, we have, and it's particularly relevant to her normal movements. She worked as a travel consultant to the wealthier sections of Australian society, and from time to time, as a tour guide when they were prepared to pay for that level of personalised service. She had her own shopfront in

Adelaide Street, near King George Square, and lived above it: an expensive area to live in. We're arranging with the Brisbane Peacekeepers to inspect the premises later today – at around 15:00, they said. On a day-to-day basis, she only took public transport once a week to visit the central food market in Margaret Street, although she could easily have walked. Other than that, she left Stanthorpe to attend university at the age of twenty-two, but chose not to study in Australia. Instead, she went to Korea and obtained a doctorate in early Japanese history, of all things.' Smithson was somewhat parochial in his attitudes and failed to see why anyone would want to study the history of a country that no longer existed. He shrugged his shoulders and continued his report. Neither Meng Jarrah nor the pathologist saw any reason to interrupt.

'After she obtained her doctorate, she travelled extensively around the world examining sites of relevance to her studies, although relatively few still exist because the Japanese isolated themselves for centuries – or so I've learnt this morning – only spreading out far beyond their own borders during the twentieth century. Still, Rhianna found enough to keep her busy until she was thirty-four, when she finally returned to Australia to build up her business in Brisbane. We don't yet know how she managed to amass enough to buy her shopfront and apartment, let alone an expensive landjet. She certainly didn't come from a wealthy family, and as far as we can tell, didn't inherit anything from some distant relative.'

The pathologist nodded, remembering the O'Connor family as he had known them in their early days in Stanthorpe. He had himself left to go to university in Brisbane, but returned at the earliest opportunity, far preferring his former quiet, country life.

Smithson checked his notes before resuming and when he once again scratched his nose, Meng Jarrah found it hard not to scratch hers. 'Must be either an insect bite or a habit,' she thought, irrelevantly.

'During the past two years,' said Smithson, 'Rhianna hasn't returned to Stanthorpe once, which is surprising as she does have family here in the form of a cousin by the name of Robert O'Connor, and his mother, Agathea. Odd fellow, I must say, though I haven't bumped into him for a long while. However, to continue, she's travelled to other countries as a tourist guide fifteen times – enjoys travelling, it seems – but there's no particular pattern as to which country, which client, length of stay, or type of tour. Still, all this seems to be normal for her style of business... That's all I have for now, but I'll start looking into her financial history after I've gone back further with her travels. I gather Nyneve isn't back yet?'

'Thanks, Smithson, and no, she isn't,' answered the pathologist. 'They seem to be having rather a long talk with Margrethe. By the way, we'll be getting Robert in to formally identify the body, now that we know what you've found – and haven't found. In the meantime, we'll get back to work.'

CHAPTER FIVE

At eight years old, Rhianna O'Connor was thin and bony. It wasn't that she was undernourished; this was just how she grew. Her short hair accentuated the thin features of her face, so much so that the dark blue eyes seemed enormous. Whenever she viewed herself in a mirror, which wasn't often, it was to wonder how she would look if her hair were long, but her mother wouldn't hear of it. 'Too difficult to wash and brush,' was her impatient answer whenever Rhianna asked.

She had attended school now for two years, one year longer than most children her age; her mother had pestered and pleaded to allow her daughter to enter earlier than the usual age of seven. Once the preceptors realised Rhianna was not thriving at home, they decided the lesser of two evils would be to allow the little girl to come to school, where at least she would have company and good food. They even allowed her to bring her small grey cat, after she became hysterical when her mother tried to part her from this constant companion. Rhianna had hugged the young animal to her slender chest, the tears flowing from her eyes as she gasped and cried out. The cat seemed to cling to the child almost as fiercely as she clung to it.

None of the other children at the local school owned a cat and so were intensely curious about 'Sylvie', as she was called, but Rhianna would never let any of them touch her. When Margrethe eventually met them, she took great care not to let anyone, especially Rhianna's mother, Leihana, know what the cat was capable of – as did the cat herself. Only Rhianna, her cousin Robert, his parents, and Margrethe knew that Sylvie was able to sense emotions, and that at times could choose to influence them, particularly if Rhianna was in harm's way.

Sylvie had been a gift from Robert on Rhianna's fifth Namingday, and it was the best gift anyone could have given her. Although the cat could never replace the father she had lost a year earlier, when a freak storm caused his airjet to crash, her presence helped.

Leihana, inconsolable over her bondmate's death, seemed to find no comfort in her daughter. Her grief even made her angry and impatient, as if she was somehow trying to run away from the knowledge of her loss. At first, she frequently smacked Rhianna for small childish things, but never since Sylvie joined the household.

Sylvie stroked herself against Rhianna's legs, then sat down neatly beside her on the sofa. Today was Rhianna's ninth Namingday and any minute now, Robert would come through the door, smiling and laughing, as he always did when he saw his young cousin. He was tall and handsome, with long, wavy black hair and dark blue eyes, just like hers. Next to Sylvie, Robert was the most important person in Rhianna's life.

The security system chimed and there he was! They ran to the door to let him in. He swept Rhianna up into his arms, hugging her to him, while Sylvie danced around his feet, tail in the air, burbling happily. After kissing his cousin on the forehead, Robert set her down and produced from his pocket a small, brightly wrapped package. It took only a moment to tear it open. Inside was the most beautiful bracelet the girl had ever seen, fitting perfectly on her slender wrist, which she held up for him to see.

'It looks as lovely on you as I thought it would,' he said, smiling. 'See here, I have something for Sylvie too,' and he searched in his pocket for another small package.

Rhianna opened the present slowly this time, savouring the feeling of being cared for. There, inside, was a dainty silver bell for the cat's collar. She knelt to put it on, patting Sylvie on the head to reassure her.

'Go on,' she cried, 'run around and let's hear how it sounds!'

Sylvie leapt into the air, did a somersault, and then careered around the sunlit room, skidding on the handmade rug in the middle of the floor. The bell tinkled musically when the cat threw herself into the middle of the rumpled rug to preen contentedly in her newly made nest.

'I've made a special cake,' Rhianna said shyly, taking Robert's hand. 'Do you want some now? I waited until you got here before cutting it.'

Robert picked Rhianna up, held her high in the air for a moment, then set her down again. Giggling contentedly, she led him into the kitchen, where he beheld the funniest Namingday cake he had ever seen, and promptly burst out laughing. 'No one but you could think of this!' he exclaimed.

The cake was shaped to look like a brushtail possum, with chocolate buttons for eyes, a sugared almond for a nose, ears moulded from skilfully painted marzipan, and a tail that definitely wasn't edible, being made from artificial fur.

'I washed the fur before I put it with the body, honestly,' said Rhianna, glancing at her tall cousin and waiting for his approval before she carefully sliced a generous piece from the middle of the cake.

'It almost seems a shame to cut it up,' he replied, his mouth full of the sweet pastry, which was filled with a mixture of sweetened ground almonds, cooked cherries, and beaten butter-cream between thin layers of vanilla-flavoured cake. It was a remarkable feat for a child so young, he thought, enjoying the next mouthful while she cut herself a portion and placed it onto a plate. Robert didn't ask if her mother had helped with the cake. He knew Leihana rarely made time for such things, even though this was her daughter's special day. She clearly wasn't even home.

Rhianna put her plate back onto the table and looked at him gravely. 'I think I should make some tea, don't you? Or would you prefer coffee?' She was trying hard to be the perfect host.

'Oh, coffee, please. It would go better with the cake. I'll help myself to another piece while you make it, if you don't mind?' Robert knew better than to offer to make the coffee. 'Do you think your mother would object if you came to our house today for an early dinner?' he asked instead.

Carefully holding the coffee pot with both hands, the little girl smiled adoringly at him and shook her head. She loved visiting Robert and his parents, Agathea and Eirann. Sylvie rubbed herself against Robert's knees and purred happily. She too loved visiting his house. Agathea always prepared a good meal for her, and Eirann was fond of giving her a thorough brush, even when the long, soft fur didn't particularly need it.

Eirann was Rhianna's father's brother, and she adored him almost as much as she had adored her father. Kind and patient, her uncle always managed to find time for his niece, to tell her stories, and to teach her how to use some of the tools he kept in his work shed. Her aunt, Agathea, was a short, plump, comfortable woman, who delighted in fussing over the young girl, hoping to make up for the neglectful habits she felt Leihana had fallen into since her bondmate died. Leihana, however, unable to bear the resemblance between Eirann and his dead brother, avoided the family as much as possible, although at least had the sense not to prevent Rhianna from seeing them whenever she wanted to. For this, they were all grateful.

When they had finished their coffee and cake, Rhianna covered the remainder of her creation and placed it in the thermolyte.

'She's amazingly adult,' thought Robert sadly, knowing that not only had his cousin taught herself to cook, she washed and mended her own clothes, and cleaned her own bedroom. Sometimes, when Leihana had forgotten to do it, she even used their household computer to connect to the lattice and order the week's food.

After Rhianna had tidied the kitchen, Sylvie fetched her leash from the hook by the front door and dropped it at Robert's feet, gazing up into his face with her beautiful light green eyes. Robert knelt, attached the leash to her collar, and once they were all outside, swung Rhianna onto his shoulders.

They walked in silence along the yellow-flowered trafficway, enjoying the peace and stillness of the countryside, only interrupted now and again by the call of a bird. Dusk had fallen, although it was only a few minutes past 17:00, so by the time they had almost reached their destination – a distance of just over two kilometres – the first stars had appeared in the evening sky. Rhianna sighed contentedly, and Sylvie quietly agreed with her. Robert patted his cousin's hand and walked steadily onwards. The door of his parents' house opened and lights shone warmly as they approached along a path lying between neat beds of aromatic herbs. A wonderful smell of the Namingday dinner being prepared greeted them when they entered the small lounge room, where Eirann sat relaxing in his favourite armchair by the wood stove. He stood up, holding out his arms to Rhianna, while Sylvie ran excitedly around the room, tail in the air and sniffing all the delicious scents.

Agathea called out from the kitchen: 'We're almost ready. I'm just putting the finishing touches to the soup Eirann made earlier today. Sit yourselves down and I'll be right there.'

Everyone, including the cat, made haste to go into the dining room, where Robert lit the red candles in the silver candelabra holding pride of place at the centre of the big table. The table was covered with a crisp, white, linen cloth, and each place was laid with a deep blue earthenware setting and red cloth napkins. Freshly polished silver cutlery and a blue vase of yellow chrysanthemums completed the festive effect. Rhianna laughed in delight before taking her place at the head of the table. She knew this was her place because a beautifully wrapped gift lay there.

'What do you think it is?' she whispered to Sylvie, who had taken her own place next to Rhianna's chair, tail wrapped neatly around her trim body, ears erect and alert.

The cat purred gently and projected, just to Rhianna, an image of bright anticipation.

Agathea came in with a pot of steaming pumpkin soup, made with vegetables from her own garden, and ladled an ample portion into each bowl. 'You could get the bread from the kitchen and cut it up for me, Robert, there's a dear,' she said to her son, who promptly obeyed and then handed the breadboard to each in turn. Sylvie had her own bowl of soup, cooled to room temperature beforehand.

They all savoured their food for a few minutes before Eirann spoke. 'I asked your mother if you could stay here tonight, and she didn't mind. Would you like to?'

Rhianna grinned and nodded.

'Good, that's settled. Tomorrow's not a school day, so you can come with us to Girraween, if you like. If the weather holds, which we expect it will, we could take a picnic lunch and go for a long walk. What do you think?'

'Yes, please!' Rhianna laughed from sheer pleasure. Since this was not the first time she had stayed overnight, there was a small set of spare clothing kept in 'her' room. Not long after her father's death, they had made a special place for her in their home, though Leihana never asked to see it. Rhianna didn't mind. She knew her mother had so many other pressing concerns.

After Margrethe had finished telling them about Rhianna's childhood, Nyneve, Gwenllian, Freddi and Shela left to go to Robert's house. Once there, they noticed a greenhouse to their left, large and well maintained, yet inside, nothing grew. Behind the house, the forest crept almost to its walls and everywhere was the sound of birdsong, some of it melodic, some eccentric and raucous as so many Australian birds were. On each side, vast fields of lavender grew, now dormant, the flowers having been harvested months since.

The house itself was situated on the side of a low hill and was unusual in having been built entirely from stone: hand-cut granite, Nyneve told them, as they walked up to its door. The door was unusual too, being made of solid wood – real timber, and very, very old. It came from the original Stanthorpe courthouse, salvaged after the building was almost completely destroyed by fire. Lovingly restored, the door gleamed with polish, its brass handle shining in the late afternoon light. Apparently the roof was made from slate, also salvaged from some ancient building and carefully restored. As with many of the other houses in Stanthorpe and the district, there was a chimney, but this one was topped with an ornate chimney pot, in the form of a gargoyle depicting an angry raven. They noticed the windows all contained leadlighting – without colour, but with different textures in each piece, all combining to form a lustrous pattern. It took a short while before Freddi and Gwenllian realised that each subtle design included a bird.

They stood at the front door, waiting, expecting either Robert to open it or for some form of electronic communication, as was usual, but nothing happened. Freddi moved over to the nearest window to peer inside, feeling a little like an intruder. All she could see was a quiet, comfortable room containing several armchairs, a black metal stove, a large display cabinet filled with antique books, and a low side-table that appeared to be made from mahogany. The floor was partially covered by a brightly coloured carpet, with a pattern that, from her brief inspection, seemed to match the windows. 'A man who cares about detail,' she thought, before turning back to the others. Aloud, she said, 'He must be around somewhere. When we checked earlier, his security system said he was home.'

'He's in the forest,' answered Gwenllian, whispering, which somehow seemed appropriate. 'I can sense him.'

She led the way to the rear of the house and then a short distance in amongst the tall eucalypts. Robert had his back to them when they found him, but turned slowly as they approached. He was the most beautiful man any of them had ever seen – as beautiful as Rhianna O'Connor had been in life, yet his face was expressionless and his eyes dead – almost as dead as hers.

Shela whimpered and crouched down at Freddi's feet, reluctant to come closer. Robert looked at the cat and then at Gwenllian, but turned away again. He stood with his back to them, his arms folded, his head bowed.

'He knows she's dead,' whispered Gwenllian to her companions.

'Yes,' answered Robert, although still turned away from them. 'I buried her body at Girraween, but the Rhianna I knew died a long time ago.'

Gwenllian started. How had he heard her?

'I also know your name, Gwenllian...and yours, Peacekeeper. I heard the cat's thoughts.' Robert now faced them, arms at his sides, his hands clenched. 'Nyneve, I'm sorry to see you again under these circumstances.'

Nyneve moved towards him and then stopped, wary.

'No,' he said, as if in reply to her unspoken question, 'I didn't kill her, but I didn't prevent her from being killed either, even though for so long I did all I could to look after her.' He fell silent. Shela whimpered again when he glanced in her direction. A tremor of pain caused him to bring a hand to his face, as if to wipe away a memory.

Three small grey wallabies hopped slowly into the clearing to stare curiously at them, before moving towards Robert and nuzzling his hands to see if he had brought them any food. He stroked their heads, then automatically patted the pockets of his tunic, appearing almost surprised to find that he did indeed have something for them. Finally, while his visitors waited patiently, Robert spent a few minutes feeding the creatures.

For a long moment, a deep stillness came over the forest, seeming to hold them all suspended in time, and then, at long last, Robert turned to them, slowly wiping his hands on a kerchief. 'I'll come with you. I don't want to speak about her here.'

The pathologist had prepared Rhianna's reconstructed head in the most sympathetic manner possible for Robert to identify, but was taken aback by the appearance of the man and deeply disturbed by the extremity of grief Robert displayed when he saw the likeness. Gwenllian tried her best to support him, yet even with Shela's help, he was completely overcome, weeping uncontrollably, unable to even stand. Gwenllian sat close beside him, waiting. Freddi waited with her, ready to begin the interview, Nyneve having decided one peacekeeper was quite enough, given Robert hardly seemed to be attempting to hide anything.

Robert eventually dried his face and, almost like a vulnerable child, blew his nose. 'She was my responsibility and I failed her,' he murmured to himself, then looked at Gwenllian, who had taken her arm from around his shoulders. 'Thank you,' he said simply. She nodded and remained silent, while Robert shook his head, sighing deeply.

'Freddi,' he said at last, 'the main sense of what either of you think is transmitted to me by your cat. I don't have a mind like them, or like Gwenllian's, but I can form an immediate bond with cats that allows me to hear other people's thoughts, though not all the details come through in the translation. I can also bond with *your* mind, Gwenllian, because it's similar to a grimalkin's.'

Freddi immediately led Shela to the door of the room and asked her to move as far away as the layout of the medcentre allowed. Understanding, Robert nodded, his expression grim. He then listened quietly while Freddi told him the interview would be recorded and his answers used, if necessary, as evidence. When she asked if he wanted a Witness present, he shook his head.

'After I found out about my abilities,' Robert told her, 'I gave Rhianna a cat, when she was five years old. I was only sixteen at the time, but already knew I needed to take care of her. Giving her Sylvie seemed the best way.' His face distorted in a grimace of pain, but with a struggle, he managed to prevent himself from weeping again.

'I don't know exactly how she died,' he continued, 'but I do know who was with her *when* she died and what they were doing. You may already know too... I have no idea how far you are with your investigation... Each year, a certain group of friends who went to school together in Stanthorpe meet for a reunion dinner, usually somewhere in Brisbane. Rhianna wasn't part of that circle when she lived here, but joined them some time after her mother died, which was a few months after she came back to Australia, eight years ago.'

'Rhianna was gone a long time. Do you know why she returned?' asked Freddi, placing one foot onto the chair next to Robert, her face stern as she towered over him.

'Oh yes. My father died in an accident. She came back for my mother's sake...and for me, or so I thought.'

Freddi made a mental note to check the details, deciding not to press him further on this point. 'I'm sorry to hear your father died,' she replied, taking her foot off the chair and sitting down next to him instead.

Robert glanced at her, then, with his eyes fixed on some distant point, said, 'Rhianna had changed a lot in the time she was away. She was hardly my little cousin at all and didn't stay long: only long enough for the memorial service, which was held at our new house, and then to visit her mother for a few months. She liked my house, especially the fruit trees in the greenhouse.' He saw Gwenllian eyeing him curiously.

'Yes,' he replied, 'it's empty now. Before she left Australia to go to university, Rhianna lived with my parents for some years. She loved their garden and trees and made me promise that when I finished my own house, I would take some of the plants with me and look after them until she returned. I had just started building then, and she was helping with the design. I kept my promise and planted the fruit trees in her memory, although I let them die after her last visit. It seemed fitting.'

Gwenllian could sense a desolation in his mind, profound and beyond anything she had ever felt from anyone before, yet she could not sense his actual thoughts at all and realised he was most likely able to block her.

'You're quite right, Gwenllian. If I want to, I can block your mind from reading my thoughts and feelings.' He abruptly stood, regarding them both sadly, his beautiful face grave and silent. 'I have nothing to hide, but it's hard to speak of Rhianna. She was like a sister to me and I loved her dearly. I think she loved me in return, but it was not enough to keep her from becoming someone I barely recognised.'

'Why do you think Rhianna changed so much?' asked Gwenllian.

'She had already begun to change when she came to live with my parents...because of Sylvie.'

'Her cat? What do you mean?'

Robert explained, and they listened, horrified...

The group of children confronting Rhianna frightened Sylvie. She could sense they wanted to hurt her, and worse, they wanted to hurt her friend. The grey cat crouched down, ready to spring if necessary, tail slowly curling back and forth, eyes narrowed to slits. One of the children bent down, picked up a stone and threw. It hit Rhianna's forehead and the twelve-year-old girl yelped in pain. She put her hand up to her face, then stared at the blood on it. The children laughed cruelly, and a second one picked up a stone. The others followed suit. After all, there was no one to see them.

School had finished for the day, so the children had followed Rhianna and Sylvie along the creek bank, where the two often walked, wanting to take as long as possible before reaching home. Usually Rhianna and her companion wandered along, playing with anything that caught their attention and searching for any new flowers that might have blossomed. Sylvie also hunted for small creatures underneath the twigs and branches scattered on the ground. Not that she would have harmed them, but it amused her to see the lizards and insects skitter away from her enquiring paws. She was happily investigating a small pile of leaves when the children appeared on the path a short distance away. They were all familiar to her, of course, so at first the cat took little notice, but something in the tone of their minds caused her to stop what she was doing. Snarling, she backed away towards Rhianna, hackles raised, tail fluffed out to its full size. Startled, Rhianna dropped the small preying mantis she held, crying out when she saw the expressions on their faces.

They were all a year or two older and all of them made her uneasy, even in the school grounds. Sylvie had agreed with her that it was best they avoid them. This time, it was not possible. Rhianna looked around to see if there were any other walkers nearby, but they were quite alone. Calming herself as best she could, the young girl stood ready to defend them both if necessary, although she doubted that she *could* against this many. There were five of them and the biggest had already earned a reputation for being a bully. Her name was Ruth.

Rhianna silently called Sylvie to come closer. The cat growled, then fell silent as she concentrated on sending her plea for help to Robert. That was when the first stone struck Rhianna. The next followed soon after. She held up an arm to shield herself and swung around to face Ruth, who had crept up behind. Rhianna struck the girl in the face, breaking her nose and splitting her lip. Blood poured down Ruth's face, yet she didn't let that prevent her from doing her best to hurt her victim. Lashing out in rage, Ruth kicked at Rhianna's left knee, but Rhianna managed to block the kick and return it, connecting with Ruth's midriff. The older girl grunted in pain, then made one last attempt, aiming a blow at Rhianna's throat. Rhianna sidestepped and used the palm strike she had learned in her martial arts classes. It connected beneath Ruth's jaw. With satisfaction, Rhianna saw her opponent drop to the ground, unconscious, but had little time to enjoy the sight before the others were upon her.

Sylvie screamed and attacked the first one, who leapt back in pain and astonishment as her claws raked his face. The others stopped to stare at the cat, whose teeth were bared, ready to defend Rhianna. She hissed at them, lashing her tail, then leapt when another of the group threw the stone they still held. The child fell to the ground with the full weight of the cat on top. Sylvie bit into the girl's throat to hold her, not to kill. Ruth, who had woken up, staggered to her feet and stared in horror.

'Call her off, Rhianna! We'll go! You win...this time.'

Rhianna stood nursing her upper arm where one of them had managed to hit her, but said nothing. She merely stared scornfully at them all, and then silently told Sylvie to let go and come to her. The cat reluctantly released her captive, doing as she was asked, but sent Ruth a message the girl would never forget. Ruth's face paled and her breathing became laboured as she was overcome with a sudden, overwhelming fear of the younger, smaller girl she had thought to be an easy target.

By the time Robert arrived, Rhianna and Sylvie were nearly home. He had heard the cat's cries for help from a distance of almost three kilometres and nearly fainted from the impact. Even he had never anticipated such power of mind from the creature. Dropping the rake he was using on the vegetable garden, he ran faster than he had ever done in his life. He arrived to find them huddled together in the shade of an old apple tree, well hidden from the nearby house and certainly not within hearing distance. Sylvie was tenderly licking Rhianna's face while the girl cried as if her heart would break. When Sylvie showed him what had happened, Robert groaned in horror as he crouched down to take Rhianna in his arms. She cried even more loudly, but gradually calmed as he stroked her short, dark hair.

'Why? Why did they want to do that?!' she wailed.

CHAPTER SIX

'Give me one good reason why that cat shouldn't be put down!' shrieked Leihana, as her daughter stood before her, weeping, shoulders shaking, her whole body trembling with fear. Sylvie was locked in the tiny woodshed and her howls of desolation echoed in Rhianna's mind. In desperation, she turned from her mother and fled the house, not bothering to put on shoes or a coat.

Outside was bitterly cold. A fierce wind caused the trees to moan and to roar like the surf of the ocean Rhianna had never seen. Ignoring the twigs and stones bruising her bare feet as she ran, she stumbled when her mother grasped her arm. Vainly trying to shake Leihana off, she struck out blindly. Her mother swore loudly when the blow connected with the side of her head, but it was not enough to make her loosen her grip. She managed to grasp Rhianna's wrist, holding on fast as her daughter tried to strike again.

Saying nothing whatsoever, Leihana hauled her back into the house and then into her bedroom, where she grabbed Rhianna by both shoulders and shook her fiercely, before slapping the girl as hard as she could. Rhianna spat directly into her mother's face then kicked her on the shin with all the strength and skill four years of martial arts training had given her. This time, Leihana let go, crying out in pain. The girl lost no time in running as fast as she could towards the open door her mother, in her rage, had forgotten to close. She hoped for just enough time to release her cat and then to keep running – running towards the only friends they had.

A faint light came from behind the curtains, drawn to keep out the cold. Rhianna pounded as hard as she could on the front door, while Sylvie crouched beside her, shivering. It had begun to rain and both were drenched and freezing. Robert flung open the door to quickly pull them inside.

'By the Sun, Rhianna, your feet are bleeding! Where's Leihana? What's happened?' He picked Rhianna up and carried her into the warmth of the room, where Agathea and Eirann were standing, having leapt up when they heard the noise.

Agathea ran to her linen cupboard for a warm towel to wrap the freezing child in, then gently examined her feet. 'Get me a basin of hot water and another towel, Robert,' she said calmly, rubbing Rhianna's hair dry.

The girl was shaking so hard with cold and fear that she couldn't speak. Sylvie was hardly in any better condition, though was soon swathed in the towel Eirann fetched for her. He spoke to the frightened animal, softly and slowly, while he stroked her head and dried her sodden fur. Robert soon arrived with a salve, a towel and a basin of water, which he set down by Rhianna's feet. Her shivering gradually lessened, but tears trickled down her pale, woebegone face.

Without warning, Sylvie retched, and then vomited. Rhianna cried out and reached for her, the towel dropping to the floor. She almost threw herself at Sylvie, burying her face in the cat's fur and gripping her so tightly that she vomited again. Robert was horrified to realise he wasn't receiving anything at all from Sylvie and gently prised Rhianna away, while Eirann cleaned up the mess without a word, shaking his head in disbelief. He had begun to guess what the cause of all this might be.

'Rhianna...Rhianna,' murmured Robert, stroking her hair, 'try to calm down and tell us what happened.' He made her sit on the sofa, with her feet in the basin of hot water, then carefully placed Sylvie by her side. The cat nestled in, hiding her head under Rhianna's arm, curling herself up as tightly as she could.

'She wants to kill Sylvie! She locked her in the woodshed... I couldn't stop her and Sylvie couldn't stop her! She was so angry and I kicked her. I *had* to come here! Please don't send us back!' Rhianna was sobbing again and frantically stroking Sylvie's damp, grey fur. The cat was still quivering and hiding her head.

'We won't send you back, dear,' said Agathea, still calm. 'Is it your mother you're speaking of?' Rhianna nodded. 'And why do you think she wants to kill Sylvie?'

'The school's Council of Parents is thinking of having her killed because she defended me yesterday! They told my mother that Sylvie's a dangerous animal. She isn't! She's my friend and tried to help. If it wasn't for her, they would have hurt me...badly! I couldn't have fought them all off!'

Rhianna's ashen face contorted in pain and her chest heaved with the sobs she could not control. Sylvie's face came out from under her arm and she reached up to lick her on the cheek. Rhianna clasped her tightly, rocking to and fro, her wet hair standing up in dark spikes, her eyes unfocused.

Robert stood up and looked at his father. 'We won't let them do that, will we?' It wasn't really a question. It was a statement.

'No, Rhianna, we won't let them kill Sylvie,' replied Eirann, taking Robert's place by Rhianna's feet and placing his large warm hand over her small cold one. 'Agathea and I will talk to the Council tomorrow and tell them what really happened. Robert was there soon enough to see the state you were in. He would have spoken with them sooner, but we didn't realise they'd take this attitude. We'll talk to your mother too and try to get her to understand that without Sylvie's help, her little girl would have been in a far worse condition than she already was.'

Agathea handed Eirann a hot cup of cocoa, which he held out to Rhianna, coaxing her to drink. 'Here, let me take Sylvie now and give her something warm to eat. You're both safe now. We won't let anyone hurt either of you ever again. That's a promise.'

Sylvie allowed herself to be lifted and placed onto the floor, close to Rhianna, where she tasted the warm, sweet porridge, first slowly and then eagerly. She had been frightened in that cold, dark place. She had never been locked up before, nor kept from her companion, so couldn't understand what she had done wrong, but suspected it was to do with the children she attacked. But she hadn't hurt them very much... Only enough to stop them hurting her Wight!

The comfort of the food helped and Sylvie began to feel a little better. Though still wary, and with her eyes half-closed while she ate, the cat glanced at Robert, then quickly looked away. She didn't want to open her mind to him just yet. Her feelings were too chaotic, too confused...

'That was only the beginning,' said Robert. 'Rhianna lived with us for almost four years, until she was a few months past the age of sixteen. Leihana didn't want her back after that night. She preferred her freedom, though didn't make much use of it as far as we could make out.'

'Despite her appalling treatment of Rhianna, my parents used to visit her fairly often...when she would let them. They even took her rock climbing at Girraween.' He ran a hand through his thick hair, then shook his head, as if to break away from an unpleasant memory. 'They were all good climbers, and Leihana seemed quite happy when they went on those trips, but otherwise kept to herself, letting the house and garden go to ruin. Rhianna told me she sometimes used to stand nearby, just to look, but never approached her mother, until one day she suddenly went back. I think she pitied her. By then, Rhianna had grown into an extraordinarily beautiful young woman, excelling at everything she did, in particular her martial arts, but had no friends other than us...and Sylvie, of course.'

He paused to consider. 'No, that's not entirely true. Margrethe was her friend. She knew what happened the day Ruth and her gang of bullies attacked them. Once I'd spoken with the Council of Parents, I told her the full story, as well as what happened here the night after. From that time onwards, Margrethe kept a closer eye on Rhianna. She was the one who managed to get Sylvie to talk to us again. It took a while though, poor little cat.'

Everything Robert had told them thus far fitted exactly with what Margrethe herself had related in her beautiful sunlit garden. 'Didn't she even have a young beau?' asked Freddi, thinking how a girl like Rhianna would have attracted attention.

'Yes, she did have admirers, though as far as I know, never had time for any of them. There was one in particular, Edric, who was with the gang who attacked her. He evidently got over his dislike, because he followed her everywhere, and even made such a nuisance of himself that Rhianna finally took matters into her own hands and reported him to the peacekeepers. He kept his distance afterwards, yet oddly enough, he was one of the small group of people who were with Rhianna when she died. In fact, he was the one who called me.'

Robert stopped speaking. Eventually, he cleared his throat and said, 'There seems so much to tell, it's hard to keep it all straight. Do you mind if I continue Rhianna's story, rather than telling you exactly what happened that night? I really need you to understand *who* she *was*, first.' He looked directly at Freddi, who nodded, understanding completely.

The garden, once expertly and proudly maintained by her father, was now a tangled mass of overgrown paths, dead and dying shrubs, and rotting limbs fallen from the towering eucalypts surrounding the property. The tidy rows of vegetables were gone too, and except for one by the verandah, the climbing roses were dead as well. Rhianna suspected Leihana poisoned them; they were too tough to have died of neglect. She gazed at the dilapidated house and, for the first time, pitied her mother. Taking care to avoid the thorns entangling the small gate, she pushed it open, wincing at the harsh grating of the hinges. It had begun to lean even before she left, but now the gate was almost unusable. Rhianna wondered how long it was since her mother had been out of the house. There was a rear path, so perhaps her food and other necessities were delivered and they used that?

The front door and verandah, well sheltered from the weather and strongly built, looked more like she remembered them from four years ago. Debating whether to knock or to simply go in, she chose to walk around to the rear door in case her mother was outside. Sylvie had been left behind, since Rhianna did not want to risk another confrontation. Without her cat's perceptions, she was therefore completely unprepared for what she found when she finally entered the house. It literally stank, as if it hadn't been cleaned for many months, possibly even longer. The kitchen sink overflowed with dirty dishes and the floor was greasy with spilled food and neglect. The light coming into the room was dimmed by the dirt on the windows and a thick coat of dust lay everywhere. It also appeared as if the security system either had malfunctioned or was turned off.

She slowly turned away and walked silently into her mother's bedroom. Leihana was there, lying on her side, her hair filthy, clothes bedraggled, on a bed that looked as if the sheets hadn't been changed in a long time. Rhianna felt like walking out again, yet managed to overcome her revulsion, choosing instead to stay. Pushing a pile of dirty clothes from the one chair in the room, she sat down, waiting for her mother to wake. Leihana turned over, groaning in a low, weak voice. Rhianna realised then that her mother was not merely sleeping. She was ill. If the security system had been functioning, the medcentre would automatically have been notified and someone would have come to her aid, but this situation made it impossible to know how long Leihana had lain there.

Wasting no further time, Rhianna called them. As she spoke to the practitioner on duty, the young woman studied her mother more closely. She was painfully thin and appeared far older than Rhianna remembered. Pity stirred in her, but not love – that was long dead.

Only some ten minutes went by before Rhianna heard the front door open and then the footsteps of the ambutechs walking towards the room. They hesitated in the doorway for only a moment, assessing the situation, then, with hoverbed in tow, examined Leihana. Before long, they had her neatly covered and ready to be taken to the medcentre.

'She's very anaemic, Rhianna,' the older of the two ambutechs told her, 'and has a blood alcohol reading eight times the healthy limit. By the appearance of her skin and its texture, she's also extremely dehydrated. If you hadn't arrived, your mother would almost certainly have died in another day or two. It's highly doubtful she would even have woken up. Do you want to come with her? I think you should.'

Rhianna considered what to say, then made a quick decision. The woman was, after all, her mother. Perhaps she owed her one last chance.

A feeble hand scratched helplessly around on the bedspread and Leihana moaned faintly several times before Rhianna could bring herself to take the hand in her own. Immediately, her mother breathed more deeply and the moaning ceased. They stayed like that for a long while, until one of the practitioners came to check on her patient. She greeted Rhianna and smiled kindly.

'She'll need to stay here for several days at least, Rhianna, and shouldn't be left alone once she goes home. Are you able to be with her, or do you want someone to assist?'

'I can be with her when I'm not at school, but I'd feel happier if there was someone else to help.' Rhianna felt distinctly uneasy at the idea of taking sole responsibility for this person who had almost become a stranger to her.

'I'll arrange it, then. They can live-in for a week, or until your mother is fully stable. I suspect it's best that way. She didn't get into this state because she's managing her life well. I'm amazed we haven't admitted her before.' The practitioner briefly touched Rhianna's hand in sympathy before leaving them alone again.

Rhianna called Agathea to tell her what was happening. 'I think I have to move back in to live with her, at least for a while, until she's able to look after herself properly.'

Agathea's expression was grim, her face drawn into unfamiliar lines of disapproval. 'I'm not happy, Rhianna. You could be putting yourself into danger, staying there with her once the assistant leaves.'

'I'll have Sylvie with me. Robert would know straight away if anything went wrong, and I don't think she'd let my mother lock her in again. It only happened because Sylvie never expected such a thing was possible...and besides, I promise to call every single day to let you know how it's all going.'

'Alright, my love, but if you change your mind, no one will think the worse of you. You're still only a girl and not really old enough to take on this sort of responsibility.'

Rhianna grimaced. She quietly agreed with Agathea, yet her determination to make the attempt remained. 'If it makes you feel any better, you could visit. Visits might even help Mother get well.'

'We'll try, although how welcome we'll be remains to be seen. Last time we asked her to come walking in Girraween, she was quite dismissive, and even told me she wanted to be left alone. That could well be typical of depression, but we can't force your mother to come with us if she refuses.'

'No, but coming to visit's different,' said Rhianna. 'She wouldn't close the door in your face. At least *I* wouldn't, and once you were there, she might even enjoy having someone come to see her.'

Agathea nodded. 'Well, I'll send Robert over tomorrow evening at about 18:00 with some dinner and the rest of your things. You won't have to cook anything then, and afterwards, you can both visit the medcentre. He can tell me how it goes and we'll take one step at a time from there. What do you think?'

'Thanks, Aunt Aggie! That'd be wonderful. I'll probably leave now and come home to pick up some clothes and school things, then go back to Mother's house to do some tidying up. It'll take forever, which means the sooner I begin, the sooner it'll be done.' Robert's company never failed to cheer Rhianna, and to have him there for what might be the first time she would see Leihana awake would help the situation enormously, or so she hoped, heaving a sigh.

Agathea smiled, said goodbye, and blew her niece a kiss.

Rhianna surveyed her mother's bedroom in disgust. How *could* she have let it get into such a state! She started with the rubbish, putting it into a bag, going from room to room until the worst mess was gone. Fortunately, the recycling unit still worked, so it wasn't long before it was all disposed of, but that still left the cleaning and washing to be done. Picking up the discarded clothing lying in the bedroom, bathroom, lounge room – and kitchen! – Rhianna wrinkled her nose at the smell and gingerly stuffed it all into the washing machine, which, thank the Sun, was also working. The bedding would have to wait until another load could be done.

Rhianna was working too hard to notice how the temperature had dropped, but as the evening drew on, it became far too cold for her not to notice. She realised that without a functioning security system, the climate controls were unlikely to be working either. It was too late in the day to get someone out to fix it, she concluded, and an inspection of the wood stove found it to be surprisingly clean. Although the woodshed was the last place Rhianna wanted to go, there was little choice. Taking the old-fashioned back-up key from its hook by the rear door, she found the emergency torch and then manually turned on the outside light, before cautiously making her way along the overgrown path until she reached the shed. At first, the key wouldn't turn in the lock, but with some persuasion, the door eventually opened. As it did, she jumped when her comlink chimed, seeming unusually loud in the still night air. It was Robert.

'What are you doing out in the garden?' he asked, concerned.

'Fetching some wood... It's getting a bit cold,' she replied, peering cautiously into the shed.

'I sincerely hope you've got gloves on.'

'No, I forgot. Do you really think I need them?' Rhianna decided she did, spotting a cobweb up near the ceiling. The shed was meant to be spider-proof, but like everything else, the small outbuilding had been allowed to become run-down. 'You're right... I'll go back in and get some.'

'Don't work too hard tonight,' Robert was saying as she walked. 'I'll come and help you tomorrow evening like my mother promised. By the sound of it, Leihana won't be home for some time; she's far too ill mentally and physically. Just make yourself comfortable.'

'The house is an awful mess, Robert. I've never seen anything like it. But you're right. I promise to only get rid of the worst of the stink, then make myself a bed somewhere. I dread to think what my old room is like! I haven't even gone in there to see. I don't think I want to, until you're here.'

After hunting around in the laundry cupboards, Rhianna found some gloves, put them on and held out her hands for Robert to see. He laughed. 'You look like you can tackle the woodshed now, but please, be careful. Anyway, I'll leave you to it. Have a good sleep and I'll see you tomorrow.'

Rhianna hummed to herself while she collected enough wood and kindling for the evening. This was the first time she would spend a whole night almost entirely alone and was enjoying the sense of independence it gave her. If the house and garden could be put back into good repair, her mother might begin to feel better, she thought optimistically. She might even get better enough to take care of herself... Rhianna sighed. She was probably hoping for too much. It also felt strange to think about her mother again and to wish for something from her.

Sylvie had been nosing around the house, silently reacquainting herself with memories and places, though definitely had not wanted to accompany Rhianna to the woodshed. That was one memory she did not want to relive! As the wood fire began to warm the lounge room, the cat decided the best thing to do was to find herself a suitable place to sleep – although she kept an ear cocked and half an eye open in case anything untoward should happen in this quiet, solitary house. In the kitchen, her companion was trying to decide where to start, and how much to do before making her own bed next to the spot Sylvie had chosen. At least there were clean blankets in the linen press. She was young enough not to mind sleeping on the floor: it seemed the easiest thing to do.

Putting on a pair of waterproof gloves, she rinsed some of the filthy dishes and packed them into the washing unit, then switched it on. It seemed to be operational, so Rhianna turned her attention to rinsing and neatly stacking the remainder before tackling the benchtops and sink. There was far too thick a layer of dirt to make much headway tonight, she decided, so cleaned only enough space to unload the dishwasher when it finished. The cupboards were in no fit state to put the clean items into, but at least the smell of stale food was beginning to disappear.

After taking off the gloves and hanging them up to dry, she opened a window a few centimetres to let in some fresh air. Closing the door to the kitchen to prevent the cold air from coming into the rest of the house, Rhianna made her bed, removed her shoes, checked the fire was safe for the night, then curled up next to Sylvie and was soon fast asleep.

Robert's narrative was interrupted by a knock at the door. They had almost forgotten the time and it was now late evening. Meng Jarrah poked her head into the room and looked at the intent faces.

'I think it's time you stopped,' she said, with a hint of a smile. 'It's past midnight. I've done more than enough for today, *and* tonight, and there are things we should talk about...which we can do tomorrow.' She held up a hand to forestall Freddi's question. 'I've taken the initiative and arranged for Robert to stay in the communal house tonight to save him having to go all the way home... I hope you don't mind? No? Good. In that case, Robert, you can join us in having something hot to eat and drink, and afterwards, we'll all find our beds.'

Gwenllian chuckled, highly amused at the way Meng Jarrah had taken over. With a grin, Freddi folded her arms and met her eyes, while even Robert had the ghost of a smile on his face. He hadn't met Meng Jarrah until now, but immediately responded to the obvious sympathy he could feel radiating from her. They all obediently followed her out into the anteroom, where the promised food and hot tea were waiting. As they all ate and drank, Robert let himself relax a little, settling back into one of the comfortable armchairs. He had grieved for the Rhianna he once knew for so many years that it was almost a relief to share his memories of her.

A small, distant sound in his mind suddenly caught his attention. The peacekeeper's cat, Shela, was voicing her disgust at being left alone for far too long. 'I think your cat wants to be allowed back in, Freddi,' he said.

Freddi gazed at him, startled Robert had heard Shela before she herself did.

Robert answered her unspoken question: 'I can amplify their range, but don't worry, only if they want me to. I couldn't hear her while we were talking. Your cat knows her role extremely well.'

Freddi frowned, but accepted what he said and, without saying a word, got up to fetch her.

While she was gone, Meng Jarrah introduced herself properly and Robert stood up to solemnly shake hands, then sat down again.

'I'm helping the pathologist,' explained Meng Jarrah. 'I gather you and your mother are the only relatives of the deceased living here in Stanthorpe? You have my deepest sympathy.'

Robert nodded, but said nothing for a long moment. 'Thank you,' he eventually replied, his expression showing he meant it, then, just as Freddi and Shela returned, added, 'I think it's time I accepted the bed you've arranged for me. I'm exhausted!' The cat approached and pressed herself against his legs, purring. He leaned forward to stroke her head and ears, then straightened up and said, 'May I ask you for a very large favour, Freddi? May I keep Shela with me tonight? It would be a great comfort.'

Robert hunched his shoulders as if to ward off refusal, yet he needn't have. Freddi was more than happy to agree. Shela made a better guard than any peacekeeper could have, but more to the point, since Robert hardly required guarding, she would help him gain some much-needed peace. There was no doubt in her mind that although Robert committed a great wrong in not reporting Rhianna's death immediately, he had no hand in her death.

Without further discussion, they gathered their things and walked silently to the nearest exit, then out into the cold night air, shivering when it touched their skin. After wishing each other good night, Gwenllian,

Robert and Shela made their way to the communal house, while Freddi and Meng Jarrah walked on towards Nyneve's home.

CHAPTER SEVEN

Rhianna woke the next morning to feel Sylvie curled up against her back, warm and soft, and still fast asleep. She yawned, then stretched and slowly sat up, feeling the strangeness of this house which had once been her home. Sylvie murmured in her sleep, then opened her eyes, ears twitching. It was still early, barely light outside, and cold. When Rhianna pulled on her jacket, before standing up to put on her boots, Sylvie tried to entice her into coming back to bed, where it was so lovely and warm.

'Sorry, puss, there are things to do, and besides, I'm hungry.'

Yawning hugely, Sylvie moved over to the spot Rhianna had vacated and curled up in the blankets again, one front paw over her face.

An icy wind blew in through the open kitchen window, although at least the air was fresh. Filling the sink with hot water, Rhianna quickly washed herself, teeth chattering, but she couldn't have faced the filthy bathroom for anything other than the essentials. Once fully dressed, she brushed her long hair and looped it into an elegant coil that made her appear older than her sixteen years.

There was breakfast for both of them in the pack she had brought with her. The best place to have their food was the lounge room, where, in comparison to the rest of the house, it was a few degrees warmer. Sylvie opened an enquiring eye and stretched out her long front legs, then showed her strong white teeth in another wide yawn, before making her way carefully over the bedding to sniff at her breakfast, which she contentedly sat down to eat. Rhianna was relieved to find her this amiable. She had half-expected Sylvie to flatly refuse to enter either the house or the garden ever again.

With breakfast finished and the bedding tidied away, Rhianna called the local security contractors. 'The whole system, including the climate controls, is down,' she explained. 'We have power, but that's all.'

'We can be there in about two hours. Will that suit?' The woman knew Rhianna, due to it being a small community, and was surprised to see her in Leihana's house.

'Yes, but I can't be here; I have to go to school. If I engage the manual locks, can you still get inside?'

'We'll be fine. There aren't many systems, mechanical or otherwise, that can keep us out.' She sounded faintly smug, though in a comforting way. 'Do you want us to call you when we've finished?'

'Just send a message, in case I'm in class. I'll notice. Oh, and please forgive the state of the house. It's a dreadful mess, but I thought I'd better get the systems back online before I did much else. It's awfully cold in here.'

'Don't you worry; it'll be nice and warm by the time you get back. We'll set the system to your mother's ID, voice pattern and thumbprint, as it was before, and add yours if you can transmit the details. Do you have them stored?' Fortunately, Rhianna did, so she sent them the file. 'Fine, I've got it,' confirmed the woman. 'Now, who do we bill for all of this?'

'Oh! I suppose you can bill my mother. She must have something in her account. If not, let me know and I'll work it out. My uncle or cousin would be able to pay if she can't. Is that alright?'

'We'll let you know how much it comes to once the system's up and running, and then you can check and let us know. I think that would be best, don't you?'

'Yes, of course, if you think so.' Rhianna wasn't used to paying for anything, other than the occasional food delivery when she was younger and still living with Leihana.

The woman smiled, understanding. 'How *is* your mother?' she asked, her curiosity getting the better of her.

Rhianna paused, considering what to say, then replied, without giving much detail. The woman nodded sympathetically, wondering just how big a mess the house was in, particularly if all the systems had been allowed to go offline. They were robust enough to last at least two years without any maintenance whatsoever.

Before leaving for school, Rhianna made one more call: to the medcentre. The practitioner who answered was looking a little weary, but nevertheless tried to be helpful and cheerful.

'Your mother hasn't regained her senses yet,' she said, in response to Rhianna's questions. 'It may be a day or two yet before she does. She's severely dehydrated and was also suffering from hypothermia. Presumably the house lost its climate controls? Yes? She *will* recover physically, but we won't know how she is mentally until she wakes up. We've done the most important brain scans, and remarkably enough, given her blood alcohol reading, there doesn't seem to be any actual damage, though sometimes these things can be quite subtle. We'll contact you when she wakes up, if you like?'

Rhianna accepted, unsure of how she felt, and politely thanked the practitioner.

*

Later that day, sitting alone with Sylvie, as was her custom, Rhianna felt perfectly content solving a particularly difficult mathematical equation. When the last line in the proof was completed, she paused for a moment to prolong the satisfaction, then moved on to the next problem in the class assignment. The other students ignored her, in the main. They had long since lost interest in this silent, self-contained girl, and were used to the sight of her working alone, accompanied by her cat. The only time they spoke with her was when the preceptors designed some form of team learning exercise, and then they were all polite and friendly enough, yet always maintained a wary distance. Rhianna hardly noticed them, preoccupied as she was with her own thoughts and with excelling at everything required of her. There were also further interests to pursue in her free time. Recently, she had chosen to learn Japanese, after having easily mastered French, but since there were no local experts in the language, did so using the lattice; which was fine, as far as Rhianna was concerned.

Finishing the last problem, she raised her arms above her head to stretch luxuriously. This was the first time she had truly appreciated how lovely it was simply to be warm! Sylvie mentally agreed, and stretched as well, then stood up to place her head on Rhianna's knee, smooching and asking to be stroked. Rhianna obliged, before looking around to see if any of the other students had finished their work. Most of them had, although two or three seemed to be struggling. The preceptor was helping one of them, but glanced inquiringly at Rhianna. The girl nodded, and walked over to the student whom she knew from experience would need the most help *and* who wouldn't resent the help coming from her. His name was Edric. He smiled at Rhianna when she sat down next to him. Sylvie stayed behind, studying Edric, but for the time being she was content to watch and listen.

The class over, they went outside, into the bright winter sunshine, for a short break. Rhianna, as usual, walked alone, thinking about her mother. A tall girl, a young woman really, given she looked to be at least two years older, approached her. 'She must be new to the school and to the town,' thought Rhianna, pausing in her walk and gazing at the stranger with frank interest. Her face, dress and manner were quite different from anyone else she had met in Stanthorpe.

'Vous avez un chat! Elle est très belle. May I pat her, do you think?' said the young woman.

Sylvie took a small step backwards and sat down, ears pricked, whiskers erect.

'No, I don't think that would be wise,' replied Rhianna, and then, unusually, added a brief explanation: 'She doesn't like being touched by strangers.'

'Bien, alors nous devrons devenir des amis au lieu des étrangers.' The new student smiled, showing small, even teeth of a startling whiteness; startling in contrast to the jet black hair framing her heart-shaped face in a short, straight mass cut evenly across her forehead. Dark eyebrows arched delicately above beautiful, deep brown eyes, while a small, pert nose complemented her dark red, bud-like mouth.

'My name is Marietta,' she said, in a rich, mellow voice. 'Do you like it? There is an ancient operetta called *Naughty Marietta*. That is me...naughty Marietta!' She laughed, stretching out an elegant hand and taking Rhianna's strong, muscular one in a quick, firm grasp.

The winter sunshine still shone through the dirty kitchen windows while Rhianna, her sleeves rolled up above her elbows, cleaned the cupboards. As she worked, she thought about the stranger, Marietta. Sylvie sat beneath the table in the centre of the room, watching. The cat made it perfectly clear to Rhianna that *she* didn't like this wight.

'No, puss, I don't think I do either, but she *is* unusual, and could be interesting. Ah well, I don't think you'll need to worry, my love. She probably won't talk to me again anyway.'

When Sylvie said that she hoped not, Rhianna laughed, flicking some soapsuds at her. The cat dodged, then licked at the spot where they had fallen onto the now clean floor. 'Ugh!' she 'said', and Rhianna laughed again.

The house was wonderfully warm, now that its climate control was back online, but the first thing Rhianna had done on coming back from school was to check the woodshed. The door was now electronically secured, which meant the shed was freed of any spiders and insects, as well as secure against any fresh intruders. She had thumbed open the small door and collected an armful of wood, having grown accustomed to a real fire and wanting its company in this house that was now quite strange to her. From the kitchen, she could hear the occasional crackle of the cheerfully burning wood, and then heard the front door open. It was Robert!

Hastily drying her hands and rolling down her sleeves, she ran out into the hallway to meet him, followed by a joyful Sylvie, who leapt up and almost knocked him over in her enthusiasm. Robert gazed in amazement at the state of the house, meanwhile restraining Sylvie with one hand and holding a large picnic basket in the other.

'She never let us inside, you know,' he told Rhianna, after giving her a quick kiss on the cheek, 'but we should have guessed what was happening from the way the garden had been neglected. We should have done something!'

Rhianna looked at him in silence, unhappy he should feel guilty. He walked into the lounge room then out to the kitchen, while she followed a few steps behind.

'You've made a good start though,' he said, noticing how clean the floor and the benches were. 'I don't suppose there's any use blaming ourselves. Instead, we need to accept that your mother won't get better in a hurry and that we'll all have to help, even if she tries to stop us. Otherwise, she'll most likely die, and we need to decide if that's something we're prepared to allow. I can see you've made *your* decision, but I hope you realise how hard it will be. Do you?'

'How can I say, Robert? I've never taken care of anyone before, except for Sylvie. How can I possibly know how it's going to turn out? All I can say is that I want to try. *Someone* has to.'

Her cousin considered her thoughtfully before he replied: 'You won't be able to be her daughter. You'll have to be her friend instead. She won't like it, to begin with. She may even try to bully you into doing as you're told again. Do you think you can stand up to her if she does?'

'I don't know, but somehow I think I *can* because I don't actually love her any longer. I can try to care for her as a person whom I know and who needs the help I can give. I don't need her approval or her love, but I do want her to get well again. If I fail, then perhaps there was never any real chance of her ever getting over my father's death and becoming a person in her own right again.' Rhianna's shoulders were slightly hunched, her face troubled and serious.

Robert took her firmly by the hand. 'You can rely on us to help, and if it gets too much, you know you can come home...even if it's in the middle of the night!'

She gave him a quick, hard hug. 'Yes, I know. That's why I think I can do this. I have a choice.'

'She stayed with her mother and looked after her for three years,' continued Robert, standing up to stare out the window, turning his back on Freddi and Gwenllian. It had been so cold the previous night that a heavy frost covered the earth, almost resembling a light fall of snow and sitting strangely on the gum trees, which seemed more suited to sunshine and warmth, yet were hardy and resilient in their twisted shapes. For a long time, he said nothing further. When he did eventually speak again, his voice was a mere whisper:

'Despite everything her daughter did for her, Leihana killed Sylvie after all.'

*

'You love your cat, but you don't love me, do you!' hissed Leihana, leaning forward over the dining table. She and her daughter were eating their evening meal, prepared, as usual and with considerable care, by Rhianna.

Rhianna looked up at her mother, and for an instant the contempt she felt passed across her face. It was enough to confirm Leihana's words – all too clearly. The woman picked up her plate of food and threw it to the floor, then with all her force threw the wine glass against the nearest wall. The dark red liquid splashed out, running onto the polished floor, where it spread out into a small pool. Sylvie, who had been lying close to Rhianna's feet, dozing peacefully, sprang up in alarm and fled the room, heading for the rear door; but it was closed. She crouched, with shoulders hunched and ears flattened, waiting for what was to come next. This was not the first time the cat had witnessed these scenes, and not the first time she felt the hatred in Leihana's mind.

'Do you really wonder why I don't?' replied Rhianna in a low voice, not even bothering to take notice of the mess her mother had made.

Tears ran down the older woman's face. She had sunk to the floor, holding her head in her hands, but looked up as her daughter spoke. 'Then why don't you leave!' she cried.

'Is that what you want? To leave you to kill yourself? Like you almost succeeded in doing three years ago?'

Rhianna knelt down in front of her mother, took her by the wrist and forced Leihana to look into her face. 'Tell me, is that what you want?' she repeated, her voice harsh, even to her own ears.

'Yes! Yes, it's what I want! I don't want your pity and I don't want that beast here! If I want to kill myself, it's none of your business! You shouldn't have saved me before. I didn't want you to!'

Rhianna had heard these words of self-pity many times before, yet all of a sudden couldn't bear to hear them one more time. She felt there would never be an end to the recriminations, the self-hate, and the morbid fixation on her father's death so many years ago. More importantly, she could no longer bear the irrational hatred her mother felt towards Sylvie.

She released her mother and stood up, staring down at the figure on the floor, then turned and walked slowly to her own room to collect her few belongings. It took only moments to put them into a travel bag, yet she hesitated, overcome with a sudden sense of doubt. Wishing that the courage to keep trying had not deserted her, Rhianna sat down on the edge of the bed, staring out the window at the full moon, which had just risen above the horizon. A feeling of great emptiness grew, as if something that had been there for a long time had all at once vanished. Starting up in alarm, she cried out: 'Sylvie!'

A scream of sheer terror came from the kitchen. Not a human scream. A cat's scream, high and wailing. Rhianna saw her beloved grimalkin cowering abjectly, cornered by her mother wielding the razor-sharp knife used to prepare the evening meal. There was blood on the floor near the door where Sylvie had been crouching, and there was blood on the cat's neck: her fur was dripping with it. Rhianna hurled herself forward and swiftly disarmed Leihana, throwing the knife as far away as she could before striking her mother on the side of the neck. The woman slid to the floor, unconscious but unharmed.

Sylvie was also unconscious as Rhianna tore her kerchief from her pocket to bind it around the gaping wound, bringing its edges as tightly together as possible. She sobbed as she begged her cat not to die, then called frantically to the security system to contact the medcentre. The request was confirmed, in its usual bland tone, while Rhianna cradled Sylvie in her arms as well as she could without moving her from the floor. Almost immediately, a practitioner appeared on the screen, blanching at the sight before her.

'Rhianna! What's happened to your mother?'

'Damn my mother! She's fine... It's Sylvie! Mother attacked her with a knife and she's bleeding to death! Please, please, send someone now, or she'll die!' Tears streamed down Rhianna's face as she stared up at the screen.

The practitioner hesitated for only a moment, then spoke to someone who was out of view. 'They won't be long,' she said, turning back to the screen. 'We'll send the animal healer with the ambutechs. In the meantime, keep the cat still. I'll stay with you until they arrive.'

The practitioner understood the situation, as did most people in the small town. That Leihana O'Connor was attempting to kill herself with alcohol was common knowledge. She flatly refused the help that could have overcome her addiction, and Rhianna was not prepared to have her taken forcibly to a treatment centre. Nearly everyone, including the practitioner, was of the opinion that the young woman should have allowed this to happen.

Leihana moaned faintly, and when the ambutechs arrived, began to wake up. She tried to sit, but failed, sliding back onto the floor in an undignified heap. The ambutechs were closely followed by the animal healer, who immediately brought out his equipment from his copious bag and began to work on Sylvie, right there on the floor. Despite Rhianna's care, the cat had lost a great deal of blood. Even the trauma of the attack itself might kill her.

Meanwhile, the ambutechs were having trouble persuading Leihana to allow them to examine her. 'No!' she screamed. 'Go away! I don't want your help. Just leave me alone. Take that accursed daughter of mine and her damned cat instead. Didn't I manage to kill it? Then maybe I'll make a better go of it this time!'

She leapt to her feet, her insane rage giving her strength, and snatched the nearest thing that came to hand to throw in Sylvie's direction. The animal healer ducked and the saucepan bounced harmlessly off a cupboard door and onto the floor, where it rolled about for a few moments before becoming still – as still as the room, until the ambutech nearest Leihana took her in an expert grip and applied a fast-acting sedative. The second ambutech neatly caught her and lowered her onto the waiting hoverbed.

'Sylvie's body didn't die, but her mind did.' Robert turned to look at Gwenllian, his own mind open to her for the first time. 'You understand, don't you?' he said.

Gwenllian slowly nodded, appalled at what she had heard and at the deep sorrow in Robert's mind. 'You tried everything you could,' she replied, trying to comfort him with the words that are so often used, yet which, in themselves, rarely do bring any real comfort, 'but you still feel there should have been something else that could have been done. Robert, no one knew as much about cats back then as we do now, not even the Breeding Centres. Individuals might have known what they were really like, but the medical knowledge wasn't there to treat them if they became totally traumatised. This quality they have, it's only during the past five years that anyone's fully understood just how powerful it is, as well as how sensitive they are.'

She moved closer to Robert and placed her hand on his arm. He briefly touched it, then turned away. Gwenllian withdrew her hand, but left her mind open to him. Freddi saw a faint aura of light surround them as they stood together near the window. It glimmered briefly, shifting colour, then disappeared. When Robert turned to face her again, to continue his story, his fine features were calmer and his voice stronger as he spoke.

'Once her wounds had mended, we brought Sylvie to Margrethe, hoping she could heal her mind, but after almost a year, Sylvie still could not – or would not; we don't know – speak with us. Rhianna lost a part of herself the day her mother did that to her cat. She had lived with Sylvie for fourteen years. A presence that had been in her mind for all that time was suddenly gone. Sylvie's gentle and loving thoughts had become part of Rhianna's own mind, and without them, Rhianna began to change. Slowly at first, but as time went by and her darling didn't recover, it became clear even to my mother and father. They adored Rhianna and were reluctant to admit it, but there was no mistake. We eventually sent Sylvie to the new Breeding Centre in Brisbane, yet even their nursing mothers couldn't help. In the end, Margrethe offered to keep her because Sylvie became frightened of everyone else, which was more than Rhianna could bear. It almost broke her heart to see the poor creature cower when she came near.'

'What did Margrethe's cat think?' asked Gwenllian. 'Didn't she help Rhianna understand?'

Robert bent his head for a moment, considering. 'Yes,' he said, 'Harriet did help Rhianna understand that the Sylvie she knew and loved was gone, probably forever. What remained was a timid, ordinary cat.'

'So Sylvie lived out the rest of her life with Margrethe and Harriet?'

'Yes. She became quite content after a time, as far as anyone could tell. Rhianna decided to leave Stanthorpe shortly after Sylvie finally died. There's a grave in Girraween not far from where I buried Rhianna. I thought they should be together one last time.'

Nibbling the tip of his thumb, the pathologist studied the list on the screen. There were four names – the names Meng Jarrah identified from the samples he had given her: Marietta Ross, Edric, Ruth Baillieu and Stefano Salvarez. All former Stanthorpe students, all one or two years Rhianna O'Connor's senior. It appeared that although Rhianna may have rejected Edric's advances in the distant past, he had, at least this one time, been her lover. Unless, of course, Rhianna was raped, but despite the bruises, there was no evidence to show this had been the case.

'The pollen results are relatively straightforward,' said Meng Jarrah, scrolling down to her second list. 'She hasn't been anywhere other than Brisbane since she last washed... At least, that's the highest probability. Also, there's nothing in all this to show she was taken anywhere other than straight to Girraween after she died...or before she died, for that matter.'

Musing, and nodding his birdlike head, the pathologist called Nyneve to give her the four names, together with their other results, at the same time taking the opportunity to find out if Smithson had made any further progress.

'Well, I'm amazed to hear she was in company with that crowd,' remarked Nyneve, shaking her head. 'She certainly didn't have much to do with them while she lived here, except for Marietta. They almost seemed to become friends for a while, but fell out. I think it was something to do with hunting. Rhianna reported her to the peacekeepers for shooting birds.'

'Shooting!' exclaimed Meng Jarrah, having joined the conversation soon after it began. 'But no one shoots birds, or anything else! Do they?'

'No, not usually. At least, not if they're sane.' Nyneve looked at them for a few seconds before adding, 'I'm not sure if Marietta Ross *was* entirely sane, the way she carried on. I'll send you the whole file. But you say Rhianna had been with Edric not long before she died? That's bizarre, given she disliked his attentions enough in the past to report *him* to us as well!'

'Do you know yet who paid the restaurant bill, and who was there with her the night she died?' asked the pathologist.

'Yes, we do. They'd all booked beforehand by name, it being an invitation-only event. Altogether, there were fifty-four guests, and most of them were former Stanthorpe students, not only the four you've listed. The bill was paid beforehand too, presumably from credits collected from those who were to attend. The coordinator of it all was Ruth Baillieu.' Nyneve paused to consult her comlink. 'She lives in Brisbane apparently, as do Edric and Stefano Salvarez. Marietta Ross came all the way from Melbourne.'

'For a dinner?' Meng Jarrah stared at Nyneve. 'She's keen!'

'Well, I gather the wine was exceptional,' replied Nyneve, a wry expression on her face. 'She's not the only one who came a long way. A few of them even flew in from other countries.'

'It must have been quite an event,' remarked the pathologist, one bristling eyebrow raised in surprise. 'That's also a rather long interview list.'

'Yes it is, but we'll check them all, unless we find out what really happened from the ones you've just given us. We'll start with Edric, since he's the one who contacted Robert O'Connor, and then I think Robert should tell us how Rhianna came to be buried in Girraween. Could you call Freddi in? I'd like to speak with her.'

'It's time you told us what happened the night she died,' said Gwenllian in a low voice, touching Robert lightly on the arm. Freddi had left them alone for a few moments, so she used the opportunity to reach out to him. She felt his hurt keenly and understood how reluctant he was to relive the night his cousin was buried. He turned around at her touch, looked down, and for a moment, put his own larger, finely shaped hand over hers, before fully facing her. Gwenllian moved away slightly, the better to see his eyes.

'You *need* to talk about it,' she said. 'It would help if you'd allow Shela to be here too. She can transmit the images in your mind directly to us all. I could too, but to be honest, I'd rather concentrate on helping you through this.'

Robert regarded her silently for several seconds, then startled Gwenllian by placing a soft, brief kiss on her forehead. 'Thank you,' he said, and sat down to wait for Freddi to return. As Gwenllian sat down next to him, Freddi quietly entered the room, together with Nyneve.

'I'm ready to tell you the rest of the story,' explained Robert. 'You could bring Shela in, Freddi. She can help you understand and also to see what I saw.'

Surprised, Freddi nodded and went out again to fetch Shela. When she came back, the cat walked by her side, with tail lowered and a subdued expression on her face. She sat down by Robert's knee, gave him a quick lick on the hand, and made herself comfortable.

CHAPTER EIGHT

Rhianna lazily rolled over to touch Edric on his bare shoulder. Having slept for some hours, it was time to get up, since they did not want to be late for the Stanthorpe reunion dinner. It was being held early in the evening to allow time for the tournament afterwards, and because neither they nor the other contestants would want to fight on a full stomach.

Edric murmured in his sleep, woke, and slowly turned to face Rhianna, drawing her closer. Rhianna laughed softly, tousling his thick blonde hair, then, before wriggling free, wrapped her arms around him in one last hug. When she stood up, long black hair flowed down to her waist, almost clothing her in its lustrous beauty. Edric propped himself up on one elbow to watch. He never tired of looking at Rhianna, and continued to marvel at the good fortune that had at last brought her to him.

'Will you braid my hair for me?' called Rhianna from their bathing room.

Easing himself from the bed, Edric stretched languorously and walked over to where he had left his robe. 'Just a minute... I'll be right there,' he called back, absent-mindedly picking up Rhianna's clothes from the floor where she had dropped them. He hung them neatly on the back of a chair.

Rhianna appeared in the doorway and shook her head, amused, as always, at his passion for neatness, then sat down so he could brush her hair before carefully braiding and twining the dark locks. While he brushed, he ran his hand over her brow to smooth back any escaping strands, then deftly formed a complex knot to withstand the evening's fierce competition.

'There,' he said, admiring her reflection in the mirror. 'You look wonderful. I'm sure Marietta will be so envious she'll be put off her stride and have even less chance of defeating you.' As their eyes met in the mirror image, he kissed the top of her head, dark hair against golden.

'She doesn't stand a chance... She never has,' replied Rhianna, smiling as she stood up to finish dressing.

They left their landjet in Roma Street and walked arm-in-arm through the parkland until they reached the Hotel Grand Chancellor in Petrie Terrace.

Rhianna looked magnificent in a long, dark green robe, made from fabric that shimmered as she walked. As the evening was chilly, a shawl of the same material covered her head then draped elegantly around her throat and bare shoulders. Rhianna wore no ornaments of any kind because they would only hinder her later; besides which, she didn't want to risk losing anything by having to take it off before her first round. It was superstition, she supposed, since the security would be tight. It needed to be, given the tournament was illegal.

Edric was a hand's breadth shorter than Rhianna, yet of a more sturdy build. While she was slender, with a tensile strength that was the product of more than three decades of hard training, he was naturally athletic and maintained his fitness far more readily than she. In her opinion, this led him to be somewhat lazy in his approach to their martial arts tournaments, yet in spite of this, he was still the undefeated champion.

Although Edric normally wore his shoulder-length hair loose, tonight it too was securely tied back in a ponytail. He was dressed to complement Rhianna, wearing dark green trousers and a long black tunic with ornate embroidery depicting a wyvern on his left breast, in matching shades of green. The tunic had been a gift from Rhianna not long after they met again, now almost seven years ago. At the time, she had contacted Ruth Baillieu to make it known she wanted to become a contender in the contests Edric and her former adversary helped each other organise, and which traced their origins back to their schooldays in Stanthorpe.

Ruth stood waiting just inside the grand entranceway as they arrived. She was even taller than Rhianna, with statuesque proportions that tended to be almost too opulent. For reasons she could not fully understand, Ruth remained somewhat wary of the other woman, despite managing to overcome the actual fear she had felt for her since the day Sylvie defended Rhianna against her bullying – although Ruth did not use this term. She never bothered to analyse her actions or why she wanted 'followers', but had learned to accept, if not like, the fact that Rhianna would never be truly 'hers'. In turn, Rhianna treated Ruth with distant composure, dealing with her merely as Edric's colleague, nothing more. She now held out a hand to her. Ruth briefly shook it, then kissed Edric lightly on the cheek.

'Has Marietta arrived yet?' asked Edric, after returning Ruth's kiss.

'Not yet.' Ruth grimaced slightly. 'I suspect she wants to make 'the grand entrance', as usual. Stefano can show you to your table, if you like. I need to wait here to welcome everyone, of course, so I'll see you both later.'

Stefano Salvarez had been waiting patiently to take his turn to greet the two reigning unofficial Australian champions; Edric being the heavyweight and Rhianna the middleweight kung fu and karate combined tournament winners for the past four and three years respectively. Both would fight tonight to defend their titles. Stefano himself no longer fought, having lost his sight two years previously in an exceptionally vicious bout that ended when his opponent simultaneously struck both eyes. He now enjoyed perfectly adequate artificial vision, but as it was rather more than adequate – enhanced, in fact – he no longer qualified for the contests, since any form of artificial advantage was disallowed.

He enthusiastically shook Edric's hand, then held Rhianna's and kissed her on the cheek. Neither of them had taken much notice of him while they were students in Stanthorpe. He joined the community there only towards the end of their studies, when they were both far too busy with other things to want to make new friends; or, in Rhianna's case, any friends at all. Nevertheless, Stefano had become one of the few people Rhianna was truly fond of, as well as close to. He and Edric had been firm friends for many years, ever since he became Edric's protégé in the tournaments. Being in the lightweight division, Stefano was not, however, in any danger from Edric's superior skills.

Laughing in sheer good humour, he led them to a table situated in the place of honour at the furthest end of the banquet hall. Everyone applauded Edric and Rhianna as they walked, almost regally, to their designated places, where Stefano seated them with due solemnity – then ruined the impression by grinning at the onlookers and executing a small, mock bow. With a farewell wave to his two friends, he returned to the foyer to await the other guests.

The dinner was held here in Brisbane every year, and each year great effort went into lavishly decorating the banquet hall, creating a grand, formal occasion. All the tables were furnished with white linen tablecloths, silver candelabra, red napkins, and the finest arrangements of Australian flowers obtainable. Magnificent waratahs were interspersed with fine sprays of young eucalypt leaves, as well as grevilleas in a truly superb range of shapes and colours. Elegant silver cutlery and finest pure-white porcelain tableware completed the effect.

While Rhianna and Edric gazed at the assembly in satisfaction, Marietta Ross, the last guest to arrive, appeared on Ruth's arm and the two women began walking towards them. Marietta looked stylish and highly impressive in her long, deep red, form-hugging sheath dress of pure silk printed with swirls of black. She hardly seemed older than the first time Rhianna met her, twenty-six years ago. Her hair was still cut in the same severe style that contrasted so well with her pale skin and childlike features. The expression on her face, however, was anything but childlike as she approached their table and held out her hand to Edric, before turning to Rhianna.

'Comme toujours, vous êtes très beaux ce soir, Rhianna O'Connor,' she remarked, laughing, 'but before the evening is finished your fine coiffure will be a touch less fine. Non?'

Rhianna inclined her head, maintaining a pleasantly bland expression, then firmly grasped Marietta by the hand and said, 'Well, you can try your best, as always, but I don't think you'll succeed, my dear Marietta.'

Ruth hid a small smile, kissed Marietta's cheek, then left them in order to see to the dinner arrangements. Although the banquet hall had filled, there were final touches to coordinate before the evening could officially commence.

Marietta seated herself next to Edric in the customary place of honour reserved for the highest-ranking challenger of the evening, carefully composing her expression to best advantage. While Edric respected Marietta's prowess and had worked amicably with her before he met Rhianna again, he found it increasingly difficult to tolerate the constant small thrusts she seemed unable to resist making. Sighing to himself, he did his best to enjoy the company of both women, but really did wish Marietta could have taken herself elsewhere!

The fine clothing of the guests sitting at the other tables rustled and crystal goblets chimed as the pre-dinner toasts were drunk. No speeches or announcements were necessary; everyone knew what to expect from the evening. Silent, efficient servitors brought the food, dish after exotic dish. Meats not normally available, such as tender roast venison with jellied red currant sauce, were a feature of the meal, delicacies savoured and remembered from year to year. Even those who were not intimately connected with the forthcoming tournament anticipated this annual event with pleasure, simply to taste the exquisite food. Edric, Marietta, Rhianna, and the others who were to fight, ate and drank relatively sparingly so as not to hinder their stamina.

As the evening's gaiety gradually increased, Marietta became ever more focused on needling Rhianna. At last Edric could stand it no longer. He turned to her and spoke quietly: 'You are behaving dishonourably, Marietta. Do you even understand the concept? Honour may be an old term, but it's still one that matters, particularly here. I suggest you find another table to sit at, or else we will.'

Marietta flushed a dark, ugly red, glared at him, then stood up without a word and walked over to the table where Ruth was now seated. Edric and Rhianna watched as Ruth glanced their way with a puzzled frown. Edric shook his head slightly and she looked away again.

'It wasn't necessary, Edric,' said Rhianna in a light tone. 'She was only upsetting herself, not me, though I must admit, I *will* enjoy the rest of this meal far more without her. Thank you.'

Edric kissed her lightly and they continued to eat in companionable silence.

*

The referee, dressed in a loose black tunic and trousers, bowed, with hands pressed together before him, then addressed the audience and the contestants in the traditional terms:

'Each contest will be judged on the skill of the fighters and their ability to disable their opponent using the minimum of force and causing the minimum of damage. All strikes are allowed except those designed to kill. However, strikes causing potentially permanent damage to the opponent will cause a fighter to lose points. Any medical assistance required will be given by our own team of medtechs here onsite, while any serious injuries will be treated at our private clinic until such time the injured person can return to his or her normal life without attracting undue attention. Each contest will continue until either one person is disabled, or a contestant calls a halt. If a halt is called, they and their opponent must immediately retreat to opposite ends of the arena, as far as practicable. If this rule, or any other, is not followed instantly, those breaking it will be disqualified from this and all future tournaments. I wish you all an honourable event.'

The referee bowed once more and left the arena. A sigh of satisfaction ran through the audience.

Rhianna and Marietta carefully assessed each other. They wore no protective equipment, just their black uniforms and soft shoes. This, and the right to use almost any form of strike, was the reason the tournaments were illegal. Although Rhianna had already won two previous bouts this evening – one against a young man from Sydney whom she had not formerly met – she was not tired. Instead, she faced Marietta with calm anticipation, her mind and body in harmony. They had fought many times before and each time Rhianna had forced Marietta to concede. Marietta's technical skills were as great as her opponent's, but she had yet to learn to lose her desire to hurt and not to be distracted by this desire.

Marietta made the first move, attempting to land a low, sideways kick to Rhianna's shin, but Rhianna stepped aside and moved forward to strike the other woman beneath the jaw. Marietta deflected the blow, moved inwards to return the strike and, to her own intense surprise, connected. Rhianna instantly dropped to the floor, unconscious. The audience rose as one and a great clamour sounded throughout the hall as the referee leapt into the arena to check the fallen woman. He felt for her pulse, which fluttered faintly beneath his fingers and then ceased. Immediately applying every resuscitation technique he knew, he was completely unaware of Marietta, who stood as one struck dumb, staring in horror at her opponent of so many years. She hardly noticed when Edric frantically thrust her aside to kneel down by Rhianna's body, although he knew enough not to interfere with the referee's ministrations unless asked. When the referee met his eyes and nodded, Edric joined the vain attempt to bring her back to life. After more than thirty minutes, they were finally forced to admit their efforts were hopeless.

The referee stood up, shaking his head, while Edric held Rhianna in his arms, weeping. Marietta also wept, hiding her face with one hand. By now, Ruth and two medtechs had joined them, along with Stefano Salvarez, who was doing his best to comfort Marietta. One of the medtechs examined Rhianna and scanned her as thoroughly as his equipment allowed, yet could find nothing to explain this sudden death.

'I don't think your blow killed her, Marietta,' he said eventually, as the woman gazed wanly at the body. 'She must already have been ill, but what the cause was, I cannot tell.' He turned to Ruth and the referee. 'What do you want done now? If we report the death to the peacekeepers now, everyone here will face questioning.'

The referee surveyed the audience. They all knew the risks involved in holding these tournaments, but this was the first time someone had died. He made a difficult decision.

'We must put some distance of time between this tragic death and tonight's event in order to allow the audience to leave safely. There are no records of who is here or even of this venue being used. It is a great risk, I know, yet I believe it is necessary. It's unavoidable that some of you will be called to account, but a delay will allow you to deliberate and to order your affairs. Edric, what do you think? You were her lover and friend. What do *you* want?'

Edric stood up with difficulty, wiping the tears from his face. He was ashen pale and shaking. 'I want her to go home. I can't stand the idea of her being violated in a morgue. I want her to have time to rest in the earth first. Can you understand?'

His face twisted in grief, while his listeners stood by mutely. They could understand.

'You should call Robert, her cousin,' suggested Ruth, heaving a great sigh. 'He was close to her, and has a right to know and to help decide.'

Stefano nodded when Edric looked to him for support. 'We first need everyone to leave as quietly as they can. A lot of people are beginning to panic. I'll arrange with the stewards to speak with them and afterwards to unlock the doors. We have to keep everyone calm.'

The referee agreed, then made his announcement: 'Our champion is dead. It appears to have been an appalling accident and not the fault of her challenger. We ask you to remain calm and to leave quickly and quietly in an orderly fashion. The stewards will speak with you about your arrangements. Afterwards, they will unlock the doors and supervise your departure. We do not want a crowd leaving here all at once, attracting attention. We ask that you respect Rhianna O'Connor and talk of this to no one...not your family, your friends, or your colleagues. In due course, there will be an inquest, but we hope these arrangements will help avoid any of you becoming implicated. We, the organisers, will unavoidably be involved, although perhaps not for some days yet.'

The members of the audience muttered to each other and to themselves, both frightened and dazed, but ready to cooperate. They understood the consequences of being caught up in an inquest that would bring these tournaments to light. So, slowly, one by one, they filed out into the foyer, where the stewards were waiting for them.

A strange, heavy silence settled over the hall once all the guests had departed. None of those remaining had spoken since the referee's announcement. What, after all, was there to say? Edric retrieved his comlink from his pocket, hesitated, then asked for a connection to Robert O'Connor. More than a minute passed before Robert's sleepy face appeared on the small screen. It was almost 01:00 and he had been deeply asleep.

'Yes?' he mumbled, blinking and rubbing his eyes.

'Robert, my name is Edric. You may remember me from when I lived in Stanthorpe. I have terrible news for you. Rhianna has had an accident and is dead. We need your help.'

He stopped, waiting for the shocked response, but at first, none came. Robert just stared at him, then took a deep breath. Eventually, his face almost expressionless, he asked, 'How did she die?'

'We don't actually know what killed her, but it happened during a martial arts tournament. The medtechs who attended don't think a blow was the cause, even though she *was* struck.'

Robert grimaced, not at all surprised at Rhianna's involvement in a tournament. When last in Stanthorpe, she had told him of her continued interest in fighting. 'Was it a legal tournament?' he asked.

'No, it wasn't,' Edric replied, feeling unsure of himself, 'but that's not the only reason we're asking for your help. We know you were once close to her and would want to help decide what to do next. I don't want her to be taken to a morgue.'

Edric's voice broke and it was some time before he could compose himself. Robert waited, then asked, 'Were you and Rhianna lovers?'

'Yes,' Edric managed to say.

'Bring her here and we'll bury her in Girraween, where Sylvie is buried. Not *in* the earth, but above the earth, where she will soon be found. She *will* have to be found, you know that, but it will give everyone time to make whatever arrangements they feel are necessary. I'll be glad to see her home one last time, though I wish it were alive and not dead.'

Unable to continue, Robert held a hand to his eyes. After regaining control, he said, 'Come now, and I'll meet you at the entrance to the reserve. Only you, Edric, no one else. We loved her and we alone will bury her.'

*

Completely engrossed in their task, beneath a cloudless night sky ablaze with stars, the two men did not feel the bitter cold. Their small lanterns lit their faces and, as they walked, caused the tors and boulders to cast strange patterns on the earth, yet they had little mind to enjoy the surreal landscape. Robert showed Edric where Rhianna's beloved cat, Sylvie, was buried, and they chose a place close by. Edric then removed Rhianna's soiled clothing and loosened her hair. She now wore only the silver ear circlets he had bought in readiness some time ago, sure of her winning the contest and retaining her championship. He wanted to give her this parting gift, even though she could no longer smile and kiss him in return.

It was not possible for them to simply build a cairn over her without first protecting her face and skin from the rocks. They needed to give her every respect, although they knew it would not be long before the person they loved ceased to exist in her current form; but for now, they could not bear to think of this. Robert covered Rhianna's body with the fine, deep red, alpaca blanket kept in her landjet and which Edric had brought with him. 'In case of an accident,' she tartly informed him when once, a long time ago, he laughingly suggested the blanket could have interesting uses if they ever went on a visit to the countryside together. That was before they became lovers.

Each stone was placed with tender care, as if Rhianna could feel and be hurt by their heavy coldness. When the last one was put into position, Robert straightened up and studied Edric. He could see the exhaustion in his face. 'Come and sit down,' he told him, taking him by the shoulder.

Edric followed Robert to a large, flat rock nearby – the rock Robert had used as a marker for Sylvie's grave – and sat down beside him. He shivered, suddenly cold and immensely lonely. He had loved Rhianna for almost three decades, yet the love had been returned for only the last three years.

'She was incredibly beautiful, Robert, even in death,' he said, his eyes fixed on the place where Rhianna was now buried. 'Even though she eventually left Australia and didn't keep in contact, Rhianna has been part of my life since I was a child! How am I to go on without her?'

'The same way I did, Edric. We go on because we must. Anything else is a betrayal of those we love. Her mother betrayed Rhianna when her father died, and paid the price. I wonder if that betrayal has led Rhianna to be here now.'

Edric turned to Robert and stared at him. Robert gazed back steadily, then, speaking softly and slowly, explained. 'I haven't seen her for more than seven years. She came back when my father died, here at Girraween. I hardly recognised the person she had become. We kept in contact after she first left Stanthorpe to attend university in Seoul, but Rhianna gradually became more and more distant, until she stopped accepting my calls altogether. I almost expected her not to come back when I sent a message about my father. Even then, she didn't stay long...only until her mother died a few months afterwards.'

'She never spoke about her mother at all,' said Edric, his voice subdued. 'I wondered why, but felt I shouldn't ask. I remember people talking about Leihana and what she did to Sylvie when Rhianna was still at school, and how Rhianna left Stanthorpe soon after Sylvie died. I always supposed she went to Korea to get away from her mother and the horrible memories, so didn't want to bring it all up again. What happened to Leihana? How did she die?'

'She felt herself to blame for my father's death... Once Leihana returned from the treatment centre, after the time she attacked Sylvie with a kitchen knife, my parents took her rock climbing and visiting friends as often as they could. On the surface, she *seemed* quite well again, but never asked after her daughter. I think she wanted to move as far away from the past as possible. Also, despite all the help she received, we could see Leihana still couldn't really cope, perhaps because of the guilt she felt for the way she treated Rhianna, and possibly even Sylvie – although she may not have cared about Sylvie. Some people still don't care much about animals...

'One day, when they'd stayed here at Girraween for some hours, my parents took an afternoon nap and awoke to hear Leihana screaming for help. She'd taken it into her head to climb alone, and then slipped to a ledge below. My mother went down to fetch her back up again while my father held the ropes, but somehow the combined weight of the two of them was too much for him and he slipped as well. He wasn't young any longer. Still, I think it was just an unlucky chance. He didn't die immediately, but by the time the ambutechs arrived, he had. It happened in summer, and there was an unusually long delay before they could get here because of the bushfires which had been burning for several days – all the emergency crews had already been called out. Again, just bad luck, but Leihana began drinking again. I think this time she really did want to die. Rhianna found her, choking on her own vomit. Horrible! The problem is, Rhianna could have saved her and chose not to.'

'No, I don't believe it!' Edric jumped up to face Robert. 'She would *never* have let anyone die without trying to help! She was a good person!'

'She *was* a good person once, possibly even a good person during the last few years you've known her, but I'm telling you the truth. After her mother was cremated and the ashes scattered, Rhianna told me herself what happened.'

'Not this time, Mother, not this time...' and Rhianna waited, her fingers on her mother's throat, waiting for the faint pulse to cease.

CHAPTER NINE

For most people, examining financial records would be a most tedious way to spend a morning, yet for Smithson, the activity usually provided a fascinating insight into a life – except in the case of Rhianna O'Connor, he found instead a yawning chasm. To be sure, he *had* managed to identify the incoming fees from her clientele, going back to the time she started her travel consultancy eight years ago, as well as the usual outgoing expenses associated with daily private and commercial life. A clear title to the shopfront apartment in Elizabeth Street, Brisbane, also existed, although no records of the financial transaction itself were to be found. Similarly, she had owned the landjet for six years, yet once again no record of its actual purchase could be located. Furthermore, the expenses associated with setting up her business must have been substantial and would surely have far exceeded her apparent income, but no source of the required credits could be established. The conclusion seemed obvious: the sources were either extremely well hidden or someone else had paid.

Smithson's freckled brow wrinkled in thought as he slowly ran a hand through his short red hair. Finally, rubbing his chin, he contacted the Lands Archival Office in Brisbane and asked for a detailed trace of the previous owners of her apartment. It did not take long before a very upset employee told him that the relevant files for the entire twenty-fourth and twenty-fifth centuries had disappeared.

'What about your back-ups?' asked Smithson, absent-mindedly scratching an eyebrow. 'Surely you have back-ups?'

The employee typed furiously on his keyboard for some time. 'No!' he exclaimed, his face a picture of astonishment. 'They've gone too! That's impossible!'

'Apparently not,' replied Smithson dryly.

The situation was the same for the landjet. It had been new when first purchased – which meant locating the dealer was simple enough, given the model and year – but when they searched for the original transaction records, they too were gone. The woman responding to Smithson's polite request looked guilty and confused; a common enough reaction, he knew, when dealing with a peacekeeper, despite having done nothing at all wrong.

His gloomy reflections were interrupted by a call from the Brisbane Peacekeeping Force to report the results of their inspection of Rhianna's apartment; as well as the homes of Ruth, Marietta and Stefano, primarily in order to retrieve the clothing they wore the night of Rhianna's death. They had, of course, enlisted the help of the Melbourne Peacekeeping Force to search Marietta's home. 'Good,' he thought. 'Now we might learn something.'

'We've found an item in Rhianna's apartment that might tally with one of the autopsy findings,' said his colleague cheerfully. 'It's a jar of something called 'Sensa', made in Bolivia and exported around the world. I gather from our pharmacist that it's used by women who want to improve their sex life, though why chemicals are necessary is beyond me. However, none of my business in that respect... We're having it analysed now and should be able to send the results through to your pathologist in about twenty-five minutes.'

'I'll let them know to expect it,' replied Smithson, then listened as she continued:

'By the condition of the apartment, it was clear Rhianna shared it with someone by the name of Edric, at least part of the time. Quite a few of his personal belongings are there, and the two of them appeared to be lovers. They were in bed together not long before she died, which corroborates another piece of your evidence, and his prints are on her hairbrush and comb, suggesting he may have helped with her hair before they left. That's a nice touch, don't you think?'

Smithson nodded, remembering Rhianna's beautiful long black hair. It had also been carefully brushed before she was buried: a small but interesting point. It said something about their relationship; or even about the love Robert felt for her, since it might have been he who brushed it that last time. He must remember to ask. Not that it mattered to their investigation; he just wanted to know. In the meantime, he said, 'Were there any business documents that might help us?'

'Yes and no. She appears to have been methodical, as well as meticulous, in keeping her client lists and the records of all her business dealings for the last six and a half years, but the language used in a number of the agreements is peculiar. Destinations and interim stopovers are often given as coded numbers, not actual place names. We can't find keys anywhere to explain what the codes mean, either. And didn't you say she started her business eight years ago? In which case, there's one and a half years' worth missing.'

'Damnation,' muttered Smithson. 'Well, send me everything you have and I'll see if I can do some pattern checking with it all. If nothing turns up, we'll start tracking down her clients. Were there any prints or DNA on, or in, the jar of Sensa?'

'No,' she replied, shaking her head regretfully, 'none other than her own.'

'What about travel souvenirs...something that might not have been purchased in Australia? Was there anything like that?'

'Surprisingly few. Only this.' His colleague held up an item for him to see – a small grey figurine of a slender cat, made from African soapstone. 'It sat on her bedside table.'

'Was there anything at all from Argentina?'

'No, nothing. Why?'

'She went there regularly every three or four months for the past two years, and at irregular yet fairly frequent intervals for the one and a half years before that...although we still don't know why, or who she may have visited. I must say, this woman appears to have been particularly good at hiding her tracks when she chose to.' Smithson pulled a wry face.

'Well, one thing we do know is that Rhianna O'Connor was evidently a martial arts fan. There are two kung fu uniforms and a whole cupboard full of championship awards. They go back to when she was a child. I gather from Nyneve's report she was at an illegal tournament when she died?'

'Yes, she was defending her title, primarily against an old foe by the name of Marietta Ross. They went to school together for some years here in Stanthorpe, but weren't friends. Marietta wasn't popular in the town at all, although she soon joined the local gang of bullies led by Ruth Baillieu – and I'm sure *her* name would've appeared in Nyneve's report, because she was the organiser of the tournament. Now, one last thing: I understand the BPF will investigate these events?'

'Oh yes, we're looking forward to it.'

His colleague smiled and Smithson returned the smile.

Thinking about Marietta Ross, Smithson remembered the time quite clearly when Rhianna came storming into the Reconciliation Centre, rage contorting her young face.

'I want you to arrest Marietta Ross for shooting a bird!' she had cried.

The peacekeeper on duty had spoken calmly and kindly to her, asking her to explain what, exactly, Marietta had used to shoot it.

'A sonic rifle! Here, I've got it in my backpack. I took it from her,' and Rhianna looked grimly pleased with herself as she handed him the broken pieces of the extremely expensive rifle.

'And where is Marietta now?' asked the peacekeeper, doing his best to keep his astonishment from showing.

'Probably on her way home. I don't suppose she'd still be lying where I left her. I had to hit her to get the rifle, you see. She tried to hit me first, but didn't succeed...and here's the poor bird.'

Rhianna, more carefully this time, brought out a small package and opened it, to show the bright red and blue feathers of a dead rosella, tenderly wrapped in her kerchief.

'Look at the poor thing! Why would anyone want to kill anything so beautiful? Why would anyone want to kill anything at all?'

The peacekeeper shook his head. Killing these or any other creatures was certainly illegal, and Marietta Ross was definitely not licensed to own or carry a rifle: very few people were. 'Well, she'll be charged,' he said, his voice gentle in an attempt to comfort the young woman, 'although we'd better make sure you didn't hurt her too much, don't you think? Can you take me to where you left her?'

'Oh don't worry, I know how to hit someone without really hurting them,' Rhianna reassured him, in a slightly prim tone, 'but I must admit, I did kick her as well.'

A furious Marietta was eventually discovered sitting on her front verandah nursing a badly bruised shin as well as a painful midriff, but was otherwise unhurt, as promised. While Rhianna watched in satisfaction, she was duly arrested. Rhianna was even more satisfied when she discovered Marietta would be required to spend an entire twelve months cleaning the animal healer's premises and learning to assist him in the simpler procedures required by his practice. Evidently, Marietta's attitudes improved somewhat as time went by, much to the healer's credit.

Smithson sent a full transcript to Nyneve of everything he had learned, then called to follow up on the latest developments. He found her at the medcentre morgue, where she was discussing the final details of his results with the pathologist. Based on the type of kidney and liver damage, it appeared that Rhianna had indeed died from amanita poisoning.

After thanking the pathologist for his work, Nyneve paid close attention while Smithson gave her a summary of his and the Brisbane peacekeepers' findings. 'Well,' she said, 'it shouldn't be long now before their analysis of the contents of the jar of Sensa comes through. We'll wait for the results before fetching Edric back here for an interview, though I think he should see Rhianna before we speak with him. It might help us get to the truth. For all we know, he may have poisoned her. Not that I can see any reason why he would... Still, there's a lot we don't yet understand. Now, you said the homes of the other three have been searched?'

'Yes, they have. The items worn by Marietta have been sent from Melbourne to Brisbane and those belonging to the others are being examined now. Also, the examination of the clothes and shoes Edric wore has already been done and found pollen from plants indigenous to Girraween.'

'Good, that agrees with at least part of what Robert told us. Hopefully the rest will be confirmed once we interview Edric and get the evidence from the remaining clothing and footwear.'

The trip from Brisbane to Stanthorpe took far less time than the previous one Edric had taken, accompanied only by Rhianna's dead body. On this occasion, there were two burly peacekeepers for company, who kept a watchful eye on him, particularly since being informed he was an unofficial Australian heavyweight martial arts champion. Edric had spent the week since the burial in a state of extreme depression, now doubting whether they had done the right thing in not reporting her death immediately. They should have held the entire audience captive in the hall in case any of them were involved. Damn the illegality of the tournaments! What did it matter compared to his beautiful, wonderful Rhianna's death? Well, it was too late now, but he felt totally unable to deal with seeing her again in the state the body must now be in.

On their arrival, the peacekeepers immediately escorted him to the morgue, then into the viewing room, where Freddi, Shela, Gwenllian and Nyneve were waiting. Except for the reconstructed face, the body lay within its containment field, on a narrow, raised dais, and was covered in a dark blue shroud. Rhianna's hair had been arranged to hide her neck and the damage it sustained while lying beneath the cairn of stones. No one spoke while Edric looked at her this one last time. She did not appear lifelike, or even asleep; more like a waxen artist's model of the woman he loved so dearly. Tears ran down his face as he remembered their final day and evening together, and how he had arranged her hair. He stretched out a hand to stroke it, but abruptly withdrew. It was as icy cold as Rhianna herself.

Edric turned around, finally able to speak: 'Do you know how she died?'

Nyneve answered. She was known to Edric, although they had never actually met before. 'Rhianna was poisoned. We discovered the source of the poison in her apartment...which apparently you shared, at least part of the time?'

She studied the obvious astonishment on Edric's face. Shela burbled softly and lay down, paws stretched out in front of her, the tip of her tail moving to and fro while she drew in the wight's emotions, as well as the images in his mind. Meanwhile, Gwenllian stepped forward, held out a hand and introduced herself. Edric shook hands, and experienced a momentary jolt of recognition, as if something of Rhianna had somehow associated itself with this stranger. It passed immediately when he released Gwenllian's hand. Edric thought he had imagined it – perhaps the trick of an exhausted mind.

Freddi then introduced herself and asked him to accompany them to the Reconciliation Centre, where he would be required to make a formal statement about his recollection of the events leading up to Rhianna's death, as well as his involvement with her subsequent burial. She also asked if he wanted a Witness present. Edric nodded and silently went with them. The sun shone on their faces while they walked the short distance. It was a bright, clear winter's day, with a mild, fresh breeze that blew Edric's long golden hair into his eyes. He brushed it away, scarcely noticing what he was doing. His mind was focused on the strange sculptured face that was Rhianna's, and yet not. Unable to bring himself to contemplate the reason behind the reconstruction – why they had needed to recreate her features – Edric did his best to remember Rhianna as she was when alive, not dead, even though it was no longer possible to escape the reality.

Once inside the Reconciliation Centre, the small group seated themselves around a low table in a comfortable, colourful room, pleasantly warm after the cold outside. Nyneve fetched fresh coffee, made sure everyone had what they needed, then asked the Centre's computer to take an official record, which would be used at the eventual inquest. The Coroner would formally determine fault or accident, and afterwards, make recommendations relating to guilt or innocence should this death not be considered accidental. When the computer replied in its bland voice that it had commenced the recording, Nyneve privately wished someone would program some character into its voice! Still, perhaps it would become tiresome and not to everyone's taste...

Edric relaxed slightly, comforted by the familiar, homely smell of the coffee, and almost glad he had these three people to talk to, strangers though they were. The Witness kept herself inconspicuously in the background and her presence was soon forgotten, at least by him. However, he noticed the cat, which blinked at him with her golden eyes, fluffing out her whiskers.

'How long had you and Rhianna been lovers?' Nyneve asked him.

Edric studied his hands before replying. 'Lovers,' he repeated, looking up at her. 'Yes, I suppose we *were* only lovers for the last three years, not bondmates. I have loved Rhianna ever since we were at school together. She treated me as a nuisance, though, and no doubt I was. She even reported me to the peacekeepers for being a nuisance, but it didn't make any difference to my feelings for her. Of course, it *did* stop me from following her around.' Edric grimaced and looked down for a moment.

'After she left Stanthorpe,' he continued, 'I was afraid I'd never see her again, particularly since she'd left the country as well. Then, without any warning, about seven years ago, Rhianna turned up as a contestant at one of our tournaments. Ruth hadn't even told me she was going to be there! Ruth loves playing little games... Still, I can put up with her because she *is* extremely good at organising the annual Stanthorpe reunion dinners, as well as the tournaments, and can also be incredibly funny at times, though usually at some poor sod's expense.' Edric shook his head and frowned.

'At first Rhianna was quite distant towards me, but I kept my own distance, so before long I suppose she realised that I didn't intend to repeat my 'nuisance' behaviour of old. She eventually asked to have me as a sparring partner when she found everyone in her own weight division too easy to defeat, except for Marietta. Marietta was almost her equal, although Rhianna didn't like fighting with her – quite possibly because she knew perfectly well that, even after all this time, Marietta still hated her.' Edric looked at each of them in turn. 'Did you know that?' he asked.

'No,' replied Nyneve, 'not exactly, but we knew there was some rivalry between them when they lived here in Stanthorpe, and at one time, Rhianna reported her to the peacekeepers for having killed a bird. Rhianna took somewhat drastic, though probably warranted, action. She was really very brave, taking on someone wielding a sonic rifle, and even had the presence of mind to take comlink footage before challenging her.'

'Rhianna was courageous in everything she did,' said Edric, pride in his voice. 'She was honourable. Marietta fought in the tournaments because she enjoyed hurting people, although she always kept just within the rules. If she hadn't, she would have been disqualified. It's one of the problems with these types of contests. They attract people like her.'

'So why did Rhianna want to join?' asked Freddi.

'Purely for the competition and to maintain her skill levels. Rhianna was a touch rusty when she first joined our group... My impression was that she'd once had a highly talented sparring partner, but for some unknown reason, they no longer saw each other. Her former practice stopped more than a year before and she hadn't found a group to suit her since.'

'But why full contact contests with no protective gear?' asked Gwenllian, genuinely puzzled.

'In our opinion, it simply isn't possible to fully develop all the techniques without this type of fighting. You see, the point is to do the minimum amount of damage, while at the same time disabling the opponent. The first priority is to avoid a blow, the second to deflect, and then, if necessary, strike. The strike then has to be effective, because at this level of competition it can't be assumed a second chance will be given. If shielding is worn, it's difficult to learn how to strike accurately enough, and it's also difficult to lose all fear of being struck if one hasn't experienced it, particularly in the more vulnerable areas of the body. To be completely honest, it also adds a certain frisson to the whole exercise.' Edric smiled, but only for a moment.

'How often does anyone get seriously hurt at these tournaments?' asked Freddi, leaning back in her chair, hands loosely clasped together.

'It's fairly rare, but the audience knows it could happen and many of them thoroughly enjoy the danger. I think it's an instinct some people have more than others. I don't personally care for the audience being there, but Ruth, and others like Marietta, thrive on having spectators. It's the ego factor. Rhianna was different, which is one of the reasons she was such a good fighter. Ego wasn't something she was interested in.'

'Do you think Marietta could have hated Rhianna enough to kill her?'

'Yes, but not at a tournament,' Edric replied, honestly considering the question, just as he had already done many times over the past week. 'She was genuinely horrified when Rhianna collapsed; I'm sure of it. She was amazed her strike even connected. They've had countless bouts over the past three years and not once has Marietta ever succeeded in seriously slowing Rhianna down, let alone landing a difficult blow such as the one she attempted that night. I must admit, the blow was capable of killing Rhianna if Marietta had chosen to deliver it fully, but she's skilled enough to pull back at the last instant. Still, she would probably have been disqualified from entering any tournaments in the future. Like I said, she hated Rhianna, but if she had wanted to harm her, Marietta would have thought up a far more devious method.'

Nyneve nodded, and said, 'We found traces of someone else's DNA on Rhianna's skin. Do you know a Stefano Salvarez?'

'Yes, I do,' answered Edric, wondering at the question. 'He's one of my closest friends. Rhianna was very fond of him as well. He did shake hands with her when we first arrived and gave her a brief kiss on the cheek...that's all, other than a hug at one point when Rhianna won a bout. He used to fight in the tournaments himself, but lost his sight when an opponent used a prohibited strike.'

'How very unfortunate,' said Nyneve, standing up. 'I hope his sight was able to be restored.' She went outside for a moment, returning with the jar of Sensa that Edric's guards had brought with them from Brisbane. She placed it on the table. 'Have you ever seen this before, Edric?'

Edric put out his hand to pick up the jar in its protective covering, but Nyneve quickly prevented him. 'Why yes, or something exactly like it,' he admitted. 'It was a joke! Rhianna didn't need to use anything like this, but she came back with it after her last trip to Argentina and said it might be fun to try.' He blushed. 'We had a very satisfying sex life, although I noticed she was usually a bit less enthusiastic after her overseas trips, particularly the Argentinean ones. I thought the problem was just fatigue, since I knew she worked hard ensuring each tour was a complete success. Rhianna was quite the perfectionist in many ways. I didn't ask her much about them, because right from the beginning she made it clear she didn't want to share any of the details with me. Her business dealings were kept strictly separate from our personal life. I didn't mind. She gave me enough of her time and I had my own life to lead.'

'So you don't know where or how she obtained it?'

'No, why? Is it important?' Edric was becoming agitated. 'Is this something to do with how she died?'

Nyneve glanced at Gwenllian, who nodded briefly. 'Yes,' she said. 'It contains the poison that killed her. I'm so sorry.'

'You mean I helped kill her!'

Edric jumped up and crashed his fist into the nearest cupboard door, which splintered under the impact. Shela leapt to her feet, growling, while Freddi moved quickly to the distraught man's side and placed a hand on his shoulder. Edric shrugged her off, and then, just as quickly, forced himself to become calm before turning to face them. 'I'm sorry too. I hope for Marietta's sake it wasn't her who gave it to Rhianna!'

'I think it's unlikely, don't you?' replied Gwenllian, moving over to him as well. She touched him, and quite suddenly, he relaxed and began to weep, softly at first, and then openly. While Gwenllian did her best to soothe his mind and help him heal, he gave in to the grief he had tried hard to control for so many days.

They waited until the worst was over, and then Nyneve said, 'Do you happen to recall whether the jar was already open before Rhianna used it?'

'I think so,' answered Edric, putting away the kerchief he had used to dry his eyes. 'Yes...I seem to remember she had already opened it.'

'I see. Thank you. One last question... Is there anything at all about her past or her work you can think of that might help us find out who gave this to her, or who sold it to her?'

'No,' replied Edric helplessly, 'Rhianna never spoke about her past or her work. She had no friends other than me, and of course, Stefano. She never felt the need for many friends, even when she was a child. It was one of the reasons Marietta hated her... She wanted Rhianna's friendship, but never had it, and obsessed over Rhianna's rejection for years.'

'Well, I think we can probably assume someone else may have hated her as well,' remarked Freddi thoughtfully. 'The question is, though, who would she have trusted enough to accept something like this from? Or, on the other hand, where did she buy it, if it wasn't a gift?'

With the interview over, Gwenllian walked back to the communal house, where she wanted to be alone to mull over the impressions received from Edric and Robert. She hadn't yet made up her mind whether to stay a little longer in Stanthorpe, return to Melbourne, or accompany her two friends back to Brisbane the next morning to continue helping with the case. It depended to some extent upon what their further investigations brought to light.

Meanwhile, Freddi went back to the medcentre to find Meng Jarrah, who was poring over the results of the Sensa analysis provided by the Brisbane pathologist. She kissed the top of her curly head, but instead of looking up, Meng Jarrah mumbled something Freddi couldn't catch.

The conversation with Edric had reminded Freddi how much she loved this woman, and how bitterly she would have grieved in a similar situation. She shuddered at the thought and put a warm hand on Meng Jarrah's shoulder. Meng Jarrah absentmindedly took Freddi's hand in her own, giving it a light squeeze, then continued with her work. Smiling, Freddi patiently sat down to wait, using the time to reflect upon the gaps in Rhianna's life and how best to proceed to fill them. Eventually, Meng Jarrah stopped what she was doing and turned to face her, saying, 'Did Edric know how she got hold of the Sensa?'

'No, he said he had no idea, which was the truth. Shela and Gwenllian could both confirm it. Edric is devastated by her death. His escort has taken him back to Brisbane. I thought he might want to stay here a while, but he didn't. I gather his family lives in Brisbane, and there's no one else here he wanted to visit at the moment, not even Margrethe.'

'I see. While you were interviewing Edric, Smithson's been busy again, tracking down the Sensa distributor, as well as allied companies who produce the ingredients. It's not out of the question that the entire batch was accidentally contaminated, which would be catastrophic.'

'By the Sun, I hadn't thought of that!' exclaimed Freddi, horrified. 'Are you telling me this could be an accidental death and there might be others who could die the same way?'

'No, calm down, Freddi. He's just being thorough. It's extremely unlikely, or an emergency would already have been declared. The poison is so incredibly obscure that accidental contamination is almost impossible. None of the usual ingredients are even faintly related to fungi, and none of them are sourced from companies who deal in fungal products – I've already checked. Even so, Smithson will contact the distributor and all the retail outlets and ask them to place a halt on sales, and for the distributor to put out a general recall to the public. He's already notified the manufacturer, who has stopped production, pending an investigation. Also, the Brisbane Peacekeepers are sending out a notice to Federation medical facilities to put them on additional alert for anyone needing treatment for symptoms that could be caused by amanita poisoning. They're often hard to detect initially, but if an alert is issued, there's a higher chance they'd be recognised. Fortunately, this isn't a high-use product and the symptoms can be successfully treated if they're detected early enough. Rhianna's obviously weren't, poor woman... Did Edric say if there was anything unusual about her in the days before she died?'

'No, he didn't. Is it possible this particular species of amanita might not cause any early symptoms?'

'It's highly unlikely, but she was exceptionally fit and strong. She could even have felt unwell, yet didn't bother telling him. It happens. Given the tournament was coming up, she may not have wanted to tell him, or anyone else, in case they stopped her from fighting. I'm sure it's not the first time someone's made a decision like that. Either way, I haven't found any records of her having gone to a medcentre for treatment.'

'It's certainly plausible. Well, I'd best leave you to your work. I've finished everything I need to do here in Stanthorpe, except to say goodbye to Margrethe. She deserves to know how Rhianna died, and I'm sure we can rely on her not to tell anyone else. I won't tell Robert, though. He'll want the full story, not a partial one... Will you be finished in time for dinner at Nyneve's, or do you want me to bring you something?'

Meng Jarrah considered for a moment. 'I think I should be finished in time for dinner. I like her, don't you?'

'Yes, I do,' agreed Freddi, touching Meng Jarrah briefly on the shoulder before leaving her to stare at the screen, lost in thought.

It seemed strange to Freddi to enter Margrethe's peaceful garden again after having witnessed such deep grief and spending so long listening to first Robert's highly emotional account of the past, and then Edric's account of his relationship with Rhianna. Margrethe's cat, Harriet, had sensed Freddi's arrival and was seated comfortably in the front garden to greet her. She stood up to rub herself against Freddi's legs, in the process shedding large amounts of white hair on her black uniform.

'Aren't you ever combed, cat?' asked Freddi, attempting to brush away the hair, which was futile, because Harriet simply kept winding herself around her legs. Sighing, Freddi gave in to the inevitable, picked Harriet up, and cradled the cat against her chest as she walked towards the rear of the garden, where Harriet told her Margrethe was working. The front of her uniform would be a mess, she thought, glad Shela was black and didn't shed hair. Shela, close at her heels, smugly agreed.

As they approached, Margrethe stood up and slowly straightened her back, clearly happy to see them. 'Ah, I see Harriet's being a bit of a nuisance. She's always shed hair. Pity about your uniform. Still, I can see you don't really mind. There, give her to me and clean yourself off. I've a good brush inside...and I do comb her, but it doesn't make as much difference as one would expect. *Your* cat's lovely and shiny. Do you groom her?'

'Yes, often,' said Freddi, patting Shela on the head, who purred loudly.

'Now, I don't expect you've come here to discuss cat fur, have you. It must be that you've found out more about poor Rhianna. Come inside and tell me all about it. It's getting a bit chilly out here, don't you think?'

It *was* becoming cold, and black rain clouds were gathering. They both looked up at the sky, deciding there would most likely be a storm before the day was finished.

Inside, the house was cluttered and untidy in a homely sort of way, although everything appeared spotlessly clean. The air smelled of dried herbs and flowers. Bunches hung from the ceiling in a bewildering array of colours and types, yet strangely enough, the scents were not overpowering; the climate control systems were evidently in good order. The furniture consisted of oddly assorted pieces which had seen better days, but Freddi felt wholly at ease and thought Margrethe must clearly be fond of colour since nothing she could see was colour-matched in any usual manner. Instead, vivid hues were combined with muted autumn tones in such a way as to create a sense of harmony both unusual and exciting. It closely resembled the effect achieved in her garden, which, she imagined, must be even more striking in spring and autumn when many more plants would be in bloom, with leaves either fresh or changing colour.

As if to enhance the effect of homeliness even further, Margrethe hadn't stored her collection of preserves in a pantry or cupboard. Instead, they were lined up on shelves in the main dining room, almost as if to tempt visitors to ask for a sample. Row upon row of sparkling, transparent jars of all shapes and sizes contained a vast array of fruits and vegetables, preserved over many years. Some of the jars held sugared flowers, still retaining their colour, while others held sweets made from nut pastes or dried fruits.

While Freddi gazed in delight at this culinary masterpiece, Margrethe gently took her by the elbow and steered her towards a deep, well-padded armchair, inviting the peacekeeper to sit and put her feet up. A handmade embroidered footrest sat ready for her to use and a small table stood at just the right spot for serving refreshments. Once her guest had made herself comfortable, Margrethe produced a tray with a plate of biscuits and a dish of samples from her store of preserves. There was even a small glass of deep red Davidson Plum wine, which, she explained, was a good vintage from five years ago.

'Try the macadamia shortbread,' Margrethe invited. 'I managed to get a good supply of nuts from up north this year and stored away quite a lot. If you like it, you can take some back with you to Brisbane. Now, tell me about Rhianna.' She sat down in the armchair opposite, while Harriet nosed around Freddi's feet in case the peacekeeper was careless enough to drop a crumb of shortbread.

Despite the purpose of the visit, Freddi felt reluctant to introduce the subject of someone's death, and possibly even murder, into this cosy, everyday setting. Still, she was sure Margrethe was not an ordinary woman, and had seen and heard many strange and difficult things in her long life. Speaking carefully, she said, 'Rhianna owned a highly successful travel consultancy in Brisbane, together with an apartment and a landjet, and spent her spare time training for and competing in martial arts tournaments. She died from being poisoned, but we're still not sure whether her death was accidental or not. We've spoken with Robert O'Connor at great length, and it appears that although he had no hand whatsoever in Rhianna's death, he did bury her at Girraween, with the help of her close friend, Edric, whom I imagine you might remember.'

Margrethe made no comment, only nodded, with the hint of a wry smile on her lips.

'We've interviewed Edric, and it seems he and Rhianna met some years ago when she developed an interest in fighting in certain tournaments involving full contact and not many disallowed strikes. They eventually became lovers, and he was with her at one of these tournaments when she died. It might not come entirely as a surprise to you that at least some of these contests follow an annual Stanthorpe reunion dinner, organised by Ruth Baillieu, who, with help from Edric, also organises the fights.' Freddi raised a questioning eyebrow at Margrethe, who nodded again; it did come as no surprise.

'Rhianna was the unofficial Australian middleweight kung fu champion, and she died during her championship challenge,' continued Freddi. 'And here's another name you'll know... Marietta Ross was her opponent when she died.'

This time, Margrethe shook her head and frowned, yet still did not comment.

'We are as certain as anyone can be that it was not Marietta who killed her, even though she did manage to land a blow capable of killing were it delivered with full impact. We think this blow connected only because Rhianna was already ill and it was coincidental that she died. From Edric's account, Marietta had never before managed to defeat Rhianna, despite being a member of the tournament group for some years.'

'Yes,' said Margrethe at last, 'it sounds likely. Marietta was fond of baiting Rhianna in their martial arts classes, but never succeeded in troubling her in the least. Rhianna kept her head and fought well even in those days, though I'm sorry to hear she took part in tournaments that presumably weren't legal?'

'No, they're not. The Brisbane Peacekeeping Force will be investigating them now, so it's unlikely they'll continue; or at least, I hope not. I intend to return to Brisbane tomorrow, which means I should be able to conduct some of the initial interviews, since they overlap with this inquiry into Rhianna's death. Which reminds me, did you know someone by the name of Stefano Salvarez?'

'Yes, I did. He was here in Stanthorpe for only the last few years of his schooling. His parents bought a winery, then sold it and moved to New South Wales to live on a larger property. Stefano was a sweet young man, good humoured, and mischievous in an engaging sort of way. Why? Was he involved?'

'We don't yet know to what extent, but he was there the night Rhianna died, and was close friends with both her and Edric. He was also a former fighter, and it seems he lost his sight during a tournament.'

'I hope he has good replacements. Did Edric say?'

'No, but I'll let you know once I've met him, if you like.'

'Yes, please, I'd appreciate it. I must admit to being surprised Rhianna joined up with that crowd. She kept her distance when they lived in Stanthorpe.'

'According to Robert, she had changed a great deal during the time she was away. For example, he claims Rhianna could have saved her mother, yet chose not to.'

'I can well believe it, although it's doubtful she would have let her die if there was much chance of Leihana surviving to become well again. Still, I could picture Rhianna choosing to wait just a few minutes too long before calling the ambutechs. Her mother became intent on killing herself after Eirann died trying to save her. Fortunately, Agathea is a far more courageous woman and has made a good life for herself. She shares Robert's house, did you know?'

'No,' answered Freddi. This was something Robert hadn't mentioned, and no one else had either. The initial family listing on the Federation database she and Nyneve consulted gave only identity numbers and general location, not full addresses, and at that point in time there had been no reason to check.

'She's hardly ever there, though,' continued Margrethe. 'Agathea keeps in contact with me, you see. At the moment, she's in Africa, after spending the winter in Norway learning cross-country skiing. An extraordinary thing for a woman her age to take up, but she was always very fit and strong. Her view is that Eirann would have wanted her to be happy, and naturally, so does her son. Of course she grieved for her bondmate when he died, but when Robert finished building his house, it seemed the best thing to do was to leave the past behind and move in with him. Only her dearest possessions went with her, as well as anything Robert wanted. Afterwards, Agathea became a wanderer...goes wherever the fancy takes her...and good luck to her, I say. I'm sure the reason she hasn't come back now is because Robert hasn't told her what's happened. He most likely doesn't want to upset her, which is a bit silly. I'll have to talk to him. His mother has a right to know and make her own decision about coming home, don't you think?'

Freddi could only nod. To her mind, this piece of information showed even more keenly just how disturbed Robert had been by Rhianna's death, as well as the manner of it. Seeing her again, dead, and then burying her, must have been unbearable, yet it seemed almost unnatural not to have told his own mother at the earliest opportunity.

As if she had read her mind, which in a sense she had, Margrethe asked Freddi about the one thing that so far hadn't been explained: 'Why did Robert bury her at Girraween?'

'Apparently Edric contacted him immediately after Rhianna's death. They wanted to take her body away from Brisbane in the hope of giving the people at the tournament a chance to remain uninvolved, as well as to give Robert an opportunity to help decide what should be done. Edric also said that he couldn't bring himself to allow her body to be taken to the morgue. Robert agreed, and wanted to bring her to Girraween since Rhianna had loved the place and because it was where they buried Sylvie. It all makes sense, oddly enough, given the emotional impact it would have had on them at the time.'

'Ah yes, Sylvie. If ever I saw a death in the making, it was that poor little cat's. I often think that if she and Rhianna hadn't been able to defend themselves the day Ruth and her bullies – and Edric, remember! – attacked them, they would have killed Sylvie. That's one of the reasons I wonder at Rhianna taking up with Edric again... How could she have forgiven him for being there when it happened?'

'I expect, as Edric told us, she was truly courageous. It takes courage to forgive. He told us that he has loved her ever since, which is a long time to wait for someone.'

'Yes, I'm sure you're right, my dear. Do you know, Rhianna used to write to me after she left Stanthorpe. Real, handwritten letters! She was learning Japanese calligraphy at university in Seoul, so may have wanted to try her hand at English lettering as well. They were beautifully done. The borders were sometimes decorated with tiny cats in comical poses. I've kept them all. Would you like to see them?' Margrethe stood up, taking Freddi's agreement for granted, and left the room for some time.

While she waited, Freddi fed Harriet a biscuit, then watched, fascinated, as the old cat cleaned every tiny crumb from the floor before delicately licked herself clean. Shela looked wistfully at Freddi and was rewarded with one as well. When it quickly disappeared, pleading eyes asked for more, but Freddi shook her head, pointing instead at the crumbs. Shela did her duty, snuffling around until they were gone, then curled up again at her companion's feet. Harriet curled up next to the big cat, laying her head on Shela's stomach and wheezing faintly, then snoring as she fell asleep. Shela shifted slightly, but purred and fell into a light doze, although one ear remained on alert.

Margrethe returned with a thick sheaf of paper in her hands. 'There's rather a lot, isn't there,' she said, handing them to an amazed Freddi. Despite having had some practice herself five years ago, during the Willsmere inquiry, when they were unable to trust the lattice for a period of time, she had never before seen this much handwriting in her life, certainly never such fine calligraphy.

'It would be best if I made a copy for us both, and then you can take the originals as well. You never know, there might be something helpful in there, although I'd like them back at some stage, if possible.'

Freddi silently handed over the letters and Margrethe left the room again. Shela raised her head, 'biscuit' plain to see in her mind, but disappointed, rested her head on her paws and sulked.

'You can give Shela a biscuit, if you like,' Margrethe called out from the next room.

Freddi laughed, and Shela stood up, dislodging Harriet, who merely curled up more tightly, still snoring, with hind legs twitching as she dreamt of her younger days when she could run and leap after butterflies.

Before long, Margrethe came back with the letters, gave Freddi a small storage module containing the scanned copies, and said, 'Rhianna met someone over there and wrote a great deal about him. I'd almost forgotten. Here, have a look at this one in particular.' She carefully turned over the pages until she found the one she wanted, then pointed to the paragraphs in question:

> ...I've met the most intriguing person. He's descended from an old Japanese family and is here in Seoul to improve his knowledge of Japanese history and culture, so is studying at the university – but not to obtain a degree, only out of interest. He's also unbelievably handsome! I think he likes me, because he's asked me to observe one of his kendo classes. He's a master, not a student, and I think he might invite me to learn if I demonstrate the right attitude. I met him one evening in the grounds, just before sunset, where I had been quietly practicing *chi sao* with another student from our history class, who also studies kung fu. When we finished, he bowed and congratulated us on our technique, then asked if we would like to join him for supper. Marianne declined, saying she needed to go home, but winked at me as she left (!). We went to a small Japanese teahouse in an out-of-the-way part of the city, where he said we could get the very best service and food in Seoul. I don't know if that was true, although everything *was* marvellous.
>
> We talked for hours, Margrethe, about all the things that interest us – about architecture and poetry, about gardens and martial arts, about Japanese history and art. It was early in the morning when we left the teahouse and he walked with me all the way back to the university house where I still live.
>
> There's a good chance I'll see him tomorrow – we share some classes, though I can't understand why I haven't noticed him before...

Reading this short passage, Freddi was struck by how much it sounded like any other young woman about to fall in love with someone she had already begun to idealise. 'Does Rhianna mention him by name?'

'Oh no, never by name, which is odd, don't you think? There are references to this man for almost three years, then all at once she stopped writing. You might want to ask Robert if she wrote to him. He may have some more recent letters; or if not letters, he may have kept some comlink calls. It's not out of the question.'

Outside, the sky had darkened considerably and they heard the first distant rumble of thunder. 'I'd better go, Margrethe, before this storm sets in,' said Freddi. 'Do you have something I can put these letters into, in case it begins to rain before I get back?'

Margrethe quickly fetched a waterproof folder, then held out a hand. 'I'm grateful to you for coming here, and hope you discover how and why my dear Rhianna died. Could you let me know when you do? Yes, of course you will. I needn't have asked. Oh, and before you go, do take this small jar of jam back to Meng Jarrah for me, together with these biscuits. I'm sorry I didn't get an opportunity to meet her, but she'll most likely know what this is and enjoy it.'

Freddi clasped her hand and accepted the gift...but how did she know Meng Jarrah's name?

Margrethe smiled and saw Freddi to the door, where Shela was already waiting, staring mournfully up at the dark sky.

When she reached the outermost boundary of the garden, Freddi waved and called out, 'Take care of yourself, Margrethe. I think we'd better run now.'

Margrethe waited until they were out of sight, while Freddi and Shela literally did run, Shela keeping pace with her companion's long strides, although she could easily have outdistanced her. The first heavy drops of rain began to fall just as they reached Nyneve's house.

CHAPTER TEN

Although heavy rain and lightning prevented Freddi, Meng Jarrah and Shela from returning to Brisbane in the morning as planned, the prediction was for relatively fine weather later in the day. Taking advantage of the delay, they slept late, after having stayed up until past midnight reading and discussing the letters Freddi brought back from her visit to Margrethe. The two women snuggled up to each other in their warm bed, listening to the rain outside and watching the lightning through the window. The shutters had been left open so they could follow the progress of the storm, although Shela had crawled underneath the coverlet, forming a large lump by their feet. From time to time, the cat poked her head out from beneath the quilt, but hastily withdrew when yet another rumble of thunder convinced her it was not yet safe to come out. Even the prospect of breakfast couldn't persuade Shela to emerge from her haven.

Freddi was lying on her back, comfortably propped up on the soft pillows and enjoying the contrast between the warmth and peace inside the house, and the turbulent weather outside. Meng Jarrah rested her head on Freddi's shoulder, relaxed and content, with one shapely leg lying on top of Freddi's, her other foot touching Shela to comfort her when she became alarmed. Stroking Meng Jarrah's hair as it lay on her breast, Freddi sighed, then murmured, 'We should get up.'

Meng Jarrah kissed her warm, dark skin and smiled. 'Just a little longer,' she answered softly, before falling back into a light doze. Freddi smiled, moved down beside her, and fell asleep.

It was almost 09:30 when Nyneve knocked lightly on the door, opened it a fraction, knocked again, then peered in to see if they were awake. She grinned at the sight of them, held in each others arms, fast asleep, their long curls intermingled on the white, hand-embroidered pillowcases. Shela's head appeared from under the covers to blink sleepily at her. A 'loud' image of oatmeal porridge formed itself in Nyneve's mind as the cat slid out of the bed and onto the floor with a soft thump. She padded over to rub herself against Nyneve's legs, tail winding around her knees, asking for food. Nyneve bent down to stroke her, then went back to the kitchen, closely followed by the hungry cat.

After satisfying Shela's needs, Nyneve made breakfast for her other two guests and carried it back to their room, sure that by this time they would be awake. She was right. The smell of freshly brewed coffee had permeated the whole house, bringing them back into a world where there was work to do and a death to be investigated. They were dressed in loose morning gowns, though not yet showered. Nyneve smiled. She was a true romantic, thoroughly enjoying the sight of two people who cared so much for each other, and even better, seemed to be well suited.

'I decided to let you sleep,' she said. 'Shela's been fed and is now curled up in front of the fire, pretending the storm is over. I lit the stove especially for her. She really is an extraordinary cat, that one; so brave and yet still frightened by lightning!' Nyneve set the tray down on the bedside table, accepted their grateful thanks, and left them to enjoy the food.

Some forty minutes later, Freddi and Meng Jarrah presented themselves downstairs, with empty tray in hand.

'Here, I'll fix all that up for you,' said Nyneve, taking the tray and efficiently disposing of the dishes. 'Now, I've done what we discussed last night and asked Robert to see if he can find any of the old comlink calls or letters he might have received years ago from Rhianna. I could see he was curious as to why, even if he didn't ask, and of course I didn't tell him about the other letters, or anything else.' When Freddi and Meng Jarrah both nodded, without commenting, Nyneve added, 'He was looking a little better, which is good. Gwenllian may be the one to thank for that. She called earlier this morning to say she'd be staying on for a while. Apparently Stanthorpe agrees with her, and personally, I think she's taken rather a liking to Robert. Perhaps that's why he's feeling happier. He's an odd one, you know. He's never had a close female friend, and he's more than fifty years old!'

'That *is* odd,' replied Meng Jarrah, helping herself to another coffee from the fresh brew Nyneve had made. 'Why do you think that might be?'

'I'm quite sure his feelings for Rhianna were never anything other than that of a brother for a sister, even though they *were* only cousins, but I think he loved her so much that no one else ever measured up to her standard – although he probably doesn't realise that's the case. I also think he was so hurt by the change he saw in her when she came back that he withdrew into his own solitary life and made no effort to meet anyone, not even people from Stanthorpe, whom he could at least have formed friendships with. All of which means I'd be glad to see him form a bond with Gwenllian, who really is rather special! She *is* still unbonded, isn't she?'

Meng Jarrah nodded, sipping her coffee and munching on the fresh crumpet smothered in honey that Nyneve had prepared while she spoke. 'They both have cat-like minds,' she said, swallowing her last mouthful and grinning broadly. 'I'd call that a good start for forming a relationship, wouldn't you?'

Nyneve laughed, then asked Freddi if she wanted a crumpet too. Freddi eagerly held out a plate to accept the hot, honey-laden delicacy. As they ate, Nyneve's comlink chimed, and when she answered, Robert appeared on the larger, household screen. They all turned to look at him, making haste to wipe away the small drops of sticky honey from their fingers.

'I still have five recorded calls and all her letters,' he announced, without any preliminaries. 'I thought I'd thrown the letters away after I allowed the trees in the greenhouse to die, but it seems my mother retrieved them. She must have been very quick about it, I must say... Anyway, they've been scanned, so I'll send it all now.'

They soon had the files, and then, thanking Robert, told him that unless anything else came up, the Stanthorpe part of the investigation was now finished; at least for the time being.

'What will happen to Rhianna's body?' he asked, his voice hesitant.

'She will be taken to the Brisbane morgue and kept there until the inquest is held and we're able to give the Coroner enough evidence to make a determination. If a trial is deemed necessary, we may need to keep her a while longer. Afterwards, you may conduct a funeral ceremony, if you wish. We can assist if you need us to.'

Robert nodded abruptly and ended the connection.

'I think Gwenllian should be here to see these recordings,' said Freddi.

'Yes, she should,' replied Nyneve, while Meng Jarrah only waved a hand, her mouth full again as she tasted the jam Margrethe sent over with Freddi the previous day.

'Quandong!' she exclaimed.

'What?' asked Freddi.

'It's quandong jam,' Meng Jarrah announced. 'I haven't eaten it since I was a child! Mmm...lovely... I wonder how she knew I'd like it?'

'It's one of her specialities,' explained Nyneve, 'as well as riberry chutney with wild lime. You can try some of it with our midsun meal, if you want. She gives me a few jars every year.'

Shortly afterwards, Nyneve managed to contact Gwenllian, who took longer than usual to respond. 'Decided to go back to bed and sleep in,' thought the peacekeeper. 'It's that sort of morning.'

She was right. Gwenllian had also stayed up late the night before, poring over copies of some of the letters given to them by Margrethe, trying to sense the person behind the writing, and to form a picture of the unknown man with whom Rhianna had clearly established a strong connection. Disturbed by her impressions, she slept badly, and now appeared slightly grumpy, with her short, fair hair standing up in spikes and her hazel eyes half-closed as she listened to Nyneve asking her to come over as soon as possible. Yawning and sleepily rubbing her eyes, she said, 'I've been dreaming about those letters. It wasn't a good dream, either. I'll see you in about fifty minutes, if that's alright, though it's still raining, I see. I'll have to get someone to bring me. It's too wet and windy to walk.'

'I'll come and fetch you myself,' offered Nyneve, 'and I'll make some coffee for you when we get back here. That's one thing the communal house isn't good at making!'

'It certainly isn't,' agreed Gwenllian, grimacing at the memory of the last cupful she'd sampled, 'though I can't understand why not.'

'No, it's one of the small, local mysteries. I'll see you soon.'

While they waited for Gwenllian to get dressed and have breakfast, a bright and cheerful Smithson called to say that the distributor of Sensa had succeeded in withdrawing all the remaining jars from the batch Rhianna used, and had also provided a list of their retail outlets.

'They're panicking, actually,' he added, grinning. 'Still, it doesn't hurt for them to keep panicking if it makes them this efficient. They're a private company, and because it's a luxury product, naturally they don't want their licence terminated. Fortunately, they keep meticulous records of all batch numbers and their destinations, which means it wasn't difficult for them to give us the locations where this particular batch went. However, they and the manufacturer will still need to check their other batches for contamination, even though we haven't received any reports of anyone coming down with symptoms that might be related...or any other deaths.

'All the returns should be in by this time tomorrow, when we can check them off against the manufacturer's list. That leaves us with the ones already sold, which is a shade more difficult, because although we should be able to trace the transactions fairly readily, catching up with the people who bought them may take a little longer. We *could* send a message to their comlinks; then it just depends upon how long they all take to respond... By the Sun, they'll be put out if they receive a Federation request for them to return a jar of herbs they're using for rather private reasons!' Smithson laughed. He couldn't help it, but his listeners didn't join in.

'Sorry,' he said, 'I know it isn't at all funny. Still, I'd prefer to laugh about it than think someone else might be unlucky enough to get killed. Let's just hope we end up being able to account for every single jar of the dratted stuff. I'll let you know how it goes the minute I have anything further. Oh, and Brisbane pathology called to say there was no pollen from Girraween on any of the clothing worn by Stefano, Ruth or Marietta on the night Rhianna died, or on any other clothing found in their homes. Therefore, unless they've disposed of what they wore and lied to us about it, it would appear Robert and Edric are telling the truth when they say no one else was with them when they buried Rhianna.'

'Well, it's good to have that confirmed,' replied Nyneve, 'although I would have been surprised to hear otherwise.'

'Right, I'll get back to herb hunting,' said Smithson, waving to them. 'Bye all!'

At this point, Nyneve realised it was time to collect Gwenllian and took Shela with her. The cat had finally decided a trip in the landjet was worth braving the storm for, although she kept close by Nyneve's side as they walked the short distance to the vehicle, with her tail was well down and ears lowered. In their absence, Meng Jarrah and Freddi sorted the letters Robert had sent them, then put their entire collection into sequential order. There were more than a dozen from each year, but gradually the number lessened, until about six months after she stopped writing to Margrethe, Rhianna also stopped writing to her cousin.

In order to have the correct sequence for all the correspondence, they arranged the letters into groups, leading up to each of the comlink recordings Robert had supplied. Just as they finished, Nyneve, Gwenllian and Shela returned, wet from their brief exposure to the rain. Shela shook the water from her coat, flinging it over anyone standing nearby, then while Freddi fetched a towel to rub her dry, sat down to thoroughly clean herself in front of the wood stove.

Gwenllian, looking wide awake now and her usual calm self, was wrapped warmly in a bright, multicoloured, full-length coat that reached high up under her chin. After taking off the coat and matching mittens, she sat down, brought out her hand reader from its small carry-bag and was soon ready to receive the correspondence. Once the files were transferred, they all systematically worked through the first set of letters until one of the comlink calls fitted into the sequence.

As they watched, a very young Rhianna appeared on one side of the screen and her cousin on the other. The physical resemblance between the two was remarkable. Gwenllian wondered how many times Robert had watched these recordings, and whether he could now bear to see them again. The ease with which they spoke to each other was to be expected from the close relationship they had enjoyed. Rhianna spoke of her studies, of the places she had seen and the interesting people she observed – not of the friends she had made, since it appeared she did not attempt to make many, nor of the people she left behind in Stanthorpe, other than to ask after Eirann and Agathea. Rhianna clearly did miss *them*.

The recording lasted almost an hour, after which they tackled the next batch of letters. As time went on, Rhianna seemed less and less at ease when she spoke with Robert, while the tone of the letters became more formal, more distant. At no point did she mention the man who featured in the letters to Margrethe.

'The only conclusion I can draw,' said Gwenllian, rubbing the tip of her nose thoughtfully, 'is that she developed a sexual relationship with this unknown person and wasn't entirely comfortable with the situation. Otherwise, Rhianna would surely have written and talked about him at every opportunity. Another possibility is that although Robert may have been like a brother to her, he was, and still is, an extremely attractive man.

As Rhianna grew up, she could hardly have failed to notice, and as she spent more and more time away from her family, she would most likely have noticed even more, so may have felt reluctant to speak about the relationship, particularly if it was difficult in some way.'

'In that case, why would she have been happy to write to Margrethe about him?' asked Freddi, puzzled.

'Well, he's being idealised. Writing about him to Margrethe, a much older woman, would have added a romantic dimension. We should contact the university to see if we can put a name to him.'

'Let's see,' Freddi calculated quickly, 'she left here in 2436, obtained her doctorate in 2443, and returned to Australia in 2448. The letter in which this man is first mentioned was written when she was twenty-five, in 2439, and the last letter to Robert was written in 2443, when she was twenty-nine. That means we need their class lists from at least 2439 until 2443. We can only hope he had a Japanese name. It's highly likely, based upon his interest in studying his family's original culture and history. Even if he didn't have one from the outset, he may well have chosen one later on. If not, it's going to be difficult to work out who he was after all this time...unless there are records of kendo masters teaching in Seoul.'

'That's assuming it's important,' said Meng Jarrah, leaning back and stretching her arms high above her head, easing her muscles after sitting still for so long. 'She could have died from accidental poisoning, or else one of her former Stanthorpe enemies finally worked out how to hurt her. They may not have intended to kill her, you realise. Just make her ill enough to lose the championship.'

'It's another possibility, I agree,' replied Freddi, 'which means Ruth Baillieu can't be excluded. I expect she would have preferred by far for Marietta to win. Still, until we know for certain whether the death was accidental or not, we had better assume someone killed her on purpose; we need to cover all bases. Rhianna wasn't close to many people, so would hardly have accepted a jar of Sensa as a gift from someone she barely knew or didn't like, or didn't trust. Presumably this rules out Marietta or Ruth giving her the Sensa in person. It might not rule out Stefano Salvarez, though. According to Edric, he has a mischievous sense of humour and was close to both of them. As Edric said, they considered using it as a sort of joke.'

'I think you should interview Stefano first, as soon as you get back to Brisbane,' suggested Nyneve.

'Yes, you're right. I was thinking we should speak with Marietta first, but I doubt whether she had anything at all to do with Rhianna's death — unless she used Stefano and put him up to it. They were friends, from what I can gather, so it's something to consider. After all, she did hate Rhianna. Personally, though, if anyone used Stefano to give her the Sensa, I think it was more likely Ruth. It seems more in character to me.'

'Do we know where Marietta is at the moment?' asked Gwenllian.

'Yes, she's in Melbourne. We can track her down easily enough, and I believe Ruth and Stefano are still in Brisbane. Nyneve, while I contact Seoul University, could you contact him and make a time for later this evening for us to interview him in his home? The storm should be finished soon.'

Nyneve made the necessary call to a downcast Stefano, who agreed to be home at 21:00, without fail. He evidently knew why. Freddi, in the meantime, contacted the student records office in Seoul, where a flustered administrator immediately protested at the amount of time it would take for them to obtain the information.

'This is an unnatural death we're investigating and it involves one of your former students, so it's unavoidable that you cooperate and transmit the information to me without delay,' insisted Freddi, while steadfastly maintaining a friendly expression and tone.

The administrator grudgingly asked for the details he would need in order to perform a search of the records, then went away from the screen and an unnecessarily lengthy fifteen minutes later, gave her what she wanted. There were one hundred and twenty-six students who had shared Rhianna's classes during her time at the university, fourteen of whom had Japanese names, and of these, nine were men.

'He may have changed his name,' said Freddi dubiously, studying the faces of the nine men. None of them were strikingly attractive in her opinion, nor in the opinion of the other three women.

Meng Jarrah peered at them, searching for signs of exceptional character that might have made Rhianna view one of them as "unbelievably handsome", but failed to see any. 'What about the kendo connection? There must be a list of current and former masters somewhere.'

'Perhaps, but first we'll have a look at the faces of all the other men to see if any of them have Japanese features, though no doubt a lot of them will have Asian features, so we'll have to take them into account as well.'

They scrolled through the pictures of the seventy-one men, finding forty-three who looked 'Asian'. They all agreed that at least twelve were unusually handsome.

'Many Koreans, for example, are of Japanese descent,' remarked Gwenllian. 'Perhaps he's one of them?'

'True,' replied Freddi. 'We'll simply run them all through the Federation database and see what we come up with.'

'This is interesting,' she said, a little while later. 'I extended the search into the DNA profiles to double-check their ancestry, and none of the men, except those with Japanese names, are of Japanese descent. So, unless Rhianna's taste was quite different from what we might expect, our man has no university record left.' Freddi sighed. 'This really is peculiar. If his records *are* missing, why would anyone go to the trouble of removing them? I don't suppose it would be an easy feat by anyone's standards.'

Gwenllian agreed. 'It could be accidental. It happens, but the odds are against it, and anyway, it's too much of a coincidence.' She spoke from experience, having worked for many years at the Central Computer Site in Melbourne, and she also had a Doctorate in Information Technology.

'In other words,' said Freddi, 'given Rhianna's most significant financial records are missing as well, I'd say whoever killed her – assuming it wasn't accidental – was once closely involved in her life and has now gone to a great deal of trouble to remove any trace of the connection. Meanwhile, the only other clue we have at present is kendo. Let's see what can be found if we use that, although it'll be remarkable if anything turns up. There's no requirement for any official records to be kept of who does, or does not, practice martial arts, unless, of course, they're professionals earning an income, or competing in official tournaments. No keepsakes relating to kendo have turned up in Rhianna's apartment, have they?'

'No, nothing at all,' replied Nyneve, after consulting the extensive, itemised list of everything the Brisbane peacekeepers had found.

'Thanks. In that case, I'll make a request to the Federation Special Investigation Unit to do a crosscheck between known kendo practitioners and our list of people who attended Seoul University. It shouldn't take long.' Using the secure lattice link available to the Brisbane peacekeepers, Freddi entered the request in the required format. Acknowledgement of the request and an estimate of the time it would take to be met were received after about half a minute. It appeared they would receive their answer within the hour.

The greenhouse was cold and almost dark when Robert decided to leave the warmth of his house to see it again. He hadn't gone in there for a long time, although he scrupulously maintained the external structure and kept the security system functional. Standing in the gloom, he stared at the barren ground and arrived at a decision. Rhianna was dead. The past was dead with her, so there was no point remembering the pain for any longer than he could help. Perhaps it was time to replant and to think about the future. He turned on the climate controls, blinking as the lights came on. When a faint hum signalled the beginning of the heating cycle, he waited until he could just detect the slight increase in temperature. Satisfied, Robert left the building and returned inside, feeling happier than he had for many years.

CHAPTER ELEVEN

While they were waiting for the Federation to return the results of their query on the former Seoul students, Nyneve took Gwenllian back to the communal house and Meng Jarrah returned to the medcentre to work. Having discovered nothing more in the jar of Sensa to give any clue to either its purchaser or the origins of the amanita, she turned her attention to the silver ear circlets Rhianna had worn.

They were a masterpiece of design and precision manufacture. The minute, ornate engraving covering their outer form consisted of a series of intertwined serpents, each with the tip of its tail in the mouth of the following one. Even the expression on the serpents' faces varied. Putting them under her enlargement scanner, she wondered if they were machine or hand made. Handmade items usually revealed some telltale irregularity that differed in character from manufacturing faults. Eventually, Meng Jarrah came to the conclusion they were handmade, then noticed something very odd. There was a tiny inscription on the inside of the left ear circlet, which presumably Edric requested. It hardly seemed likely such an exquisite piece of personal ornamentation could contain a mistake, yet it definitely did: the inscription read "MY Rhianna", instead of "My Rhianna".

She leaned back in her chair and considered what to do, but decided not to call Edric just yet. First, it would be better to determine exactly what type of silver they were made from and where the silver had been mined. With luck, she could also find out relatively easily who had made them. Some twenty minutes later, Meng Jarrah frowned as the silver analysis was completed. The metal came from Patagonia, which for some reason tugged at her memory. She called Freddi, who looked slightly annoyed.

Guessing at the reason, Meng Jarrah said, 'Are the results back?'

'Yes, and it still gives us nothing. Only one of the students with Japanese ancestry is listed as practicing kendo, but at a grading far below that of someone who could be termed a master. I think it's fair to conclude that the man Rhianna met has definitely had his records erased. The problem is, where to go from here?' Freddi paused, and then smiled, making an effort to dispel her annoyance. 'Is that what you called about, or do you have something we can use?'

'I may have. Does Patagonian silver mean anything to you?'

'Yes, it does.' Freddi looked puzzled now. 'It's famous for its high quality and is used extensively in jewellery making. Was it used for Rhianna's ear circlets?'

'Yes...and wasn't there something associated with the Willsmere case made from this same silver?'

'Yes, Michiko Yamada used it for all her designs.'

'That's what I thought. "MY"... She used to put her initials on all her pieces too, didn't she?'

'As far as I recall, yes. Why?'

'The inscription on the ear circlets is peculiar.' Meng Jarrah showed Freddi the scanned image.

'It may be either a mistake or a point of emphasis. On the other hand, it might not be. There *could* be another designer with those initials. Can you track down where Edric bought them?'

'I'll call him now.'

'Thanks. I'll make the arrangements for the airjet to take us back in about two hours. Will that be enough time for you to finish up here?'

'Yes, that should be fine. There's just one other thing to do before we go. Due to its somewhat unusual design, the pathologist took a closer look at Rhianna's tattoo. It's quite old, and he's sure it dates from the time she was at university. The quality of the work is exceptionally high, so we may be able to trace whoever did it. People usually have some definite aim in mind when they have a tattoo made, and I don't think this particular pattern would be chosen simply for its beauty.'

'No, I agree,' said Freddi. 'There could be some meaning that's relevant. I'll see what the Federation database has. All tattooists need to be licensed, and many keep records of their better work.'

When Meng Jarrah contacted Edric, he looked surprised to see her, rather than Freddi or Nyneve. 'I help the BPF with specialist forensic work from time to time,' she explained. 'I've called because I need to know where you bought the ear circlets Rhianna was wearing, what you asked for in the way of an inscription, and if there was any particular reason you chose that specific design.'

Edric raised his eyebrows, but answered readily enough: 'Rhianna owned a silver necklet that she used to wear fairly often, so I took it to one of the better jewellers here in Brisbane to have a matching set of ear circlets made. I didn't specify which silver to use, but he may have chosen to match that as well. They *were* fairly expensive. As to the inscription, I wasn't entirely happy when I read it. I just asked for her name, nothing else. The jeweller explained that they were designed and made by the same person as the first piece and it was their custom to incorporate their initials into the design; which was true...he showed me where the "MY" had been placed on the necklet, though it didn't have Rhianna's name on it.'

'Did he tell you who the designer was, or when it was made?'

'No, I didn't ask. Sorry. Is it important?'

'I don't know. It might be. Did Rhianna ever tell you who gave her the necklet?'

'I asked once, but she laughed and said it was a former lover, and didn't want to make me jealous by telling me his name.'

Meng Jarrah paused for a moment before asking, 'Were you jealous anyway?'

'No, of course not!' he replied, flushing. 'She had a long life before we met again and the past is the past. I had no reason to be jealous in the present, and that's what counted for me.'

'Alright Edric, thanks. Now tell me, who was the jeweller who obtained the circlets for you?'

Edric gave her the name of a company in Margaret Street, not far from Rhianna's apartment.

'Thank you. We may well be able to give you some news before long. We'll do our best for her.'

'Thank you, as well. One question though... Will her belongings eventually be returned? I would very much like to have her personal things...to remember her by.' He lowered his eyes and put a hand over his face, but quickly regained control.

'It depends upon what the Coroner determines. If a trial isn't pending, all her possessions will be returned once the inquest is over. Otherwise, it may take a while, and it's possible some of her things will be kept as evidence. Do you know if she left a will?'

Edric nodded. 'Yes, I'm the executor, and she left everything to me, excluding the consultancy, but specifically mentioned that Robert and Agathea were to choose any keepsakes they wished to have. The consultancy was to be wound up and the proceeds were to go to the Breeding Centre here in Brisbane, in memory of Sylvie.' He paused. 'How *is* Robert?'

'He's getting some help from Gwenllian. They have an affinity, it seems.' Meng Jarrah allowed herself a slight smile. She didn't think she was breaking any confidences by giving him this small piece of information.

Edric briefly returned the smile. 'I'm glad,' he said. 'No doubt I'll be hearing from Freddi again? She'll be wanting to look into the tournaments, won't she? Or will they get someone else to do that?'

'I'm not sure, but I think you'll most likely be hearing from her fairly soon anyway. However, I need to do some work with the information you've given me, so I'll wish you goodbye.'

Edric wished her the same, and closed the connection.

Shortly after her conversation with Edric, and having decided it would be best to speak with the jeweller in person during normal business hours, Meng Jarrah returned to Nyneve's house, where she found Freddi engrossed in examining a vast variety of tattoo designs.

'Will you take a look at them all!' exclaimed Freddi, as she heard Meng Jarrah enter the room. 'Can you imagine having these put on? Some of them are truly gorgeous, but others are hideous... They wouldn't show up on my skin anyway,' she added, peering at her forearm as if considering the possibility.

'You weren't thinking of trying it, surely!' Meng Jarrah instantly hated the idea, although she couldn't precisely say why.

'Why not... A fire-breathing dragon? Your name below an eagle? No? Okay, I promise not to. Still, some of them are incredible. Look at these Maori designs...all over their entire bodies! And here: the Japanese once used them extensively. I wonder if that's why Rhianna had it done...to please him, whoever he was. Anyway, let's go home. I can finish this later.'

Smiling, Freddi stood up, hugged Meng Jarrah, and kissed her. Shela looked up from her place in front of the hot stove, thought it was time to join in, and leapt to her feet, tail in the air. She danced around her two companions, pouncing on Freddi's feet until they gave in and took notice of her instead. By the time Nyneve decided to check in on them to find out how things were progressing, all three lay in a tangled heap on the floor. It seemed a pity to interrupt, but it was necessary, so she made a polite sound to attract their attention then waited until they sorted themselves out. Freddi grinned as she held out a hand to help Meng Jarrah to her feet, but soon became more businesslike when she realised Nyneve wanted to speak with them about something other than their departure.

'I'm sorry you're going,' Nyneve began, meaning what she said. 'It's been good having you all here. But before you leave, there's just one last thing... Smithson has narrowed down the search for the batch of Sensa containing the jar which killed Rhianna to outlets in Bolivia, Paraguay, Argentina and Chile. One thousand and twelve jars were sold, of which four hundred and eighty-two have been returned due to the recall. Also, the company has already received return samples of previous batches from all over the world, together with samples from the two batches following the one we're interested in. Everyone has reacted swiftly and efficiently, which is a relief. The samples have all been independently tested and there doesn't seem to be anything in them that shouldn't be. They've still to finish testing all the four hundred and eighty-two returns from our batch, and there's still a lot of work to be done trying to track down the remaining five hundred and thirty that haven't come back yet, but I don't think it should take too many days before it's all done. At least, I hope not. The distributor has had their equipment checked and tested too, and no trace of amanita was found either there or anywhere in the manufacturing plant.'

'Well, that's definite progress, and very promising. I have news for you too,' said Meng Jarrah. 'We may have a link to the past in the ear circlets Edric bought for Rhianna. It turns out that he wanted them to match a necklet she often wore. The jeweller he commissioned for the work managed to have the circlets made from the same silver and by the same designer, rather than attempting to make them himself. Perhaps the design was registered and it would have been unethical to copy it? At any rate, look at this.' Meng Jarrah showed Nyneve the enlargement of the inscription that had caught her attention.

'The "MY" is typical of a designer by the name of Michiko Yamada, whose name I'm sure you'll remember. She's quite famous for her work and always uses this silver, which is of exceptionally high quality.'

'Great heavens!' exclaimed Nyneve, recalling the name immediately. 'The Cultural and Artistic Director of Wyvern Meridian!'

'Strange, isn't it,' replied Meng Jarrah dryly. 'Do you have the silver necklet amongst the things listed from Rhianna's apartment?'

Nyneve consulted her comlink. 'Yes, I do. Here it is,' and she showed them the image. 'You'll have a chance to see the original when you get back to Brisbane. The airjet's ready to take you now. Gwenllian promised to be here to say goodbye. Do you want to wait? I thought you might want to call Robert as well.'

'No need,' replied Freddi. 'He's already arrived...with Gwenllian.'

They came in, shivering from the cold. The storm had passed, although the remaining breeze was icy. Freddi was looking forward to the milder climate in Brisbane, but was too polite to say so. Shela silently agreed, although she would miss the wood fire.

Robert was looking far better than he had the day before – in fact, remarkably so in such a short time. Gwenllian appeared more than usually cheerful as well. Although they weren't actually touching, they were definitely standing closer together than usual. When Shela pranced up to Gwenllian and burbled a greeting, Gwenllian blushed, and Robert followed suit. Freddi, however, was unable to read what was in Shela's mind, the cat being perfectly capable of shutting her out when she felt like it.

Robert took the initiative by solemnly shaking Meng Jarrah's hand and then Freddi's. 'I would be glad if you could come back when we're able to hold Rhianna's funeral,' he said, his voice sombre, despite his better humour.

Touched, they both agreed. 'We've done all we need to do here in Stanthorpe for the time being, though we may well be back before the funeral,' said Freddi. 'It depends upon how the investigation goes. We can't yet tell you anything definite, but once we have a better understanding of how Rhianna died, we *will* let you know. You'll be required to attend the inquest in any case. Did you realise that?'

'I hadn't thought about it,' said Robert, considering the question. 'Well, I doubt it'll be harder to deal with than anything else that's happened so far. Still, I'd better let my mother know so she doesn't hear about it from someone else. That would be dreadful.' He appeared distracted, realising again how difficult it would be to speak to his mother about her niece's death. Gwenllian reached out to touch his hand. He appeared to relax immediately, and nodded, as if to thank her.

It was Gwenllian's turn to wish them a safe trip home. 'I'll be staying here for a while, but if you need me for anything, just call. I don't yet know when I'll be returning to Melbourne, though it will most likely be in about two weeks time, unless the Breeding Centre wants me for something sooner.'

Meng Jarrah hugged Gwenllian, then on impulse, turned to Nyneve and hugged her as well. Pleased, Nyneve laughed and returned the embrace, before turning to Freddi and shaking hands, saying, 'If you need to come back to Stanthorpe for any reason, you're welcome to stay with me again.'

After thanking her warmly, Freddi, Meng Jarrah and Shela made their way to the waiting airjet and were soon high above Stanthorpe, heading for home.

The return trip to Brisbane was uneventful in the sense that the storm seemed to have almost completely passed over. However, it was not uneventful in terms of the conclusions both Freddi and Meng Jarrah reached.

'Let's put a list together,' began Meng Jarrah, as she settled down more comfortably in her seat. 'We have an unusually attractive Japanese man, studying Japanese history, and who was a kendo master. Rhianna O'Connor forms a relationship with him that doesn't appear to be sufficiently 'normal' for her to feel able to tell her cousin and closest friend, Robert, about it. She eventually receives a great deal of financial assistance to set up a consultancy, acquires an extremely expensive apartment and landjet, then after some years, frequently visits Argentina, and continues to do so. All records of the mysterious man from the time she met him are erased, as are any records associated with the financial assistance. The consultancy itself used encoded information, which is unusual, to say the least. Furthermore, it appears she owned a necklet made by Michiko Yamada and given to her by a former lover. Her current lover orders a pair of ear circlets to match, and shortly after her most recent visit to Argentina, Rhianna dies of amanita poisoning. Is there a name that springs to mind, do you think?'

'Oh yes,' replied Freddi, feeling as if a hand from the grave had gripped her heart. 'Kenjiro Kakura.'

The interview with Stefano Salvarez was conducted soon after they had eaten an evening meal – in some haste, since the time was fast approaching 21:00. It seemed almost an anticlimax compared to the conclusion Freddi and Meng Jarrah came to on their return trip, intuitive though it may have been. Stefano lived in a small, neat, colourful house with two friends, both of whom were martial arts practitioners – although, he informed them, not participants in the tournaments. He was downcast and very subdued, quite unlike the mischievous, happy person Edric described – which was, of course, easy enough to understand. It was dreadful to have lost a close friend to death, no matter what the circumstances.

'Come in,' he mumbled as they entered, after hanging their wet apparel on his hallway coat stand. Meng Jarrah removed Shela's leash, then wondered what to do about her wet fur. It had started raining just as their airjet landed, though thankfully, only a light drizzle – an aftermath of the storm.

'It's cold out there. Would you like something hot to drink?' offered Stefano, hospitably enough, under the circumstances.

'Yes, thank you,' his visitors replied. Despite his subdued manner, the charm of the man still managed to shine through and immediately affected them both. In any event, there was nothing to gain by adopting a heavy-handed manner. 'Do you happen to have something we could use to dry our cat?' added Freddi.

Stefano managed a brief smile and brought a towel, then watched while Shela was rubbed dry. She wriggled with pleasure, but knowing this was a serious occasion and not one she should 'enhance', didn't purr. Stefano carried the wet towel into the laundry, went into the kitchen to make a pot of tea, and when he returned, led them to his comfortable lounge room, which was gaily decorated in vivid greens and blues, with deep yellow cushions liberally sprinkled on both floor and furniture.

'Are your housemates out?' asked Freddi, accepting the bright red mug of hot tea he handed her.

'Yes, and they won't be back for at least two hours, which gives us plenty of time to talk and not be interrupted,' he replied, giving a similar mug to Meng Jarrah. She noticed there were dark smudges under his brown eyes and that his finely sculptured face was pale and drawn. His hand also shook a little when he handed her the tea.

Stefano sat down, gesturing to the others to join him. Warming his hands on his own tea mug, and with a tremor in his low voice, he asked, 'Do you think you'll find out how she died?'

'We already know what she died from,' replied Freddi, after sipping the scalding hot tea. 'What we don't know, is whether her death was accidental or not, and if not, who killed her and how it was done. Do you?'

Stefano flinched, anticipating the question and dreading it. Still, he hadn't been a fighter for nothing. He breathed deeply, calming himself before replying: 'I gather Marietta's strike didn't do it, otherwise you'd hardly ask. I don't suppose you'll tell me what did kill her?'

'No, not yet.' Freddi drank more of the tea, then said, 'What I'd like to know is, did you ever give Rhianna any presents?'

Stefano raised his eyebrows in surprise. 'Well, of course I did. We were close friends. I gave her many small things; for example, when she won a particularly difficult tournament. Why?'

'Did you give her anything in the month before she died?'

'No, I didn't. I had something ready to give her after the fight...a small figurine. It's very old...from Japan. I knew she was interested in Japanese history and art, so when I saw this, I thought she'd like it. It's a Samurai warrior. Do you want to see it?'

Freddi shook her head. 'Thank you, but that won't be necessary. Do you know if anyone else gave her any presents recently?'

Stefano shook his head in turn, shrugging his shoulders. 'Not that she mentioned. Rhianna didn't have many friends... Just Edric and me, really. No one I know would have given her a present, unless one of her clients did.'

'Is there any chance Ruth Baillieu or Marietta Ross might have given her something?'

'No! Not a chance!' Stefano made a sound of disgust. 'They both avoided Rhianna, except for the reunion dinners and the tournaments. The last thing either of them would do is give her a present, unless it was a poisoned apple!' He blanched. 'That's it, isn't it? She was poisoned, and you think one of us gave it to her somehow, which explains why Marietta managed to hit her for once! She was as shocked as we were. She was horrified when Rhianna collapsed and didn't get up again. I'm certain she wasn't pretending!'

Stefano put his hands over his face and quietly began to weep. Shela walked over to him, gently nudging his hands until he took them away, whereupon she licked his cheek. The young man stroked her broad forehead, caressing the silken ears. When Shela purred softly and licked him again, he hugged the great cat to him and wept unrestrainedly. Freddi and Meng Jarrah waited until the sobs had subsided, then stood up.

Freddi put her hand on Stefano's shoulder, looking into the forlorn face that raised itself to hers. Shela moved away a little and sat down to one side, front paws tucked neatly together, tail wrapped around her body. 'We'll leave you now. Rhianna was fortunate to have a friend who loved her as much as you did. You'll need to attend the inquest, of course, and in the meantime, if you feel there's anything at all you should tell us, please call me immediately. However, please don't discuss her death, or this interview, with anyone other than Edric, whom we've already interviewed. Also, until the inquest, I must warn you to be careful. I don't want to alarm you, but it's not impossible that you and Edric might be in danger.'

Stefano looked at them, startled, and suddenly afraid.

'For the time being, I want you to keep Shela here with you and take her everywhere you go, though it would be better if you stay in tonight. We'll be assigning a cat to Edric as well.' Freddi checked her comlink for the time, then glanced at Meng Jarrah, who nodded.

'We're due to see him first thing tomorrow morning. We'll be taking him to the Breeding Centre to find a suitable guardian, and we want you to come too. Once you've selected a cat, Shela can come home with us. You'll both receive some intensive instruction in how to take care of them, but don't worry, they usually tell us very loudly what they want if it hasn't already been provided.'

Freddi permitted herself a sympathetic smile and was relieved to see that at the prospect of such a diversion, Stefano already appeared slightly less miserable. She noticed he had put his hand back onto Shela's head and strongly suspected her cat would be spending the night on his bed. Shela enthusiastically agreed.

PART II

CHAPTER TWELVE

Cats slept, played and cleaned themselves on every available surface, or so it seemed to Edric and Stefano as they gazed in awe at the creatures. So far, the two men had not been allowed to enter the living area. Instead, they were subjected to a lengthy interview about their personal lives and habits, as well as a detailed explanation of how cats functioned, how they were trained, and what their future responsibilities were to be as guardians. Whether the relationship was to become permanent or not, was a point still under intense discussion.

'Although we have determined you are both suitable candidates to have a cat as a companion, and not only as a guardian, I suppose you realise that not everyone is as fortunate?' The gentech blinked a few times, his expression serious, then waited for them both to agree, before adding, 'This is a tremendous opportunity for you to have a cat for life, assuming one of them agrees to come with you, naturally. So, if you can, you should make a decision before going in there, otherwise the cats may prefer not to come with you. They don't generally like a 'wait and see' attitude, and if you take one as a temporary guardian only, there's no guarantee they'll stay if you change your mind later on.'

Edric and Stefano looked at each other, still unsure. They were both feeling intensely vulnerable, so the opportunity to have a cat seemed highly attractive from an emotional point of view. However, their lives seemed to have assumed a level of uncertainty that did not bode well for making such a long-term commitment.

'I think I'd better just have a temporary guardian,' Edric told the gentech, a somewhat regretful expression on his bearded face. 'We don't know how things will turn out, and it would be unfair to say I could form a permanent relationship with one of your charges.'

The gentech slowly nodded, then turned to Stefano for his decision. Stefano was obviously torn by having to make one. He had seen the most beautiful longhaired silver-grey tabby, which seemed to be studying him through the plastiglass barrier.

'If I asked the cat, telling her I'm not sure what the future holds for me, could *she* make the decision?' His dark eyes pleaded with the gentech, while his hands were unconsciously clasped together.

'If you are *so* uncertain, in this instance the cat may decide,' the gentech replied, with some reluctance, yet understanding his dilemma. 'If you open your mind to her, she can make a judgement. I see you have already chosen the one you would like, yes?'

Stefano nodded, strangely overcome by emotion. The gentech opened the door to the habitation enclosure, and when they entered, the air seemed to be electrostatically charged, tickling the skin on their hands and faces. They stared at him in astonishment.

The gentech laughed softly. 'All the cats in here are guardians and a little different from those in our other groups. What you feel is quite normal in this particular enclosure. We've become used to it and don't much notice any longer. It's because there are so many of these highly trained and specialised creatures in the one place. Let's just sit quietly over here and see what happens. Edric, try to keep the decision you've made clear in your mind and look around for a cat you like. I don't mean only in appearance. Get in contact with your feelings. They'll be doing the same. If you feel strongly towards one of them, slowly go over and introduce yourself.'

'Introduce myself?'

'Yes, do whatever feels most natural. There aren't any rules.'

Stefano was hardly listening to either Edric or the gentech. He could feel a tightening in his chest as his breathing became shallow and rapid. A picture formed in his mind of the silver-grey cat sleeping in his gaily-decorated bedroom while he made her breakfast. Without noticing, he had closed his eyes, sitting as one in a trance. The dreamlike state continued as he saw himself waking the cat, then stroking her small, tufted ears and furry head until she rolled onto her back, purring contentedly and batting playfully at his hands with her paws. With quiet curiosity he noticed that even the underside of her paws was furry, and gingerly touched one of them. The skin of the pads was rough and pink, the claws long and curled. She flexed her claws and rolled onto her side, meowing for food.

He opened his eyes and there she was, sitting calmly at his feet, front paws neatly tucked together and gazing up at him with big golden eyes. He looked into them and said her name: 'Peri.'

The cat rubbed her forehead against his knee and then twined herself around his legs, plumed tail high in the air. Her long fur hung almost to the ground. When he put out a hand to stroke her silky back, she arched in pleasure and licked his hand, her front paws kneading the thick carpeting of the floor. Stefano sighed, almost forgetting the reason that brought them here.

The gentech interrupted his reverie by placing a hand on his shoulder. 'She accepts your terms. Peri is a wonderful cat. They all are, but she's not young and has completed many assignments before this one. She'll know how to protect both you and herself, despite appearances.'

As if in answer, Peri yawned, showing long, immensely sharp teeth, then closed her mouth with a snap and with her full dress of fur flying out at the sides, bounded off at full speed towards one of the other cats, who was sitting closer than the rest. She came to an abrupt halt, just short of toppling the cat, and sat down, looking over her shoulder at Edric. He watched and waited for a while, eventually realising he was being asked to 'introduce' himself. Surprised and pleased, Edric did exactly that, bending down and allowing the cat to sniff his hand. She appeared to be a delicate creature, not quite the type he had expected to be a guardian; but then, size and muscle weren't everything. He 'heard' the cat agree, and laughed out loud.

She was sand-coloured, with short, ticked fur and a long, thin, dark tail. Her face was also long and narrow, with large, dark ears and long whiskers, which at the moment were fully erect. Small, neat paws and long shapely legs made him think of a ballet dancer. The cat immediately leapt into the air to execute a perfect somersault, landing neatly at his feet. When she 'grinned' up at him, Edric noticed that her eyes were a deep sea-green.

'Beautiful,' he thought. Aloud, he asked, 'And what is your name, you incredible creature?'

'What name would you like to give me?' he heard in his mind.

Completely taken aback, Edric stared at this astonishing animal, then knelt down to look into her eyes, saying, 'Why, what about 'Zarifa'?'

When the cat purred in agreement, placing one delicate paw on his knee, he held her paw in his own large hand and stroked its silky softness. Then, with some effort, he picked her up – although smaller than many of the others, she was still a large cat. As he held her, Edric felt surprisingly happy, despite his grief for Rhianna, and smiled at the gentech.

The gentech strolled over to them. 'The cats have this effect on nearly everyone,' he said, a slightly amused expression on his face. He patted Zarifa and she pushed her head into his hand as he kneaded it gently with his fingertips.

'She seems pleased with the name you've given her. Some of the guardians prefer to have a different name with each new companion. It seems to give them a better sense of identity...the companion's identity, I mean. Others, like Peri, eventually prefer to keep their name. They're the ones who are ready to be with the same person for the rest of their lives, if someone suitable can be found.'

The gentech turned to look at the other guardians, who were no longer taking much notice of their visitors. 'Well,' he said decisively, facing them again, 'I think it's time we did the paperwork, so to speak. You've a great deal to do and the cats will want to familiarise themselves with their new homes. I suspect Freddi and Meng Jarrah will be wanting to get back to work by now as well.'

*

Freddi and Meng Jarrah were, as it turned out, waiting patiently, Freddi fully understanding just how intense the selection of a cat could be. Shela was staring intently down the corridor towards the habitation area, concentrating on all the layers of thought that were blending and growing into new forms as the humans and cats interacted. She lay on her stomach, her front legs stretched out, ears and tail twitching to and fro, black nose occasionally sniffing the air. As the two men approached with their new guardians, Shela stood up, then sat down again, head forward, waiting expectantly.

Edric and Zarifa were the first to reach them, with Stefano and Peri only a few steps behind. After touching noses with Shela, Zarifa sat down to watch while Peri did the same. Satisfied, Shela turned to Freddi and Meng Jarrah and told them the cats' names. The image contained more than just the words: it contained *who* they were, and what they had committed to in order to protect their new Wights. Freddi, therefore, was also satisfied, although she'd expected no less. Her own life would be almost unimaginable without Shela and the intense bond they shared.

Meng Jarrah squatted down in front of Peri, gazing into the golden eyes, outlined in black. The cat's face was the sweetest she had ever seen, with unusually long whiskers, a reddish-brown nose, and long tufts of hair growing out from her small ears, giving her a whimsical appearance. Purring softly, Peri gave Meng Jarrah permission to stroke her. Looking up at Stefano, Meng Jarrah said, 'You're very lucky, but I can see you know that.'

Stefano, still overcome by his good fortune, yet acutely aware of why he required a guardian, simply nodded, unable to say a single word. Peri sent him a comforting thought, and when he smiled wanly, she immediately turned from Meng Jarrah to rub herself against his legs, tail high in the air.

Sighing, Stefano gathered himself together to think rationally. 'We have to pick up some supplies of food. They've given us a list of what to get. Maybe we should do it now?'

Peri and Zarifa enthusiastically agreed. Zarifa had in the meantime introduced herself to Freddi by leaping onto a high window ledge that happened to be nearby, butting her forehead against Freddi's shoulder and waving her tail in the air, then pacing back and forth in the small, enclosed space, purring loudly. At the mention of food, she leapt back down and scampered towards the entranceway, her feet thudding on the hard surface of the floor. Peri followed more sedately, with Stefano not far behind. Edric stood surveying all three, shaking his head in amazement, an uncertain smile on his face.

'Do you want to order the food and have it delivered, or do you want to go for a walk?' asked Freddi, smiling at them all.

'Walk!' chorused the cats in everyone's mind.

Edric laughed, yet at the same time felt bewildered that he could. It was as if Zarifa was somehow urging him to take pleasure in life, despite the loss of Rhianna – although he felt a sharp sense of grief as soon as the thought entered his mind. Zarifa immediately returned to sit at his feet, gazing up at him, her green eyes, it seemed to him, full of sympathy. He picked her up again and walked over to the others, feeling the cat's softness and warmth against his chest and in his arms like a balm. When tears trickled down his cheeks, Edric felt the small, rough tongue of the cat licking them away. Heaving a great sigh, he set Zarifa down, patting her gratefully.

'We're meant to attach a leash to their collars, or so we've been told,' he managed to say. 'Is that really necessary? It's not as if they'd run off or attack anyone.'

'Well, I expect it's a leftover from the days when hardly anyone realised what they were capable of, or from when they didn't have the mental powers they have now,' replied Freddi. 'There are still many people who don't know much about cats, so they feel safer seeing them on a leash. Perhaps one day it won't be necessary.'

'They don't seem to mind,' remarked Stefano, fastening Peri's.

'We don't,' echoed Peri in his mind. 'We understand wights are sometimes afraid of us. We *can* be very frightening.'

'By the Sun,' exclaimed Stefano, 'do you know what they call us?'

'Yes, 'wights',' answered Meng Jarrah, with a laugh. 'Gwenllian told us they call themselves 'grimalkins'.'

'Who's Gwenllian?' asked Stefano, as he straightened up.

'A good friend of ours, who happens to have a cat-like mind. Her new abilities developed without any warning about five years ago,' she explained, while Stefano gawked, open-mouthed, at her.

Edric stared at Meng Jarrah. 'She was there when I was interviewed in Stanthorpe. Do you mean to say she could virtually read my mind?'

'Not exactly,' Freddi reassured him, slightly embarrassed by the revelation of Gwenllian's powers. 'She senses strong emotions and images, so can tell if what a person is saying is consistent with what's in their mind. We needed to know if you were telling the truth, and she helped confirm it. Shela was there for the same reason.'

'Is it usual for peacekeepers to have cats, and people like Gwenllian, present at interviews without warning someone what they're capable of?'

'As far as we know, there aren't many people like Gwenllian, but yes, the cats are often used in that role now, although it's a fairly new procedure. We only realised fairly recently just how useful they could be. The Judge accepts their input as evidence, in conjunction with other information that helps confirm their impressions.'

Edric chose not to pursue the matter, but had a decidedly thoughtful expression on his face as he walked out into the midsun light.

Outside, the air felt fresh and cool, and a light breeze blew in from the river. Before proceeding confidently in the direction of the marketplace, the two grimalkins stopped for a moment to savour the scents it brought them, then walked in companionable silence across the Victoria Bridge and along Queen Street, which was lined with small shops along its entire length. Many people were shopping, although not to the extent that the marketplace was overcrowded. A few paused to watch the unusual group as they passed, and most smiled in pleasure to see three cats in the company of four such strikingly handsome people. Neither Edric nor Stefano were used to being noticed in the street and found the experience a touch disconcerting, yet soon realised they would need to become accustomed to the phenomenon, because it was actually the cats attracting most of the attention.

The first place at which they stopped sold a variety of herbs, spices, fresh produce and dried goods. Meng Jarrah produced shopping bags from the pockets of her coat, since she'd had the foresight to realise this expedition might be necessary and had come prepared. With a grin, she handed some to each of the two men and took the leashes from them. They walked slowly around the shop, lists in hand, examining the wares on display. When Shela calmly reminded them that she could do with some food as well, Meng Jarrah produced yet another bag and without a word, handed it to Freddi.

While she waited with the three cats, Meng Jarrah began to feel hungry. The shop smelled wonderful. It *was* midsun after all, she thought, wondering if there might be something she could buy to eat while the others found what they wanted. The shopkeeper, as if sensing her dilemma, came over, smiled pleasantly and asked if she wanted anything for herself.

'Could I have a mixture of dried fruits, and a small bag of macadamia nuts? About four hundred grams of the fruit and two hundred grams of the nuts, please.'

'Certainly,' replied the shopkeeper. 'Is there any particular fruit you would like?'

'Oh, I like everything. Whatever you feel like putting in,' said Meng Jarrah, feeling hungrier by the minute.

Before long, the shopkeeper returned with her purchase. Selecting a particularly juicy piece of mango, she munched happily and watched the cats as they lay on their sides in a small patch of sunshine coming in through the front windows. The light gleamed on their fur and formed a delicate pattern of ripples on the dark, slate floor. Meng Jarrah looked more closely at the windows, wondering what was causing the pattern, then saw that the glass was uneven, distorting the view outside. 'How odd,' she thought, and turned to ask the shopkeeper about it, but saw he was busy putting the food for the cats into the shopping bags.

When he had finished, and before he could disappear into the darker recesses at the back of the shop, Meng Jarrah called out to him. 'Hello... I was admiring your windows. They're very unusual. What type of glass is it?'

The shopkeeper turned around, his eyes lighting up with pleasure. 'You're the first to notice...or at least, the first to ask. It's *old* glass. *Very* old glass. In fact, it's over five hundred years old. Remarkable, when you think about it... These windows are real glass, made from sand. They came from an old restaurant that used to be at the end of a long pier that went out from the beach when the old Saint Kilda still existed, in Melbourne. Of course, the area was drowned long ago, but someone went to the trouble of saving what they could and then kept it in their family for generations. It's a miracle this set survived at all. My great, great grandmother, who owned this shop at the time, bought and installed them. Lovely, aren't they? I've read that most old glass was slightly uneven and produced this effect. Anyway, I'm glad you noticed. It's nice to have the old things appreciated.'

Meng Jarrah nodded, agreeing wholeheartedly, and feeling gladdened that something as simple as a plain glass window could be valued enough to have survived for so long. 'Thank you,' she said. 'I hope they last another five hundred years.'

The others were listening and looked curiously at the glass. They could see the difference now it had been pointed out to them.

'Isn't it odd how, in spite of everything, we can turn our minds to something as relatively inconsequential as some old windows,' remarked Edric, astonished at himself.

Meng Jarrah handed him Zarifa's leash and patted his arm. 'It's the perspective that's important. That's what ran through my mind when I noticed the glass was unusual. We get caught up in so much that *seems* important, and usually most of it is, but a sense of time – the passing of time and the small things that matter – somehow helps us manage. At least, that's what I feel. The ripple in the glass – it's a type of perspective, if you like. Not one we see very often, but if you think about it, how many people have looked through this glass since it was made? All those eyes and minds seeing something different each time the windows were put somewhere else or the scene outside changed.'

Freddi, understanding exactly what Meng Jarrah meant, took Shela's leash from her as she absentmindedly handed it over, quite absorbed. Peri pressed herself against Meng Jarrah's legs, reminding her it was time to go.

Collecting herself, Meng Jarrah offered her bag of fruit to the others, and they soon left the shop, each preoccupied with their own thoughts. The shopkeeper watched them, nodding to himself, then turned back to rearrange his display. He liked what the woman had said. She reminded him of his mother, who had spoken similarly about the windows, which was one of the reasons he took particular care of them, washing them regularly so that not a speck of windblown dust ever marred their clarity. Humming a popular tune, he selected a few bright yellow lemons and placed them with careful precision next to a basket of Australian limes, then stood back to better admire the effect, before placing more lemons of another variety and a darker shade of yellow next to them.

Gwenllian had spent the previous two hours inspecting every nook and cranny of Robert's house, marvelling at the craftsmanship in every detail. He had insisted on showing her each room, although little insistence was necessary because she genuinely enjoyed his enthusiasm, touched that he wanted to share it all with her. It was as if Robert had made a decision to free himself from the past and was now eager to move towards the future – which, it seemed, might include her.

As Robert showed her through the house, Gwenllian grew to know both him and Rhianna O'Connor far better. Rhianna's hand was everywhere. They had shared so much of their taste, and had been so much in tune with each other's feelings and sense of achievement in the creation of something beautiful and lasting, that there was little which reflected only the one and not the other. It made Robert's sense of intense betrayal at her eventual isolation of herself from him all the more understandable, and perhaps her death, in its finality, was the only thing that could begin to free him from the grief.

It was bitterly cold outside and the wind crashed through the forest like surf at a beach. The earlier passing of the storm had been temporary, having now returned in full force, yet Robert was eager to show Gwenllian the greenhouse as well, completely ignoring the fact they would need to battle the weather to get to it.

'Come on,' he shouted above the roar of the wind, 'let's run!'

Laughing, Gwenllian set off, and they both arrived at the same time, exhilarated. Robert opened the door, and when they were both inside, closed it behind them. Gwenllian's hair was in disarray from having pulled off her hat, but she didn't bother to settle it down with her hand. Once, she would have taken great care to do so, but somehow, her self-conscious vanity disappeared when she finally came to terms with the changes that had taken place in her mind five years ago.

She turned to Robert and grinned. 'It's wonderfully warm in here. I'm glad you've decided to replant. Would you mind if I helped? I know a little about soil, as well as what grows best here and there.'

'Yes,' he said slowly, 'I would be glad to have your help, whether you know a little about soil and plants or not.'

They regarded each other in silence for almost a minute, and the strangeness of the link that had developed between his mind and hers seemed less strange. These past five years, Gwenllian hadn't met anyone else whose mind was in the least similar to hers, yet now, in the space of only days, she had met two. Robert sensed her thoughts and put out a hand to briefly touch her cheek, then withdrew, suddenly shy, but only for a moment. The reassurance he immediately felt from Gwenllian's mind made him grin, and they stood for a while longer, enjoying the quick understanding they had reached.

'You know rather more than "a little", don't you,' said Robert, grinning even more broadly.

Gwenllian laughed. 'Yes, a great deal more than just a little. My brother, Owain, has a position with the Department of Agriculture as a research coordinator, and we've worked together for many years on private research into methods of soil regeneration. We use a knowledge-based modelling technique which analyses the biological and physical structure of soils and then compares it to standards that show whether it's healthy or not, and if not, what needs to be done to make it healthy. The next step is to track the soil over time to make sure it's all going in the right direction, and then if anything seems to be wrong, we try to work out how to put it right again. Are you impressed?' Gwenllian put her head to one side, trying hard not to laugh again, but failing.

'I'm definitely impressed,' Robert agreed. 'How long have you been doing this research?'

'Oh, years and years. We used our system to help Meng Jarrah and the Federation put together a strategy for regenerating the soils over at Lamington. Owain and I helped with the reforestation trials as well, although Meng Jarrah and the Federation's own research coordinator did most of the work. It was when we were at Lamington that I discovered I'd turned into a cat. It was a shock, that's for sure! To begin with, I didn't want to accept it, but of course, I had to. Once I did, my whole life changed – or at least, my attitude towards life. I don't think you'd have liked me very much the way I used to be.' As she said this, Gwenllian suddenly looked unsure of herself, remembering how arrogant and defensive she had once been.

'Well, it's certainly not the case now,' said Robert in a low voice, his eyes studying her face.

'No, I guess not. It's a humbling experience being treated like a young kitten by the nursing mothers at the Breeding Centre. My research took second place for quite a long time, and even now, I tend to spend more time working with them than with Owain. He gets a bit jealous at times. We've always been close. Not many people are as incredibly lucky as us to have a brother or sister, and we used to do everything together. I think that's why I can understand how you felt about Rhianna. She must have been like a sister to you. I don't know what I'd do if Owain didn't want to see me, or talk to me any longer...'

Gwenllian's normally pale face became a touch paler as she spoke. She had never examined this idea before, and felt distinctly dizzy at the thought of no longer having Owain as part of her life. Looking around, but finding nowhere to sit, she leaned against one of the greenhouse supports and took a deep breath. Concerned, Robert reached out to touch her shoulder.

Rubbing her face with a mittened hand, Gwenllian smiled and said, 'Don't worry, Robert, I think it's your loss I'm over-empathising with; I almost did lose Owain five years ago. It's this ability of mine that saved him. I still get the horrors thinking about it. It's as if I developed my powers just in time...and it could so easily have been too late.'

'What happened?' asked Robert, some of her memories seeping into his mind. He felt the fear that had momentarily overcome her.

'Have you ever heard of the Wyvern Meridian case?'

Robert nodded.

'We were caught up in it. While we were working at Lamington, there was an attempt on Owain's life. I had been trying to ignore the fact that something was happening to my mind, giving me these new powers, when all of a sudden I knew Owain was about to be killed. Without my consciously trying to, *I* killed the two men who were about to murder him.'

Gwenllian paused, staring at Robert, her heart racing as she recalled all too clearly how she and Owain had felt at the time. Making an effort to keep her voice even, she explained further: 'If you remember, Wyvern Meridian was trying to compete with the Federation in most areas of forestry, and wanted to lease a huge tract of Australian land for plantations. The company used every means they could to fast-track their own research while slowing down ours, including takeovers of any small company that could add to their reputation or knowledge base and putting bugs into Federation research models. They even sabotaged other competitors, bribed government officials, and murdered anyone who got in their way.'

She carefully studied Robert's face to see how he would react, equally carefully refraining from looking into his mind. Under the circumstances, it seemed wrong to do so.

'I gather you mean that you killed the two men with your mind, rather than with a weapon?' asked Robert, frowning and gazing into her eyes.

'Yes, that's exactly what I mean. I managed to kill them from a distance of several hundred metres. I didn't even fully realise what had happened until I arrived at the spot where Owain had been working. You can see why I had to spend a long time at the Breeding Centre...and it's not something I tell the whole world about, either.'

'No, that I can easily understand,' said Robert slowly. 'It must have been horrible for you. Strangely enough, it reminds me of how Sylvie protected

Rhianna from school bullies when she was little. Sylvie didn't have the training cats receive now. She simply reacted as well.'

By now they were both sitting on the earthen floor, resting their backs against the foundation stones. They had forgotten the wind and rain outside. Despite the roaring of the storm, it seemed quiet and peaceful in here. Gwenllian sighed, remembering just how very horrible it all was.

'Did the case come to trial?'

'No. Once all the evidence had been gathered and evaluated by the Judge, the peacekeepers decided not to lay charges. Instead, my Federation records were amended to show that I have these abilities, which is fine. It just means I'm officially weird.'

Robert gently took her hand in his and they sat there in silence for a long time. Eventually, when Gwenllian leaned against his shoulder, he put an arm around hers, holding her close.

CHAPTER THIRTEEN

Once more, Smithson was in his element. Of the five hundred and thirty jars of Sensa previously unaccounted for, only six were still in question, and no reports had come in of anyone who had developed any untoward symptoms. However, he was still not satisfied. Those six jars worried him. The purchase records were incomplete, and could not be traced to any Federation citizen, so allowing for the fact that even in such a well-ordered society as theirs occasional computer and human errors were possible, six was still too high a number.

Intuitively, the peacekeeper was sure the jar Rhianna used was amongst those six. He knew they had been sold in Argentina over a period of four months, in six individual transactions, from three different shops in Córdoba. The final transaction took place during the time Rhianna last visited the country. Smithson concluded that the lack of traceable records opened up the possibility that someone had planned to murder her well in advance. Nevertheless, proving this was altogether another matter.

He settled back in his comfortable chair, deep in thought, and after a while called Freddi. When she answered, the intensely colourful background formed by the room where his colleague was standing momentarily distracted him and he peered more closely at the scene.

Freddi smiled slightly, explaining that she was with Stefano Salvarez in his home. 'We've just delivered him safely, together with his new guardian, and were about to take Edric home. He has one now as well. Do you want to see?'

Smithson nodded, intrigued, then burst out laughing when two cats pushed their faces up to the screen. The cats drew back a few centimetres, before stalking off, insulted.

'You may need to apologise, Smithson,' joked Freddi. 'They expect to be taken seriously, and believe me, they do make exceptionally good bodyguards. We've just been to the Breeding Centre so Edric and Stefano could choose – or be chosen, whichever way one looks at it.'

'Is it for their protection, or instead of appointing a peacekeeper to keep an eye on them?'

'Mostly for their own protection until we know whether or not they're in any danger. I've sent an encoded report to Nyneve of an idea that occurred to both Meng Jarrah and I during our flight back to Brisbane. You can ask her about it later, if you like...but I gather you've discovered something? You can speak freely. Edric and Stefano aren't in the room or within hearing distance.'

'Yes, I have,' and Smithson told Freddi of his tentative conclusion about the missing jars of Sensa.

While he was speaking, Meng Jarrah came over to listen. 'What you've said fits in with our own thinking,' she remarked. 'There are far too many 'missing records' in this case to be coincidence. We have to work on the assumption that Rhianna's death wasn't accidental.'

Freddi agreed, a grim expression replacing her earlier more light-hearted one. 'Thanks, Smithson, I'll make sure I keep you and Nyneve up to date. In the meantime, if anything relevant occurs to either of you, just say so, and we can discuss how best to proceed. We still have some interviews to do here in Brisbane, as well as one in Melbourne, after which we'll be taking a little trip to Argentina. With any luck, someone in at least one of the three shops will remember a customer buying the Sensa, particularly if they only sell fairly small quantities. Did you happen to notice whether that was the case?'

Smithson consulted his computer. 'Over the period we're looking at, one shop sold between seven and twenty-one jars a month, the second sold between three and fourteen a month, while the third sold between eight and nineteen. That's a lot of customers to remember.'

'Unless the person in question was somehow memorable.' Freddi's face expressed a mixture of resignation and hope.

'Ah, the eternal optimist,' replied Smithson, grinning.

'Well, why not? We need to be in this job or we'd never do it.'

'True,' he agreed, scratching an eyebrow with his little finger.

Meng Jarrah prodded Freddi in the ribs, and she turned to see both Stefano and Edric coming back into the room, closely followed by Peri and Zarifa. Smithson winked at Freddi and closed the connection.

'Are you ready to go, Edric?' asked Freddi. 'Or more to the point, Stefano, are you ready for us to leave?'

Stefano stroked Peri's silky head. 'Yes, I feel perfectly safe. But I felt safe before. It's *your* fears for my safety that brought this gorgeous creature into my life, not any fears of mine. Thank you, though. It would never have occurred to me to apply for a cat.'

Peri twined herself around Stefano's legs, purring loudly, her paws kneading the carpet. She glanced at Freddi, then sat down to clean herself, delicately licking one paw and rubbing it over her unusually long whiskers and eyebrows.

Meanwhile, Zarifa sat quietly shifting her gaze from one person to another, listening to everything being said – and thought – but made no comment, other than she was happy to leave. Zarifa was keeping a little reserve between herself and her Wight, because unlike Peri, she was not yet committed to staying with him, nor he with her.

Edric, ready to leave as well, looked at Zarifa and smiled, almost unaware he was answering her without actual words, then attached her leash. 'I must admit to being glad not to have to return to Rhianna's apartment alone,' he told them. 'I still think of it as *her* apartment, not my home, even though it is. Odd, isn't it.'

'Not really,' replied Meng Jarrah, sympathising with him. 'She owned it and lived there before you formed your relationship with her. You know you don't have to stay there if you don't want to. *Do* you want to?'

Edric considered the question for a moment. 'Yes, I do want to stay in the apartment. It hurts terribly when I remember her being there with me, but I'd prefer that to nothing. I feel as if a piece of my heart has been torn out! Sorry...' His face crumpled, but he collected himself with an effort and began walking to the door. Zarifa followed, more subdued than before.

Stefano gripped Edric by both shoulders and hugged him, briefly and fiercely. 'Come over to dinner tomorrow, will you?' he said.

Edric nodded, then silently turned away.

Freddi and Meng Jarrah finally returned home late in the afternoon, by which time Mount Cootdha was shrouded in misty rain. The trees in the garden dripped steadily as the moisture they collected on their leaves formed huge drops before falling to the ground. The air smelt of the clean, wet earth. After climbing the stairs to the verandah, they both turned to admire the view of the river, then, holding hands, walked the last few metres together in silence, glad to have each other, and of course, Shela.

Once inside, and as soon as her leash was removed, the cat flew along the broad hallway and into the kitchen, skidding on the polished floor as she ran. The main objective in her mind, loud and clear to both her companions, was 'Food!'...naturally.

Freddi soon obliged, and while a large bowl of cheese and cooked rice was demolished with relish, Meng Jarrah made coffee and hunted through the larder for something to eat. Finding some shortbread biscuits, she put them on the circular wooden table standing in the centre of the room. They sipped their steaming coffee for a few minutes and munched their way through several biscuits, each thinking about Rhianna and what their next tasks should be.

'Perhaps you'd better finish looking into the origins of her tattoo,' suggested Meng Jarrah. 'You could be lucky enough to find something useful before today is over. Or else I could do it while you contact Ruth and Marietta. There's the jeweller to interview, too.'

Chapter Thirteen

'Yes, I might interview the jeweller today. It should be fairly straightforward.' Freddi held her coffee with both hands, sniffing its fragrance, elbows resting on the tabletop. '*You* could stay inside where it's lovely and warm and dry, and look at tattoos, that's true.'

Meng Jarrah laughed. 'I promise to have dinner ready for you when you come back. Would that compensate?'

Pleased, Freddi grinned, then finished her coffee and one last biscuit before standing up and looking over to where Shela was in the process of cleaning her paws.

'Ready to go out again?' she asked the cat.

Shela stopped what she was doing to gaze steadily at her, making no move towards the door.

'Oh, you're going to desert me as well, are you?'

Freddi sighed theatrically, called the jeweller's establishment to check whether he would be available, then made her way out into the drizzling rain. She opened a large black umbrella and, hunching her shoulders against the cold, turned to look back at the house for a moment before quickening her pace.

Having preferred to take public transport for such a short trip, it wasn't long before Freddi reached the callstation, and only minutes later, the light railcar arrived to take her to the city centre and Margaret Street, where she would find the jeweller from whom Edric had bought the ear circlets. After reaching the elegant building, Freddi hesitated just long enough outside its glass doors to form an impression of what type of company it was: old, well established and expensive.

As she entered, Freddi could see an elderly man arranging various items in a display case with great precision. He immediately noticed her, put down the small box he held, and gave the merest hint of a bow. 'May I help you?' he asked.

'Yes, I hope so,' replied Freddi. 'Are you Anthony Markham?'

'Yes, I am. And you are?'

'My name is Freddi. I called earlier and spoke with your assistant. As you can see, I'm with the Brisbane Peacekeeping Force. A recent client of yours, by the name of Edric, gave me your details. He commissioned a set of ear circlets to match an existing piece...an exceptionally fine silver necklet. Do you recall?'

'Of course. May I ask why you need to know?'

'Yes, you may. The person for whom the ear circlets were made has unfortunately died in, shall we say, odd circumstances, so her death must be investigated in order to ascertain whether it was natural or otherwise.' Freddi found herself speaking in an unusually formal manner, as if in response to the grave dignity of the man before her, as well as the ambience of the shop.

Anthony Markham bowed again and shook his head, one hand making a small flourish. 'Well,' he said, 'I accept that you have your reasons for asking, so please, come with me and I will show you our transaction records.'

Leading the way towards the rear of the shop, the jeweller soon found what Freddi wanted then stood back while the peacekeeper studied the designs, the details of the order, as well as the final payment.

'Do you often deal with Michiko Yamada?' she asked him.

'No, not often. Only when someone wants a certain type of design, as well as exceptionally high quality silver.'

'I see you have an image here of the necklet Edric brought with him. Do you know when it was made? The date isn't mentioned here.' Freddi noticed she was holding her breath while she waited for the answer.

'Oh no, it wouldn't be. Those records are held in another file. I will bring them to the screen for you.' Markham keyed in a few characters. 'There,' he said, satisfied. 'This is a complete catalogue of all Michiko Yamada's commercial creations. We should be able to find out quite readily, although I did not use this to determine who made the piece. It was obvious from the workmanship, the design, the type of silver, and of course, the initials 'MY'. When I contacted her, she confirmed it was one of her pieces and agreed to make the matching ear circlets.'

He looked at the catalogue again and then hesitated, confused. 'How odd,' he murmured, peering more closely at the screen. 'It doesn't seem to be here.' Markham turned to Freddi, his expression both perplexed and apologetic. 'The only conclusion I can draw is that the necklet was a private commission and not a commercial product. I *am* sorry.'

Freddi paused before replying, trying hard not to become exasperated by yet another missing piece of information. 'Thank you,' she said. 'You've been most helpful. We may require your transaction record as evidence, so it would be best if I take a copy now, if you don't mind?'

'No, not at all. Please, help yourself.'

Markham stood back while Freddi transferred the copy to her comlink and then asked him to verify that it was complete and unaltered. He slowly examined the record, comparing the copy with his original before placing his thumb on the keypad, sealing the information.

'We need to seal your original too, as well as your back-up copies.'

Markham gave the computer the necessary instructions. With the records secure, Freddi left the shop. The jeweller quietly returned to his display cases, meticulously polishing each item and then arranging them to best effect, soon dismissing the incident from his mind.

*

Agathea's round, plump face, delicately creased and lined with her years, displayed the grief caused by the news her son Robert had given her. His call had reached her at a resort in Kenya, where she was taking great delight in feeding a few individuals belonging to the herd of elephants roaming freely throughout the vast wildlife reserve. The trunk of the youngest elephant carefully explored her free hand, searching for traces of leftover food. While she spoke, Agathea absentmindedly stroked its soft skin as it proceeded to investigate the back of her neck, tickling ever so slightly.

Her distress over Rhianna's death was increased by hearing Robert relate how they had chosen to bury her in Girraween, rather than insisting the peacekeepers be informed immediately. 'Robert, my dear,' said Agathea, controlling herself with an effort, 'I can understand why these people didn't want to be found anywhere near an illegal martial arts tournament, but surely that wasn't your concern? Still, never mind... Too late now to worry about it, though I must admit to being appalled at Edric even suggesting her body be removed from the place where she died.'

'We needed to come to terms with her death, Mother. That was more important to us than anything else. I realise it was stupid from a legal point of view, but at the time it seemed the right thing to do, both for Rhianna and for us. I don't regret doing what we did.'

As Robert stared at his mother, her deep grey eyes held his, even over the vast distance between them. Eventually, she said, 'I'll come home. I think it would be a very good thing if you called Edric and asked him to visit, for at least a few days. After all the years of wanting her so much, to have lost her now is an awful thing. I think he would benefit from being with us and talking about her. I also think it would be good for you. You need to forgive her.'

'I think I have, Mother. I've decided to replant the greenhouse.'

'Good...I'm glad. Perhaps Edric could help? He was a big strong lad the last time I saw him.'

'Oh, Edric's still a "big strong lad"! He's the unofficial Australian heavyweight combined kung fu and karate champion. Rhianna was the middleweight champion.'

'Great heavens!' exclaimed Agathea. 'How then did she manage to get killed at this tournament? Or are they so vicious that people sometimes do get killed?'

'She didn't die from a blow, we're almost certain of that, but I don't yet know what *did* kill her. The peacekeepers are still investigating. No doubt we'll find out when the inquest is held.'

'Who was the poor girl fighting when she died? They must have been dreadfully upset.'

'Well, yes, so I gather. It was Marietta.' Robert frowned as he spoke, remembering Marietta Ross with distaste.

'Marietta! This gets more and more incredible, Robert. Was all of Stanthorpe there?'

'A good part of it. These tournaments began when Marietta, Stefano Salvarez and Ruth Baillieu were still at school. Rhianna wouldn't have anything to do with them then, so it was one of the things that astounded me the last time she was here...when she told me about joining up.'

'After your father died, yes. You didn't tell me she'd done that.' Agathea mused for a few moments. 'She *had* changed a great deal, though I wouldn't have thought *that* much. I think there's a lot more to this than we can see at present. If Rhianna wasn't killed accidentally, someone must have done it on purpose – unless she was suffering from some obscure illness that suddenly caught up with her, which doesn't sound likely. Poor, poor young woman. She was such a beautiful little girl – and I still believe, a beautiful person, in spite of having changed so much.'

'She let Leihana die, Mother!'

'Yes, I know, but perhaps it was the right thing to do, cruel as that might sound. Sometimes people need to die. Everything anyone could do had been done for Leihana, yet she still couldn't find the courage to live. Life does take courage, immense courage sometimes, and when someone finally gives up, is it kind to force them to keep going? I don't have the answer, but Rhianna made *her* decision. You've assumed it was because she hated her mother, but perhaps not. It could well be that she cared for her enough to let her go this time.'

Robert shook his head and looked away for a moment. 'We'll never know... Edric certainly loved Rhianna and was happy to be with her. It's hard to say what type of person *he* is, given how little time we spent together that night, but if he agrees to visit, we might find out. By the way, Edric won't be the only visitor if he does come.' Robert's expression lightened with these last words.

'Really, dear, who else is staying?' Agathea gently pushed the elephant's trunk aside as it tugged at her hair.

'A most remarkable woman by the name of Gwenllian. She's not staying here as such, but comes to visit most days and is helping me plan what to grow in the greenhouse, as well as what to do with the soil before we begin. She came down to help with the investigation into Rhianna's death... Well, not really the investigation, but to help a distraught cat. Rhianna's body was discovered by a cat who was accompanying two Italian tourists. The cat needed expert help to overcome the shock, so Gwenllian was sent by the Melbourne Breeding Centre and soon became involved in the investigation; as it turns out, she's a friend of the two peacekeepers who were sent here from Brisbane to assist.'

'Great heavens!' exclaimed Agathea again. 'This is becoming quite a story. If these creatures will let me, I think I had better leave *now*, so you can tell me the rest when I get home.' She consulted her comlink and did a few calculations. 'I should be home in about eighteen hours. Perhaps your friend, Gwenllian, would like to meet me and have a meal together? I don't suppose you've forgotten how to cook?' Agathea smiled at her son, happy at the thought of being with him again after having been away for the past fifteen months.

The tattoo on Rhianna's thigh had clearly been the work of a highly skilled artist. The general design – a phoenix – was not unique, although this particular style of phoenix did not appear in any standard catalogue of any registered tattooist. Frustrated, Meng Jarrah drummed her fingertips on the edge of her keyboard and studied the screen, thinking, then used her encrypted pass to enter the database of the Federation's Special Investigation Unit, being one of the very few with the right to do so without having formal employment with them. Her fame as a palaeontologist and status as a Government Research Coordinator, together with her previous association with FSIU Coordinator Morag MacIain and the Willsmere investigation, had qualified her to be given this authority, yet this was the first time there was reason to use it. Even Freddi did not have this level of access, so strangely enough, Meng Jarrah would require formal permission from Morag to share any information obtained from the database. She shook her head. It was ironic, really. The investigation *was* Freddi's, after all!

Based on their earlier suspicions, Meng Jarrah performed a search on Kenjiro Kakura and immediately located the entire record associated with the Willsmere case, including all related links. Skimming through the Willsmere entry, it was easy to remember just how complex the case had been, and she shuddered to think they could once again be involved with something related to Wyvern Meridian!

After tagging the information as having been read, she looked at the next entry. It had been made since Kakura's death and contained details about his bondmate, Michiko Yamada, his three children, his parents and extended family, as well as his earlier years. At last they had something to use! He definitely attended Seoul University at the same time as Rhianna O'Connor. How then, and why, had his name been removed from their records?

The phoenix was renowned for its ability to 'return from the ashes'. Was this the significance of the tattoo, rather than the purely decorative? Was it an indelible mark of Rhianna's sympathy with Kenjiro Kakura, if indeed they were lovers at the time? She realised they knew almost nothing of his early years. Did he develop his intense desire to identify with the old Japanese empire because he felt the loss of the ancient homeland more keenly than most?

Together with the inherent instability of the earth's crust, always the bane of Japan, the manmade environmental disasters that led to low-lying countries becoming submerged by the oceans had caused millions to die, and those who remained, to lose the cultural core of their lives. Even after many generations, there would still be countless people of Japanese descent who bitterly felt this loss, as did the descendants of all the other races who lost their homelands.

Reading on, Meng Jarrah noticed that Kakura formed his bond with Michiko Yamada in the year 2441, one year before Rhianna obtained her doctorate and while he was still studying for his, having apparently changed his mind about not studying for a degree. Could her reluctance to tell Robert about her lover have simply been because Kakura was involved with someone else and she was unable to accept this other relationship, yet was still too in love to give him up? Meng Jarrah shook her head again, her dark curls glinting in the sunlight now streaming in from the window through a break in the clouds. This particular story was repeated over and over throughout the ages, and now, perhaps yet again. The obvious thought struck her: if so, had Michiko Yamada known about Rhianna?

Further hunting revealed little else of relevance, so, still curious, Meng Jarrah entered a search on Rhianna's name. Finding nothing, she exited the database and sent a message to Federation Special Investigation Unit Coordinator, Morag MacIain, requesting permission to share the information she had found with Freddi and asking for anything further Morag might know that could help them with their enquiries.

A warning note appeared on Morag's screen as she was studying her itinerary for the day. A single name appeared: "Rhianna O'Connor". She leaned forward, brushing a stray auburn curl from her forehead, and as she watched, another name appeared: "Meng Jarrah". Morag touched the screen to display Meng Jarrah's description of their investigation, as well as the strange circumstances that indicated a possible link between Rhianna and Kenjiro Kakura. She then touched Rhianna O'Connor's name, still displayed at the top of the screen. Nibbling at the inside of her pursed lips, Morag read through the latest report Freddi had entered into the lattice, ready for the Judge if and when the time came for it to evaluate their case. The coffee sitting on her desk was still hot, so she procrastinated for a few minutes longer by taking a mouthful and savouring the aromatic liquid. Finally, she decided to wait a while longer to see which direction the investigation would take before replying to Meng Jarrah's request.

*

128

By the time Edric arrived for his dinner with Stefano, the rain had ceased and the night sky was clearing, although a sharp breeze now came in from the sea. It felt good to be inside. He removed his guardian's leash and she bounded across the gaily decorated room to her friend. Peri rose up on her hind legs to throw herself onto Zarifa's neck in mock attack. The tawny, slimmer cat, somewhat more agile, quickly wriggled away to catch Peri with her front paws, before grasping her neck in strong, though gentle, jaws. The playful snarling continued for some time as the two cats wrestled and leapt around the room, while Edric and Stefano watched in amusement. Despite the play, nothing was disturbed – except for the pile of yellow cushions, which the cats had somehow arranged into a wonderfully comfortable bed. Before long, Zarifa and Peri were tightly curled up together, fast asleep.

The two men felt strangely calm and more at peace than at any time since Rhianna's death. Edric suspected this was due to the influence of the cats, but gratefully accepted their gift. Stefano was absolutely sure it was due to Peri's presence in his life; the impact the cat had made in such an incredibly short time was astounding. He had found himself smiling at seemingly nothing in particular throughout the day, and was glad his housemates weren't there to see. The two friends who shared his home seemed unaware of the cat's abilities and, for the time being, Stefano chose to leave it that way. He felt sure that if Peri wanted them to know what she was capable of, she would tell them. They were not due back until late this evening, which meant he and Edric could share their experiences with the guardians quite openly.

'Next to Rhianna, Peri's the most extraordinary creature I've ever met,' said Stefano, as he handed Edric a bright red mug of hot tea.

They had left the cats to their sleep and moved into the kitchen. Edric sat down at the battered old table standing in the middle of the floor, leaning on it with his elbows, hands around the mug of tea. The darkness was firmly excluded from this cosy room. Heavy curtains hung over the large window that, during the daytime, looked out over a wide balcony festooned with hanging plants of all descriptions. Stefano had a talent with plants, and took care of them as meticulously as he took care of everything else he owned. The fact the table was battered was not due to neglect. It was simply old, and Stefano preferred to keep the original appearance, appreciating something as simple as a kitchen table which had managed to survive such a long series of owners. A green glass vase stood at its centre, holding a bunch of golden chrysanthemums. Their faintly acrid scent tickled Edric's nose and he sneezed, but waved his hand as Stefano immediately offered to remove them.

'No, no, I like them,' he said, taking a kerchief from his tunic pocket. 'It's only the first sniff that makes me sneeze. Don't worry about it.'

Stefano sat down with his own mug of tea and pushed a plate of homemade lamingtons toward his friend.

Edric took one, bit into the soft cake, and was about to take another bite when he suddenly sneezed again. 'That's odd,' he muttered. 'Maybe you *had* better take the flowers away.'

Stefano stood up to take the chrysanthemums into the dining room, placing them in the exact centre of the sideboard and briefly admiring the effect before returning to the kitchen, only to behold Edric looking distressed, tears running down his face while he rubbed his eyes.

'I think something's really wrong, Stefano. My eyes itch and my nose has started running. It's getting worse by the minute. Do you mind if we go to the nearest medcentre? I've never felt anything like it.'

Without unnecessary comment, Stefano fetched Edric's coat and helped him into it, then put on his own warm, woollen jacket, silently telling the cats what was happening and fetching their leashes. Both cats rose and studied Edric curiously, then sat down again while Stefano attached the long leads to their collars. Sneezing furiously, Edric held his kerchief to his face as they all left the house to walk to the nearest callstation. By this time, Edric was beginning to have trouble breathing.

'It's not far to the medcentre,' he gasped, when Stefano suggested they call an ambulance. 'It shouldn't take more than about ten minutes.'

Stefano, beginning to feel frightened for his friend, made the call for their transport then contacted the medcentre anyway. A practitioner's face appeared on his comlink shortly after he had given a brief description of the situation to the medtech who first answered his call.

'We'll be ready for him as soon as he arrives,' said the practitioner, concerned. 'I'll place a priority call to the transport service to make sure there's no delay getting you here. That'll be as fast as if we sent out our own. It sounds like an allergic reaction to something. You must keep him calm in the meantime.' The practitioner broke off for a few moments to make the promised call, then said, 'It should only be another two minutes before your transport arrives. I'll stay online until you get here.'

Stefano nodded, and was just in time to catch Edric by the shoulders as he collapsed onto the trafficway, gasping for breath. Stefano shoved the comlink into his jacket pocket and quickly turned him onto his side, making sure he was still breathing, even if it was with some difficulty. Pulling the comlink out from his pocket again, he showed the practitioner Edric's condition.

'Just keep him as warm as you can and on his side, as you've done. It won't be long now,' the practitioner intoned in a soothing voice.

The light railcar arrived at that moment and the attendant helped Stefano carry Edric inside, laying him down on the heated floor. The two cats quickly leapt into the vehicle, unnoticed by the attendant, who was more concerned to get to the medcentre at the fastest possible speed, which, in emergency situations, was very fast indeed. A medtech was waiting outside with a hoverbed when they arrived. By this time, Edric's breathing was little more than a laboured gasp, while his eyelids had swollen to such an extent he could no longer see.

Once they were inside, the practitioner applied her medical scanner and took a small blood sample. She looked at Stefano and then at the two cats, who had followed them inside without anyone questioning their right to do so. 'It's the cats, I'm afraid. He's allergic to them. It's an extremely rare condition, but that's what it is. Get them out, now!'

Without hesitating, the two cats fled to the door and, when it opened for them, ran out into the night.

CHAPTER FOURTEEN

Sitting side by side at the edge of the blue flowered trafficway immediately outside the medcentre, Peri and Zarifa stared mournfully at the night-time horizon, silently sharing their woe. They took almost no notice of passers-by, although those who saw the two cats stopped briefly to peer at them, disturbed at seeing the creatures alone and unaccompanied by a human. One woman stayed long enough to consider whether she should notify the peacekeepers, but Peri swiftly diverted the thought into other, less inconvenient channels without her being any the wiser. She went on her way and, with a mental nudge from Zarifa as well, soon forgot the encounter.

Even from this distance, they could sense Stefano's main concern was for his human friend, though he was also worried about them. Edric's body was recovering rapidly due to the ministrations of the practitioner, but his mind was still dazed and confused. Zarifa probed gently, but found no way of helping. She snuffled and moved closer to Peri, who thoroughly licked her face before turning her attention to her own fur, the reliable resort of every cat at a loss as to what to do.

They eventually agreed to cautiously approach the entrance of the medcentre to see if there was a sheltered spot where they could wait for Stefano without attracting undue attention. More than one and a half hours went by before they saw Peri's Wight leave the building to come searching for them. When Peri meowed softly, Stefano immediately ran over to where they were hiding and knelt down to wrap his arms around her in a close hug. Zarifa waited politely for his emotions to subside a little before butting her head against his shoulder. Stefano immediately put an arm around her as well, kissing her silken forehead. She licked his nose and rubbed her head against his cheek, purring softly.

They sat like that for some time, pondering their dilemma and earning the curious gaze of the occasional pedestrian. An elderly man paused for several seconds, intending to ask if they required any assistance, but with a discreet and unnoticed prompt from Peri, changed his mind and left.

'There must be some way of dealing with Edric's condition,' Stefano told the two cats, who listened without blinking. This was something about which they knew nothing. He stroked Zarifa, continuing to speak aloud, even though it wasn't strictly necessary, yet preferring to hear his own voice as it helped him see the situation more clearly. 'Unfortunately, they didn't have time to tell me what could be done... They were too busy dealing with his symptoms.'

When both cats 'asked' the same question, almost simultaneously, he explained: 'Some people's immune systems react to certain proteins and cause what the practitioner said was an allergic reaction. The body sees the protein as foreign and tries to neutralise it as quickly as it can. Edric went into what they called anaphylactic shock. This happens when the reaction is so fast and so severe that tissues in the body begin to swell rapidly, which often affects the person's ability to breathe. If they're not treated immediately, they can die.'

Although they could hardly be expected to understand everything Stefano told them, both cats wailed loudly and sprang to their feet, pacing back and forth, their tails low to the ground, extremely distressed at inadvertently being the cause of so much trouble. Stefano stood up, looking down at them, astonished at the intensity of their feelings. Zarifa stopped pacing to sit at his feet and gaze earnestly into his face, her eyes large and luminescent in the dim light, her front paws kneading the ground in agitation, tail curled tightly around her trim body. She placed one paw on his knee, a question in her mind.

Stefano knelt and took her paw in his hand. 'I'll go back to see what's happening. Promise you'll stay here and not draw attention to yourselves? I shouldn't be long.'

The two cats promptly agreed and quietly settled themselves beneath the low-hanging branches of a nearby callistemon. Stefano looked back before he went inside and was satisfied to see they were almost indistinguishable from the shadows beneath the shrub. By the time he reached Edric's bed, his friend appeared to be almost back to normal, although it was easy to see he was fretting about something. His face cleared when he saw Stefano.

'They can treat this condition, Stefano! There's a small risk, but I'm prepared to take it. Where are the cats?'

'They're hiding under a bush outside, not far from the main entrance. They're pretty upset, but doing a good job of keeping themselves inconspicuous.'

'Thank the Sun!' exclaimed Edric, more concerned for his new feline friends than for himself, now the immediate emergency was over.

He turned to the practitioner, who was tidying away her instruments. She smiled reassuringly. The practitioner had seen very few cases of this type of allergy, and rarely one as extreme as Edric's. Under the circumstances, she was therefore intrigued by the deep concern these two young men had for the welfare of their cats. Edric himself was amazed at how strong his need for Zarifa had become since being separated. 'How long would the treatment take?' he asked.

'Not more than two weeks. With luck, less,' she replied, checking his pulse again and carefully feeling his throat for any lingering swelling. 'You must keep away from cats during that time, and then contact should be gradual and under medical supervision. Will that be a problem? You won't be able to go back to your home either – not until it's been thoroughly cleaned. There'll be cat hair and other cells all over the place. Can you arrange for somewhere else to stay?'

Edric and Stefano looked at each other, weighing their options and quickly coming to the same conclusion. 'Yes, I think I can manage,' replied Edric. 'Would it matter if another medcentre administered the treatment?'

'No, I don't see any problem at all,' said the practitioner, with another polite smile. 'Which one were you thinking of?'

'Stanthorpe,' Edric told her. 'I can go back to Stanthorpe. I grew up there. It's time I paid someone a visit.'

'You'll need to take new clothing with you. You can't take anything from your home.'

'Oh! Oh well, I guess I won't have to get much if it's only for a few weeks.' Without really seeing it, Edric gazed around at the purposefully cheerful décor of the room, imagining how Robert would react when he asked him to accept a guest for while. Still, if he turned him down, there was always the communal house...though there was no guarantee it would be free from cat hair, come to think of it... Perhaps the peacekeepers could provide a solution if it came to that? After all, they were the ones who decided guardians were necessary.

'I could visit with the cats later on when you're ready to be reintroduced,' suggested Stefano. 'I wouldn't mind a trip back to the old home town myself.' He looked happy at the prospect, thinking in particular of Margrethe and wondering if she still had her cat. He hadn't thought about Harriet in all these years, but with cats now so important, he remembered her.

'Good,' responded the practitioner. 'Let's say that one way or another, you go to Stanthorpe, either tomorrow or the next day, depending upon how well you do here overnight. I'll make the necessary medical arrangements. Now, I should see to some other patients, so please excuse me, and if you're hungry, you can order something to eat.'

She gave them one last professional smile and then left the two men staring at each other, unsure who should call whom in Stanthorpe, or whether it would be better if they called Freddi first. Clearly, the sooner one of them did something, the better.

'I think I'll call Freddi,' decided Stefano. 'She'll want to know. Do you feel like eating? You could get us something while I make the call.'

'What about the cats? They must be hungry too.' Edric felt a sudden gnawing in his stomach, so set about consulting the menu. 'If I get something they'd like, could you take it out to them?'

Stefano grinned. For someone who had recently been uncertain whether he wanted to keep his guardian as a companion, Edric was rapidly becoming devoted to her. He chuckled, patting his friend on the shoulder before making the call.

It took longer than Stefano would have expected for Freddi to appear, yawning and rubbing a hand over her face. 'Mmm?' she said.

'Sorry, did I wake you?'

'Yes, it's past midnight, or hadn't you noticed?'

'Ah, no, or I wouldn't have called... Sorry... Do you mind if we talk? It shouldn't take long.'

'I'm awake. Talk away.' Freddi yawned again, but listened closely while he told her what had happened to Edric and what they were proposing.

'How extraordinarily unfortunate! Still, he'd be as safe in Stanthorpe as anywhere else. In fact, if Robert agrees, it might even work out very well. Gwenllian is still visiting him, so she can help keep an eye on Edric. No one could get near him with her around.'

Stefano nodded, relieved. 'Do you want to call Robert, or should we?' he asked.

'I'll do it, and explain how important it is, but not now. I'll leave it until a more civilised time of day and then call you back. Are you going with him?'

'Yes, I might as well, though it will have to be by separate transport because both cats will have to come with me.'

'How are they doing?'

'They're confused and a bit frightened. At the moment, until I can take them home, they're making themselves invisible just outside the medcentre. Once we've had something to eat, I'll leave and let Edric get some sleep.'

'Good. I'll try to call you around midsun. That'll give you time to have some sleep too. Now, if you don't mind, I'd like to get back to mine.' Freddi grinned and ended the call.

In the meantime, Edric had managed to order some food for the cats, in the form of a cheesecake dessert enough for two, together with some chicken and asparagus soup, barley bread and pumpkin risotto for themselves. Before long, a cheerful, sturdily built man arrived with the meal and served the dishes on the small table standing by the bed.

'I brought you some iced water to go with it,' he said kindly. 'Call me when you're finished and I'll collect the empty dishes.'

Once he had gone, Stefano looked at the cheesecake, wondering how he would get it out of the medcentre without anyone noticing. The same thing must have occurred to Edric. He was carefully sliding one of the pieces onto the same plate as the other, then using one of the linen hand towels hanging over the bedside rail to wrap the whole lot into an oddly shaped, tent-like parcel, making sure not to squash the cake in the process. Finally, he tied a small knot in the top to keep it all together. 'I hope they *like* cheesecake,' he muttered.

Stefano stared dubiously at the result. '*I* hope no one asks me what I'm doing.'

'I doubt whether anyone will take much notice at this time of morning,' replied Edric. 'Just say you're taking some food you couldn't finish out to your cat and you'll bring the plate back soon. It *is* the truth. Anyway, I doubt if anyone would worry about a plate and a linen hand towel, do you?'

'Who knows... They might.'

Edric shook his head and then sampled his soup. It was very hot and very, very tasty. Stefano joined him and they ate in silence, each of them thinking about Stanthorpe...and Rhianna. Edric sighed. Without Zarifa nearby, her loss weighed heavily upon him. 'I wonder if the peacekeepers are any closer to finding out who killed her, assuming it wasn't an accident,' he said, his mouth full.

'They haven't had much time yet to look into it properly, and I'd be surprised if it was an accident. I can't see how it could have been.' Stefano ate some bread, drank more of the iced water, then stood up. 'I'd better go and let you sleep. The cats will be frantic if I don't get back to them soon. Give me the parcel and I'll see if I can leave inconspicuously.'

Stefano felt horribly self-conscious as he carried the plate of cheesecake out of the building and over to the callistemon, where he could see two pairs of eyes shining in the semi-darkness. The cats sniffed the air and crept out from their hiding place, tails high, sensing his concern for them and also that Edric was feeling a great deal better. Stefano put the parcel onto the ground and undid the knot at the top. Each cat daintily tasted the confection then crouched down to quickly eat the cake. Maybe not the healthiest of food to give them, he thought, but it would do until he got home and gave them something better.

Peri and Zarifa immediately dismissed his concerns, giving the plate one last lick before settling back to clean their faces and paws. Stefano watched for a few moments, then ran back to the medcentre with the borrowed items – leaving them just inside the door, too embarrassed to personally hand them to someone – and ran back to the cats. After fastening their leashes, they all walked to the nearest callstation and were soon at the door to his apartment. Once inside, they made their way to his bedroom, being careful not to disturb his housemates. Within another few minutes, they were warm and fast asleep beneath his bright yellow quilt.

The smell of fresh coffee began to wake Freddi from a dream in which she was staring down a long avenue of trees at someone in the distance, whose face and form she could barely distinguish. Shela was in the dream and had left her side to run towards the form, ready to attack if danger threatened. Freddi's conscious mind began to take over in an attempt to see who was standing there, at the end of the avenue, but she still couldn't make out their features. When she finally woke, feeling uneasy, sunlight was falling on her face from the window, where Meng Jarrah had drawn back the curtains. The coffee sat on the bedside table, together with freshly baked scones, butter and cherry preserve.

Sitting up and propping the pillows into a comfortable position, Freddi stretched, quickly forgetting the dream and revelling in the fact that today neither she nor Meng Jarrah were required to work unless they wanted to. The view from the window showed a blue, cloudless sky. 'Wonderful,' she thought, picking up the coffee and savouring its taste. A second scone had disappeared the way of the first when Meng Jarrah appeared at the door, wearing nothing at all but her beautiful brown skin. Smiling, she slid into bed beside Freddi and snuggled close, putting one lithe arm around her waist and kissing her on the neck, just below the ear. Meng Jarrah's breath was warm and sweet. Freddi rolled onto her side to return the kiss and they spent the next delicious hour oblivious to anyone or anything but each other, afterwards falling into a light sleep, content and at peace.

When they awoke, the sun had moved from the window, yet they could see the day was still fine. Meng Jarrah wriggled her toes in pleasure, stretched her long legs, then twined them around Freddi's and tickled her lightly beneath the chin. Freddi caught her fingers and kissed the tips, drawing her even closer. They lay in satisfied silence, listening to the occasional bird singing in the garden, thinking of very little other than the comfort of being together and not having to hurry off anywhere.

Eventually, Freddi remembered it was time she made the promised call to Robert in Stanthorpe. Sighing, she caressed Meng Jarrah one last time, then sat up, yawned widely, and got out of bed. Leaning over and pressing her lips to Meng Jarrah's hair, Freddi murmured that she should go back to sleep: there were only two calls to make and they wouldn't take long. Meng Jarrah mumbled something incomprehensible and curled up, drawing Freddi's pillow to her breast and soon falling asleep. Freddi pulled on a morning gown and tiptoed from the room into the kitchen, where Meng Jarrah would not be disturbed by her voice.

Curious, Shela slid off the foot of the bed and followed. She could sense something unusual had happened, although not exactly what...something to do with the dead wight and the other grimalkins. While Shela 'listened', her chin resting on Freddi's foot as she sat at the kitchen bench, Freddi found Robert in his greenhouse, hands covered in soil. He appeared relaxed and happy. The change was remarkable, thought Freddi, wondering how much Gwenllian had to do with it.

As if in answer, Gwenllian appeared by Robert's shoulder, her hair standing up in unruly spikes; a result of her having run her hands through it after Robert accidentally showered her with earth while he was digging. 'Hello, having a late and lazy morning, are you?' she said, grinning. 'We've been hard at work since sunrise. Robert's decided to build a fountain in here, so we're laying the foundation. It's to be in memory of Rhianna and Sylvie. She drew a design for him before leaving Stanthorpe to go to university, but it was never built. Now it will be. Don't you think that's a wonderful plan?'

'How would you like a bit more help?' replied Freddi, returning the grin. 'Edric's developed a problem and a visit to you might help solve it.'

'That's odd,' said Robert. 'I was talking with my mother just yesterday about inviting him to stay with us. She's coming home, and should be here soon. We thought it would do him good. What's his problem?'

'We want Edric and Stefano to each have a guardian – a cat – in case there's more to Rhianna's death than might appear. They were her only close friends, so there's a remote chance they could be in danger. We just need to cover all possibilities until we finish our investigations... Don't become worried about it,' she added, when she saw the frown appear on Robert's face. 'It's most likely an unnecessary precaution, but it's also a good thing in itself. They've both been badly hurt by Rhianna's death. The cats may help them get over the worst of their grief faster and more easily.'

'However,' and Freddi paused, 'it appears Edric is allergic to cats. He went into anaphylactic shock last night and was admitted to a medcentre. Fortunately, Stefano was with him when it happened and brought him straight there. He's taken both cats home and is waiting for me to call to let him know if Edric can visit you while he's being treated for the allergy, which might take a week or two. He needs to be in a cat-free environment, and with Gwenllian on hand, he'd be just as safe. He could have his treatments at the medcentre in Stanthorpe and Stefano can bring his cat back to him when he's ready for a gradual reintroduction. What do you think?'

Gwenllian's grin faded as she listened. She knew from experience that the steps Freddi had taken to obtain a guardian for each of Rhianna's friends meant there was more than a "remote possibility" of their being in danger. Taking care to shield her mind from Robert, she forced herself to adopt a light tone.

'If Robert and his mother are happy to have us both stay here for the time being, I think I can help keep him safe. What do you think, Robert?' She turned to him, one earth-grimed hand lying lightly on his shoulder.

Robert looked into her eyes, considering. Turning back to Freddi, he hesitated for only a moment, then said, 'Yes, I think it would be good for Edric to be here in Stanthorpe, and it could be good for me as well; there's a great deal we can do to help each other. When do you expect him to arrive?'

'I'll let you and Stefano make the arrangements. It depends upon how well Edric's feeling today, I imagine. I'll call Stefano now and ask him to contact you when he knows something definite. Is that alright?'

Robert nodded, then linked arms with Gwenllian, putting his hand protectively over hers. Freddi noticed she didn't draw away, and was both pleased and faintly surprised that they seemed to have developed such closeness in so short a time.

'You're being careful with me, Gwenllian, I can sense it,' said Robert, when Freddi's call had ended.

Gwenllian sighed. 'Yes, it's become a habit. I should have realised you'd be able to tell. Freddi was also being 'careful'. Allocating a guardian isn't done when there's only a remote chance of someone being in danger. It means that they think the danger is very real and immediate. She probably guesses, quite accurately, that I'd tell you – Freddi wouldn't put you into a situation you didn't fully understand. I suspect she just didn't want to put it all into words over a public comlink channel...and no, I don't know exactly what the danger is, but we'll find out when the time is right. I trust her completely, so whatever it is, once she can tell us more, she will. If necessary, Freddi can contact me on a secure lattice link.'

They worked steadily in the greenhouse, stopping only for a quick mid-afternoon snack, which they ate seated on the pile of stones that were to be used for the new fountain. Towards early evening, a small, plump woman appeared at the entrance and called out to them, beaming and holding out her arms to Robert. He dropped his tools and swiftly went to his mother, picking her up bodily and kissing her on each cheek. Agathea laughed, and once he'd put her down, looked around the greenhouse in delight. She sniffed the air appreciatively. The sweet earthen smell was back: life was replacing the dead, cold air and dark memories. That was good – very good.

Smiling brightly, Agathea held out her hand to Gwenllian, who stood waiting, a little shyly, wiping her hands on her tunic. 'Gwenllian, I presume. Welcome, and may the Sun warm you. Has Robert settled you into the house properly?'

Gwenllian was startled by the old-fashioned greeting, not having heard it since her grandmother died, but she felt a sense of peace emanating from this woman that was deep and certain. 'And may it shine for you every day of your life,' she replied, in the traditional manner, the old words coming easily to her, even after so many years.

'Here, give me a hug,' said Agathea, and pressed the taller woman to her ample breast, holding Gwenllian in a warm embrace before letting her go, deeply satisfied her Robert had found a friend at last. 'Are we expecting Edric as well? I hope so.'

Robert smiled, delighted to have his mother home again. 'Yes, we are. By an extraordinary coincidence, he's decided to visit for a while. He's developed an allergy to cats and has to stay somewhere near where he can be treated, and where there aren't any. There's a bit more to it, I gather, but it appears Stefano might be visiting as well, once Edric is ready to come into contact with the cats again.'

'I think you've left something out,' replied his mother. 'What have they to do with cats at all?'

'Oh, yes... The peacekeepers decided they needed a pair of cats to keep watch over them while they're investigating Rhianna's death...just in case.'

Agathea laughed. 'Remind me to tell Margrethe about this. It would amuse her, and would certainly amuse Harriet. I hadn't heard about cats being officially employed by the peacekeepers, but it makes sense, that's for sure. Now, do you have our dinner under control, or do I need to help, after having travelled all the way from Africa?'

Robert smiled again, putting an arm around her shoulders and leading the way out into the waning sunlight. After he and Gwenllian had washed their hands, they helped bring in all the luggage, taking it to Agathea's room and unpacking the things they thought would help her settle back in. Before long, they asked her to come with them into the kitchen to see what was being prepared. Admiring the neat and orderly room, where the last rays of the sun shone through the leadlight windows and onto the dark, slate floor, Agathea nodded, pleased. Everything gleamed. The light reflected from a polished copper kettle and from glass jars containing herbs, dried fruits and teas, each with a translucent green lid. A large bowl of fresh fruit stood in the middle of the kitchen table, the warm colours complementing the dark wood, while a skilfully arranged vase of flowers stood next to it: grevilleas and banksias in reds and yellows, mixed with pale green orchids.

A broth was cooking on the hearth range. Agathea lifted the lid to taste it. 'Lovely, my dear. How long before it's ready?'

'Another hour should do it, I think. We'll have the soup, followed by cucumber salad and an asparagus quiche I prepared last night, and afterwards, an apricot strudel with fresh cream. Will that do?'

'Oh very nicely, as long as we have a good semillon to go with it.'

Agathea enjoyed a glass of wine with her meals, as did Robert, so there was little doubt an extremely fine semillon would be produced. The house was built over a large, cool cellar, where some twenty dozen bottles of wine had been laid down over the years, although in recent times the collection had become somewhat neglected.

As the evening progressed Gwenllian felt increasingly comfortable in Agathea's company. At around 20:30, Robert's comlink chimed, and when he answered the call, she felt sure it would be either Stefano or Edric, and it was. Stefano was calling to confirm that Edric would be arriving in Stanthorpe, at the medcentre, at 14:00 the next day, and would it be possible for Robert to meet him there?

'Don't worry, Stefano, he'll be well taken care of. My mother's home and looking forward to seeing him again, and Gwenllian has agreed to stay on, which means he'll be perfectly safe. I gather you might want to visit in a couple of weeks, assuming his treatment goes well?'

'Yes, thank you, I really would appreciate it. I'll be there tomorrow as well, with the cats, but by separate transport. I'll stay at the communal house until Edric's ready for them. When he is, do you have enough room for us all to stay, if necessary? It would save travelling back and forth each day.'

'Plenty...and that'd be fine. In the meantime, is there anything special Edric will need?'

'No, I don't think so, but he'll have to go to the medcentre every day for treatment. Will that be a problem?'

'No, I can take him in and bring him back; or come to think of it, it might be better if Gwenllian takes him in.'

'I gather that *is* what Freddi had in mind...just in case.'

Robert turned to Gwenllian, one eyebrow raised. She nodded quickly. 'Yes, she's agreed. So...how are you?'

Stefano smiled. He liked Robert, though rarely had much to do with him. Knowing how fond they once were of each other, he'd always wondered why, since coming back to Australia, Rhianna hardly ever mentioned her cousin and even avoided answering any of his questions when he inquired after him. 'Under the circumstances,' he replied, 'I'm exceptionally well. May I introduce you to my new friends?' Stefano turned away for a moment while two curious and alert furry faces presented themselves to view.

Gwenllian, hearing the faint sounds coming from the two cats, approached, peering over Robert's shoulder to see what was happening. She laughed gleefully when she saw Peri and Zarifa. 'Which one is Edric's?'

'I gather you're Gwenllian?' answered Stefano, with a lopsided grin and a quirk of one finely outlined eyebrow.

'Oh! Yes! I am. Pleased to meet you at last. Let me guess, this gorgeous grey creature is your guardian and the other divine grimalkin is Edric's? Am I right?'

Stefano's smile broadened and he raised both eyebrows. 'You're quite right. I'm informed that you know a great deal about cats. Does this mean you know a great deal about people too?'

Gwenllian didn't answer this time, instead putting her head to one side and returning the smile, instantly liking the young man. She gave him a small farewell wave and then stepped aside to allow them to finish their arrangements. The cats gave the screen one last scrutiny before settling down to clean themselves.

CHAPTER FIFTEEN

'Would you kindly keep still!' exclaimed the practitioner sharply, for the fourth time, while Edric squirmed impatiently as the vaxxin was administered. He was totally unused to being the focus of this much medical attention, particularly over such a short span of time, and as a result was heartily tired of it all. It was not that the procedure was unpleasant; more that he disliked having an illness requiring prolonged treatment.

As soon as the practitioner had finished her ministrations, and warned Edric for the fifth time not to go near *any* animals at all, if he could help it – including birds, just in case – her patient jumped up, said goodbye, and hurried out of the building, to find Gwenllian waiting patiently where he left her.

Gwenllian had amused herself by picking a bunch of flowers from the side of the trafficway, where they tended to grow taller than usual because of the water runoff from the gently curved surface. The flowers were gathered into a posy, trimmed with leaves from a melaleuca growing near the front of the medcentre and which bore new, tender, pink shoots. She presented the bouquet to Edric as he came towards her and was delighted to see him take her offering seriously, handling the flowers with care and bringing them to his nose to find out if they had any scent, which they did, very faintly.

Sturdy and deep-chested, he was a handsome man, although quite dissimilar to either Robert or her brother, Owain, who were both fine-boned and slender, yet also strong. Gwenllian could see why Rhianna might initially have been attracted to Edric. Of course, his personality would have needed to withstand the test as well – which she rather thought it would, and wondered what Owain would make of either of the two men if they ever met. She missed her brother, even though only a relatively brief period of time had gone by since she left Melbourne. They spent so much of their lives together – living in the same house, sharing their research and most of their interests – that this was one of the few instances when they had spent more than two or three days apart. Even most of their world travelling had been done together.

Edric interrupted the reverie by suggesting they take in the sights of Stanthorpe, particularly the nearest winery. 'Do you think that's a good idea?' replied Gwenllian. 'Someone might have a cat with them. What about taking a stroll along the riverbank instead? We could see anyone with an animal from a distance and avoid them.'

Edric sighed, but agreed that, yes, it *would* be more sensible. They spent the next half hour walking slowly, arm-in-arm, along the riverbank pathway, enjoying the sound of the water and the winter sunshine, which felt wonderfully warm against their backs. A trio of currawongs flew from tree to tree before them, shy and wary of people, even though they were large birds. Their keening cry was in keeping with their dark, predominantly black, plumage.

'Do you mind if we visit Rhianna's old house?' Edric said at last.

'No, of course not. Where is it?' Gwenllian wasn't overly surprised he should mention it.

'Not far. She was walking home along this path when I and other kids from the school taunted and attacked her. Did you know about that? I still feel ashamed, even after all these years.'

'Yes, I've heard the story. You were a small boy, and from what I've also heard, you didn't stay with that gang of bullies.'

'No, but it's ironic, isn't it, that I associate with Ruth now, and even Marietta, and that they were both there when Rhianna died?'

Without replying, Gwenllian gently pressed his arm, sensing that he needed to talk about the past.

'They both hated her, thoroughly and completely. When Rhianna collapsed at the tournament, I was sure Marietta had killed her. She was always a good actor, so despite the horror and disbelief she displayed, I still thought it could have been her, although the referee was almost certain it wasn't. He should know – he's attended enough tournaments. By the way, do you know if Marietta and Ruth have been interviewed yet?'

'No, I haven't heard, though I assume so. Freddi doesn't hesitate to do what's necessary.'

'How long have you known her?'

'About five years. She was part of the investigation team in a case I was involved with. I was initially one of the suspects.'

'What were you suspected of?' Edric stared at Gwenllian.

She stopped and returned his gaze. 'Murder,' she replied, after a long pause, 'and sabotage of a research site.'

'Well, only petty crimes, I see. Nothing to worry about.' Edric's tone was light.

'No, nothing at all, though believe me, I was worried at the time and for a long time afterwards. It took almost a year for the case to be resolved. Let's hope this one doesn't take as long! It's not a lot of fun, but you know that already. Sorry... If you want to read about the investigation, a search of public trial records on 'Willsmere' should bring it up for you.'

'I may just do that,' said Edric, taking her arm again. They walked on in silence until they reached a pretty house situated on a gentle rise. 'There it is. That was where her family lived, and where Rhianna lived until she moved in with Robert's family. I'm glad to see it looks well kept.'

'I wonder who owns it now?'

'I don't know. As far as I do know, the property was sold soon after Rhianna's mother died. Whether it's the same people now, I haven't heard.'

The old rose, neglected during Leihana's last years, now crept happily over the verandah, its bright red, new shoots bursting forth with the small buds that were already forming.

'Do you know what type of rose that is?' asked Gwenllian.

'Yes, I do, as a matter of fact. It's a Climbing Edith Holden – a sport from an older, pillar rose. It has flame-coloured flowers and a spicy perfume. It's one of my favourites.'

'You're fond of roses and gardens?' Gwenllian was faintly surprised, although she couldn't say why.

Edric picked up on her surprise and seemed slightly affronted, withdrawing his arm from hers.

'Don't be annoyed, Edric,' Gwenllian told him, taking his arm again. 'It's just that you're a bit of an enigma. An extraordinary mixture of strength and gentleness. It's a wonderful mixture. Was Rhianna like that too?'

'Yes, she was, Gwenllian. She was...'

Gwenllian briefly put a hand over his and suggested they pay a visit to someone he might be interested in seeing again: Nyneve. 'I can sense she's home. I'm sure she'd like to see you.'

'Which reminds me... It only occurred to me recently to wonder why the poison that killed Rhianna didn't affect me.' Edric stopped walking and turned to Gwenllian, waiting, his blue eyes half closed while he studied her face, his own expression sombre, almost hesitant, as if uncertain he wanted to hear the answer.

'I suspect it's because it took some time for the toxin to be released from the extract and that you weren't exposed to it long enough. There's no other explanation. As far as I know, no one would be immune to it, but given it's an unknown species, that's not entirely certain.'

'Oh... I see.' Edric paused, then began walking again and said, 'There's something else I've wanted to ask you... This ability of yours – to sense things the way cats can – aren't you ever tempted to pry or to influence others? I admit to being angry when I discovered you were present at my interview to help work out what I was really thinking, and whether I had anything to do with Rhianna's death.' Without realising it, Edric was frowning at her.

Gwenllian nodded, understanding completely. 'Cats have been proven, at least so far, to be incapable of harming people, or even each other, under normal circumstances. They're also vegetarian and don't do the things their ancestors did: killing birds and small animals for fun. All that's been bred out of them. This power of mine seems to be the same. I can't even contemplate using it for the wrong reasons without feeling something like panic at the mere thought. In fact, just speaking about it makes me feel quite strange.' She stopped for a moment and felt herself having difficulty breathing. Nothing marked – just enough to be noticeable. It was the first time anyone had asked her this question directly.

Edric was immediately contrite. 'Let's forget about it, Gwenllian, except for one last question, if you don't mind?'

'I don't mind. I'm all right. Honestly...'

'Can Robert sense things too? I have the feeling you two communicate far better than can be explained by simply liking each other a lot.'

Gwenllian laughed, relieved to think about Robert instead. Thinking about Robert was a pleasure she indulged in as often as she could lately. 'Ask him yourself. I don't reveal other people's secrets either!'

Raising an eyebrow, Edric smiled, and they walked on again until they reached Nyneve's house.

Interviewing Marietta was not the most pleasant experience, so Freddi was glad Shela was there with her. The cat helped her stay calm and focused when in the presence of someone she intuitively detested, particularly while Marietta spoke about her distress at seeing Rhianna collapse at the tournament:

'The whole situation was appalling. So sad and upsetting for everyone. Edric was devastated. Rhianna, poor woman, is past feeling these things, so it is the living who continue to suffer.' She paused for dramatic effect. 'You understand, me, I suffer. Ruth suffers, Stefano suffers... Even the people who enjoyed the tournaments suffer, because, mais certainement, they cannot continue. This we must accept...' Marietta waved a hand in the air as if to dismiss the tournaments from having any future part in her life.

'How do you and the other participants intend to maintain your skill levels if there are no longer any tournaments for you to practice your more 'advanced' techniques?' replied Freddi, stroking Shela's head.

'Well, perhaps we will all become peacekeepers, yes?'

Marietta laughed unpleasantly. Completely at ease, she leaned back into the remarkably elegant armchair, upholstered in slate grey. Freddi was sure Marietta had chosen the armchair, not for its innate beauty, but in the knowledge that it would complement her skin and hair, as well as the clothes she appeared to prefer: deep, vibrant colours, with well-defined contours that enhanced her lithe, muscular form and which gave an overall appearance of self-contained strength. Were it not for the underlying arrogance and profound sense of self-importance, Freddi could almost have admired her, but as it was, could easily see how Marietta and Rhianna quickly became adversaries. She wondered if at some level Marietta found satisfaction in having been directly involved in the death, despite not necessarily having caused it.

Shela shifted to lie on her stomach, front paws neatly folded together, and stared at Marietta. She could sense a level of deception difficult to analyse. It did not seem to be directly associated with Freddi's questions, or even with the answers. It went far deeper. Her ears flattened, as if in anger, but then she relaxed, laid her head on her paws and closed her eyes.

'Your cat is becoming sleepy, non? Elle est très belle. Does she accompany you everywhere, Mademoiselle Peacekeeper?'

Freddi smiled slightly at the title and also at Marietta's tendency to use the occasional French word or phrase, which seemed more an affectation than anything else. 'Almost,' she replied. 'Sometimes Shela prefers to stay at home, especially if it's raining. Have you ever considered having one yourself?'

Marietta grimaced. 'Mais non! The cat hairs would not suit me.'

Shela sent a quick image to Freddi of Marietta densely covered in cat hair. Her companion almost laughed, but managed to control herself.

'I understand you and Rhianna weren't fond of each other, ever since you went to school in Stanthorpe. Why was that?' asked Freddi, crossing one long leg over the other and settling back into the armchair.

Marietta inclined her head a little, pursing her mouth as if deliberating. 'She was too sentimental. I am not. It is as simple as that, n'est pas? We all live so nicely in this Federation of ours, yet underneath we are the same as we have always been. It is natural for people not to like everyone and to have their differences, yet we did have one thing in common... We enjoyed a true fight. None of this holding back nonsense.'

'Did you ever want to kill her?'

'Many times. She was exasperating... So moral, so very right in all she did, even trying to help that mother of hers. My precious Rhianna should have let her die, if that was what she wanted. Well, for all I know, she did. I have heard the possibility spoken of.'

Marietta, expecting Freddi to be shocked, was disappointed. Instead, the peacekeeper merely nodded slowly and asked if she *had* killed Rhianna. Marietta laughed, throwing her head back so that the shiny black hair swung around her face. Her perfect white teeth almost glinted in the light streaming in from the skylight and she looked positively feline: a highly satisfied feline, but her laughter stopped as suddenly as it began and she leaned towards Freddi, patting her on the knee.

'No, mademoiselle, I most certainly did not. At times I wish I had... It would have been something, would it not, to have done that to our dear champion? In all the years we fought each other, I hate to admit that I never had any chance of landing such a blow, even though I was tempted to try on many occasions. No, no, I was as amazed as everyone else when she fell at my feet. Whatever she died from, it was not at my hands... At least, not by design. I can only surmise that she was ill and it was her exceedingly bad luck to have fought with me that night. Tell me, do you know what killed her?'

It was Freddi's turn to laugh, but her laughter was soft and controlled. 'Oh yes,' she replied, 'but you'll have to wait until the inquest to find out. Now, were you in the habit of giving Rhianna gifts of any kind? We discovered some unusual items amongst her belongings and would like to know who gave them to her, just to ensure we have a complete list of all her recent contacts.'

'I have never given Rhianna O'Connor a gift and she has never given one to me. That type of thing was not part of our relationship – we were neither of us hypocrites. We may not have liked each other, but were honest about it and accepted this to be the case. It does not mean we had no respect for each other. Rhianna would not have chosen to compete with me if there had been no respect...and I had a great deal of respect for her as a fighter. It is a shame there is no one left now to challenge me. I will be the Australian champion, you realise, yet somehow there is little satisfaction in it. A pity...'

Freddi noticed how quickly the woman turned the conversation back to herself and her own feelings. Marietta truly seemed to have little regret that Rhianna had died. She sent a quick query to Shela, who agreed, without raising her head or opening her eyes. The cat was still trying to decipher what it was about this wight that didn't fit with the otherwise honest answers she gave.

'One last question before I leave, Marietta. Did Rhianna ever discuss her travels with you, or her business dealings?'

'Oh, only in the most trivial way. Sometimes, you understand, she forgot her dislike of me and behaved naturally, yet soon remembered.' Marietta laughed again, her eyes crinkling at their corners. 'No,' she continued after a short time, 'I know almost nothing about what she did with her time, or her life, other than the obvious. There is only one thing I do know, and that is she occasionally introduced refinements of technique into our contests which I am sure did not originate from within our particular circle. I had the feeling that she practiced – or fought, I am not sure which – somewhere else. In another country...that is possible.'

Freddi found herself biting the inside of her lower lip while she listened. Marietta had given her a potentially valuable insight that Edric might be able to elaborate upon. She rose to leave, feeling as sure as anyone could, based on the information currently in their possession, that Marietta had nothing to do with Rhianna's death – as much, perhaps, as she might have enjoyed the idea.

Marietta stood up as well and reached out to stroke Freddi's upper arm, saying, 'You are going? What a pity. Tell me, do you fight? You would make a delightful opponent.' Freddi jerked her arm away and Marietta, satisfied, smirked.

As they left the small, ultra-modern house, Shela was still unsure what bothered her, so simply told her companion not to trust this wight. Freddi promptly reassured Shela on that point!

Their next appointment was with Ruth Baillieu. Fortunately, Freddi had plenty of practice dealing with objectionable people, otherwise two such interviews in one day would have seriously tried her patience. Such was the lot of a peacekeeper, she supposed, and sighed, before mentally shrugging her shoulders and concentrating on the positive aspect of the experience: she was making progress. Seeing Marietta in her own environment had been well worth the trip. Her personality seemed well framed by the odd mixture of deep pastel colours adorning her home's interior, with its strange angles that created optical illusions, and for Freddi, a sense of unease. The home was consistent with everything else they had learned about Marietta: beautiful, controlled, expensive, and somehow, soul-less.

The flight to Melbourne had taken two and a half hours, and the journey from Tullamarine to Marietta's house in Kew, thirty minutes. They now had the return trip to make, which suited Freddi quite well since it meant the time could be used in thinking about her impressions and what she wanted to ask this next potential suspect. As an added bonus, the food served during the flight back to Brisbane was ample and surprisingly tasty.

The day had turned into early evening by the time Freddi and Shela arrived at Ruth's home. They walked up the short flight of steps to the rather ordinary house, which occupied a small piece of land close to Moreton Bay. Despite being ordinary, the property was presumably valuable due to its attractive location and convenient distance from the airport. Almost ten minutes went by before the door opened. Freddi checked her comlink: no, they were on time. If they were early, being kept waiting might be understandable, but this appeared to be either deliberate rudeness or an unwillingness to have them in the house.

When they were finally given entry, Freddi received neither apology nor explanation. Ruth merely stood to one side, waving them into the first room, which seemed to be a dining room. She appeared dishevelled and ill at ease. The room was untidy and the air smelled stale, which was peculiar because normally the climate controls would have kept it fresh and clean. Shela sat by the entrance to the room and sniffed the air, raising her head and turning occasionally, ears pricked. Ruth ignored the cat, seating herself at a table near the window and motioning Freddi to sit as well. As she did, Freddi winced at the sight of several unwashed plates and other dishes heaped untidily at one end of the table. Portions of uneaten food had also been left, becoming squashed into small, unsavoury messes. She thought this was where at least some of the smell came from and wondered what state the rest of the house was in. Could this behaviour be normal, or was it the result of Rhianna's death and the subsequent investigation? Making a mental note to ask Edric, Freddi carefully avoided a pile of crumbs lying near her elbow and formally explained the reason for her visit, although this had been made clear when the appointment was first made. Still, it was a legal necessity, since their conversation, as well as the earlier one with Marietta, would become a matter of record for the Coroner to consider.

In response, Ruth nodded listlessly. Her face had a defeated look and her manner was totally inconsistent with the descriptions Edric and Robert had given.

'Are you ill?' Freddi asked, concerned.

Ruth shook her head and absentmindedly pushed a small piece of tomato lying near her hand towards a dried-up green pea lying nearby, as if in a vain attempt to make the table appear tidier. She fiddled with a dirty fork, put it down, then picked up a spoon and made random patterns on the dusty surface, until Freddi could barely resist taking it from her.

'Are you sure nothing is bothering you?' she prompted.

Ruth stopped what she was doing to stare at Freddi. 'Of course something is bothering me!' she snapped, her voice distinct for the first time, and then burst into tears, hiding her face in her hands. Freddi waited until she looked up again, wiping away the tears with a crumpled kerchief. The tears left streaks on her skin. It appeared likely she hadn't washed in many days. Freddi was beginning to think Ruth was quite seriously depressed, and wondered if she should suggest they go to the nearest medcentre and continue the interview in the presence of a counsellor.

When Ruth blew her nose and rubbed her eyes, which were already red from crying, Freddi touched her lightly on the shoulder and said, 'I'm here to listen.'

Ruth blew her nose again, noisily, and tried to speak. She succeeded on the next attempt. Taking a deep breath and sitting straighter, she said, in a low, sad voice, 'It's all gone.'

'What's all gone, Ruth?'

'My circle. It's gone. Rhianna defeated me after all. I thought I'd won, but she defeated me and took away everything. All my friends, all my work, my whole life. I've nothing left now.'

Freddi shook her head in amazement. Just like Marietta! It was all about herself and not about Rhianna's death at all, or even Edric's loss.

'Have you spoken with Edric or Stefano recently? Or Marietta?'

Ruth shook her head, but didn't elaborate.

'Why not?'

Shrugging her shoulders, Ruth sniffed loudly, her face contorted in misery.

'Do you think they don't want to see you?' prompted Freddi, managing to sound sympathetic.

'Why would they? The tournaments are over. It's all over. There's no other reason for them to talk to me, is there!'

'Aren't you friends with Marietta, as well as Stefano and Edric?'

'Friends? No...not friends. While I had something to give them, they were happy to be part of it all, but that's over. There's nothing left. There was never anything else. I'm not a fool, Peacekeeper. I know perfectly well what I've done all these years. I may be many things, but not a fool.'

'Ruth, did you kill Rhianna?'

She stared at Freddi again, seeing her properly for the first time. 'Kill her? Of course I didn't kill her. Her death ruined everything! Why would I have wanted her to die? She was one of our star attractions. She and Edric were the beautiful ones...the two champions. Marietta was the dark challenger...always dangerous, yet never quite succeeding...until now. They said her blow wasn't the real cause of Rhianna's death, but maybe Marietta somehow weakened her before the tournament. Was she ill, do you know?'

Freddi paused, debating how much to tell. 'She *was* ill, Ruth. We think she had been ill for some days, although even Edric didn't know, or I'm sure he would have tried to stop her fighting that night. We're not sure what caused the illness. It was rather unusual.'

Ruth nodded. 'She travelled a lot. Maybe she caught something in Argentina. Rhianna went there every year, and told me she often took long walks alone in the mountains behind Córdoba. What type of illness was it?'

'Something that came into contact with her skin, we believe. It may have been something growing in the mountains. It's certainly possible. We can't precisely identify the substance. Do you know if Rhianna visited anyone while she was there?'

'I think there was someone, though she never mentioned a name. It sounded like a close friend and someone she'd known for a long time. Rhianna was rather vague when I asked about it all, and only spoke to me about her trips because she wouldn't be able to fight in all the tournaments. As organiser, she probably felt I was owed *some* explanation.'

Ruth seemed to be feeling a little better, making feeble attempts to arrange her hair, which hung in lank strands.

'Did you like Rhianna?'

Ruth gave a wry smile. 'Yes, despite what everyone else might think, I liked her a great deal, though that didn't prevent me from pushing her around at school, did it? Maybe it was the only way I felt I could get her attention. It worked, but not how I expected.'

'What do you mean?'

'She stood up to me. Rhianna didn't want to join our group. When she came to Brisbane and contacted me, I thought I'd finally won.'

'There *are* other ways of making friends.'

'I don't know of any, which is why I'm alone now, isn't it.'

'Yes, I imagine it is, Ruth. I'm sorry.'

Ruth shrugged. 'I believe you, strangely enough. I can see you really are sorry. I just don't know whether you can do anything to help. You can't bring her back, can you?'

'No, I can't, but if you like, I can take you to a medcentre to see a counsellor. It might help if you spoke with someone about all this. I think you need to.'

Ruth sighed and scratched her cheek where the drying tears made the reddened skin itch. 'Well,' she said, 'there's not a lot to keep me here. Maybe it's the best thing to do. Can't do any harm, can it. Would you wait with me until it's all arranged, if we go now?'

'Yes, I can do that. Shall I call them first to explain your situation, or would you like to make the call?'

'No, you do it.'

When Freddi called her from the medcentre, Meng Jarrah's eyes widened in surprise. 'Ruth is there speaking with a counsellor? I never expected that. From what I've heard people say about her, I was almost sure she would have maintained her bravado. Was she really a total mess?'

'Not only her, but also her house. I don't think she'd cleaned anything or possibly even washed herself since Rhianna died. The smell was appalling. The climate controls were obviously out of order, and she hadn't bothered to have them repaired.'

'What did Shela think?'

'She didn't object to the smell... I've noticed she never does. Cats seem to find smells of almost any description interesting. It *is* understandable, considering how they clean themselves.'

Meng Jarrah laughed briefly. 'True. How long will it be before you come home?'

'It's hard to say. The counsellor wants me to stay in case Ruth decides to go home again; in which case, she'd prefer her to have an escort.'

'How long have they been talking?'

Freddi checked her comlink. 'About fifty minutes now. I don't imagine they'll come out in less than another half hour. No doubt Ruth has a great deal of unburdening to do. Almost a lifetime's.'

'No doubt,' Meng Jarrah agreed dryly. 'Have you eaten anything?' she asked, concerned as always for her bondmate's welfare.

'Don't worry, I'm fine. We were given something to eat during the flight from Melbourne and I've just had a mushroom lasagne, as well as some fresh pineapple. The small restaurant here is quite good, and they don't charge patients or carers for a meal. Now, how would you like to take that trip to Córdoba?'

'I assume in Argentina, not Spain?'

'Yes.' Freddi smiled, as they had once considered taking a holiday in Spain, yet somehow it never eventuated. 'If you wouldn't mind checking,' she added, 'I think Michiko Yamada will still have a house in Córdoba, where she and Kakura lived with their children. And I also think that if we check with residents and shops in the city when we get there, someone will have seen Rhianna.'

CHAPTER SIXTEEN

The airjet landed smoothly at the Taravella airport and taxied to a stop, just as Shela almost managed to escape from the seatbelt keeping her firmly in place during most of the flight. She had insisted on sitting by the window, but the sight of the Andes was almost too much for her, never having seen such high mountains before. Her excitement became so intense it transmitted itself to the other passengers, who rose in their seats to stare out the windows, gaping at the view, even though many of them had seen it before. Everyone was transfixed and silent, in awe of the grandeur stretching in both directions as far as the eye could see. Too soon, it seemed, they passed over the mountain range and began their descent. The passengers sighed and returned to their seats, but Shela continued to press her nose against the windowpane, ears forward and tail twitching. Freddi and Meng Jarrah were also entranced, both vowing to take time to do some sightseeing before they returned to Australia, even if only for one day.

After collecting their luggage, they quickly found transport to the city, where a room was booked at one of the old hotels in the historic quarter, near the National University of Córdoba. It was possible the university's facilities would be required during their investigation, so to be within walking distance was a sensible precaution. The air felt cold and dry as they finally walked the short distance to their hotel, although with the warm clothes they had brought, the temperature wasn't a problem. However, it was difficult not to wish they were in this ancient and beautiful city for a holiday, rather than to look into an unnatural death.

They arrived to find their hotel room to be large, wonderfully comfortable and beautifully furnished, if somewhat more opulent than their taste required. Shela jumped onto the enormous bed and rolled onto her back, stretching luxuriously. Freddi joined her, leaving Meng Jarrah to unpack their relatively few belongings. She also wanted to check that the private landjet Freddi had prearranged would be available when they needed it.

'What do you think,' asked Meng Jarrah, when everything had been put away to her satisfaction, 'shall we take a walk before it gets dark? We can book an early dinner and afterwards pay an evening visit to Madame Yamada, assuming she's home, of course.'

154

Freddi looked up, disentangling herself from Shela's playful embrace. 'If she isn't, we can leave the message we discussed and ask her to call us. If we're right about her, Michiko will want to know Rhianna is dead.'

'We *could* be wrong, or she may want to pretend we are, but either way, presumably she'll respond to the message.' Meng Jarrah felt instinctively sure Michiko Yamada would speak with them. Everything pointed to her home in Córdoba as Rhianna's mystery destination.

They walked down the avenue Obispo Trejo, which still contained some of the city's oldest and best-preserved buildings from Argentina's colonial days. Even the seventeenth-century church, Compania de Jesus, was still there, as remarkable as ever. Unfortunately, there wasn't enough time to explore properly, so Shela and her companions continued on, stopping occasionally to admire the old buildings and eventually returning to their hotel for the evening meal.

The hotel manager was initially somewhat reluctant to have Shela in the dining room, but after a certain amount of discussion and reassurance that her 'table manners' really were extremely good, he agreed, although insisted she remain with them and not wander around. 'The other guests may not like to have her here, if you see my meaning. Fortunately, most will be eating later on; otherwise I honestly do not think I could agree. Cats are not people, and dining rooms are for people, not cats. Please, please, I do not wish to offend you, or her, but what if our other guests wanted to bring animals in with them, or their pet birds?' The little man shrugged and shook his head in dismay.

Shela put her head to one side and pictured the dining room full of birds flying about. 'No,' she thought, 'I don't think I'd like that either – at least, not the droppings,' and sent a sympathetic image to the manager, who, startled, bent over to examine her more closely, a distinctly puzzled expression on his earnest face. Freddi hid a smile, but decided not to elucidate.

They were eventually escorted to their table, which was covered in a crisp white linen tablecloth, with red serviettes and brightly shining silverware. 'Please be seated. Your meal will be ready shortly,' said the servitor, who immediately joined them once the manager had gone. He deftly placed a pitcher of iced water onto the table, together with a bowl of freshly prepared sliced fruit.

Their order, which included Shela's meal of scrambled eggs, mashed pumpkin and plain yoghurt, had been made at the same time as the booking, and the servitor managed to keep his expression perfectly neutral as he brought the cat's food, placing it on the floor near the table, in the most inconspicuous space available. Shela sniffed all three items appreciatively then crouched down to eat delicately and quietly, keeping her tail well out of the way of Freddi and Meng Jarrah's feet.

Their table was situated in the most remote corner of the dining room, which, Freddi realised, was quite likely due to their request to have Shela with them. At this point, they were the only guests, so it was no surprise when, true to the servitor's promise, their own food arrived only a few minutes after Shela received hers. It smelled delicious! The nearby Suquia River had supplied the grilled fish on their plates, cooked to perfection and accompanied by scalloped potatoes and tender green asparagus. A glass each of good Torrentés, a wine neither had tasted before, completed the simple, but excellent, meal.

They kept to only one course in the hope they would be back early enough to have supper served in their room before going to bed: they were looking forward to a good night's rest after their long flight. The visit to Michiko might have been left until the next day when they were feeling less weary, but a sense of duty, and some other instinct neither could define, prompted them to go this evening rather than later.

It was now quite dark and very cold. Freddi parked their landjet near the base of an old gnarled tree, then left Shela with Meng Jarrah while she walked swiftly to their destination, about fifty metres away. A high and graceful gate made of dark, polished wood seemed to be the main entrance to the property. She pressed one hand against the stone wall that appeared to surround Michiko's home and found it to be faintly warm, which was hardly surprising, given it faced west and therefore retained some of the sun's earlier warmth. The facade of the building itself was simple and tasteful, its many windows shuttered against the night. Deciding they might as well announce themselves, Freddi returned to where Meng Jarrah and Shela were waiting, and beckoned.

The gate opened silently for them as they approached and a broad path of dark, multicoloured raked pebbles led to the wide, double doors of the house. The sound of the pebbles crunching underfoot as they walked seemed unduly loud in the stillness. Small lantern-shaped lights turned on as they neared, turning off again once they passed by, until, upon reaching the shallow, curved steps leading upwards, a larger, stronger light filled the entranceway with a warm, yellow glow. One of the doors opened and they were greeted by a tall, shapely woman, dressed in a red and blue robe. She bowed, and with a graceful motion of her hand, welcomed them. Meng Jarrah glanced at Freddi, who shook her head. This was not Michiko Yamada, so presumably the woman was a housekeeper or companion.

Freddi introduced herself and then Meng Jarrah, both confirming who they were by holding their forearms, with their embedded Brisbane

Peacekeeping Force identification chips, up to the household security scanner. 'We wish to speak with Michiko Yamada, please,' said Freddi. 'We have news that may be of interest to her, and hope she can help us clarify certain questions.'

The woman bowed again before answering: 'I will ask. Please, come inside and make yourselves comfortable in the meantime.'

As they entered the wonderfully warm entrance hall, Shela kept close to Freddi, her tail down, her sensitive nose taking in all the new scents. The woman indicated a room to one side of the entrance hall and then left them alone. The room contained, amongst various other things, several upright chairs, ornately carved and made from mature oak, a rare and precious commodity. Meng Jarrah raised an eyebrow and nudged Freddi, before carefully sitting down. The chair was remarkably comfortable, with curved arms and legs and a tapestry-upholstered seat. She stroked the silken surface of one arm. The grain of the wood was exquisite.

'Nineteenth-century English, I'd guess,' she remarked.

Freddi nodded, but said nothing, instead silently taking in the atmosphere of wealth, extraordinarily fine taste, comfort, and serene beauty. Looking up at the ceiling, a full four and a half metres above them, they were both astonished to see that it too was made of wood, intricately carved and delicately painted to depict a mythic scene of demons, dragons, gargoyles and various forms of sea serpent.

They were suddenly aware of being watched from the doorway by the person they had come to interview. 'I gather you like the room?' Michiko Yamada tilted her head to one side, smiling.

Freddi and Meng Jarrah immediately stood, extending their hands in greeting and formally introducing themselves. Michiko gravely shook each hand in turn, folded her own within the sleeves of her deep green kimono, and bowed.

'You are welcome here. Please sit down again and if you like, I will have some tea brought for you.'

'Thank you,' replied Freddi, 'that would be very pleasant.'

They sat in silence while Michiko pressed a small, unobtrusive indentation in the moulding of the mantelpiece decorating the ornate hearth that filled almost half the end wall.

'Surely she doesn't burn real wood in it!' thought Meng Jarrah, appalled by this one particular feature of the room.

The tea, accompanied by small sweet biscuits and a tray of artfully arranged fresh fruit, soon arrived, carried in by the young woman who greeted them at the door. They waited in silence while the tea was served in fine porcelain cups, then once the woman had left the room, Freddi began her carefully prepared account of the reason for their visit. Shela listened, one ear twitching occasionally when she detected some nuance of thought that twisted itself into the conversation, creating vague, disturbing images which she could not understand.

'You may already know my name from some years ago, when your bondmate was still alive.' Michiko inclined her head, but did not comment, so Freddi continued: 'Meng Jarrah is currently working with me on a case that, strangely enough, may have links to him as well. We were hoping you could help us. Naturally, if at any point you wish to have a Witness present, please say so and we will obtain one.'

Michiko inclined her head again, yet still said nothing, delicately sipping her tea in its fine, translucent green cup.

'Do you have a friend named Rhianna O'Connor?' asked Freddi.

Michiko raised her chin and paused. 'Yes, I do,' she answered at last.

The room seemed strangely quiet while they waited for her to continue. It would have been normal for someone to ask why they wanted to know, yet Michiko Yamada kept her thoughts to herself.

'Do you see her often?' prompted Freddi after a while.

Michiko seemed to reflect for a moment. 'Yes, several times a year. She likes to walk in the mountains and visit the wineries.'

It would, apparently, take quite some time before they obtained more than this, but Freddi was patient. 'How long have you known Rhianna?'

'Since 2452. I can clearly recall our first meeting, three months after the death of my bondmate, Kenjiro Kakura. She attended his funeral and introduced herself. It appears they studied together for several years, in Seoul. I was a little put out not to have heard my bondmate speak of her, but then, we had many other things to occupy us, and perhaps his student years were not important enough for him to mention such details. Rhianna and I did not see each other again until the following year.'

It was Freddi's turn to nod and remain silent, hoping Michiko would say more without further prompting, but she didn't. 'Does she stay with you here in this house when visiting,' asked Freddi eventually.

'Yes, always. We enjoy each other's company immensely. I am expecting to see her again in the spring.'

'Did you know that she is a martial artist of considerable skill?'

'Yes, certainly. We train together. I am also a student of kendo, which is unusual for a woman. My bondmate was a master. Since his death, I have taken up the practice, and have taken up kung fu as well. Between us, Rhianna and I developed various new techniques. I understand she takes these techniques with her to Australia.'

'Rhianna fought in full contact tournaments there, which are illegal. Do the two of you practice full contact routines?'

Michiko noticed Freddi's use of the past tense, yet made no remark. Instead, she merely answered the question: 'Yes, we do. Full contact is necessary to properly develop. It is foolish to think otherwise. Rhianna needs the practice and I help provide it for her. I enjoy fighting with someone who is more than a match for my own abilities and who can teach me many things.'

'Are you aware of any illegal tournaments here in Argentina?'

This time Michiko smiled openly, shaking her head. 'No, I was never one for public display.'

'I understand,' replied Freddi, with a slight smile. 'It certainly isn't to everyone's taste. How much of her life in Australia has Rhianna described to you?'

'She has told me about her lover, Edric, and her friend Stefano, as well as her association with Marietta Ross and Ruth Baillieu. She has told me about her mother's death many years ago and of her grief over the death of her cat, Sylvie. My friend has also spoken of the deep admiration she felt for my bondmate and her great sadness at his death. I feel I know her well.'

'Rhianna conducts a highly successful travel consultancy. Did she ever discuss her work with you?'

'Not directly. She comes here to relax and I help her do so. I only know there is sufficient income for her to live well and there are no financial concerns for the future.'

'Did you ever give Rhianna any gifts?'

'Not usually, but this last time she visited me, I gave her something. It was nothing...a small jar of herbal ointment...something we saw in a boutique. It made us curious, so I suggested she try some next time she and Edric were together...to enhance their lovemaking, which is always a pleasant thing.' Michiko smiled briefly.

'Where did you buy it?' Freddi and Meng Jarrah both managed to hide their complete surprise at this admission. They had certainly not expected it.

'Here in Córdoba. We rarely travelled outside the region. There is so much beauty and interest here, it is not necessary. There is a small shop I often visit specialising in cosmetics and herbal products, and very occasionally, Rhianna goes there as well. It is in the Plaza San Martin. One moment, and I will send you the details.' She retrieved her elegantly designed comlink from her pocket, located the information, and quickly transferred it to Freddi's comlink.

'Thank you,' said Freddi, as she checked the incoming message. 'Did either you or Rhianna break the seal on the jar or show the ointment to anyone else before she left to go home to Australia?'

'I did not, but am not aware if Rhianna did. My companion might know. Would you like to speak with her?'

'Yes, we would. What is her name?'

'Felicity. It is very suitable.'

Freddi's eyebrows rose slightly at this last remark, although she refrained from asking for an explanation. Hopefully its meaning would become apparent.

Michiko stood and went to the mantelpiece again. Before long, Felicity appeared and bowed elegantly to them all, remaining silent while she waited patiently for Michiko to speak.

'I will leave you alone with Felicity. She can call me when you have finished.'

Michiko left the room without waiting for their acknowledgement, while Felicity stayed where she was, near the door. Freddi, now standing, asked her to come further into the room and take a seat. Hesitating, she sat down in the chair Michiko vacated, but did not relax into it. Both Freddi and Meng Jarrah noticed how fine her hands were and also the rich, luxuriant appearance of her long black hair, elaborately dressed in the ancient Japanese style, although she did not obviously seem to be of Japanese descent.

Every now and then, Felicity cast a glance at Shela, who sat with front paws neatly together, tail curled tightly around her lower body, her eyes wide open and glowing in the lamplight as she closely studied Michiko's companion.

'We have come from Australia to investigate certain crimes and were hoping Michiko Yamada could assist us,' said Freddi, sitting down again. 'We think you may be able to help, too. She has spoken of a certain jar of herbal ointment that she and Rhianna O'Connor purchased during her last visit not long ago. We would like to know if you saw this jar at any time.'

The tip of Shela's tail twitched and she narrowed her eyes while they waited for an answer. Felicity's expression did not change, but eventually, very softly, she said, 'I did not see that particular jar, but herbal ointments of many different types are often in this house. I can show you what we have, if you like?'

'Thank you,' replied Freddi, 'but before you do, would you mind telling me what your relationship to Michiko is, and whether you are an employee here?'

'I am her dependant. She cares for me. I have no one else. I have lived here for many years, long before her bondmate died.' Felicity bowed her head, then looked up again, a proud smile on her face. 'Kenjiro Kakura was kind and loving towards me. I have never wanted for anything while living here.'

'How did you become their dependant, if you don't mind my asking?' There was no reason for anyone to be someone's "dependant" within the Federation.

'Both my parents died when I was very young...in an accident...and none of my remaining grandparents felt able to care for a child, so this family adopted me. I have been a sister to their own children, who are all much younger than me.'

'Is Felicity your original name, or did you choose it?'

Felicity smiled again. 'I chose it when the time came to make the decision. I did not wish to keep my original name and saw no need to have a family name. It was better to simply show how grateful I was to live with them.'

'Yes, that's understandable and very commendable. However, I would like you to give me your Federation identity number, please...just as a formality.' Freddi returned the smile to remove any sense of threat from her words.

Felicity gave her the number. Freddi's comlink was recording the conversation, so she quietly asked it to do a search before they continued speaking with Michiko's adopted daughter, of whom they had never before seen or heard any mention. Freddi then stood up and asked her to show them the household's collection of herbal preparations.

They followed Felicity from room to room, becoming increasingly astonished at the great array of medications, ointments, lotions, bath oils and other items they were shown. Meng Jarrah had had the foresight to bring her sample kit in case they were fortunate enough to be given a reason to examine the house, but hadn't thought there would be this many items to deal with! They would simply have to ask Michiko's permission to take them all away, have the contents tested, and afterwards return anything that was clearly innocent. The assistance of the local peacekeepers would be needed to store and analyse the material and even to take it away; it would be patently ridiculous to do anything else.

When Freddi and Meng Jarrah had finished peering into every cupboard and room in the entire, large house – including one rather curious outbuilding – they thanked Felicity and asked her to fetch Michiko, then returned to the 'guest' room. As the exercise had taken a long time, it was now quite late in the evening.

While they waited, Freddi called the Córdoban Peacekeeping Unit, who were, of course, well aware of the reason for her visit to their city. 'We need to remove a large number of items from this house...far too many for us to carry or to process. Could you send someone around as soon as possible?'

The peacekeeper Freddi spoke to was more than willing to send someone. Since Kakura's death, and the continuing close scrutiny of Wyvern Meridian, the peacekeepers had felt it their duty to keep a watching brief on the entire family, although nothing suspicious had ever been reported.

Michiko quietly entered the room just as Freddi was finishing the call, not even a hint of inquiry on her beautiful face. She did, however, appear faintly amused.

'The call I have made,' Freddi explained, 'was to the peacekeepers. We wish to take all potential plant-containing substances – other than foods, flower arrangements and suchlike – for testing. Since you seem to have an unusually large collection of herbal preparations and medications, we need some assistance. Do you have any objection to our taking these items?'

'None at all, but before you begin your work, perhaps it is time to tell me what you are investigating.' Her tone of voice did not phrase the words as a request.

Freddi told her, and after she and Meng Jarrah eventually left the house, with Shela following closely behind as they walked towards the gates, Michiko summoned Felicity.

The art of pain was Michiko's private delight. A devotee of all things traditionally Japanese, she had become an adherent of rope bondage, taking pride in achieving the exquisite balance of pain and pleasure, the erotic satisfaction, that the art and its more modern enhancements brought both to her and to those who shared her passion. In the room located some distance from the main house – and which was forbidden to their children during her bondmate's lifetime, as well as to the servants other than at specified times – Michiko, in her grief over her bondmate's death, had spent many hours studying the finer points of this art form.

Heavy iron rings and hooks had been strategically inserted into the black beams that formed part of the structure of the room, both on the walls and in the ceiling. Neat coils of fine, soft rope were kept in an ancient wooden cabinet of Japanese design. In the past, each of its many drawers contained only her metalworking tools and pieces still in progress, but now there was much, much more. Tonight, while her companion waited submissively, Michiko selected a long, black, single-thonged whip with a finely etched bronze handle shaped in the form of a snarling wolf. She ran the whip through her strong, slender fingers, checking that it was supple and well oiled, admiring its perfect finish.

Next, Michiko selected three ropes and gestured to Felicity to stand beneath one of the heavy beams, where two of the strong rings were located. The young woman was still dressed in the red and blue robe, but her feet were bare, while her hair was now loosened to form a veil hiding her lowered face. Michiko caressed it tenderly. Felicity raised her dark eyes to those of her mistress, who stood before her with bare, finely shaped breasts and arms. Turning Felicity around, Michiko drew the robe down to her waist, expertly tied her wrists together behind her back, and next, knotted the rope upwards and around her upper arms in an intricate, beautiful pattern that held them tightly together. Felicity's back arched as the ropes tightened.

Using the second rope, Michiko knotted and wound it several times around the base of Felicity's left breast, forming a comfortably tight coil. Grasping one of the fine, strong chains hanging from the ceiling, and which were connected to a pulley, she attached the rope to the chain. A third, longer rope was then used to form a web between the first breast and the second. The pattern was repeated, until each formed a symmetrical globe encased in coils of rope and knots. Taking hold of another chain, Michiko connected it to her artwork and tightened it. Felicity, despite being tall, was not heavy, otherwise this particular form of bondage would have been even more difficult than it already was.

Michiko gradually worked the pulleys until Felicity was suspended from the heavy wooden beam, bare feet hanging together, toes pointing inwards, long hair cascading in gleaming waves. The robe dropped to the floor and her head fell back as the whip flicked out to catch one nipple. She screamed, twisting and turning in pain as strokes to her thighs and buttocks raised a pattern of welts on the sensitive skin.

Lowering the chains just sufficiently to allow her toes to rest lightly on the ground, Michiko took two more coils of rope from the cabinet, wound and knotted them around Felicity's legs and ankles, then attached them to each of two further chains. A set of interlaced knots to support the waist completed the arrangement, allowing her companion to be raised until she was again suspended from the ceiling, this time with legs a little apart and knees bent to form a pleasing arch. Satisfied, Michiko ran the whip slowly between the woman's legs until she heard her moan, then drew back her arm and struck. As Felicity screamed again, she felt herself being gripped by the hair and kissed lovingly.

CHAPTER SEVENTEEN

Unable to make sense of the images in Michiko Yamada's mind when she was told of Rhianna O'Connor's death, Shela could not convey anything useful to Freddi, and as a result, was annoyed with herself. She licked a paw, rubbed it over her face and then listened more carefully while Freddi spoke with the first shopkeeper on their list about whether he recalled anyone in particular who had purchased Sensa over the past five months. At the same time, Freddi's assistant, an infotech from the university, was diligently examining the back-up drive used for the shop's routine transactions and most of its other commercial activities.

The shopkeeper, a short, sturdy man, had begun to perspire. 'I am sorry, but I pay little attention to who buys this product. It is a sensitive matter and not for me to remember, if you see what I mean. Naturally, we automated the recent batch recall process... But I am sorry, very, very sorry, not to have realised that all my records were not completely correct. For them to have been changed! It is not to be understood! Believe me, please, we normally have nothing whatsoever out of place. Never!' He wiped his hands, as well as his receding hairline, with a kerchief.

Freddi ignored his protestations as the infotech looked up, a grin on her dimpled face. 'There, that's done, and I must say, it was almost too easy. I even have the ID number of the person who did this.' She adjusted the screen to allow both the rotund shopkeeper and Freddi to see. Two Federation identity numbers appeared against the resurrected records: Felicity's, as having purchased three of the jars of Sensa so far unaccounted for, and the other, that of the person who made the unauthorised change to the drive. A quick search on the latter gave them a name.

'But this is the same young man whose services I terminated only three and half weeks ago!' exclaimed the shopkeeper. 'We caught him, you see, stealing an extremely expensive perfume, unique to this shop and which we have spent a great deal of time and resources developing from plants which grow only in our particular region of the Andes! The imbecile! The wicked, wicked young man!' He ran a hand over his remaining hair, shaking his head and muttering to himself: 'May he rest in peace.'

'What do you mean?' Freddi frowned down at him.

'He was found in the river only two weeks later...drowned. It is thought that he killed himself and I have blamed myself ever since. It is not a good thing to drive a young person to despair.'

'You think he killed himself because you sent him away? Surely not.'

'It is possible. He seemed troubled and was frequently late, but as he had worked here for several years, I did not want to do more than speak very sternly to him. That is, until the theft. It was too much. But for him to die so soon afterwards, this was not good.'

'I think you may be able to take some comfort from what we've just discovered. Obviously there was more going on in his life than you were aware of.'

'That is true. Well, you will let me know? I mean, if you find out why he died?'

'If we can. It may take a while. For the time being, however, I need you to authorise this release, please. The back-up drive will be used as evidence.'

'Oh! Yes, I see.'

'Thank you. There's one last question. Have you ever seen either of these two women in here?' Freddi showed him an image of Michiko, followed by one of Rhianna.

Peering conscientiously at them, the shopkeeper shook his head. 'No, I would have remembered two such beautiful women.' He sighed and shook his head again.

Their next stop was the elegant establishment in the Plaza San Martin. This time the manager of the boutique did remember seeing Rhianna and Michiko, and that they had purchased a jar of Sensa, but could not confirm the exact date.

'Michiko Yamada is well known to us, as we have many other products that please her. Still, it is not often two women spend so much time laughing together over such a purchase. Our customers are usually more discreet. Do you wish to see our records to find out when they were here? Please, come with me,' and she led them into the office where their main computer was kept.

'How strange!' exclaimed the manager soon afterwards. 'There is no record of Señora Yamada having bought Sensa here at any time.'

'Did she introduce you to her companion?' asked Freddi.

'No, and I am fairly certain Michiko paid. I noted it with some little amusement.'

'Would you mind searching for transactions paid for by this person?' Freddi handed the manager Felicity's ID number.

'Certainly...one moment... Ah, yes, I remember this woman. She lives with Michiko as one of the family. She has bought many things at various times and just nine days ago, one jar of Sensa, which I feel I must mention was not from a batch that was recently recalled. So, it seems the curiosity has persisted!' The manager laughed softly, hiding her mouth with one beautifully manicured hand.

'Thank you. That's very helpful. Do you mind if my colleague examines your back-up drive, assuming you have one?'

'Not at all. If you come over here, I will show you. We make sure all our commercial dealings are secure, so our back-up is kept in a lock-safe.'

The infotech was pleased to see that the drive was indeed kept inside a reinforced, locked safe made especially for the purpose, a not uncommon precaution against physical theft, though not against unauthorised access via the lattice. She identified herself and was soon absorbed in studying the contents of the drive. Before long, the infotech found what they wanted and, with a shake of the head, said, 'Look, Freddi, it wasn't hard to find at all.'

Freddi and the manager looked. Here again was an amended record, now restored, together with the identity number of the same young man who had recently been found dead in the river. The transaction showed Michiko had indeed paid for a jar of Sensa at around the time the manager thought likely. They were now left with one more shop to visit.

As Shela munched her way through a thoroughly delicious piece of tomato and zucchini tarta, Freddi sat at a small café table sipping a coffee, while the infotech, sitting opposite, was drinking her second cup of Russian tea. Shela had protested strongly at being taken to yet another place without even having the chance to investigate all the fascinating smells coming from a particularly attractive bakery along their route. Her nose had been over-worked in the two boutiques, and consequently, her temper suffered. When she decided to sit down on the pavement and sulk, nothing, other than the promise of food, would persuade her to budge.

'What are the odds, do you think, that this pattern will repeat itself at the next shop?' Freddi asked the infotech, whose name was Anna.

'Very high, I'd say, wouldn't you?' Anna was eating a somewhat crumbly apple and custard pastry and she hastily dabbed at herself with a serviette when a piece of apple fell out.

Although Freddi hadn't given her a full account of their investigation, she was able to answer without revealing anything confidential: 'Yes, I think I would. Of course, it makes no sense at all. Why make such an amateurish attempt to hide the Sensa purchases? Michiko admitted to having bought some; though mind you, she didn't mention Felicity had as well. Still, we didn't find any in the house, so I wonder what happened to the jar she picked up recently? Surely it couldn't all have been used by now? I looked up the recommended dosage, and even with fairly enthusiastic use, it should last at least a month.'

'I should hope so. It's expensive enough!' Anna's blue eyes crinkled in amusement and she laughed, showing her small, even teeth. 'But to answer your question, the young man may not have understood how amateurish his efforts were. Not everyone realises that records can often be recovered even if they *have* been overwritten. However, given that he *did* overwrite them, rather than simply deleting them, I think he'd put a fair bit of thought into the exercise. After all, how did he manage to bypass the security systems then access the back-up drives unless he had a reasonable amount of knowledge?'

'So how do you think he *did* manage it?' Freddi had ordered a strawberry tart with cream, which had just arrived. She took one large bite, raised her eyes to the heavens in delight, then concentrated on their conversation again.

'He had authorisation to access the specific section of the lattice used by the traders to place and receive orders, as well as to store their accounting and stock information,' said Anna. 'I checked while you were speaking with the manager of the second shop. Also, the first shopkeeper forgot to have the authorisation cancelled when he terminated his employment. Strangely enough, this should have happened automatically after his death was registered, but it didn't. It's something we need to follow up with the peacekeepers. I suspect that whatever prevented this type of routine change being made also extended his authority to use the lattice to remotely access other computers: which means we'll have to go back to the second shop to check for prints and DNA, in case I'm wrong.'

'Yes, that makes sense. I'll pick up a kit from our hotel now, before we go on to the third shop. Come on Shela, we're leaving.'

The trip to the hotel and back to check for prints didn't take long as the business centre of Córdoba was quite small. While the manager looked on, Freddi checked the office where her computer and back-up drive were kept. It turned out the infotech was almost certainly right: no prints or DNA belonging to their suspect were to be found. At the third shop, no evidence was found of him having been physically present there either, but they did locate two more changed records, each identifying Felicity as having bought the remainder of the missing jars of Sensa during the period Smithson had calculated as being relevant.

By this time, Freddi had obtained an image of the dead man to show to the nervous shop owner. 'No, I have never seen this person before,' he said immediately, 'and I most definitely do not give unauthorised individuals access to our databases, or any other confidential information. Please, can you assure me that all this will not become public knowledge? It would be most distressing for our customers to think their transactions could be at risk of being tampered with. Most distressing!'

'Yes, I quite understand,' answered Freddi. 'You can rest assured that the only other ones to use this information will be the Judge and the Coroner. There's no reason I can think of for a detail such as this to become public knowledge, even at a trial...if it comes to that.'

The man waggled his head from side to side, unsure that Freddi would not immediately broadcast to all and sundry that his information systems were not one hundred percent secure. 'It's the lattice, isn't it,' he said at last.

'I'd say so,' Freddi replied. 'I wish I could tell you these things didn't happen, but obviously they do. Still, I see you don't keep your back-up drive in a lock-safe. I could at least suggest you take that precaution in future, and I understand there are security routines you can use to periodically check the integrity of your databases.'

As Freddi spoke, her comlink chimed. 'We've found nothing suspicious so far in any of the items from Michiko's house,' Meng Jarrah told her, when she answered the call. 'What about you? Have you found anything yet?'

'We certainly have. Anna and I should be back at the university in about twenty minutes. I'll give you the details then. We're still speaking with the third shopkeeper, but should be finished soon.' Freddi had moved away from the others, so added, 'He'll be glad to see us go. *Very* jumpy. If I give you his ID, could you check his background?'

'Yes, I'll search the Federation databases. Oh, and I've had a call from Felicity. She wants to speak with us, but wouldn't say why. What's a good time for her to come in? From her manner, I'd say it'd be best for her to come to the university, rather than to the Reconciliation Centre. She sounded frightened, so an informal meeting could help settle her down.'

'Well, considering what we've just discovered, the timing's perfect. Tell her to meet us in the main student lounge at 14:00. That's only an hour and a half away, but enough time for us to catch up before we speak with her.'

Outwardly calm, Felicity sat with hands folded in her lap, in a small, private room where no one would interrupt their conversation. 'I have brought you something you should have been given last night,' she said, her voice soft, her eyes meeting Freddi's. 'Please accept my apologies.' Felicity reached into her pocket and withdrew a small container, which she handed to Freddi, averting her eyes as she did.

Freddi placed the jar of Sensa in an evidence bag. 'Thank you. Where was it?'

'In my pocket. I had forgotten it was there.'

'I understand, and it's just as well you decided to bring it to us now, because this morning we discovered that you've purchased a number of jars this year, and even one quite recently. Taking into account its purpose, we can't help thinking this is all a little unusual.'

Without answering, Felicity lowered her head.

'Would you like to tell us anything else, or is this the only reason you contacted me?' Freddi paused as Shela conveyed a disturbing image to her. 'We may be able to help, if you want us to,' she concluded, after suppressing an urge to place her hand over Felicity's in a gesture of support.

'Thank you. I do not think you can help me, but your kindness is appreciated. It is best I leave now.' Felicity abruptly stood, then bowed and left the room.

As the door closed, Shela padded over to the place where Felicity had been standing, sniffed the ground and dabbed at it with her paw.

'What is it, Shela? What have you found?' Freddi went over to her and crouched down. There, on the floor, was a small drop of fresh blood.

Meng Jarrah came over to see. 'What under the Sun is it? Don't tell me she was bleeding. How could that be?' Always the scientist, she produced a specimen jar from her bag, swabbed the drop and labelled the jar. 'I'll get it analysed. We can at least find out if she's ill, and confirm for the sake of our records that it's Felicity's. Weird, though... What do you think has happened to her, Freddi?'

'Shela has just told me that Michiko slapped Felicity this morning. Something else may have happened as well, though as you say, how she came to have a wound and how it could still be bleeding is *very* odd. Still, let's see what the analysis has to tell us, and afterwards, we should do another, even more thorough, search of the house. We'll see what Michiko has to say about Rhianna's necklet at the same time. Shela may be able to tell us more once we're there, too. I could sense she felt confused during the first interview and that it was something to do with Felicity, so before we go, we should have this Sensa analysed as well.'

The examination of both samples did not take long. No obvious medical condition was found to explain the bleeding and the jar of Sensa contained only what the manufacturer intended. As a result, Freddi and Meng Jarrah were still left with very little other than questions.

'Yes, the necklet is one of my pieces,' said Michiko, smiling gently and handing the image back to Freddi. 'I made a pair of ear circlets to match after Rhianna's friend Edric ordered them last year. It was a great surprise to see it again as I was under the impression Kenjiro had given it to his grandmother some years ago, on the ninetieth anniversary of her Namingday. I concluded he had changed his mind and given it to Rhianna instead when they were students together in Seoul. She was such a beautiful woman, and Kenjiro had great admiration for all things beautiful. Fortunately, there was no inscription on it.'

'Yes, most fortunate, I agree. Thank you. On an entirely different matter, tell me, do you ever have reason to discipline Felicity? She came to us this afternoon with a jar of Sensa that was in her pocket last night but which at the time she had forgotten. There was a slight mark on her face.' Freddi thought this last small lie was better than the truth. Shela's abilities were best kept hidden, at least for the time being.

Michiko hesitated, then said, 'I did slap her, yes. It was an unkind thing to do, but sometimes her forgetfulness is extremely frustrating. Felicity is otherwise the perfect companion, yet this morning I saw she had failed to clean and refill the water dispenser for our collection of rare plants. Unfortunately, several died. Still, I should not have lost my temper with her. It is not often I do.'

Shela's tail twitched. Lying on her side, with one silken paw folded over the other, she stared at Michiko without blinking. Michiko ignored her, but Freddi and Meng Jarrah did not, and glanced at each other. They had both received the same dreadful image.

'I see,' said Freddi, managing to keep her tone even. 'In light of what Felicity brought us today, we'd like to examine your house more closely. These two peacekeepers will help, if you've no objection? No? Good. Then we'll begin with your outbuilding, which I gather you use as a workshop?'

'Yes, I do. The décor is a little unusual, but it inspires me and has practical uses. Before he died, Kenjiro and I spent many happy hours in there.' Michiko lowered her eyes for an instant before meeting Freddi's again. 'I still grieve for him, but have managed to find a life both satisfying and useful. It is enough, although I will miss Rhianna O'Connor very much.'

'Yes,' answered Freddi, standing up. 'You have my sympathy.' Meng Jarrah stood up as well and, together with Shela, they led the way to the outbuilding, while Michiko and the two Córdoban peacekeepers followed closely behind.

Two hours later, as the evening drew in around them, they arranged their samples in the forensics laboratory for analysis the next day.

'What do think she uses that room for, other than relaxation and her metalwork?' asked Meng Jarrah, puzzled by several of the things they had seen and found.

'I'm not sure,' answered Freddi, frowning, 'but I have a bad feeling about this. Shela definitely has. She sat in a corner the whole time instead of exploring as she normally would, and the only impression I received from her while we were in there was one of general confusion and unhappiness. What about the rest of you? Did she convey anything else?'

Both peacekeepers shook their heads, remembering the strange fittings and the small selection of implements that could, at a stretch, be used for artistic purposes, yet which seemed out of keeping with Michiko's usual work. Listening to them talk, Shela suddenly growled, then hissed at something invisible to everyone else. Freddi crouched down and tried to touch her, but the cat spat and ran off.

'What on Earth is wrong?! I've never seen her do anything like this before!' Freddi followed Shela, and after hesitating, Meng Jarrah went as well, to find them sitting on the floor, Freddi holding Shela as she purred, in a frantic, high-pitched tone. Meng Jarrah all at once 'knew' what was wrong.

'It's Michiko and Felicity!' she exclaimed, her hands clenched. 'There's something very sick going on in that house, and Shela can't understand it at all. I want to check the blood sample again. I think I know what I'm about to find.' Meng Jarrah briefly grasped Freddi by the shoulder, then marched off, a fierce expression on her dark face.

Meanwhile, as suddenly as she became upset, Shela began to calm down. The purring stopped and her body relaxed. Freddi stroked her smooth, silken head, waiting until the cat's mind began to link with hers in its usual, contented manner – a comforting background murmur that 'spoke' mainly of everyday things, such as food and the surrounding scents.

'Come on, my sweetie,' said Freddi, standing up. 'Are you ready to go back to the others?' Shela meowed softly and rose to her feet, winding herself around Freddi's legs, tail in the air. When they returned, it was to find Meng Jarrah staring at her computer screen. The other peacekeepers were peering over her shoulder.

'It's an overdose of Sensa,' she said, with a grimace of disgust. 'It may have contributed to the bleeding, which could have come from the reopening of a fairly new wound. Sensa can slow healing if it's used too often...which has to be far beyond the recommended rate; otherwise the product wouldn't have received a distribution permit. Therefore, given Felicity bought so many jars over such a short period of time, there's an obvious link, although whether it was used because she wanted to, or was put under pressure, we don't yet know.'

'I suspect those ropes we found might tell us more...possibly more than we'd prefer to know,' answered Freddi, speaking slowly as she considered the implications of what they had discovered.

The other two peacekeepers' eyes widened. 'Do you mean this is some form of sex play?' said one of them.

'Yes, most likely. What we need to know is whether it's consensual or not. Felicity is Michiko's dependant, so although she's an adult, there could still be an element of coercion, even if it doesn't involve physical force. For example, if we assume Michiko has the power in the relationship, she could potentially exercise it to influence Felicity's behaviour and get her to submit to this form of activity, perhaps even by using emotional blackmail.' Freddi turned to Shela. 'You simply wouldn't know what to make of any of this, would you?'

Shela looked into Freddi's eyes, her paws kneading the floor, then made another attempt to convey something that made sense...this time, succeeding. They all saw a tearful Felicity standing with head bowed while Michiko disrobed in preparation for her evening bath. With her slender back to her adopted daughter, she descended the steps leading down into the hot, scented water and sank beneath its surface, long hair streaming out in black ripples. She then rose, ran her hands over her face, opened her eyes and gestured to Felicity to join her. Felicity slowly removed her own gown and entered the water. Smiling, Michiko stroked her companion's face as she knelt down to wash her hair. The final image Shela showed them was of Michiko kissing Felicity – although not as a mother, but as a lover. Tears ran down the younger woman's face, just as they did during the scene Shela showed Freddi and Meng Jarrah when they interviewed Michiko during the afternoon – the scene in which she was shown viciously hitting Felicity on the palm of the hand and about the legs with a bamboo cane.

In Melbourne, Marietta Ross measured her chances of bringing her opponent to the ground. 'One good kick and you would go down, mon ami,' she thought, but the rules of this club were very different from those she had followed previously.

Although she had hated Rhianna, there was now an emptiness in her life that nothing could fill. Ruth had folded completely, huddling in her pathetic house, hiding from everyone. Poor plump pigeon... Without her little crowd of followers, she was nothing. Pah! Marietta's hair swung in a neat, shiny black arc as she gave in to temptation and struck. As expected, the man opposite fell and did not get up again. Their Sifu, the one person there who could have matched her skill, gazed calmly at her from across the room and raised one hand in a gesture of dismissal. Marietta pressed her own hands together in the traditional manner, bowed and left.

When she reached her home, there was an envelope pinned to the door. Pinned to the door! Why not a message sent to her comlink? Taking care not to damage the door's surface any further as she removed the heavy metal pin, Marietta hissed in surprise when she opened the envelope and saw the signature on the letter inside – then sent a coded reply to Michiko Yamada, which was ignored for several hours.

Meanwhile, with Edric's help, the fountain was progressing well and Robert was proving to be both a true artist and a highly competent craftsman. Elegant and strong, the fountain was designed to complement the ornamentation of the house exterior, and would not simply have one central waterspout, but five.

As the three of them worked, an undercurrent of friendship and trust had developed, flowing around the small group in an almost tangible manner. Sometimes, when Gwenllian immersed herself in this new experience, it did become visible, in the form of a delicate rainbow outlining their work. The fountain had become a symbol of healing for both Edric and Robert, so even before the water was given the chance to play and to create its own brilliant display, these rainbows gave it the illusion of life.

Today, the work had been underway since 07:00, interrupted only by Gwenllian and Edric's trip to the Stanthorpe medcentre for his treatment. Now well past midsun, they were beginning to tire. Agathea either received the message or was generally in tune with her 'young people', for just as they began to think about food, she appeared at the entrance of the greenhouse with a large tray of sandwiches and a basket of fruit.

'Robert, dear,' she said, with a bright smile, 'would you go to the porch and bring back the tea things I've left there? I don't want any of you going inside with all that soil on your clothes, but there's no reason to clean up. Just sit you all down and have something to eat.'

Robert grinned, put down his trowel, and wiped his hands on the sides of his loose trousers before kissing her on the cheek. Still smiling, Agathea patted his face and wiped away a small smudge of earth. On his way out, he dodged the pieces of granite lying in neat piles, intermixed with tools and equipment for bronze casting. When he returned, Gwenllian quickly fetched a seat for Agathea, set it down near the makeshift table where Robert had placed the teapot and cups, and poured some tea for her.

'Thank you, Gwen. Ah, that's better.' Agathea wriggled her toes inside the comfortable slippers she habitually wore when at home and gazed at their work, saying, 'Now, I *am* impressed... And how are you feeling, Edric, after this morning's vaccination?' she added.

'Good,' mumbled Edric, his mouth full. 'I felt even better when I received a long-distance message from Zarifa soon after we finished. She wanted to let me know that Stefano and Peri are looking after her properly. Does she talk to you too, Gwenllian?'

'No, I think most of them prefer to share their thoughts only with their companion, once a bond has been formed. Do you think it has, in your case?'

'Hard to say. We haven't spent much time together yet, but I sort of hope so. I guess we'll know more in a few weeks.'

'What about Stefano? Do you think he and Peri will stay together?'

'Definitely. He's besotted. They went over to visit Margrethe yesterday and he was amazed that Harriet's still there. He felt a lot better, because he wasn't sure how long cats live. Losing Rhianna has made him a bit preoccupied with death, you see, which I can understand. I must admit, it's crossed my mind too.'

'You mustn't let Rhianna's death spoil the rest of your life, Edric my dear,' said Agathea, pouring him another cup of tea and handing him the tray of sandwiches. 'We must all take our chances of happiness when they come our way, and we can't be worried about how long the happiness will last. Otherwise, what would be the point of anything?'

'From the cradle to the grave in one leap... No, you're right, Agathea. Thanks.' Edric grinned, concentrated on his food for a while, then hastily swallowed the last of his tea and the remaining bite of his second sandwich before standing up, ready to go back to work. Robert and Gwenllian soon joined him.

CHAPTER EIGHTEEN

Having finally reached a decision, Morag MacIain consulted her comlink to check the time in Córdoba before making her call. She smiled when it was answered.

'Hello, Morag!' Freddi had just finished breakfast and was putting the final touches to her uniform.

Meng Jarrah's face soon appeared on the screen as well. 'You got my message,' she said, grinning broadly. 'Good to see you again.'

'What message?' asked Freddi, turning to Meng Jarrah, who allowed Morag to answer for her.

'Your bondmate contacted me about your investigation, wanting more information about any links that might exist between Rhianna O'Connor and Kenjiro Kakura, and asked if she could share what she found in the FSIU database with you,' she explained. 'I'm sorry to have taken so long to get back to you, Meng Jarrah, but I needed to feel sure that what I'm about to tell you will be relevant to your enquiries.'

'Ah, I see. You've been following the case, I gather...' Freddi's tone was slightly peevish. Even though it was perfectly reasonable, she was still annoyed by her limited access to FSIU records.

'Yes, I have,' said Morag, 'and can now confirm that Kenjiro Kakura did attend Seoul University at the same time as Rhianna O'Connor. I removed the records a few years ago.'

For several seconds, her friends were at a complete loss for words. 'Why?' asked Freddi.

'Rhianna was working for us as an agent, and I didn't want anyone to find the connection if they happened to be looking. I was hoping her death was unrelated, but suspect not.' Morag's green eyes narrowed as she frowned for a moment.

Meng Jarrah stared at the screen, too surprised at first to say anything.

'Working for the FSIU!' exclaimed Freddi. 'That's just about the opposite of what we were thinking.'

'I can well imagine,' replied Morag, with a sad smile.

'So did Kakura and Rhianna ever meet?' asked Meng Jarrah, wondering if they were just as mistaken in any of their other ideas about the case.

'Oh yes. They met at university and were both studying for their doctorates at the time he formed his bond with Michiko Yamada, in 2441. Despite this, he and Rhianna eventually became lovers, in 2442.'

'Which at least confirms one of our suspicions,' replied Meng Jarrah, her hand resting lightly on Freddi's shoulder. 'Rhianna never mentioned Kakura's name in any of her correspondence with an old friend from Stanthorpe named Margrethe, or even to her cousin Robert, with whom she was extremely close until relatively recently. I did wonder if Rhianna was either hiding something or was somehow ashamed.'

'I'd say both, Meng Jarrah. *I* only found out about the situation three years ago, after Rohan Maerz died and I was going through all his records. Apparently Rhianna was recruited by Rohan in 2447, after he found out about their relationship from a number of comlink calls he 'overheard'. She was devastated when Rohan told her what he knew of Kakura's activities and for a long time refused to accept how widespread they were. Mind you, Rhianna accepted Rohan's offer because she herself suspected Wyvern Meridian of art theft and had even taken to testing him.'

'Art theft!' Freddi's eyes widened in surprise.

'Indeed. Rhianna was quite the expert, you see, and after finishing her doctorate, travelled extensively, particularly to sites of historical interest related to Japan. She used to enjoy sharing stories of her travels with Kakura, together with her studies of important Japanese artefacts. Then, in 2445, one of the artefacts she told him about was stolen, and another three disappeared over the next fifteen months. She couldn't help but notice the pattern, so set a trap for him. He didn't fall into it, but that was about the time Rohan contacted her. *He* paid for the travel consultancy in Brisbane. It was an undercover Federation operation to watch Kakura and Wyvern Meridian. He also paid for her landjet.'

'How extraordinary!' Freddi paused, then said, 'Still, this certainly clears up a second mystery, and could explain all the coded records we found. Our colleague in Stanthorpe – Smithson – is still trying to work out what they mean. May we tell him what you've told us?' She was sure Smithson would be able to decipher the records once he had this vital piece of information.

'Yes, if only to put his mind at rest, but he won't need to decode it all.' Morag smiled, a touch grimly. 'I have copies... The files are a record of her travels and clients, and include details relating to Wyvern Meridian's activities during her tours to countries where artefacts and artworks went missing. They also contain the information she occasionally fed to Kakura. She gave the earlier records – about one and a half years' worth – to Rohan. She thought keeping them was too dangerous.'

'Smithson will be happy to hear this. He was upset to find so much missing.' However, Freddi knew he would also be disappointed at not having the chance to decipher the coded documents.

'The art thefts,' prompted Meng Jarrah. 'They continued? For how long, and how many are we potentially looking at?'

'We think at least some, and conceivably even most, of the important works that went missing from 2445 onwards until Kakura died were stolen by his people. There may be more than one art thief in the world, yet very little was subsequently lost, until about a year ago.'

'Is it just me, or is it a touch coincidental that Michiko took up Wyvern Meridian's new position of Cultural and Artistic Director one and a half years ago?'

'No, Meng Jarrah, you've made the same connection Rhianna did. We've kept Michiko Yamada under surveillance for a long time, not only because of the ongoing search for the lost artworks and the possibility that she knew about and was involved with the thefts, but more recently because we began to suspect she has a distribution network for a drug called Mandrax. From time to time, a few reports have come in of certain incidents in various parts of the world that have led us to believe it's being sold at martial arts tournaments...the illegal ones.'

'Mandrax?' Although Meng Jarrah knew what Mandrax was, she had never heard of it being used in recent times. Surely it was an old drug, long superseded by more 'effective' forms?

'Yes,' said Morag, 'Mandrax. Nasty stuff. It's not illegal to use, but it's illegal to manufacture or distribute.'

Freddi had never heard of the substance. 'What is it and what does it do?'

'The active ingredient is methaqualone, which is a sedative and hypnotic that acts on the central nervous system. The initial effects are euphoria, followed by a feeling of relaxation, although people sometimes have various forms of sensory distortion as well. That's the 'up' side, if you like,' answered Morag, with a wry grimace, 'but the down side is that it's highly addictive and can cause anything from seizures to coma, and even death. Mandrax was initially marketed by a number of companies back in the mid-twentieth century as a sleeping tablet, amongst other things, but was soon banned after its addictive properties were established. There are less serious side effects too. Sometimes users become very slow in their speech, may show poor judgement, often become very drowsy, and can briefly lose consciousness.'

'Hmm... Strange it should reappear now,' said Freddi. 'What happens if people stop using it once they've become addicted?'

Having already consulted her comlink, Meng Jarrah answered the question: 'Insomnia, muscle tremors, seizures, delirium, vomiting, anxiety, irritability, depression. Quite a long list. Why on Earth would anyone want to do this to themselves?!'

'It's a particularly difficult drug to break away from,' explained Morag. 'Some people think these things are harmless...a bit of fun...but Mandrax users often keep going to counteract the side effects and eventually take more and more to achieve the initial high.'

'Was it being distributed while Kakura was alive?' asked Meng Jarrah. This story was becoming far more complex than she had anticipated. Although, when she recalled how far-reaching Wyvern Meridian's operations once were, it should not have surprised her – if indeed they were involved this time.

'Not as far as we're aware,' replied Morag. 'The question of Mandrax only came up about fourteen months ago, and from Rohan's records, as well as my own investigations since, I don't think illicit drugs were Wyvern Meridian's style at all. To confirm the reports we received concerning the recent incidents, and then, if necessary, to find out how it was being distributed and to what extent, I asked Rhianna to attend the full contact tournaments we knew were being held in Argentina.'

'And which the Federation hadn't closed down,' Freddi remarked, frowning. 'Why not?'

'Yes, I know it sounds a bit strange,' answered Morag, shaking her head slightly. 'You see, Rohan was aware of these and other tournaments for a long time, but chose not to attempt to close them all down. He wanted to find out more about the people Kakura trained to do his bidding: his assassins. They needed somewhere to practice their skills, and what better place than this type of tournament? However, some *were* shut down, although it turned out that immediately one was closed, another would spring up somewhere else.'

'Did Rhianna know all this?' Freddi was staggered at how much she had been prepared to risk. No wonder Rhianna changed!

'Yes, Freddi, she knew. Rohan had already asked her to join the martial arts club in Brisbane, in 2449, due to its association with the Australian tournaments, and also because of the Stanthorpe connection, making it easy for her to foster contacts. I realise he put her into great danger, but Rhianna was remarkably good at taking care of herself...and desperately wanted to know what Kakura was really up to. She was deeply in love with him, you realise, so needed to find out just how far he and his company had gone before she could give him up. Also, being an extremely angry young woman at the time, Rhianna may even have wanted an outlet for her anger.' The sympathy in Morag's voice was clear.

'*Did* she give Kakura up?' asked Meng Jarrah.

'Yes, she did, once she found out that one of Kakura's killers trained in Australia...and also what he was about to do when he was discovered and captured. That was in 2450, several months before the attacks on Willsmere and Lamington.'

'How dreadful!' exclaimed Meng Jarrah, easily able to imagine the pain Rhianna must have felt – and surely, an almost overwhelming sense of betrayal.

'Did Rhianna play any part in the Willsmere investigation and everything that happened afterwards?' asked Freddi, wondering if there was more information which had been suppressed.

'Not that I'm aware of. Rohan felt enough was enough, and that she shouldn't take on anything new, but after he died, I asked her to play a central role in keeping an eye on Michiko, by making friends with her. It was quite easy, given they had martial arts in common.' Morag looked down for a moment, remembering, nonetheless, how reluctant Rhianna had at first been.

Rhianna, with her vast knowledge of technique and superior ability, soon obtained a position as a senior student and sessional instructor with the club Michiko had joined as a novice. The class, having just finished their *Shil Lim Tao* training ritual, at which Michiko was already remarkably proficient, bowed to their Sifu, as was customary. Rhianna then took Michiko aside and showed her one of the two-arm *Chi Sao* drills, which they practiced for some time, until she was satisfied her pupil had understood, if not mastered, the basics. Afterwards, they continued with various kicks, finishing the session with punching practice.

The club had its own showers and small, heated swimming pool, which, this evening, they both chose to use. Bathing costumes were not required, although some members preferred to wear them, but neither Rhianna nor Michiko felt the need, being quite unselfconscious about their bodies. Unselfconscious Michiko might be, yet Rhianna noticed how often her eyes strayed to where she was leisurely swimming back and forth along the length of the pool, and how Michiko's eyes followed when she climbed out to dry herself. Rhianna was fully and calmly aware of just how striking she was, and also that Michiko herself was a highly attractive woman: although not to her. Besides, she had a job to do, and a highly dangerous one at that. There was no good reason to add to the danger by exploring. Instead, she simply behaved towards Michiko as she would towards any promising pupil, chatting about martial arts and their session.

'You appear to be almost as accomplished as our Sifu,' said Michiko, while she put on her clothes. 'For how long have you trained?'

'Since I was a child. In Australia, nearly all children begin Wing Chun kung fu by the time they're eight years old. Most give it up once they've finished their formal education, but I continued. As a matter of fact, it was how I met your bondmate. He attended classes in Seoul, which I suppose he told you, and even taught me a number of new techniques. Unfortunately, once I finished my doctorate to go travelling, it was hard to maintain my skills, although I managed to find enough practice partners here and there to do reasonably well.' Rhianna turned away to finish arranging her hair. Now dry, it flowed down her back, black and gleaming, not unlike Michiko's, except hers was almost straight.

'Kenjiro did not tell me he was learning kung fu in Korea. How interesting. Did he only attend kung fu classes, or kendo as well?' Michiko's dark eyes probed Rhianna's face, wondering how well she had known him.

'He actually taught kendo, but I preferred not to learn, other than when he could adapt the techniques to kung fu. Kendo itself doesn't appeal to me. Did you ever see him fight, or practice?'

'No, I am embarrassed to admit I was not aware my bondmate was a master until after he died. There were many things Kenjiro did not tell me. I found out only when I discovered his armour. I have begun to learn, but it is very difficult.'

Rhianna made no comment, only nodded, and wished Michiko good night.

'Everything you've said fits in with what Michiko told us,' said Freddi. 'So, going back to the Mandrax question, did Rhianna obtain any evidence of it being distributed at the martial arts tournaments?'

'Yes and no,' answered Morag. 'One night in Brisbane, Rhianna noticed some rather strange behaviour amongst a small number of spectators, and when it happened again, eventually became sure that drugs of one type or another were being used. Unfortunately, she never found out for certain what they were or how they were being obtained. On the other hand, she did manage to obtain proof that the tournaments in Argentina were a distribution point. The information came from a user who ended up in a Córdoban medcentre due to an overdose of what turned out to be Mandrax.

'The young man refused to tell the peacekeepers who sold, or gave, him the drug, or where he obtained it. However, he knew Rhianna from the tournaments and didn't want to be banned as a contestant, so thought it was better to confess than take the chance of being found out. He asked her to speak to the organisers on his behalf, promising never to use drugs of any type again, and told her that he was introduced to it by someone who regularly attended the fights, though wouldn't give her a name.

'This put Rhianna in a difficult position. Firstly, if the young man confessed and it turned out the organisers were involved with the distribution of the Mandrax, then both he and Rhianna might be in danger. Secondly, if she told the peacekeepers, the tournaments would be shut down. We had already agreed they should keep going...at least until we gained a better understanding of what was happening and if there was any connection between the incidents in Australia and those in Argentina. Also, earlier on, I thought it best not to close them down because there was still the possibility that some of Kakura's former 'associates' might have a connection with them. The tournaments provided a convenient net, if you like. Anyway, as a result, Rhianna advised the young man not to confess, but to simply be thankful he'd had a lucky escape and to keep away from the person who gave him the drug. Afterwards, she kept an eye on him, and apparently he took her advice.'

'And how did you come to suspect Michiko might be involved?' asked Freddi.

'It takes a great deal of organisational skill and financial backing to make and distribute drugs, particularly if it's on an international scale. Neither Rhianna nor any of our other agents in various places around the world could find traces of anyone making it locally; therefore, as Wyvern Meridian still manufactures pharmaceuticals, we checked their warehouses and records. There were a few things out of the ordinary, but nothing to make a case from...mainly a higher than expected stocktaking of some of the raw ingredients used in the manufacture of Mandrax. As it turns out, these ingredients were accounted for in their documentation – or at least, seemed to be. Nevertheless, with Michiko having recently assumed a prominent position within the company, it was only natural we'd take a closer look at her.

'When she took up kendo after Kakura died, and then kung fu, we thought that martial arts may have provided a way of maintaining a connection with him. It was even possible she had learnt of his other activities and wanted to follow in his footsteps... If so, we can only hope she's nowhere near as sophisticated!' Morag paused, compressing her lips as she remembered just how ruthless and imposing Kenjiro Kakura had been, then continued her narrative:

'After Rhianna joined the same martial arts club as Michiko and they had become 'friends', Michiko confided in Rhianna about her interest in the Argentinean tournaments and that she had attended them for some time. Ironically, she even asked Rhianna if she wanted to be a contestant, but this happened before we needed her to become involved, so at first, she declined. However, based on this information, it seemed reasonable to suppose that if Michiko was attending the tournaments, she may have realised they would be a good place to begin distribution of a drug like Mandrax. Therefore, later on, Rhianna was able to pretend to have changed her mind about competing in them.'

'I see,' said Freddi. 'We certainly have a far better understanding now of Rhianna as a person, but on the other hand, the situation is a great deal more complex than we anticipated. Do you have any theories as to why she was poisoned, assuming it wasn't accidental, and if so, who might have done it?'

'No, not exactly,' answered Morag, 'but my concern is that Michiko, or even someone else, discovered she was an FSIU agent, and that she was investigating the Mandrax distribution and the art thefts. Although how anyone would find out is beyond me. Rhianna was extremely careful, and so were we.'

'Well hopefully we'll learn more soon. Do you think any of the artworks or other valuables Michiko has now should be checked?'

'No, Rhianna managed to do that for us and there's nothing in the house that isn't legitimate... Nothing she could find, at any rate.'

'Good... That's at least something to be grateful for. Now, before we finish, Morag, we need to tell you that Shela has shown us something quite dreadful. It's about Felicity, Michiko's ward. It seems Michiko may be abusing her, sexually. Do you know anything about this?'

'What! No! I've heard nothing. If Rhianna knew anything at all, it must have been recent and not certain enough to pass on to me. It's out of the question that she could have known something definite and not told me. What are you planning to do?' Morag frowned in concern, tapping her fingers against the desktop.

'We've taken some instruments, including ropes, which were found when we searched the house yesterday, and expect to have a DNA analysis finished today. The problem is that even if, for example, Felicity's is on the rope, we can't prove it wasn't consensual. I understand some people like this sort of thing.' The corners of Freddi's mouth turned down in distaste. Meng Jarrah took her hand and gently pressed it.

'The only thing to do may be to offer your help, if she wants it,' suggested Morag, looking thoroughly unhappy.

Freddi agreed, ending the conversation with a promise to keep Morag informed, a promise which Morag returned.

Rhianna drank the last of her wine, and with their evening meal over, Michiko announced that she and Felicity would have tea, followed by a bath, and that Rhianna was welcome to join them. Having a headache, she declined, but an hour or so later, feeling a great deal better, Rhianna made her way to the outbuilding, taking her time and admiring the perfumed plants lining the path. When she arrived and was about to open the heavy wooden door, she heard a muffled cry, so stopped to listen. From inside the building, muted words of pleading mixed with harsh tones of command and sudden, soft sounds that were difficult to identify. For what must have been at least the thousandth time, Rhianna wished Sylvie was with her. Her cat would have known what was happening in there. Without this knowledge, there were only two choices: enter and risk embarrassing both Michiko and Felicity, or leave and investigate later. Rhianna chose to leave.

While Michiko and Felicity were out shopping together the next day, she opened the door to the outbuilding, its security setting child's play to overcome for someone with her training and connections. Not having been inside before, it was impossible to know what to expect. At first glance, everything seemed perfectly normal, perfectly silent. A brazier, its coals still warm to the touch, stood at one end of the room, with a tea service on an elegant black table next to it, together with an array of perfumed oils. At the other end of the room was a sumptuous, sunken bath, and Rhianna grimaced as she pictured Kakura and Michiko enjoying its pleasurable warmth. The floor, made from rich, golden wood, was strewn with large, crimson cushions, so she sat down on one and looked up at the ceiling, admiring its design – which was when she noticed the iron rings, placed surely not for aesthetic reasons, but for some other purpose.

Having for many years travelled the world and studied its art and history, Rhianna was no stranger to the darker side of humanity and its desires, so quickly rose and went over to the only cabinet the room contained. The drawers held Michiko's metalworking tools, yet some held more. She swore, took images of it all and left the room.

Bounding from boulder to boulder in ecstasy, Peri and Zarifa had never before experienced such freedom. The breeze ruffled Peri's long fur as she turned her face towards it, sniffing and learning many things about this wonderful place. Shadows from the tors lay along the ground, strange in their many and varied shapes. To the cats, the shadows were playthings to leap into, then out of again into the bright sunshine. Stefano had taken them on this outing to Girraween, needing the exercise and thinking the cats would similarly enjoy being out in the open. Letting them off their leashes was an experiment, but he saw no reason for them to remain tethered out here. There was no one to see or to disapprove.

Watching them, Stefano realised they were even more imaginative than he had thought possible. Sometimes their images strayed into his mind – perhaps intentionally, perhaps not? Either way, he was able to share their play and to experience something entirely new: a strange, surreal world he never before suspected could exist, even with his enhanced vision. In sheer joy, he raised his face to the sky and shouted his name: 'Stefano Salvarez!'

Both cats stopped in their tracks to stare at him, then immediately realised there was nothing wrong. On the contrary! They both pounced on their young Wight, and all three were soon rolling around on the ground, wrestling and laughing. That is, Stefano laughed, and in his mind 'heard' the cats joining in, although the sound was difficult to describe, being more a sense of joy than an actual sound. He felt liberated, experiencing a sense of contentment more profound than anything he had ever felt before.

As Peri lay sprawled out on her back, now completely relaxed, Stefano slowly stroked her furry stomach, the silken fur irresistible. When she reached up to touch his face with her paw, he held it gently for a short while, smiling and meeting her gaze. Purring, Zarifa sat up to watch, then raised her head to look at two king parrots with their young, their high-pitched, piercing call like a swing in the wind, asking for attention. The birds put their heads to one side and chattered for a while, before flying off again in search of food. They made a brilliant display: red and green, the male with its distinctive lightning bolt of paler green on its strong wings. All three followed their flight until the birds were gone, then stood and walked on, Peri and Zarifa searching the ground for anything that told a story to their sensitive noses, Stefano turning over in his mind the visit they paid to Margrethe the previous day...

'Sit down, my boy! Over here, that's right. Now, let me have a good look at these two cats you've brought with you. Well, well, aren't they beauties!' The nearby path was strewn with gardening tools and a bag of bits and pieces Margrethe had snipped from her roses. She rubbed her hands clean on the sides of her tunic and held one out to Zarifa, who sniffed delicately then pressed her head against it, purring softly. Meanwhile, Peri stood nose-to-nose with old Harriet, who had never before met so many new grimalkins in such a short period of time. She gave Peri a lick on the forehead before waddling over to Stefano to investigate him as well, her thin tail waving back and forth in the air.

The bench where Stefano now sat was situated beneath an ancient apple tree, wonderfully twisted and deformed by age and weather. In spring, the tree would burst forth with its sweet flowers, which in late summer or early autumn would provide fresh fruit for Margrethe and her friends, as well as for her wonderful collection of preserves. At present, however, it was bare of everything other than its fine, grey bark.

While Harriet finished her inspection of this young wight, whom she could remember from many years ago, Margrethe settled down next to Stefano and studied him. Peri and Zarifa had, in the meantime, begun to explore, still taking advantage of their newfound freedom.

'Losing Rhianna was a great blow to all of us,' said Margrethe, patting his hand. 'I can sense you felt almost as much for her as Edric did...and still does, naturally. Do the cats help?'

Stefano looked down at his feet. 'Yes, they do,' he said, his voice low, almost breaking. 'How does something like this happen, Margrethe?' While he spoke, Harriet jumped onto his lap and bumped her forehead against his chin. He stroked her head and tattered ears as she kneaded his thighs, her claws prickling a little because they no longer retracted as well as when she was young.

'We don't yet know,' answered Margrethe softly, 'but I'm sure the young peacekeeper and her friend will work it out. Have you met them?'

'Yes, I have, and like them a lot. The three of them are amazing together... Freddi and Meng Jarrah with Shela, I mean.' Stefano shook his head in admiration, while Harriet curled herself into a more comfortable position, sighing and wheezing as she dozed off. 'Meng Jarrah doesn't often say much,' continued Stefano, 'but when she does, it's worth listening to. I'd say she and Freddi work well together, so I think you're right. If anyone can find out what really happened, they can...particularly with Shela's help, if my experience with these two is anything to go by.'

By now, Peri and Zarifa had returned from their wanderings and were taking great interest in Margrethe, sitting by her feet and staring up into her face, tails and ears twitching. Stefano suddenly received a clear image from Peri: in that image, Margrethe beamed at him as if she knew exactly what he was feeling – which, of course, she did.

He turned to look directly into her eyes. 'You're just like the cats! That's how you always knew what we were up to at school! Well, I'll be damned! You're a grimalkin, or at least, that's what Peri's just told me. I'll be damned!' Stefano burst out laughing, long and loud, while Margrethe gently patted his hand again.

PART III

CHAPTER NINETEEN

Freddi and Meng Jarrah studied the cold, pale face of the young man whose body now lay in the Córdoban morgue, one and a half weeks after having been found dead in the river. Forensics could find no suspicious marks on the body, nor any suspicious substances in his bloodstream or organs. The condition of his lungs indicated he had died after entering the water, and so, based on this evidence, the official verdict given by the Coroner was accidental death by drowning. The case appeared straightforward and no further investigation by the local peacekeepers seemed warranted. However, considering the current circumstances, both women wondered if he could, after all, have been murdered, although without further evidence there could be no justification for reopening the case. The problem was, how best to proceed, given they already had Rhianna's death to deal with, as well as the other issues Morag MacIain had raised? There was also Felicity to consider.

'Should we ask for Morag's help in following up on the question of why his lattice rights weren't cancelled once his death was official, or do you think your infotech from the university has enough expertise to find out more?' asked Meng Jarrah.

'Anna is confident she can follow up with the peacekeepers, and will let us know later today what she discovers,' said Freddi, then added, 'Could they have missed an overdose of Mandrax?' She stood with arms folded, still staring fixedly at the young man's face, as if it could reveal exactly how and why he died.

'No, the full blood and tissue examination would have found it, and anyway, taking into account the situation with Rhianna's acquaintance from the tournaments, they'd have been on alert for Mandrax. So how could someone lure this young man into the river and cause him to drown? There were no signs of force, nor any disturbances on the riverbanks that might be related.'

They had both read the transcript of the inquest. His name was Guillermo, and his parents had confirmed him as being restless and prone to mood swings for quite some time, often becoming depressed enough to seek help from the local medcentre, where he had seen a counsellor on several occasions. The counsellor testified to his being troubled by his conscience over having done something illegal to help a friend, although was unable to say what exactly he had done because her client consistently refused to explain further. However, the main theme of their counselling sessions had apparently been associated with a feeling of despair over an unsatisfactory love affair.

An examination of Guillermo's private accounts had shown unusually large expenditures on exotic flowering plants, but revealed only income that could legitimately be accounted for. None of the plants were found in his home, where he still lived with his parents, and his parents knew of no one to whom their son could have wanted to give such expensive gifts. They were at a complete loss as to his reason for buying them.

Meng Jarrah bent over to look more closely at the body. 'He's quite attractive...or would have been when he was alive. There's a mark on the third finger of his right hand. It looks as if he might have worn a ring. Is there a ring mentioned in the list of his effects?'

Freddi consulted her comlink. 'Yes, there is. Silver, handmade.'

'We need to see it, as well as his clothing.'

'His things haven't been returned to his parents yet. Do you want to see them now?'

'Yes, it shouldn't take long.'

Shela was waiting impatiently for them as they crossed the small courtyard dividing the morgue precinct from the properties office. She had been lying in a patch of shade formed by a large urn containing a brilliant display of orchids, but now sat up in anticipation of being released from her 'captivity'. Freddi undid the knot holding her leash to the decorative iron ring set into the side of the heavy urn.

'Sorry, sweetie, but you couldn't come in there with us. You wouldn't have liked it anyway.'

Shela agreed, and forgave them their temporary desertion on condition Freddi promised to provide her with a particularly tasty midsun snack. Meng Jarrah 'heard' her as well, and laughed. For some time now, it seemed she was beginning to form almost as close a link with the cat as Freddi, which was deeply satisfying.

The properties office soon located Guillermo's effects and after both Freddi and Meng Jarrah formally identified themselves, allowed the items to be taken into an adjacent room to be examined, under the scrutiny of a security camera.

His clothing was elegant and of good quality, primarily black, with a small amount of tasteful, silver embroidery on one side of the long tunic. The ring was plain yet beautiful, its only ornamentation being outer borders of minute scrollwork. Meng Jarrah placed it beneath the lens of one of the microscopes the room contained, projecting the image onto its screen. Inside the ring was an inscription: "To MY endless love".

'We should have the silver analysed immediately, Freddi.'

Freddi nodded, staring at the image. 'He's young enough to be her son! Just about Felicity's age. Could there be a connection? Could he and Felicity have been lovers and Michiko interfered out of jealousy?'

'Yes, that's one theory. The other is that he was Michiko's lover and Felicity interfered for the same reason. It's also possible Michiko played with him until he'd finished doing her bidding and then discarded him, which could explain a suicide.'

'She may even have 'played' with them both! Oh, this is becoming worse and worse, if that's what happened!' Freddi looked down at Shela, who was sitting by her feet gazing up at her, pupils fully dilated, clearly distressed by all these confusing possibilities, although they were somewhat beyond her comprehension.

'If Michiko did use him,' said Meng Jarrah, 'there's a good chance his DNA will turn up somewhere in her house, or in amongst the things we took away. There's also the perfume he stole, though by this time, if he gave it to either of them, it's most likely been disposed of. Still, there was a bottle of perfume in with the materials we first collected... It's time we went back to the lab.'

Rocking backwards and forwards, with her arms around her knees, gave Felicity the illusion of being safe...for a little while. It gave her time to think, to decide what to do. Her world had moved one step closer to hell. A never-ending hell. She stood up to open the front of her robe. The burns had begun to ache unbearably and since the peacekeepers had taken them, there were no lotions left in the house to use this time. Michiko's demands were becoming increasingly difficult to satisfy and last night had driven Felicity to the point of rebellion. A very short-lived rebellion. Retribution had been immediate, as these marks testified. Never had she imagined this could happen, despite all her other torments at Michiko's hands.

Deprived of a comlink, Felicity crept into the kitchen to consult the security system. Michiko was out and not expected back for almost two and a half hours, which would give her enough time to ask for help and then return. With luck, Michiko would not check the security records, although she had been known to do so before today. Felicity felt her cheeks become hot at the thought of what might happen if luck was not with her, and almost gave up. However the pain when her breasts rubbed against the fabric of her robe reminded her all too clearly of what her life would continue to be like if she did not make this attempt to free herself.

Trembling, her knees weak, Felicity managed to walk to the front entrance, check that no one was approaching the house, then slowly open the door, almost expecting Michiko to appear, as if by some appalling trick of fate. A quick glance showed the pathway was clear. She ran to the gate and pressed her thumb to its identification panel. Nothing happened. The gate would not open! Heart pounding, Felicity almost screamed in fear. This had never occurred to her. Locked in! No, there was a small side entry, partially hidden from view, behind the outbuilding! The young man had often used it. She flinched at the memory, fought down the sudden nausea, and ran – ran for her life to the side entry. It opened.

The university housed the access nodes that provided a direct link to the Argentinean Central Computer Site and they were used by peacekeepers and other authorised officials for their security requirements, as well as other high-priority transactions unsuitable for transmission over the main comlink channels. Anna had both sufficient authority to use these nodes and the skill to find answers without undue delay. Discovering the reason for Guillermo having obtained greater lattice access rights than he should have was not, therefore, difficult, nor was discovering the reason for those rights having continued after his death. Within the access security database, someone at the Site had swapped Guillermo's Federation identification number with that of one of the higher-ranking Córdoban peacekeepers. Once the inquest had determined the cause of death as accidental, the ID numbers had been swapped back. At the time, the peacekeeper in question was on extended medical leave, having suffered a brain haemorrhage, and was therefore hardly in a fit condition to notice his temporarily restricted access to the lattice. These temporary access changes were recorded as having been made by a senior systems technologist, who was himself recorded as having died four days ago of food poisoning. His inquest was still pending.

Satisfied, Anna called Freddi, and when she didn't answer, left a message. 'Freddi, I have the information you wanted. While you're at the morgue, there's another body for you to look at...that is, if you're still there?' As she spoke, Anna sent the details of her findings.

Not long afterwards, her comlink chimed. It was Freddi. 'Hi Anna. Sorry. We've left the morgue, unfortunately, and we're back in the lab, here at the university. Do you want to come over, or have you sent all there is for us to see?'

'I've sent it all, but if you need anything further, just let me know.'

'Thanks, and especially for doing this so efficiently. If we have time before we leave Córdoba, we owe you a dinner.'

Anna grinned. 'Excellent! I'll expect dessert too.'

'That's a promise.' Freddi returned the grin, even though the information the infotech had given her added yet another layer of complexity to this already overly complex case.

*

The Coroner's preliminary report on the death of the senior systems technologist listed botulism as the cause of the food poisoning. A death such as this was a relatively rare event that could only be explained by his having neither called for help nor activated the emergency alarm on his comlink before the symptoms overcame him, and also by being out of sensor range in his garden, where he was found. Household security sensors were usually effective for up to one hundred metres, and the garden was well within this limit, so initially, the circumstances seemed somewhat suspicious.

A search of the man's thermolyte revealed a jar of dill pickles well past their use-by date, which caused little surprise as by the state of his home, he was a poor housekeeper and rarely did his own cooking. He also lived alone and seemed to have little in the way of a social life. The security system was then found to have several 'blind spots' within the garden, a fault that would have been rectified if he had been a more conscientious householder.

After reading the report, Freddi presented Anna's new information to the Coroner in person, who raised an elegant eyebrow and tutted. 'Well,' she said, 'I *would* thank you, but it raises more questions than we can answer. Unless some exceptionally clever person substituted his dill pickles with ones that were less than fresh, so to speak, we still cannot rule out accidental death. There were no fingerprints other than his own and those of an apparently innocent shop assistant on the jar. The label was genuine and the pickles were supplied to him before the use-by date: we were able to trace that fact quite readily. A thorough examination of the manufacturer's and distributor's premises has revealed no production, storage or handling faults that could account for this type of contamination. Also, as far as we can ascertain, no other reports have come in of anyone having suffered from botulism poisoning during the period this batch was made available and would normally be consumed. However, we did issue a batch recall, just to be certain, and nothing returned so far has been found to be suspicious.'

'So for someone to contaminate the jar on purpose without it becoming obviously uneatable would require a reasonable amount of knowledge, I imagine,' said Freddi.

'Yes, or a great deal of luck. It seems to me that contaminating the contents of a jar of pickles would be a highly uncertain way to kill someone, although murderers aren't always logical, of course. However, needless to say, it is important to establish, if we can, why the systems technologist chose to involve himself in the record substitution. There *could* be a link with the death of the young man, Guillermo... Who knows at this stage?

Nevertheless, we cannot reopen *his* case without more evidence. You understand?'

'Yes,' said Freddi, 'I understand. Thank you.'

'Good. Well, let us know if you find anything further, and I wish you luck with your own investigation. Sometimes we can do no better than to hope the old gods are on our side.' The Coroner pursed her mouth and tutted again before turning away, soon absorbed in her work. Freddi left her to it and collected Shela from where she was blissfully snoozing outside, once again tethered to the iron ring on the urn in the courtyard, but this time, in a patch of warm sunlight.

Upon returning to the forensics laboratory, they discovered Meng Jarrah had managed to find out that over the past year, the third boutique owner, the one who was so nervous when Freddi interviewed him, had attended a number of illegal martial arts tournaments. Rhianna, it seemed, had provided Morag with footage of the crowds, not necessarily with a view to prosecution, but as potentially useful information with which to trace the source of Mandrax distribution. A comparison of the shopkeeper's face with the spectators had soon given a match, as did that of the recently deceased senior systems technologist. It turned out that on each occasion the shopkeeper was present, so was the other man, and they were always seated together. As a result, it was reasonable to assume they were friends, or at least associates, and therefore easy to understand why the shopkeeper had been nervous, beyond what might be expected of anyone receiving a visit from peacekeepers. Clearly, he would need to be re-interviewed.

'Have the DNA results come back from the things we found in Michiko's house?' asked Freddi, as Shela settled herself comfortably on the lab floor to watch and to listen.

Meng Jarrah met Freddi's eyes and said, 'Yes, they have. I wish the news wasn't as bad as it is. There were traces of Felicity's DNA on the handle of the whip, as well as Sensa. From the cellular type, it seems the DNA came from her vagina, and it would appear the cells are relatively fresh.'

'That's horrible! What about the ropes?'

'Her DNA was on them as well, but so was Michiko's, which means we can't definitively say who was the recipient, and who was the one performing the bondage... I'd say we *are* looking at bondage, wouldn't you?'

'Oh yes, I think we are. Has anything been found yet with Guillermo's DNA on it?'

'No, but he may not have been directly involved. Unless Felicity chooses to speak with us, we have nothing to justify questioning her formally, and we still can't show that Guillermo's death wasn't accidental.'

'What about the perfume we found in the house. Did it match the type Guillermo stole?'

'No, it didn't, which is a pity. If he was having an affair with Michiko and gave *her* the perfume, she probably had the sense to dispose of it, either after he died, or even beforehand.'

A sudden noise startled them. Shela stood facing the entrance to the lab, hackles raised and tail a stiff brush of rage. Her ears were laid back and her teeth were bared as she snarled at a frightened peacekeeper, who had his back to the door. They hadn't heard him come in.

'Shela! Stop it, this instant! What are you doing?' Freddi ran to where Shela now crouched, blocking the peacekeeper's path. Meng Jarrah joined them, kneeling down to speak to the enraged cat: 'Shela, what is it? What has he done? Come on, tell us what's wrong.'

As suddenly as she reacted in anger, Shela calmed down and moved to sit by Freddi's feet, turning her head from side to side, confused, looking first at one wight and then the other, questioning them. Meng Jarrah stood up and briefly put a hand on the peacekeeper's shoulder, while Freddi stroked Shela's head and spoke softly to her.

There were no images coming from the cat to tell them what she reacted to, but the peacekeeper soon managed to overcome his fright and said, 'You have a visitor. A woman by the name of Felicity wishes to speak with you. She seems close to collapse, and from the way she holds herself and the distressed expression on her face, I believe she may be ill. Please, come with me, but if you don't mind, could you leave your cat behind?' His voice trembled slightly as he made the request.

Freddi quickly assured him that Shela was harmless, yet nevertheless, told her to wait for them. The cat sighed and settled back onto the floor, ears and tail twitching, her eyes narrowed to slits, watching them as they left.

Felicity was waiting for them in the anteroom to the Coroner's Court, sitting with head bowed and hands loosely folded together. When they approached, she looked up, her face drawn and pale, eyes dark and deeply troubled. Her hair hung loose and untidy around her shoulders, so unlike the formal coiffure they had last seen. She winced when she attempted to sit straighter, then held out a hand, as if to ask for help. Meng Jarrah immediately sat down next to her and took the ice-cold hand in her own, gently rubbing some warmth into it. Tears ran down Felicity's cheeks as she began to sob uncontrollably. Meng Jarrah put an arm around her shoulders, but when the young woman flinched, she removed it, and they allowed her to weep until the worst of the storm subsided.

'Do you wish to see a counsellor or a medical practitioner?' asked Freddi, also sitting down next to her.

Felicity nodded and sniffed. Since she appeared not to have one with her, Freddi handed her a kerchief, which Felicity gratefully accepted, using it to wipe her eyes and blow her nose.

'Are you ill or hurt, Felicity?' prompted Freddi.

'I am hurt,' Felicity managed to say, between sobs.

Freddi made a quick call, and soon afterwards, a practitioner attached to the Coroner's Court made his appearance in the anteroom. It was rare for him to deal with patients not associated with cases under investigation, yet not unknown. A sympathetic man, he crouched at Felicity's knee, gazing into her face and making small, comforting sounds.

'There, there, what seems to be the problem? How can we help you?'

Felicity slowly opened the front of her gown and all saw, to their intense horror, that the nipples of each breast were swollen and blistered.

The practitioner hissed in disgust. 'Who did this to you?'

'My mother, Michiko Yamada. *Please* do not make me go back to her! I cannot bear it any longer!'

'We won't let her come near you ever again, believe me!' answered Freddi, between clenched teeth. 'Can you do something for the pain, Practitioner? Should she be taken to a medcentre?'

'I can give her something for the pain immediately, and yes, she should go to a medcentre and stay there until these burns have healed. A counsellor should speak with her too, preferably today. Do you know this woman?'

'Yes, we've met before. We're here from Australia investigating the death of someone who recently visited Córdoba, and have some evidence that Felicity has been sexually abused on more than this occasion. We intend to follow up on it immediately.'

Upon hearing this, Felicity began to shake.

'What is it, Felicity? Are you frightened of what we might find?'

Felicity shook her head, and the practitioner did as well. 'No more,' he said. 'Not yet. Let her settle down for a while. Do you wish to take her to the medcentre, or shall I call the ambutechs?'

'We can take her. At least she trusted us enough to ask for help.'

When Michiko Yamada returned to find the house empty and the side gate left open, she clenched her fists and swore, then ran up to Felicity's room and flung open all the cupboard doors, searching for anything that might lead her to where she had gone. Where *could* she have gone? Felicity had no friends, no family, no one: no one but her and the children. Not even Guillermo. Not now. Should the peacekeepers be contacted? No, she would wait until nightfall, and if her companion had not returned by then, a report would be made. Meanwhile, a walk by the river seemed wise.

*

There were only three martial arts clubs in Melbourne large enough to give Marietta competition of a sufficiently high standard to satisfy her. Having already been expelled from one club, tonight, at a second, she contented herself with remaining in the background, to observe rather than participate, correctly assuming the Sifu would not know her, either by sight or by name.

The students were quiet and disciplined, following the movements of their instructors with concentrated care. Once they completed the *Shil Lim Tao*, the beginners and more advanced classes separated and began practicing their assigned routines. Marietta was impressed by one particular woman, whom she had so far seen only from behind, and moved around the perimeter of the room to view her more clearly. The woman turned around and caught her eye. They recognised each other. Indeed, they knew each other far too well for Marietta's comfort, so without undue haste, she left and walked to the nearest callstation. To her intense annoyance, a voice accosted her in the silence of the trafficway. The callstation was relatively isolated and dusk was falling.

'Why haven't you returned my calls?' The woman was almost as tall as Marietta and slightly heavier, although no match for her superior skills. Still, this was not the place to confront someone, despite the temptation. Marietta said nothing, simply turning to face her, smiling, poised and ready.

'We had an agreement, or have you forgotten?'

'I forget nothing, but our agreement is at an end.'

'You bitch! Don't think you can simply walk away. Not from me, and not from any of the others. We won't let you.'

'And what, exactly, do you think you can do? None of you are any match for me, so do not be foolish enough to think you are. Oh, sorry, but I forget. You *are* fools, or you would not have begun this game.' Marietta neatly stepped aside as the woman attempted to strike.

'Would you like to try again? You need the practice.' Marietta deflected the kick aimed at her knee. 'Ah, très bon, but not good enough. Once more? Non? Eh bien, perhaps you are wiser than I imagined!'

'Bitch!'

'You repeat yourself. I suggest you leave before I teach you some better manners, yes?' The woman reluctantly left, yet not before Marietta saw the dark circles under her eyes and the tremor in her hand, raised to brush back the hair curling over her forehead.

The journey home was long enough for Marietta to do some serious thinking. She had been optimistic that the shock of Rhianna's death and the subsequent closure of the tournament circuit would have been enough to scare off anyone from attempting to purchase their supplies of Mandrax from her, but apparently not. Having given little thought to the withdrawal symptoms her former customers might suffer, sympathy for them was not one of her priorities when, upon her return home, she contacted Michiko Yamada. Simple self-interest was her only motive: drug addicts standing on the doorstep would be more than a little inconvenient! Therefore, yet another message was sent, without polite phrasing. This time, the words contained a threat – veiled, yet nonetheless clear enough. After all, what else was there to do, considering Michiko's reply to Marietta's message the previous day had been brief and to the point: "Suspend all operations immediately."

Before returning to the hotel for their evening meal, Freddi called Edric to hear how he and Stefano, as well as Peri and Zarifa, were managing. It was a relief to see him looking far healthier and happier than she had anticipated, given such a short time had gone by since his allergic reaction to the cats.

'Did I tell you we're building a fountain?' he said, eyes wide and with an engaging grin. 'You knew? Good! It's going extremely well. It's as if Rhianna was somehow here with us... And you wouldn't believe what Gwenllian can do! She makes the light sparkle and form rainbows while we work. Incredible! Almost as incredible as what Stefano's told me about Margrethe. Did you know she's *another* grimalkin? I can't get over it! All that time at school, she knew exactly what we were up to. No wonder we never managed to faze her in the least. I wonder how many of them there are. Robert's one as well. He finally told me when I noticed he and Gwenllian seemed to communicate rather too easily, even taking into account that Gwenllian can read his mind. Oh, and the medcentre thinks it won't be long before I can meet the cats again, which is great. I'm missing Zarifa, though she manages to 'speak' to me each time I go into Stanthorpe for the vaxxin. That's amazing, isn't it? Still, sorry for rambling on. I was just about to join the others in the greenhouse when you called. What was it you wanted to talk to me about?'

Freddi could only surmise that the combined effect of Gwenllian and Zarifa's psychic support accounted for Edric's faintly manic air, though better this than the despair and grief she saw when they first met. 'I wanted to know how you and Stefano were, but also to ask you something about Ruth and the tournaments...and don't worry about being overheard – I'm using a high-security line.'

'Right. What is it you wanted to know?' Edric's expression became serious, all the laughter gone.

'Sorry to bring you back to all this, but needs must. When I interviewed Ruth, she seemed deeply depressed and her house was a mess. Is it usually, or would it normally be reasonably clean and tidy?'

'I don't actually know, Freddi. I've never visited her. We were friends of sorts, but not of the 'visiting each other' type. Sorry. But you say she's depressed? I suppose the tournaments *were* the centre of her life and they're going to be hard to replace. I can't see it being because Rhianna's dead.' Edric frowned.

'Well, it may surprise you to hear she was very fond of Rhianna and hoped her reason for joining the contests was because she wanted to be friends. Ruth bullied Rhianna when they were at school in an effort to get her attention, that being the only way she knew how to relate. Sad, but true.'

'What! You're joking, surely?'

'No, some people are like that, and Ruth is now paying the price. She's completely alone and convinced no one will want to see her again. I took her to a medcentre to speak with a counsellor and then escorted her home. The counsellor arranged for ongoing sessions, so presumably they're managing to help her.'

'I guess I could visit once I return to Brisbane. It couldn't do any harm and might help her realise that we appreciated what she did for us. Ruth does have her good side. Most people do.'

'Yes, I think that's true...' Freddi paused, then said, 'Edric, another thing I need to ask you about is to do with Marietta. What do you expect she'll do now that she can't compete in the tournaments?'

'Try to find a suitable club, I suppose. I'm not sure what the competition is like in Melbourne, but the problem is, the clubs won't allow full contact. Without it, I doubt Marietta will be satisfied. She's highly advanced too, which you may already know, so there wouldn't be many who could even give her a good workout. To be honest, I'm not sure what *I'll* do!'

'You might want to take up international competition and learn other methods of fine-tuning your skills. I'm sure there must be a way.'

'You're probably right. Perhaps I'll study the old masters. We may have lost some of their techniques over the years, and there are other forms of kung fu than Wing Chun.'

'True, and it sounds like a good idea... For example, the monastery at Shaolin still exists... Which brings me to my last question, a difficult one. Edric, did you ever suspect or know of anyone taking drugs or distributing them at the tournaments or within your club?'

'Drugs! You're not serious! Drugs? No, never! What sort of drugs?'

'I gather from information we've recently received that a substance called Mandrax was being used and circulated. It appears to be happening over here in Argentina as well, although at this stage we don't know if it's only via the martial arts circuit. But please, I don't want you discussing any of this with Stefano until I've spoken with him myself.'

'Does this have something to do with Rhianna?' Edric's expression was one of intense concentration as he tried to remember anything at all that in hindsight he may have missed.

'Yes, it does. Your Rhianna was leading a highly dangerous life working for the Federation Special Investigation Unit as an undercover agent. Drugs were just one of the areas she was investigating.'

The blood drained from Edric's face and he became ghastly pale. Lowering his head, his hand trembled as he brought it to his eyes. When he looked up again and attempted to speak, his voice failed him. Freddi waited. She had considered carefully before telling Edric this news, and despite having preferred to speak with him in person, felt it was important to do so now. They needed to give him enough information for him to think back – think back and attempt to piece together anything at all that might lead them to whoever it was who distributed the Mandrax in Australia, or at least at the tournaments in Brisbane.

'I'm sorry,' he said eventually. 'It's just such a shock. There was never anything at all about Rhianna that made me suspect she was anything other than the person I thought I knew. This is almost beyond belief! What else was she involved in?'

'I'm sorry too, Edric, but I can't tell you anything further. Hopefully you'll learn more once we've found out how and why she died the way she did. The only thing I can tell you is that Rhianna was employed by the FSIU for many years, before she met you again, and she was deeply committed to her work. I believe the relationship she had with you helped her keep going. You should remember all the love you shared and not dwell too much on the side you knew nothing about...other than trying to help us find her killer – if indeed she was murdered. Her death *may* be connected to the drugs. That's only one possibility.'

Edric shook his head, his lips pressed together in a thin line. 'I'll do what I can, but it would help if I could talk things over with Stefano. Together, we may be able to come up with something. When do you think you'll speak with him?'

'I'll call him now, if you like.'

'Thank you, Freddi. Tell me, how do I stop Gwenllian and Robert finding out all this? It's not as if I can hide anything from them.'

'Gwenllian has our complete confidence, and if she and Robert are becoming as close as I suspect they are, I imagine we can trust him too. It may even help you deal with all this if you tell Robert what I've told you. He has the right to know, though I expect he'll just be as shocked.'

'He might not be, actually. It may help explain why Rhianna changed so much towards him and the rest of her family. Working as an undercover agent couldn't have been easy, and she must've had *some* reason for choosing that path. I can't see it being the type of work most people would want to do.'

'No,' agreed Freddi, before finishing the call. 'It wouldn't be. Take care of yourself, and let me know if you remember anything...anything at all.'

CHAPTER TWENTY

Meng Jarrah and Freddi were watching a twenty-minute recording of the recently deceased senior systems technologist. The Córdoban peacekeepers had found it on his personal computer's back-up drive after being prompted by the Australians to search for the device. This was something they hadn't already done because other than his not having activated the emergency alarm on his comlink, the case had at first seemed relatively straightforward.

'I can't believe what I'm seeing! This is horrible...and pathetic. How can someone so degrade themselves?'

'I don't know, Meng Jarrah... Will you look at him! He's grovelling and pleading, yet is obviously aroused. That's a woman in the room with him, not a man. We can just see her in the shadows. There! She moved, and I caught a glimpse of long dark hair and calf-length red boots. Can you make out her face? I can't.'

'She's wearing a mask of some sort, as well as elbow-length red gloves and the boots – nothing else. Fairly tall, slender, and based on what she just did to him, fairly strong. Pity she doesn't say anything; she just prods him and gestures. He obviously knows the script. Oh no!' Meng Jarrah put a hand to her mouth when they saw the woman heat what appeared to be a metal brand in a brazier of coals.

They watched as the glowing metal touched his buttock, then heard both his scream and the groan of ecstasy as he climaxed. The woman crouched down, allowing him to nuzzle her breasts while he moaned and gasped his thanks – only to be slapped, hard, and kicked aside. He crawled after her as she stalked out of view of the camera.

'What do you think? Payment for his cooperation, or a bribe with the promise of more?' Freddi turned from the screen and drank a mouthful of hot coffee to wash away the taste of the scenes they had just witnessed.

'Hard to know, but either way, it gives us another reason to suggest his death be considered suspicious. Whoever was in that room might have had the opportunity to adulterate his jar of dill pickles.' Meng Jarrah burst out laughing. 'Sorry, bad joke. I didn't mean it to come out like that!' She giggled, then forced herself to stop. 'Nervous laughter... It's not at all funny.'

Freddi patted her on the back, finished the coffee and stood up. 'The coincidence is too much for me. I'd say there's a circle of people in Córdoba who indulge in these fantasies and that Michiko Yamada is one of them. She may even be the woman in the room. I'll ask Anna to enhance this footage so we can see if there's some clue to either the woman's identity or the room where this took place. We should also interview his friend, the shopkeeper, again. He may be someone else who finds this type of activity amusing. None of it's illegal, of course. Still, not everyone wants to have the details of their sex life broadcast to all and sundry. He may prefer to cooperate with us rather than risk having to testify at an inquest.'

'I agree...and Freddi, we've just received the analysis of Guillermo's ring. It's Patagonian silver.' Meng Jarrah grimaced.

'Why am I not surprised? At least we now have a good excuse to check Michiko's home for his DNA, as well as the entire outbuilding, rather than just the items we brought back for analysis. We should include those boots and the mask in the search too, though I doubt she would have kept them...if they're hers...and I certainly can't recall seeing them when we were there. However, we may have missed something – it's a big house.'

'Yes, and we should do it all this morning. One thing, though. The autopsy results didn't mention a brand on the technologist's buttock. The recording wasn't new, so he may've had it removed, in which case there should be some trace. I must ask the pathologist.' Meng Jarrah immediately sent a message to the Coroner's office. Shortly afterwards, a reply arrived to say that they would check and let her know.

'Come to think of it,' said Freddi, 'if I ask the local peacekeepers to do the search instead, in the meantime, we could see if Felicity is well enough to speak with us. It's very likely she has more information and could save us some time.'

Anna felt herself blushing as she studied the computer-enhanced images. The file was four months old, but she suspected it had been viewed many times. Why else keep it? Ugh!

It seemed clear that the woman – the dominatrix – had made sure to keep as far away from the camera as possible and not show any part of her face, or even much of her body, to its scrutiny. The main focus was entirely on the man and his role-playing. A comparison of the room's details with those of the house in which he had lived showed that wherever this took place, it was not in his own home. His household security system stored full particulars of each room, so there could be no mistake. It occurred to her to ask Freddi if they had accessed Michiko Yamada's household computer for its security database. A quick call confirmed this had not been done, but would be added to the list of things to be carried out during the morning by the Córdoban peacekeepers.

The general description Anna was able to piece together of the woman fitted Michiko Yamada, but without a face, it could also fit thousands of others. There were no distinguishing marks on the body that she could see, although her hair was unusually long and luxuriant, as was Michiko's. Altogether, the woman was certainly beautiful, in contrast to the man. Anna sent her conclusions to Freddi's comlink then went back to her usual university work a little the wiser about the odd ways of the world...though perhaps, on reflection, she would have preferred not to have seen those images.

The peacekeeper at the reception centre listened to Michiko while she coldly demanded to see the most senior person on duty. 'I am quite sure, Señora Yamada,' he answered, 'that *I* will be able to help you. There is no need to bother anyone else.'

The peacekeeper was unused to being treated with such arrogance. Nevertheless, being a patient man, he had no intention of being intimidated, despite knowing his 'customer' by reputation. Her immense wealth and influential position within the world's largest private enterprise, Wyvern Meridian, would alone have been enough to make her famous, but Michiko was also well known as a sponsor of local artists.

'Very well, Peacekeeper, I will trust you to do your best.' Michiko moved closer, not wishing to be overheard. 'My adopted daughter, Felicity, is missing and has been missing since yesterday afternoon. I want you to find her.'

The peacekeeper raised an eyebrow and consulted his daily reports summary, immediately finding mention of Felicity. He read the details, muttering to himself. This would not be easy!

'Señora Yamada, I am sorry to tell you that your daughter has left your home of her own accord and does not wish to see you. She is perfectly safe, but has sought sanctuary with us for reasons that are not, as yet, quite clear.' He waved his hands in a gesture of resignation to fate.

Michiko's eyes widened and she began to speak, then changed her mind. No need to expose her thoughts and feelings to this man. She could easily guess whom Felicity first sought sanctuary with: the Australians. The coincidence of their having come to her home and having spoken with Felicity in private was too great to allow for any other explanation. Then there was the cat to consider. It may have influenced her to leave. Despite Michiko never before having come into close contact with one of the creatures, she knew their reputation, and particularly so since their role in her bondmate's business difficulties with the Federation were made public.

Thinking back, it was folly to have allowed it to be present during either her or Felicity's interview.

'Will you give her a message, Peacekeeper?' she said instead.

'Yes, I can certainly arrange for a message to be passed on.'

'Good. Tell Felicity she may return home any time she wishes. I will be glad to see her again, and if she is in any difficulty, will be ready to help in whatever manner is required.'

'Thank you, Señora Yamada. I will let her know. Is that all?'

'Yes, for now.' Michiko turned abruptly and left, seething with anger.

The news that Rhianna had worked as an agent for the Federation Special Investigation Unit left his new friends as astonished as Edric had been when Freddi first told him. He had waited until their midsun meal to pass on the news, wanting to take the morning to think about his feelings. While they continued their work on the fountain, Robert and Gwenllian were able to sense Edric was troubled, and Agathea noticed how silent he became after his comlink calls, yet they all felt it was better to wait until he told them in his own good time what was on his mind.

Robert now sat with his arms folded, a perplexed expression on his face, while Agathea, as she drank her tea, thought about the little girl she had loved and who, as the adult woman, had been revealed as someone she hardly knew at all. Her own niece, an agent! However, Gwenllian was less taken aback, due to her close involvement with the Wyvern Meridian case. During that time, Gwenllian became friends with the current FSIU Coordinator, Morag MacIain, and could therefore understand how attractive the work offered by the Federation could be. On the other hand, she also came into close contact with Rohan Maerz, the former FSIU Coordinator, who had worked undercover for many years to discover more about Wyvern Meridian's illegal activities and the role of its director, Kenjiro Kakura. Out of this knowledge and experience came an awareness of the dangers involved, something that quite possibly neither Robert nor Agathea fully appreciated.

'I've tried as hard as I can, but there's nothing at all I can remember that would've made me think Rhianna had any other work than the travel consultancy.' Still, having said this, Edric began to remember the times Rhianna came back from some of her travels strangely reserved and almost morose – although, after a few days in his company, she always managed to regain her good humour. Frowning, he took another large bite of his sandwich.

'Rhianna was a brave woman,' said Gwenllian, 'though needless to say, her martial arts training wouldn't have done her any harm. At least she was physically able to look after herself. From everything I've learned about her, Edric, I'd imagine she had very good reasons for becoming an agent and then remaining one for so long. My guess is that the travel consultancy was some type of front for her operations. Did Freddi talk about this as a possibility?' Privately, Gwenllian wondered how Rhianna had managed to keep everything from Edric. She herself couldn't have formed such a close relationship without telling her lover about this aspect of her life, at least to some extent.

'No!' replied Edric, shaking his head. 'Freddi didn't say anything about that, but it makes sense. Rhianna travelled all over the world and so had every opportunity to investigate whatever the FSIU wanted, without seeming at all suspicious. She met a large number of influential people in the process and would have formed connections everywhere. I must admit, I did wonder how she managed to purchase the consultancy, the apartment and the landjet, but didn't give it much thought. It wasn't my business to ask. I just assumed she'd inherited something when her mother died. Do you think the FSIU paid for it all?'

'Rhianna may have received some large fees conducting private tours before she set up the consultancy, but it would be hard to conceive of her earning enough to pay for it all without either taking out a loan from someone or being given what was necessary,' said Agathea. 'She certainly didn't inherit much from her mother. Leihana managed to use up all her own savings and then borrowed on the value of her house. Truth be told, it would be a miracle if there was anything left other than debts by the time she died.'

'Did Freddi say she'd tell you more soon?' asked Robert, beginning to think he'd misjudged his cousin and bitterly regretting it.

'No, she said it'd have to wait until they knew both the whole story and who killed her...if Rhianna was in fact murdered. Damn it!' Edric paused, taking a deep breath to calm himself. 'In the meantime, Freddi wants Stefano and I to see if we can remember anything at all about something else they've unearthed – to do with illegal drugs being distributed at the martial arts tournaments. Something called Mandrax.'

'Drugs!' The reaction of Edric's audience was exactly the same as his own. Illegal use of drugs was, as far as they knew, rare. There seemed little reason for people to resort to substance abuse, although given Leihana had been an alcoholic, evidently in some cases there was.

'Yes... Freddi spoke with Stefano this morning after she called me. He's as upset as I am, but didn't want to talk about it much at the time, and neither did I. We both needed to think for a while and agreed to call each other again this afternoon. Freddi believes there could be some relationship between the Mandrax, Rhianna's undercover work, and her death. Something she mentioned about Argentina makes me think Rhianna was investigating over there as well, which might explain her frequent trips.'

Gwenllian lightly touched Edric on his forearm, saying, 'I *could* call Morag MacIain. She's the Coordinator of the FSIU and a friend of mine. What do you think?'

There were so many layers to Gwenllian's personality and her past, thought Robert, raising an eyebrow in surprise; he looked forward to discovering what they all were. She read his feelings, smiled, and took his hand in hers.

'Thanks,' said Edric, 'but no. I've only known Freddi a short time, but feel I can trust her judgement. As much as I'd like her to, if she doesn't want to tell me more, then I think we should leave things as they are. Also, if Rhianna *was* working for the FSIU, wouldn't this Morag MacIain already know what's happened to her...dying, I mean...and have contacted Freddi and Meng Jarrah? Wouldn't they be working together by now?'

'Come to think of it, Edric, you're right,' answered Gwenllian. 'We'll simply have to be patient.'

'Can you recall anything related to this drug situation that could help them?' asked Robert.

'I didn't pay much attention at the time, but looking back, there were instances at some of the tournaments when a few audience members seemed to behave out of keeping with what I would've expected. I just put it down to the general excitement of being there. Other than that, no, I haven't recalled anything at all useful. I don't know if Stefano will. He knows some of the people in the scene better than I do.'

'What about Ruth and Marietta?' suggested Agathea. 'Surely they would have had *some* inkling, particularly Ruth. She organised everything, while Marietta was, and probably still is, a nasty piece of work. If anyone was involved in selling drugs, I'd suggest it could be her. Whoever was doing it needed to know where and when the tournaments were to be held...and tell me if I'm wrong, Edric...that information would have been closely guarded until the invitations went out. I'm assuming these *were* invitation-only events?'

'Yes, that's true, they were, but once the information was passed on, there'd be enough time, I guess, to organise the Mandrax, assuming the supplies were readily available. If they weren't, it'd be a different matter.' Edric was reluctant to think that either Ruth or Marietta were involved.

'I can understand your not liking the idea,' said Robert, 'but perhaps you should mention it to Freddi anyway, or at least to Stefano to see what he thinks.'

'I'll talk to Stefano and then decide. Now, I suppose it's time we got back to work and finished those bronze pieces, Robert.'

Everyone took the hint and tidied away the remains of their meal, leaving Edric to mull the situation over as the day progressed. By the end of the afternoon, the final form of the fountain had taken shape. Before they left the greenhouse, Gwenllian asked them to wait a moment, then concentrated as hard as she could. As they watched, she cast an illusion over the stone and metal. To her great delight, and theirs, for several seconds the fountain transformed itself into the finished work. This was her first attempt at such a feat, although it was something she had wanted to try since beginning the project. Alone, Gwenllian had never succeeded in creating this type of illusion, but the link with Robert gave her the additional power she needed.

'By the Sun, Gwenllian my dear, you've turned into our very own witch!' exclaimed Agathea. 'What do you think, Robert, shall we ever trust our eyes again when you two are together?' She had realised it was their joint effort, and was glad.

Robert laughed, and his mother was glad of that as well. Even Edric smiled.

The medcentre provided Felicity with her own room and gave her enough privacy and time to settle in before a counsellor came to speak with her. The woman found Felicity sitting in a corner, hands folded and her hair neatly arranged in a simplified version of its usual formal coiffure, having used the fastenings she habitually carried in her pocket. Her features conveyed little other than studied calm. The counsellor sat down to one side and waited. After several minutes passed without Felicity saying anything, the counsellor broke the silence.

'I understand you do not wish to return home because your adoptive mother has treated you very badly. Would you like to tell me what it is she has done?'

Felicity's dark eyes turned towards the counsellor and tears ran down her cheeks. 'She has betrayed my trust! When I was small, and when her bondmate, my adoptive father, was alive, I was happy. He loved me almost as much as his own children, and they were all kind to me. He gave me a home when I had none, after my own parents died. I was grateful, and so, obedient in all things. That was the least I could do for him.' She looked down and rubbed her hands together as if to warm them.

'Are you cold?' asked the counsellor.

'No, not on the outside.'

The counsellor nodded in sympathy. 'What happened after your adoptive father died?'

'The whole family grieved deeply. I helped manage the household because for a long time Michiko was unable to do anything. His loss was a blow difficult for any of us to recover from, but after about one and half years, she returned to her silversmithing. At first, it was inconceivable for her to enter the outbuilding used as a workshop, since it was there she and Kenjiro spent nearly all their evenings when he was home. I was glad to see her creating her beautiful designs again, yet was astonished at how quickly she then recovered more interest in life. Michiko stood for election to the Board of Wyvern Meridian after the Federation opened it to the public for the second time and withdrew their supervision. She was successful in becoming their first Cultural and Artistic Director.' The expression of pride on Felicity's face showed how deeply she admired her adoptive mother's achievements.

'What happened next?' The counsellor spoke kindly to reassure her.

'One evening, she invited me into her workshop. We had tea, and afterwards I was shown her workbench and the cabinet where her silversmithing tools are kept, together with some of the works in progress. I felt honoured, as none of us had ever been allowed in the workshop before. A little later, Michiko explained that it was her custom to bathe there each evening. The room contained a beautiful sunken bath and she invited me to join her. We washed each other's hair and had a pleasant time relaxing in the hot, perfumed water. It seemed important to her, this ritual, so I was happy to join her there the next evening. I understand now that she and Kenjiro were in the habit of bathing together.'

Felicity turned her face away and sighed, then met the counsellor's gaze. 'For some two weeks, this pleasant pastime continued, until one evening it became more than that.' Felicity put a hand to her eyes, unable to continue. The counsellor waited patiently. Taking a deep breath, Felicity said, 'She made sexual advances towards me, kissing me on the mouth and fondling my body.'

'Did you respond to her, or were you frightened?'

'Both. I regard her as my mother, yet know she is not. Michiko is a highly attractive woman and has been without her bondmate for a long time. It is understandable that she might want some companionship in this way, but why me? It seemed wrong, yet I felt unable to say no. I even tried to convince myself to enjoy it.'

'But you didn't?' The counsellor was moved by Felicity's simple account of these events.

'No, how could I? I wanted her as my mother, not as a lover. Our relationship has not always been as good as when Kenjiro was alive, but I knew Michiko was deeply unhappy and made allowances. Then, one evening after our bath, she asked me to allow her to practice some new skills...a new interest...on me, which involved being used as a form of live artwork...or so I was told. I still trusted her, you see.'

Felicity bowed her head and had trouble speaking. The counsellor reached out to touch her, then thought better of it and withdrew her hand. 'Trust is one of the most important things in life and sometimes even more difficult to give than love,' she said instead.

'Yes, what you say is true.' Felicity met her eyes again and drew courage to continue her story. 'Michiko, as you may know, is a skilled artist. She told me I would not be harmed and would even enjoy the process. I was told it was an ancient form of relaxation that many people even paid others to perform. It seems Michiko had been taking part in this art form...Japanese rope bondage...for some time with a master here in Córdoba, since not long after her bondmate died. She said it helped overcome her deepest grief and gave her the desire to go on living. More recently, the master had taken her on as a pupil.'

The counsellor nodded. She had heard of this form of relaxation and knew it often gave great benefit to its adherents.

'You know of this practice?' asked Felicity.

'Yes, I have seen it once, after one of my patients invited me to observe what it was that was helping her deal with some of her anxieties. It is highly respectable.'

'Respectable? Perhaps in the beginning it was with us. Cooperating with her did me no harm, and it *was* strangely relaxing. Michiko seemed to derive great pleasure from the artistic expression, as well as the trust I displayed in allowing her to do it.'

'What went wrong?'

'One evening, as a particularly advanced form had been completed and I was beginning to tire, I closed my eyes and began to drift off into strange dreams, when, without any warning at all, I was struck! Struck with one of the whips Michiko herself had created and shown me some days before.' Tears ran down Felicity's face and she slowly wiped them away. 'I screamed in fright and was struck again, this time across the breasts. I begged her to stop, but that seemed to excite her, because she continued, many times, all over my body. The more I struggled and the more I pleaded, the more she struck me. After some time, I ceased to beg her to stop and Michiko calmed down, dropped the whip and sank to her knees before me, saying she was sorry and that it would never happen again, kissing me as she spoke.'

'Did you believe her?'

'Yes, I did. She wept while taking off the ropes and afterwards cradled me in her arms. Things returned to normal for a while, but after two months, my mother wanted me to allow her one last chance to practice a new form, recently learned from her master. I was frightened, but she reassured me that it would be painless. She even had a herbal preparation to help make the experience highly pleasurable. I reluctantly agreed, so after we had our bath, I applied this preparation – internally, if you understand what I mean – and allowed her to do what she wanted. And it *was* pleasurable...extremely pleasurable. Afterwards, I felt, or at least hoped, I could begin to trust her again. However, she beat me again, this time with a cane. It happened late last year, during a visit from one of her friends, an Australian by the name of Rhianna O'Connor. I believe Michiko had somehow become angry with her and transferred the anger to me. It was the only reason I could think of at the time.'

'Were you right? Did things improve?'

'No. Michiko became more and more angry, and sometimes slapped me if I failed to do something she wanted, or if I did it badly. I did not know what to do. I had no friends or other family to speak with. Then, one day Michiko introduced me to a young man, Guillermo, and said that if I agreed, we could all three take a bath together that evening. I felt very shy to be seen by a man, but Michiko told me there was no shame in bathing together. We did so, and I found the experience enjoyable, seemingly quite normal. Guillermo was extremely handsome and appeared to find me beautiful. I suppose I am.' Felicity smiled briefly, before putting a hand to her mouth to prevent herself from weeping.

'What happened to Guillermo? Did you become friends?'

'Yes, we did. Eventually, we became lovers. He was my first and I will never forget him.'

'Did Michiko approve?'

'She seemed to, and even allowed him to spend several days at a time in the house with us. After a while, though, I sensed she had become jealous, and soon asked me to stop seeing him. I reasoned with her, saying that we loved each other, but that our love could never interfere with the affection I felt for her. This appeared to satisfy her for a time, but one afternoon, when I came home from shopping, I heard laughter coming from Michiko's bedroom and thought perhaps she had found a lover too, which made me happy. Not long afterwards, she and Guillermo came downstairs together! He was shocked and embarrassed when he saw me, but Michiko merely held him more closely.'

'What did you do?'

'I ran from the house, with Guillermo running after me. He held me in his arms in the garden and said it would never happen again, that he loved only me. I loved him so much and wanted to trust him, but he lied! One week later, Michiko again asked me to bathe with them, to show that all was well and it had been a mistake...all her fault, and would I please forgive her for having given in to temptation? I agreed, yet while we were in the bath, they began to make love. In front of me! I could have died from shame! I fled the room and could hear them laughing as I did.'

'Did Guillermo come back to the house again?'

'No, his body was found in the river not long after. He was presumed to have drowned accidentally.'

The counsellor raised one eyebrow as her eyes widened. 'Do you think he did?'

'No, I do not! I believe Guillermo was killed.'

'Why?'

'I am not sure. It is a feeling I have.'

'Have you told any of this to the peacekeepers?'

'No. Do you think I should?'

'Yes, definitely. You have nothing to be ashamed of. Your mother should not have treated you in this manner. You trusted her and she betrayed your trust. You have done the right thing in leaving her house. If you like, rather than having to repeat all this, would you prefer I show the recording of this session to the peacekeepers?'

Felicity nodded. She had been told at the outset that it was standard practice to record counselling sessions when they were related to a crime having been committed.

'Would you like to speak with me again after they have viewed it?'

Felicity nodded again and bowed her head, her hands folded loosely in her lap.

'This doesn't make sense,' remarked Freddi, after they finished viewing the recording of Felicity's counselling session held at the medcentre that morning.

'No, it doesn't. Why did Felicity allow Michiko to come near her again? The abuse this time was severe and wasn't done in five minutes! There's all that Sensa to account for as well, though I suppose either Felicity or Michiko could have used it when they were together with Guillermo. We'll have to ask, sadly enough. She's been through a lot.' Meng Jarrah's disgust showed in her voice.

'Yes, she has... Do you think Felicity might have had anything to do with Guillermo's death? Jealousy? Anger at his betrayal?' Freddi thought not, but the possibility had to be considered.

'We can take Shela with us and simply ask Felicity how she thinks Guillermo died. That's something you could understand, couldn't you, puddums?' Meng Jarrah reached down to stroke Shela's head. Shela assured her that she understood about death and wights killing each other. Experience during the Wyvern Meridian investigation had given her quite enough information for her to fully understand!

'I wonder if Rhianna knew about, or at least suspected, what was going on and tried to prevent it from continuing? Perhaps the abuse has now escalated because we told Michiko that she's dead. It's a reasonable theory.'

'Yes, I agree, it is... Aside from the possibility that Michiko discovered Rhianna was an agent with the FSIU and for some unknown reason wanted her dead, do you realise she had three powerful motives for killing her? Theft of artworks, the drugs, and the abuse of Felicity.'

'Four, actually: jealousy. Michiko might make light of Kakura giving Rhianna the necklet, but what if she put two and two together and realised such an expensive, highly personalised gift is not usually given to a casual acquaintance from university?'

'Do you think that would outweigh the other motives?' Meng Jarrah was somewhat dubious.

'Possibly not outweigh, just clinch the decision.'

'Yes, that makes sense, in a sick sort of way.'

When, at that moment, her comlink chimed, Freddi turned away to take the call. It appeared the peacekeepers had finished searching the Yamada residence, without finding any gloves, masks or red boots, calf-length or otherwise. Also, the household security database told them that the scenes of the senior systems technologist and his dominatrix had not taken place there. However, they did at least find Guillermo's DNA, both in Felicity's and in Michiko's bedroom, and upon checking the plumbing of the sunken bath in the outbuilding, discovered several of his hairs. This confirmed some of what Felicity had told the counsellor. Further confirmation was found in the form of the missing bottle of stolen perfume, hidden behind a disguised wall panel in Felicity's room, together with a message of love addressed to her by Guillermo.

'Good, and thank you,' said Freddi, running a hand through her hair. For once, the ringlets were loose and her hair shone, lustrous black and beautiful. Distracted for a moment, Meng Jarrah smiled as she watched, but immediately gave her full attention when Freddi turned around to tell her what the search had discovered.

'I'll follow up with the Coroner,' said Meng Jarrah. 'I was hoping to have heard from her by now anyway. We need to know about that brand on the senior systems technologist's rear end.' She asked her comlink to locate the Coroner and was soon deep in conversation, with Freddi listening in.

'Yes, I have accessed all the medcentre records,' said the Coroner, 'and your person did have a regeneration procedure, but no record was kept of the design of the brand. Peculiar behaviour, I must say! Still, in my profession, it is a surprise to me that I am surprised by anything at all!'

'Thank you,' said Meng Jarrah. 'You've been a great help.'

The Coroner gave her a small smile then closed the connection.

'Maybe Marietta *was* the one distributing the Mandrax,' said Stefano. 'She's the type to enjoy making others dependent on her. I think she'd even enjoy the idea of people becoming addicted. It'd give her a sense of superiority. I don't think Ruth would've been involved though. Drugs would have jeopardised the tournaments and she couldn't have stood for that.'

'What do you think Marietta will do now the tournaments are over?' asked Edric, deeply unhappy at the thought of her being involved. After all, even if he wasn't overly fond of her as a person, he had known her since their schooldays and held her martial arts skills in high regard.

'You mean about training, or drugs?' replied Stefano, also unhappy at the idea, despite the efforts of both Zarifa and Peri to keep him from being so.

'Both, I suppose.'

'I honestly don't know. From what you've told me about Ruth, she's a mess, so won't be in any fit condition to help develop another training circuit, even if it's only a legal one providing a higher standard than usual. If I were Marietta, I'd be staying well clear of the drugs, though.'

'If her supplier will let her. There must be enormous profit involved, or why else do it? I also wonder if she's in any serious danger now. She might be, you know.'

'Yes, there's that as well. Either way, I think we should tell Freddi to take a close look at what Marietta's been up to for the past few years. Surely her movements can be traced to some extent?'

'It depends upon how her supplies were delivered. She may not have needed to travel anywhere special to pick them up.'

'Do you really think she'd let someone come to her house with them?'

'Good point. I've never been there, but from what Marietta has said about the place, it's quite special, and I doubt she'd have wanted to 'sully' it.'

'Here we are, assuming it's her! The problem is, I can't think of anyone else who would've been close enough to the centre of things *and* who has the type of personality to become involved in something like this, can you?'

'No, I can't. But then again, I thought I knew Rhianna, and all this time there was this vast side to her I knew nothing about. It makes me wonder about a lot of other things.'

'Such as?'

'Did she love me as much as I loved her, for example.'

'Oh Edric, of course she did! Don't go down that track. You were incredibly important to her. I know that for sure.' Stefano, his brow furrowed in concern, leaned forward to emphasise his point.

'Did she talk to you about me sometimes?'

'Yes, as a matter of fact, she did. She truly loved you, Edric.'

They both fell silent while they struggled to overcome their renewed grief at Rhianna's death. Peri licked Stefano's hand. While he stroked her head, Zarifa leapt onto the table where he was sitting and pushed her face against his, making small burbling sounds. She couldn't project her feelings for Edric over such a long distance, but at least the cat could show him she cared by pressing her nose to the screen. When Edric smiled wanly and touched his own screen with his forefinger in a virtual kiss, Zarifa raised her paw in response, then sat down next to Stefano to 'listen' to the rest of the conversation.

'Okay, I'll call Freddi and tell her what we've discussed,' said Edric, heaving a sigh, 'not that it's much to go on.'

'Let me know what she says.' Stefano ran a hand over his face, suddenly tired. He really did hate to think Marietta could be involved in the distribution of Mandrax, but the more he dwelt on it, the more likely it seemed.

'I'll call you tomorrow from the medcentre. I'm hoping there are only another three sessions of vaxxin to go. Apparently I'm responding far better than anticipated, maybe because I'm so fit.'

'Good. Do you want to go back to Brisbane once you've been given the all-clear?'

'Yes, but I'd like to visit Margrethe and Harriet before we do. You could come with me.'

'I could, that's true. I wouldn't mind seeing Margrethe again, either. What a woman!'

'Speaking of which, you wouldn't dream of what Gwenllian can do!'

'What?'

'She can cast illusions.'

'No! Really?'

'Yep...illusions. Only when she's with Robert, though. They seem to reinforce each other's powers. How's that for true love. They were evidently meant to be together.'

'What did she do?'

'Well, we've almost finished the fountain. Just have to get the water running, and she showed us how it would look...in a magical sort of way. Totally incredible.'

'I wonder what Gwenllian could do if she had both Robert and Margrethe to work together with. World domination, here we come!'

Edric laughed, feeling far better than he had all day. They chatted about ordinary things for a while longer before Edric left to help Agathea prepare their evening meal. This was something he had promised earlier in the day, for the meal was to be in celebration of the new fountain.

CHAPTER TWENTY-ONE

Freddi and Meng Jarrah were rapidly becoming familiar with the Córdoban business district, so readily found their way to the shop where they previously interviewed the man who had now become central to their investigation into the death of the senior systems technologist. He was even more nervous than on the first occasion. A fine sweat broke out on his brow when Freddi addressed him.

'Good afternoon. We need to bother you again. Do you have somewhere we can speak in private?' Calmly studying him, Freddi placed her hand on the countertop near where the shopkeeper was standing.

Although he was around Meng Jarrah's height and could easily have met Freddi's eyes, he didn't. Instead, his gaze shifted between the front door of his shop and the door to the room at the back, where stores and other items not for display were kept. 'Yes, yes, please, come this way,' he said, hesitating and then leading them into the back room, where he gestured for them to take a seat if they wished. They didn't.

'Is there someone who can mind the shop for you while we speak? This may take some time,' began Freddi, noticing that the assistant who had been there on the former occasion was now absent.

'One moment... I will call Maria from her break.' He spoke rapidly into his comlink and a few minutes later they all heard the sound of the front door opening. Maria, apparently, had not gone far.

'We have another image to show you,' said Freddi, handing him her comlink. The shopkeeper became pale, his hand trembling when he gave it back to her.

'You know him, I gather.'

'Yes, I do, but have not heard from him in a while. Has something happened to him?'

'It has. He's dead. I'm sorry.'

The man's jaw dropped and he wiped his face with a crumpled kerchief dragged from his coat pocket, then shook his head and sighed. 'He was a friend of some years' standing, you see. How did he die?'

'Of food poisoning, several days ago.'

'Food poisoning, you say? How on Earth could that happen?'

'It's unusual, I agree. How well did you know his habits at home?'

'Not well, although he was a careful man, even if not the tidiest in all things. Did he die at home?'

'Yes, he did. How did you become friends?'

'We have social interests in common and met almost three years ago.'

'What were these social interests?'

The shopkeeper looked at his feet and mumbled something indecipherable.

'I missed that. What was it you said?' Freddi leaned closer, as if to hear better.

He took a step backwards before answering. 'It is not illegal... Do you mind if we all sit down? I am becoming quite uncomfortable.'

'Sit if you like. We prefer to stand. But, please, continue.'

The shopkeeper found a chair and sat down, crossing his legs and twiddling with a piece of loose thread on his coat front. Shela stood up from where she was lying by the door and padded over to sniff his shoes. He shrank back when she sat by his knee, staring into his face. 'Does your cat have to do that?' he asked.

'No, does it upset you?'

'Yes. I don't like cats. Could you please ask her to move further away?'

Freddi sent a quick request to Shela and the cat moved back to her former place, a position designed to prevent him from escaping. She continued to stare at him, her golden eyes glinting in the sunlight coming in from a window high in the far wall.

'Well, do you feel better now?' asked Freddi, smiling for the first time.

'Yes, much. Thank you. Where were we?'

'You were about to tell us what the social interests were that you and your friend had in common.'

'Oh. I should not be embarrassed to tell you, yet I am. I would prefer this information be kept private, if possible. Is it possible?'

'It depends upon whether it's relevant to our inquiry, and if so, whether the Judge will need to know once the inquest is held.'

'There will be an inquest?' The man was clearly attempting to sidetrack them.

'Yes, of course there will be an inquest. Now, please tell us what we want to know – although before you do, do you want a Witness present?'

Heaving a deep sigh, his narrow shoulders hunched, he finally said, 'No. No Witness, please. To answer your question: bondage and fantasy games. Quite tame and unremarkable, but nevertheless, sexual. You understand?'

'Yes, we understand perfectly. Thank you. Did you have a sexual relationship with your friend?'

'No! Oh, no! Never! No, we were only interested in women. Beautiful women, who sadly enough would normally have little interest in men such as us.'

Freddi mentally shrugged at his assumption; the man evidently had little in the way of narcissistic ego. 'Leaving that aside for the time being, please tell us where these sessions were held and with whom.'

'Ah... They varied. We preferred not to use the one venue for long because that might have attracted attention. There are a number of premises here in Córdoba available for hire, and so we usually spent no more than around one or two months in any one place.'

'Can you recall which venue was used four months ago?'

He started, and for the first time met Freddi's eyes, staring at her. 'Four months ago? Why four months?'

'Because, during a search of his home, we found a recording of your friend together with a dominatrix. We'd like you to see it and then tell us if you recognise either the woman or the venue.'

The shopkeeper's face turned an unattractive shade of dark red, but he nodded in agreement. When Freddi handed him her comlink again, he held it as if it would bite him. Shela growled softly from her place by the door. He winced. They waited patiently while he watched the recording. Finally, the shopkeeper handed the comlink back to Freddi, his expression resigned and defeated.

'The venue in this recording is by the river. It was one of our favourites because we could hear the water lapping against the outer walls. It added to the mystery of the occasion, you see.' He stopped speaking and folded his thin arms.

'And the woman. Do you recognise her?'

'Yes, I do, but I do not know her name and have never seen her face. We did not exchange names unless friendships formed, as in our case. This woman often attended these events and helped organise them, particularly in the sense of ensuring the required equipment and other accoutrements were in place. She is highly professional and popular.'

'Is there any chance at all of her having formed a friendship with him?'

The shopkeeper shrugged and tutted. 'Perhaps... I honestly do not know. He was an intelligent man and easy to be with. It is not entirely out of the question.'

'We have one more item to show you.' Freddi found the scenes recorded by Rhianna where the two friends were sitting together at one of the martial arts tournaments. After the increasingly distressed shopkeeper had viewed them, sweating profusely by now, she said, 'Well, what have you to say?'

He stuttered and cleared his throat several times. 'W...will...will you prosecute me?'

'That remains for the Córdoban peacekeepers to determine. Unless you have committed a more serious offence, we can recommend that you not be prosecuted if you cooperate with us now.'

Shela growled, more loudly this time, to emphasise her companion's words. The man jumped slightly in his chair then gathered his courage to say, 'The dominatrix told us of these events, but also warned us they were illegal. She presented us with invitations every now and again when we were more than usually obedient to her wishes. They are very exciting to watch...fascinating, even.' The man's eyes widened as he remembered.

'Did you keep any of the invitations? What form did they take?'

'Form? Calligraphy, on thick parchment-coloured paper. Quite beautiful, but we were not able to keep them. They were handed to the door attendant at each of the venues.'

Freddi sat down close to him. He cringed and held his breath, before letting it out in a long sigh.

'I am not about to hurt you, my friend,' said Freddi.

'No... No, of course not. My apologies. Beautiful women make me nervous, if you will excuse me saying so.'

'Naturally... One last question before we leave you to resume your business. Do you know what Mandrax is?' Freddi watched him closely, as did Shela and Meng Jarrah. Shela's tail twitched as she probed his mind.

'Mandrax? No, I have never heard of it. What is it?'

Freddi glanced at Shela, who purred and told her the wight was not lying.

'It's a medication used by some to help them relax.' Freddi bent the truth a little. There was no point in telling him more.

'I see. Do you think it would help me?'

'No... Oh no. You have no need for it at all, really. It was just something that occurred to me.' Freddi smiled in a friendly, reassuring manner. Thinking too much about Mandrax was not something she wanted him to do. Standing up, Freddi held out her hand, which he tentatively grasped, his own hand cold and clammy.

'Thank you for your cooperation. We appreciate it. Please, take my advice and don't attend any more of these tournaments.'

He shook his head and stood up. 'This dominatrix...should I find someone else?'

'Yes,' replied Freddi. 'If I were you, I'd find someone else.'

'What do you think, Meng Jarrah?' asked Freddi, as they left the shop.

'Sad... Very sad. I'm sorry he's lost his friend. I suspect he doesn't have many. At least he told us the truth.'

'Shela shared her opinion with you as well, did she?' Freddi stopped in her tracks to face her.

'Yes, she did.' Meng Jarrah took Freddi's arm and held her close. 'Not jealous, are you?'

'I shouldn't be, I know. It's good, actually. Saves me having to tell you all about it!'

Shela wound herself around their legs, tail in the air. They both looked down and laughed.

'Cheeky cat!' exclaimed Freddi, as she bent down to stroke her head. Shela had picked up some interesting scenes from the shopkeeper's mind and suggested that, unlike grimalkins, wights were at times extremely peculiar.

'There are some things that never seem to change, I must admit, but trust me, Shela, before cats were born in breeding centres, *they* sometimes behaved rather strangely too!'

Shela did not believe her.

They walked on until they found the venue by the river, recognisable from the image Shela had shown them. The building, set apart from others nearby, was fairly ordinary, small and self-contained, with a single doorway and several small windows on each side, placed high above the ground. In this respect, it was suitably private, since casual passers-by could not easily see inside. The door was locked and did not open to Freddi's ID. Meng Jarrah tried hers, but without success.

'We'll need a warrant.' Freddi entered a few commands into her comlink. Before long, an entry code displayed itself on the screen and they were soon inside. Meng Jarrah had her forensics kit with her, so once the door was shut behind them and Shela safely settled outside, they donned coveralls and gloves. An hour later, they had what they wanted.

Early the following morning, Freddi received a call from Edric.

'Marietta?' she replied, in response to his suggestion. 'Well, she's certainly arrogant and unfeeling enough to be involved, and from what I've seen, her lifestyle *is* expensive. Do you know where she gets the extra income from? I haven't done a trace...at least, not yet.' Freddi yawned, hiding it with her hand. Having only recently woken, she was still wearing a lovely, dark blue nightgown given to her by Meng Jarrah for her Namingday. Edric could hardly help noticing, but concentrated on her face instead.

'No,' he said, 'I haven't a clue. We were never close enough to discuss such things... Stefano and I can't think of anyone else who'd be the type to sell drugs and also have the inside connections with the tournaments to be in a position to organise the distribution efficiently. Assuming, of course, it *was* done efficiently. I suppose it must have been, or someone would've been caught by now, either using it or selling it.'

'Mmm. You're right... How are you going with the vaxxin treatment? Do you think you'll return to Brisbane when it's finished?'

'It's going well, and yes, Stefano and I will go back soon. We just want to visit Margrethe and Harriet before we do.'

'They'll be glad to see you, I'm sure. The reason I ask – besides wanting to hear how you are – is that we need Gwenllian. Obviously, we can't take her away from Stanthorpe before you're ready to have Zarifa with you again, but could you let me know when you reach that point?'

'It sounds as if you're making progress. Do you have someone in mind?' Edric's expression hardened and his eyes narrowed. He would dearly have liked to have that "someone" within grasping distance.

'We may have, but I can't say more, as I'm sure you'd realise. Tell Gwenllian from me that I'll call her soon, and to think about a trip to Argentina. In the meantime, look after yourselves.'

'Oh yes, you can trust us to do that! Same to you.' Edric smiled, rather grimly, before he ended the call.

Meng Jarrah came up behind Freddi to put her arms around her waist, kissing her on the nape of the neck. 'What was all that about?' she asked.

Freddi turned around and cupped Meng Jarrah's face with her hands, returning the kiss and caressing her bondmate's dark hair. They remained in their close embrace for several minutes, enjoying the sense of warmth, the deep satisfaction in each other's company – a small, quiet world of their own. Freddi eventually replied: 'That was Edric. He and Stefano have come to the conclusion that Marietta is the person most likely to have organised the Australian distribution of Mandrax...at least at the tournaments.'

Not having met Marietta, Meng Jarrah could hardly comment, so put her head to one side and said, 'What do *you* think?'

'Yes, it's possible. I should find out more about her sources of income and then consider what else we need to do.' Freddi paused. 'Even better, I could ask Smithson to do that while we concentrate on the investigation here. He can pass on anything interesting to Morag. I'm sure he'd enjoy doing that. After all, unless it relates directly to Rhianna's death, it's really something for the FSIU to follow up.'

Meng Jarrah agreed, so they decided their first task would be to make an appointment to speak with Felicity. Afterwards, they would examine the results of the automated DNA analysis of the samples obtained from the building by the river, which had been scheduled to complete overnight. They would also need to view and discuss the final outcome of the analysis of all the herbal and plant products collected during their first visit to the Yamada household. Meanwhile, the call to Smithson could wait until a more civilised hour. After all, it was now late evening in Australia.

*

The appointment having been made with Felicity for 13:00 that afternoon, both women returned to the forensics laboratory. As expected, the DNA analysis and other results were waiting for them.

'Nothing out of the ordinary so far,' said Meng Jarrah, scanning the DNA report and raising an eyebrow. 'Sundry members of the public, who, based on its bookings history, could have used the building for any of a variety of purposes; plus our shopkeeper; our recently deceased systems technologist...and...Madame Yamada. Ah...Guillermo is here as well. At least Felicity isn't.'

Freddi peered over her shoulder. 'Where was Guillermo's DNA?'

'Near the door leading out onto the balcony overhanging the river. We should take another look at that balcony. Do you want to do it now?'

'Yes, we'd better. What about Michiko's DNA?'

'All over the place, including on the balcony. In itself, it means nothing, of course, but I wonder if Guillermo took part in any of their 'events'? As far as we know, the shopkeeper didn't meet him, but Michiko may have had other customers who did. Or else she just enjoyed bringing Guillermo there, either to watch or to talk to him about her activities. I'd say that's something we'll never know.' Meng Jarrah turned away from the screen, shaking her head in disgust. The more she thought about it, the more Guillermo seemed to have been Michiko's pawn.

'Possibly not...unless Shela or Gwenllian can find something in her mind that we can use, assuming she doesn't refuse to allow them to be present when we interview her.'

'She may refuse to have Shela present, but Michiko won't know who Gwenllian is, so we'll simply have to wait and see. Do you think we should recommend she be placed under house arrest?'

'No,' said Freddi, looking up from reading the summary of the second report, 'I don't think we can justify doing that yet, particularly since it seems nothing containing amanita was found in any of the items we collected from her house... That is, *we* can't arrest her, and we can't recommend the peacekeepers here do so, unless Felicity can give us more definite evidence implicating her in Guillermo's death, or Michiko's DNA is found in the systems technologist's home. They were planning to re-examine the house, weren't they?'

'Yes, they were. After the recording was found on his back-up drive, the Coroner arranged for various samples to be taken. Odd that we haven't heard back from them about the results, come to think of it.'

'Not really, it hasn't been very long.'

'True, but I might call anyway to let her know what we've discovered, and at the same time ask about their progress.'

Meng Jarrah caught up with the Coroner on her way to an inquest. She had just enough time before the proceedings began to let them know that Michiko Yamada's DNA had not been found anywhere in the systems technologist's house, but Guillermo's was. Based on this new evidence, and on the initial samples from the balcony by the river, the Coroner agreed to re-open his case.

'Thank you,' said Meng Jarrah. 'We'll re-examine the balcony today and let you know the outcome. Also, we're about to interview someone else this afternoon who had a connection with Guillermo. Her name is Felicity, and she's Michiko Yamada's adopted daughter. She's currently in the care of the central precinct's medcentre and has met with a counsellor. She claims to have suffered some abuse at Michiko's hands, and judging by the marks on her body that we've seen, she's certainly suffered abuse at someone's hands. We have a recording of her counselling session that may be relevant and which we'll send to you, together with a copy of the interview later today. A Witness will be present to ensure you can use the information as evidence for the Judge, if you need to.'

'Good,' replied the Coroner, 'I will expect to hear from you then,' and she nodded briefly before ending the call.

Shortly afterwards, they made their way back to the building by the river, where it took relatively little time to examine the balcony. There were no apparent defects or signs of recent repair work to indicate a safety issue that may have led to Guillermo accidentally falling into the water. The balcony railing was slightly more than average waist height, which meant it seemed unlikely he could have leaned over too far and lost his balance, and there were no marks on the floor, nor on the railings or nearby walls, to indicate a struggle had taken place. Therefore, although the Coroner's report mentioned this general locality as being the probable entry point, to all appearances this did not seem to be where he entered the water, if he did so involuntarily.

Guillermo could, of course, have chosen to quietly climb over the railing and lower himself into the river. If his reason for being in the home of the senior systems technologist was to arrange for him to die of food poisoning, this may indeed have provided a motive for killing himself, if and when remorse struck. Although, if that was the case, why not simply either warn the man not to eat the dill pickles, remove them, or substitute the jar with a fresh one? On the other hand, perhaps he was there in the house only because they had become friends and it was because of this friendship that the systems technologist agreed to give Guillermo the extended lattice access.

After compiling their report and sending it to the Coroner, Freddi and Meng Jarrah both felt hungry enough to have their midsun meal. They chose a small, out-of-the-way café where conversation was less apt to be overheard. Keeping their voices low as they spoke, the two women both came to the conclusion that Guillermo had most likely committed suicide.

'All in all, when we add up the theft of the perfume and subsequent loss of his position; the entanglement with Michiko, which may well have cut across a genuine attachment to Felicity; the misery this entanglement caused Felicity; the possibility that he had begun to associate with the seamier side of Córdoban life; the unauthorised use of the lattice; and perhaps even the poisoning of the systems technologist as well, it isn't hard to see why Guillermo might have wanted to kill himself,' said Freddi, carefully scooping up the last remnants of a strawberry ice-cream.

'It's a great deal for any young man to cope with, unless he was already used to a life of 'unusual excitement', shall we say,' agreed Meng Jarrah, finishing off her own dessert of fresh mango with cream.

At this point, Freddi's comlink chimed. When she answered the call, a text message from Morag MacIain displayed itself: "Who has Rhianna's comlink?" Freddi showed the message to Meng Jarrah, a quizzical expression on her face.

'Interesting... Who *does* have it? Do you think she may have used it to record something important? If so, why didn't she send it to Morag?' From what they'd been told of Rhianna's life and behaviour, it would seem uncharacteristic of her not to follow-up immediately on something of relevance to a case she was investigating.

'Morag is presumably just being her usual meticulous self and making sure there are no loose ends,' replied Freddi. 'Still, it's a good question. I wonder why no one else thought of it. It's a bit too late now to call Edric, so I'll send him the same message, and with a little luck, we'll have an answer later today.'

With the message sent, it was time to meet Felicity at the medcentre. Shela rose from her warm place in the sun to lead the way. After her own midsun meal of mashed pumpkin with yoghurt, she was feeling content with life and ready for her role in the forthcoming interview.

Michiko, in the meantime, had one last arrangement to make – for the sake of her children's inheritance, should the Federation intervene in her private affairs to the extent that her fortune was threatened. A call to the Curator on a secure channel brought back memories of her bondmate's funeral...and the grief...

The Curator waited for Michiko to step away from the graveside before approaching the small family group. He bowed and murmured, 'Please accept my condolences. I knew Kenjiro Kakura well. If Madame has time, it would be an honour to speak with her, preferably alone.'

Michiko looked into the face of the oddest man she had ever seen. He was taller than average, stooped, narrow-shouldered, and had one blue eye, one brown. Almost bald, which was rare to see, his ears appeared to sit nearly at right angles to his head, while his nose was most definitely missing part of its tip. An accident? Why then had it not been regenerated? Altogether, she could only conclude that someone made a mistake when his parents applied for fertility rights! Still, that aside, his voice was remarkably pleasant: low and melodious.

'I will speak with you,' replied Michiko, putting an arm around the eldest of her children and telling them not to worry, but please, to go with Felicity and wait on the seat by the old stone sundial. They hesitated, then saw the reassurance they needed in her face, so obediently left her alone to speak with the strange man. The children sat close together, seeking comfort in each other's presence, while their mother listened with increasing agitation to what he was saying.

'What you are suggesting is offensive! My bondmate would never have involved himself in any undertaking that was less than honest!'

'Madame Yamada, I was only his humble servant, and am ready to be yours, if it pleases you. I was entrusted by Kenjiro Kakura with the collection should circumstances such as this very one arise. Your children... You *must* realise he was thinking of them. He wanted to ensure his children were well cared for. Surely you wish to do the same?'

'Naturally! But I have more than enough to care for them. There are no financial problems and we have a home fine enough for anyone. My bondmate did everything in his power to provide for us, under any circumstances. You...you are a monster! Go away and do not attempt to contact me again!'

The Curator bowed and left the cemetery.

Three weeks later, Michiko heard her security system announce the arrival of someone who said he was a former employee of Wyvern Meridian and that he had attended Kenjiro's funeral, yet would give no name. She studied the screen and at first could not make out who her visitor was. He had bowed his head and was wearing a somewhat outlandish hat, adorned with black ribbons. Curious, Michiko went to the door, opening it cautiously. The man raised his face to hers. It was the Curator again. Her first impulse was to slam the door shut, but he placed his hand against it and put his head to one side, as if to appeal her decision. Frowning, Michiko stepped back to allow him to come inside.

'Thank you. You are most kind. Please do not be offended at my insisting upon seeing you again. It was your bondmate's wish that we should meet, and his wishes are sacred to me.' He waited for Michiko to respond, patiently standing in the entrance hall and taking off his hat. The weather had turned to rain and the hat dripped water onto the floor, as did his black cloak. Michiko held out a hand to take his hat and offered to take the cloak as well. The Curator appeared to appreciate the gesture, for he smiled briefly before giving the items to her.

'Please, come with me,' said Michiko, and he followed her into a room leading off the entrance hall, where an open fire was burning. The Curator regarded the fire with satisfaction and moved closer, hands outstretched to the warmth. After a few moments, he turned around and surveyed the room.

'Ah,' he sighed. 'Everything is as I envisaged...entirely in keeping with my master's taste. The collection, you see, taught me to admire his discernment. You also are as beautiful as I expected, if you will excuse me for saying so.'

Michiko chose to ignore the compliment. 'Please, take a seat and I will order some tea, or something else if you prefer.'

'Tea would be greatly appreciated, thank you. White China tea, if you have it.'

'We do.' Michiko walked over to the mantelpiece, where she used a device unobtrusively built into the design of the woodwork to summon someone to bring the tea. Several minutes passed. The Curator amused himself by studying the ornate ceiling and humming tunelessly, while Michiko remained standing before the fire, staring into the flames. An elderly man appeared in the doorway, took their order, and before long, returned with a tray of tea things, as well as hot buttered scones and toasted muffins, arranged on antique Japanese plates of pale, translucent green. The Curator rubbed his hands together in anticipation and accepted a cup of tea, together with a generous helping of scones and muffins. Michiko sat down in one of the oak chairs and simply had some tea.

'What is it you want?' she said, after the elderly man left the room.

'I want to help you. The collection is quite safe and is kept in Korea, far from the prying eyes of the Federation. It is yours to do with as you will, whenever you choose to accept my assistance.'

'Tell me once more: how did my bondmate acquire these objects?'

'My master knew of potential private sales of artworks which had been obtained from various Federation sites. Over many years, he chose the very finest, negotiated an honest price and kept them as an investment for the future. Would you like to see some of them?' The Curator retrieved his comlink from one of the deep pockets in his trousers and nimbly scrolled through a number of images until he found one of particular interest. When Michiko nodded, he handed her the comlink, satisfied to hear her sudden intake of breath as she looked at the screen.

'May I?' she asked, raising her eyes to meet his.

'You may.' The Curator smiled, showing his uneven teeth.

Michiko studied the selection of artworks and historical artefacts, astonished at the extent of her bondmate's purchases. Handing back the comlink, she said, 'I hardly know what to say. These objects have been acquired through illegal means. It is my understanding that the Federation does not allow works of this type to be sold privately, and yet you now tell me my bondmate paid an honest price. How can that be?'

'My master paid an honest price to the person who acquired them. How that person obtained them was no business of his. Nevertheless, it must be admitted that he realised public display of his purchases was not an option, so to speak.' The Curator bit into another muffin and hastily used his linen serviette to wipe away the butter threatening to drip down his chin.

'May I inspect the collection itself?'

'You may. I will arrange for your trip to Korea and will also find suitable accommodation for you. How long would you like to stay?'

'My children will miss me if I am gone too long. I can only take three days in all. That should be enough, surely.'

'Quite sufficient. I will contact you shortly.' The Curator finished his tea and muffin, then stood, bowed, collected his hat and cloak from the entrance hall, bowed again and left.

Dawn was breaking when Gwenllian awoke, briefly wondering where she was, but then remembering. Next to her in the wide bed lay Robert, still asleep. His eyelids fluttered while he dreamt. Gwenllian hoped he was dreaming of her. She rolled onto her side, propping herself up on one elbow to watch and to listen to his soft breathing. Their growing love for each other had at last found physical expression in the most tender way imaginable. Surprisingly, neither of them had ever before slept with anyone else, so the experience was an exploration of a new world for both. Although Gwenllian's love for her brother, Owain, was deep and abiding, this man now held an altogether different meaning for her, as she did for him, compared to the others in his life he loved, and once loved, such as Rhianna.

A sunbeam crept through a chink in the wine-red curtains covering the wide casement windows at the front of the house. It landed on Robert's face, highlighting the smooth, sun-browned skin. Gwenllian kissed his cheek. He murmured and woke, his dark blue eyes searching for her. She smiled and kissed his lips.

'My little witch,' he whispered, reaching for her and drawing her warm body close to his. They lay together for almost an hour, simply enjoying the feeling of having another person in their arms, in perfect harmony of mind and body.

'Do you believe in Fate?' whispered Gwenllian. Somehow they needed to whisper on this quiet morning.

'No, but nonetheless, we were meant to meet and to be together. I feel it and so do you, my love.' Robert caressed the silken head resting on his shoulder. Gwenllian pressed her lips to the palm of his hand and then the inside of his wrist.

'Can you bear to let me leave you for a little while, to go to Argentina? I won't be gone for long, I promise.'

Robert didn't answer immediately. He could hardly bear for her to go. Now he had found her, he wanted her to stay. Gwenllian felt his sadness and gently stroked his cheek.

'Nothing will happen to me. I'll be perfectly safe with Freddi and Meng Jarrah, as well as Shela, to guard me.' Gwenllian laughed...a low, soft sound. 'Believe me, between the four of us, we could take on just about anyone!'

Robert held her even closer. 'Should I go with you? Then there would be five of us and we'd be invincible!' He grinned, feeling reassured.

'What a wonderful idea! I don't think Agathea would mind. After all, she goes globe trotting regularly, so could hardly begrudge you a trip to Argentina. We could have a holiday!' Gwenllian sat up, fully awake now. Robert laughed and pulled her back down.

'If we're to have a holiday, we should practice being in a holiday mood and do what most bondmates do when they have time to spare!'

Gwenllian giggled, and the sun was high in the sky before they finally went downstairs for their belated breakfast.

CHAPTER TWENTY-TWO

'Thank you for allowing us to watch the recording of your counselling session, Felicity. We appreciate your trust,' began Freddi, as they all seated themselves in a small, cheerfully furnished room in a quieter area of the medcentre. Felicity nodded, then lowered her head, taking no notice of either Shela or the Witness.

'Do you understand why we have a Witness present?'

'Yes,' replied Felicity in a low voice. The counsellor had already explained to her what the procedure would be during the interview.

'Good. We need to ask you some questions to clarify certain details. The first, which may seem a small point, is why don't you carry a comlink?'

'I have never carried one,' said Felicity, looking up, her eyes wide. 'Should I have?'

'Yes, it is the law, mainly for various safety reasons. I gather your parents didn't tell you?'

'No! Will I be in trouble?'

'Under the circumstances, not at all. However, we have obtained one for you and would appreciate your always having it with you and learning how to use it.' Freddi handed her a comlink, keyed to Felicity's Federation identity number and requiring only her thumbprint for activation. After she gingerly took it, holding the comlink as if it were too fragile to use, Freddi showed her what to do next.

'It won't break easily and you can't hurt it by doing anything wrong. Just relax and you'll soon find out. In the meantime, press your right thumb to the screen. Once you've done that and the comlink has recorded your voice pattern, no one else but you can activate it.'

Felicity studied the device and tentatively pressed her thumb onto its screen. The screen lit up and a welcome message displayed, giving her name and ID number. Felicity put a hand to her mouth, then smiled shyly. Freddi and Meng Jarrah both returned the smile.

'Would you like to try calling me?' suggested Meng Jarrah.

'How do I do that?' replied Felicity.

'Simply ask it, by saying 'Please contact Meng Jarrah'. Otherwise, you can use the key display to type in my name, or, if you knew it, my ID number. If there was more than one person in the world with my name, it would ask you for more details and show you the faces of the people who matched the description. You would then touch the screen when the right face was shown. If you didn't know what the person you wanted to speak to looked like, it would soon realise when you didn't select anyone and would ask for more information. It sounds a bit complicated, but in practice, works well.'

'Thank you, I will try,' said Felicity, then slowly selected and used the key display to enter Meng Jarrah's name. She laughed softly when Meng Jarrah's comlink chimed, and again when the call was answered. Shela padded over to Felicity and rubbed her head against her knees, purring.

'What do I do if someone calls me?' asked Felicity.

'Simply answer. Once you've used it, a voice recognition system begins to operate, which means the person making the call will receive a confirmation message letting them know that it really is you.'

'I see.' Felicity put the comlink into her pocket. 'Why do you think I was never given one?'

'I don't know,' answered Freddi, 'but at least you have one now and I'm sure it will be useful. Felicity, I need to ask you a more personal question. Please don't be embarrassed. We know from certain shop records that you are in the habit of buying fairly large quantities of Sensa. Did you use it when you were together with Guillermo, and do you know if Michiko used it?'

Felicity blushed, yet managed to meet Freddi's eyes while she answered. 'Yes, he wanted me to and I did not mind, knowing how pleasurable it is. As to my mother, I do not know directly, but I did buy some when she asked me to.'

Shela had returned to lie at Freddi's feet and raised her head from her paws to study Felicity for a few moments, then relaxed again. This topic of conversation was still a puzzle to her, so the cat decided to leave the understanding of it entirely to her companions, concentrating instead on simply collecting as many images as she could and relating them to the underlying emotions.

'I understand. Thank you,' said Freddi. 'Unfortunately, we have discovered you may have been overdosing yourself. Do you realise that using Sensa too often can cause a wound that hasn't completely healed to begin bleeding again?'

'Yes, I do now, but was unaware until recently that it could. I did not read the instructions closely enough. I will not use it again, ever.' Felicity frowned and looked away.

Freddi tried to speak as kindly as possible. 'That might be wise. We know how difficult it has been for you since your adoptive father died, and even more so since Michiko began to betray your trust in her. Still, there's something we don't understand. From what you told the counsellor, she mistreated you on several occasions and interfered in the relationship you developed with Guillermo...and yet you allowed her to mistreat you again, more than once.'

Felicity hesitated, then took a deep breath and said, 'My mother threatened to put me out of the house...to take my home away and leave me with nothing! What could I do?!' She hid her face with her hands and wept – heartbreaking, anguished sobs. Shela, burbling an inquiry, went over to her again, putting her paws on Felicity's knees and nudging her hands with her nose. Eventually Felicity noticed the cat, dried her eyes, and tentatively stroked Shela's head. Once the young woman had regained control, Shela curled up by her feet.

Freddi felt unhappy about having to keep probing, but Felicity was their best, and possibly only, adult witness to the relationship that formerly existed between Rhianna and Michiko. Rhianna's death needed to remain their priority. Nevertheless, Felicity's situation was appalling and required action.

'The Federation would never allow you to become homeless, Felicity. This medcentre, as well as the counsellor you have spoken with, would help you in whatever way necessary. We can explain the situation to them, if you like.'

Felicity sniffed and blew her nose. 'Yes, thank you, but I cannot remain in this city. I could not bear to live here in the knowledge that at any time I could meet Michiko in the streets. Even her children – my brothers and sister – how could I face them?'

Listening to Freddi's offer, Meng Jarrah had a sudden idea. She wondered if a complete change of scenery would actually be best. A chance for Felicity to leave her past behind and lead an entirely new life? This was not the time to introduce the idea, of course. Discussions would need to take place with several people first, but it seemed the ideal solution. 'Overhearing', Shela raised her head to stare at Meng Jarrah, then gave her decided approval to the plan and passed it on to Freddi. Freddi glanced at her bondmate, eyebrows raised, but for the time being said nothing. Instead, she replied to Felicity's question as best she could:

'I understand what you mean and will let the people here know how you feel. I'm sure something can be worked out. In the meantime, I'm sorry to have to do this, but we still need to ask you a few more questions. Can you manage?'

'Yes,' said Felicity, making an effort to appear calm, 'I can manage. What is it you wish to know?'

'We would like to know the nature of your relationship with Rhianna O'Connor and your impressions of her, particularly in terms of her friendship with Michiko.'

'Rhianna? She was a good person and showed me every respect and kindness. I am sorry she is dead and miss her friendship. We were not as close as she and my mother, yet still enjoyed pleasant times doing simple things, such as shopping and working in the garden. Rhianna liked to work outside, even though it was not necessary; the family employs gardeners, naturally.'

'What did Rhianna and Michiko do together?' prompted Freddi.

'Many different things. Sometimes they went shopping, sometimes just walking in the mountains. Other times, pleasures such as swimming in the river and dining in the local restaurants filled their afternoons and evenings. I also know they trained together. Rhianna had great expertise in the martial arts and Michiko was keen to learn more from her. We rarely went on outings as a family, but sometimes Rhianna suggested we all be together and travel into the countryside for a picnic. It seemed to me that she and my mother had a strong friendship and great mutual respect.'

'Do you know if Rhianna ever met Guillermo?'

'No, I do not believe so... I doubt she even knew of his existence. Michiko warned me not to tell Rhianna about him. I came to the conclusion she simply preferred to keep such matters private.'

'What about the problems you experienced with your mother. Did you ever tell Rhianna about them?'

'No! Never! I would have felt too ashamed.' Felicity shook her head and heaved a sigh. 'No, Rhianna did not know what happened between us.'

'Did it ever occur to you to ask her for help?'

'Yes, I considered it, but how could she have helped? I simply kept hoping my mother and I would return to our former relationship.'

'Yes, I can understand that. Thank you for being so honest with us.' Freddi had received confirmation from Shela that Felicity was telling the truth. Even though the cat was not fully able to comprehend the strange relationship existing between this wight and her mother, she could usually sense when lies were being told.

Freddi paused while she considered how best to avoid 'leading' Felicity, then said, 'Do you know how Rhianna died?'

'Michiko told me she died accidentally, during a martial arts tournament. Is that not the case?' Felicity had begun to wonder why all these questions about Rhianna were being asked.

'It is in a literal sense, but we're investigating further because we have found something in her body that shouldn't be there. Now, please think very carefully. Did you or your mother have any reason to open the jar of Sensa that Michiko bought for Rhianna during her last visit?'

'No, and I was not aware that Rhianna used Sensa! Did she really? How strange. I remember at one time her speaking about a strong preference against taking any form of stimulant or mood-enhancing substance, other than the usual beverages and the occasional glass of wine. During one of the few times we ever spoke about truly personal things, Rhianna told me about her own mother and how she was addicted to alcohol, eventually dying from its poisonous effects.'

Freddi paused again. Under the circumstances, it did seem strange. Still, Leihana's death was now many years ago and conceivably Rhianna no longer felt quite so strongly about the issue. It seemed to indicate, however, that she had trusted Michiko, or at least, could be influenced by her. Something for them to think about later... Meanwhile, the last and most difficult question: 'Felicity, did you kill Guillermo?'

Felicity's mouth opened in shock and her eyes widened in horror. 'How can you ask me such a question? I loved him! I know he betrayed me, but I loved him!' She stood up and moved quickly towards the door, but Meng Jarrah was faster and prevented her from leaving the room.

'I'm sorry, Felicity,' said Meng Jarrah, as she held her by the arm. 'We had to ask. It was our duty. Please, come back and sit down.'

Anger compressed Felicity's lips. Strangely enough, Meng Jarrah was glad to see anger. Far better anger than despair. She led the young woman back to her seat. Shela had also followed her to the door, although hadn't joined in to prevent Felicity from leaving, as she quite easily could have. Instead, she sat by the door and began cleaning herself.

'Good,' thought Meng Jarrah, glancing at Freddi, who was also watching Shela, a relieved expression on her face. Meanwhile, the Witness surveyed the scene impassively, unperturbed by anything she heard or saw. It was her profession to remain calm in all circumstances, taking in every word spoken and every gesture made, later to be called upon by the Judge or the Coroner should there be any doubt as to the veracity of the entries made by the interviewer, or the validity of the recording.

'We believe you, Felicity,' Freddi told her, once she was calmer. 'You said to the counsellor that you thought he'd been killed and hadn't died accidentally. Why is that?'

'I have no evidence either way. It is merely a feeling. What type of strange accident could have caused him to drown and for no one to report it immediately? Or for that matter, why would a young man, so handsome, so strong, and with family of his own, want to die, to kill himself? It makes no sense.'

'Perhaps not,' replied Freddi, wishing Felicity was not quite so unworldly and could give them more to go on. 'Well, I have no further questions – at least, not today. I gather arrangements have been made for you to remain here until more permanent accommodation can be provided. Are you content with this?' She could hardly ask her if she was 'happy' with the situation.

'I am safe here. That is enough for now.'

'What do you think?' Freddi asked Meng Jarrah as they left the medcentre, Shela happily pouncing on shadows as they walked.

'I think Rhianna and Michiko really did become friends, otherwise why would she have accepted, and then used, the Sensa? Surely as an agent she wouldn't normally relax her guard to such an extent? So, if we didn't have Shela here to confirm Felicity was telling the truth, I'd almost suspect her of having adulterated the stuff out of some sick form of jealousy. Just as well we have you, puddums.' Meng Jarrah stopped to give Shela a cuddle and received a joyous lick on the nose for her trouble.

Rubbing her nose, Meng Jarrah looked up, then hesitated before saying, 'Freddi, is there any chance Shela could be wrong?'

With an indignant 'Mmroww!' Shela sat down, put her front paws together and faced Meng Jarrah, eyes narrowed, tail twitching.

Freddi grimaced and turned to Shela, saying, 'I certainly hope not. I've come to rely on you, haven't I? Still, there's a lot going on here that's outside your normal experience. We're a strange lot sometimes.'

Shela confirmed the last statement, yet was still disgusted at being doubted and 'said' so loudly.

Raising an eyebrow, Freddi said, 'Shela, can you show us why Felicity was too ashamed to ask Rhianna for help?' They needed to know if she could understand the complexity of the emotions involved.

The cat kneaded the ground with her paws, laid her ears back, raised her hackles and hissed at something invisible. She then projected the awful image of Felicity being repeatedly struck by Michiko while she begged her not to, just as Felicity described to the counsellor. Even worse, Shela showed them how Michiko had used the handle of a whip to rape her daughter. It was horrible to virtually witness the pain and humiliation.

Suddenly realising this occasion was not in fact the one Felicity had described during her counselling session, Freddi abruptly told Shela to stop. This abuse was more recent, confirming their earlier suspicions... Suspicions based on the analysis of the items taken from the outbuilding, as well as the drop of blood found on the floor at the time Felicity gave them the jar of Sensa – the jar she claimed to have forgotten when they first searched Michiko's house.

Shela stood and wound herself around Freddi's legs, meowing and conveying her deep sadness at the fear she had sensed in the mind of the young wight during the interview. Fear of her own mother!

Freddi and Meng Jarrah looked at each other for a long moment before Meng Jarrah said, 'We need to ask the counsellor to speak with her about this and see if she can confirm when it happened...and we *must* help Felicity. Once Gwenllian has done everything that's needed here, she should take her back to Australia...to Margrethe. From what you've told me about her, someone like Margrethe, and even old Harriet, could surely help Felicity heal. She'd be safe there, particularly if Gwenllian was nearby and could visit regularly, at least to begin with. I have the impression Gwenllian will stay in Stanthorpe for longer than she first thought, so it might be possible.'

'Yes, I think you're right, and if Margrethe agrees, it's a good option. Gwenllian might even be able to help Felicity while she's here, as well as work out if that's really the best way forward. I'll speak with her later today. I want to talk to Edric and Smithson in any case, so may as well make one more call while I'm at it.' Freddi consulted her comlink. 'I can call Smithson in about an hour and a half without disrupting his beauty sleep. In the meantime, I'll send the recording of this interview to Morag and the Coroner, then enter all the latest evidence into the Judge. It's about time I did that. What do you want to do?'

When Meng Jarrah received a loud request from Shela, she said, 'Apparently I'm about to take a long walk by the river, where there'll be lots of interesting scents for Shela to enjoy, followed by a snack at a café, preferably one with lots of customers for her to investigate.' She chuckled, relieved to think of something so ordinary. 'I promise I'll bring you back something nice to have with your coffee. Call me when you're ready to have it.'

Freddi smiled, also relieved by the change of subject. They hugged each other before going their separate ways, Meng Jarrah with her shoulders hunched against the cold breeze blowing in from the river.

Smithson rolled onto his back and opened his eyes. A man of habit and cheerful disposition, he routinely got out of bed at 07:00 every morning. His bondmate, lying next to him in their cosy bedroom, still slept, unaware of the fond kiss placed lightly on her cheek, or the gentle touch when her dark hair was smoothed away from her forehead to make place for yet another kiss. Sitting on the edge of the bed, Smithson idly scratched his chest, where soft golden-red hair grew generously and, according to his bondmate, attractively. He yawned, stood up and quietly dressed. His comlink's message light flashed when he picked it up. As he read the message header, he smiled. Good, something from Freddi meant she probably wanted his help, but since it hadn't been marked as urgent, he decided to have breakfast first.

Twenty minutes passed before the peacekeeper returned the call. 'Good evening, Freddi,' he said when she answered.

'Good morning, Smithson! How are you?' replied Freddi, with a grin. She had thoroughly liked this man when they first met and then worked together in Stanthorpe.

'Fine, fine. How are you? And how is Meng Jarrah? I assume she's there with you?'

'Yes, we're both here, and we're both fine. Shela says hello, by the way,' and Shela did, putting her nose up to the small screen, blotting out everything else. Freddi gently pushed her aside. 'Smithson, we'd like you to find out everything you can about Marietta Ross' sources of additional income, what she does for a living, and what she spends her private income on. I've never checked because it didn't seem relevant, but it may be. Unfortunately, as I expect you know, you'll need to apply to the Speaker of the House of Representatives for permission to access all her personal records. It may take a while for them to respond, although as this is an inquiry into a suspicious death, I'd hope a little cooperation on their part might be forthcoming.'

Smithson nodded, pleased at the chance to obtain further information about Marietta. He'd been curious about her role in this case and felt in his bones there was more to her than appearances initially suggested. He hadn't forgotten her behaviour when at school here in Stanthorpe, either.

Before he could answer further, Freddi added, 'If you meet any obstruction from the Speaker's Secretary when you make the request, or if they take too long to respond, let them know the FSIU are interested, and then if you need to, contact the FSIU Coordinator, Morag MacIain.'

Smithson's bright blue eyes widened a fraction. The FSIU, eh? This was becoming even more interesting! 'I hope you're about to tell me why they're involved. Don't leave me in suspense, Freddi.' Smithson grinned.

Freddi laughed. 'No, I won't, don't worry. I've left the best bit until last. I'd like you to contact Morag MacIain anyway, once you've found what there is to find. It's all to do with another complication associated with Rhianna's death. It turns out she was an undercover agent for the FSIU, reporting directly to Morag.'

Smithson boggled and held one hand to his mouth, then recovered and said, 'She was?! Truly? Hmm...well, well. Apparently this case has even more to it than we imagined. And so where does Marietta fit in...other than being there when Rhianna died?'

'One of the things Rhianna investigated was the distribution of a drug called Mandrax, mainly at their martial arts tournaments in Australia, as well as here in Argentina. Edric and Stefano have pinpointed Marietta as being the best candidate for the Australian side of things. If so, she's covered her tracks well because Rhianna was unable to discover very much at all, which is why we want financial information. Marietta lives well, and evidently has some source of private income. If you find legitimate sources, it makes it less likely she's the one. If not, we have more excuse to take further measures. Or at least, the FSIU will have. I'm trying to concentrate on Rhianna and not get sidetracked by these other issues unless they have a direct bearing on her death.'

'Mandrax? Haven't come across that one before. It's an old drug, isn't it?'

'Yes, it is, I gather, and a nasty one. Rhianna was only able to find definite evidence that it's being distributed at the tournaments here in Argentina, but not who's responsible. There *is* at least one company we know of with the capacity to make and supply it, but so far nothing has been found to implicate them.' Freddi deliberated as to whether to tell Smithson about Wyvern Meridian's potential involvement, and decided against it. They could, after all, be entirely innocent.

Smithson was curious, but sure that if Freddi wanted him to know more, she would tell him in her own good time. 'Right, I'll get onto it today. This Morag MacIain, how well do you know her? Is she easy to get along with?'

'Meng Jarrah, Gwenllian and I know her quite well. We all worked together on a case a few years back. She's excellent. I'm sure you'll like her, and she'll be grateful for anything you can come up with. I'll let her know to expect to hear from you some time soon.'

After chatting for a few minutes about general happenings in Stanthorpe and in Argentina, they each went on to their next task: Smithson to send in his request to Parliament and Freddi to make her call to Edric.

Sunlight streamed in through the kitchen windows as Gwenllian and Robert sat facing each other, sipping their coffee and finding it impossible to stop smiling. Robert reached out to place his hand on the table, palm upwards, and Gwenllian immediately took it in hers.

Agathea had already been down for breakfast. There was a note on the household security system screen to say she was out walking in the forest and would be back for their midsun meal. After their meal, they were planning to complete the fountain by turning on the water pump. To Gwenllian and Robert, this seemed a fitting celebration of their night together – although Agathea did not yet know, since they had gone to bed later than her. However, they were both sure she would be delighted by this new stage in their relationship, based on the not-so-subtle encouragement her words and looks had given them of late.

The whole house and its surrounds had an air of profound peace, if not silence. Outside, magpies were strutting around pecking at the ground, hunting for worms and other insects, while intermittently warbling their approval of the bright morning. A pair of brightly coloured rainbow lorikeets sat in a tree nearby, busily grooming each other and generally enjoying the warmth. Cheeky and entertaining little birds, they were hard to resist. Two years ago, despite there being plenty for them to eat in the forest, Robert gave in to their demands by providing them with food, yet for once, they weren't loudly demanding to be fed. This was probably just as well, for when they chose to be more raucous, their noise was almost deafening!

At this point, Edric wandered in from the garden, where he had been working on the plumbing for the fountain since early morning. Neither Robert nor Gwenllian were aware of him as he halted, watching, entranced by the extraordinary beauty of these two people and touched by their obvious affection for each other. Edric could not help but experience a profound sense of his own loss, but managed to overcome it, feeling instead genuine pleasure at the good fortune of his two friends. Experiencing an urge to capture the scene, he took his comlink from his pocket and then announced his presence.

'Good morning! You've finally made a decision, I see. I'm glad, truly glad.' He grinned when they both turned around, blushing. 'Look,' Edric added, sending the image he had captured to the screen on the wall, located near the double doors leading out into the garden. 'Quite a work of art, if I say so myself.'

The picture was indeed lovely, capturing the emotion on the faces of its subjects, without seeming to intrude. Gwenllian considered it, leaning her elbows on the table, chin resting in one hand. Strangely enough, neither her brother nor her work colleagues had ever taken portraits of her. The only ones she possessed were from her childhood, taken by her parents, and the occasional impromptu snapshot from her travels when a companion had insisted. Having once been deeply concerned with appearance, and at that time going to great lengths to look distinctive, she had nevertheless been uninterested in any record. After all, there were plenty of mirrors in the world...

Robert was also intrigued, but mainly by Gwenllian. He knew his own physical appearance was striking, yet thought nothing of it, being more concerned with his family, his home and his work. Nevertheless, it had to be admitted that together, he and Gwenllian were certainly a pair who would stand out anywhere. Turning to Edric, he said, 'You've a good eye for composition and lighting. May we keep this? I think my mother would like it too...and thanks. It's a wonderful gift for a wonderful day. Perhaps you should take some shots of the fountain once we have it working.'

Edric opened his mouth to say something just as his comlink chimed an incoming call. 'Excuse me,' he said instead, and went into the next room to answer. 'Hi Freddi. What can I do for you?'

'Did you get my message?'

'No, I don't think so. Let me check, in case I didn't notice. I've been working in the greenhouse since early this morning and must admit that for once I just shoved my comlink into my pocket and didn't check to see if anything had arrived. Also, the birds around here are sometimes loud enough to drown out its ring tones. I must turn up the volume. Anyway, I have it now... Rhianna's comlink? Yes, it was in the apartment in Brisbane. Why?'

'Did you try to use it?' asked Freddi.

'No. I'm not even sure I can. Rhianna never mentioned setting it for my access.'

'I see. There may be something on it we could use. There might not be, but we've only just realised, fairly late in the day, that there could be.'

Edric frowned. Why hadn't *he* thought of this? Obviously, because there were too many other things to deal with. 'Is it urgent?' he asked.

'Hard to say... May we have your permission for the Brisbane Peacekeepers to enter the apartment and take it away to be examined?'

'Yes, of course.' He knew she was just being polite, though he still appreciated it. During an inquiry into a suspicious death, they had every right to enter at any time and examine whatever they wanted.

'Are you able to let me know what you find, if anything?'

'It depends upon what we find...if anything...and it won't be us who'll look at it; it'll be the FSIU, although they'll tell us once they've finished. You'll eventually have it back, so if there's anything personal that might interest you, I'll let you know. Would you like them to set the comlink for your access before it's returned?' Freddi understood the comlink might have sentimental, if no intrinsic, value.

'Thanks, yes, I would. I might use it rather than my own, come to think of it. It was such a personal item of Rhianna's. However, if you don't mind, I came in for morning coffee and I'm getting desperate. I've earned a break, with all the work I've done. If you like, I'll send you a picture of the finished product once the fountain's working.' Edric tried not to think about what might be on Rhianna's comlink. It was pointless. He'd know soon enough and didn't want to spoil the mood of the day.

'Thank you. I'd like to see the fountain and so would Meng Jarrah, I'm sure. Now, I need to speak with Gwenllian. Is she there?'

'Yes, right here. I'll get her for you.' Edric transferred the call to Gwenllian's comlink, waving his own to let her know to expect it. 'Freddi,' he told her.

Gwenllian hastily swallowed the last mouthful of her second cup of coffee and picked up the call. Robert raised an eyebrow, stood and stretched, then joined Edric to discuss progress with the plumbing works while he made his coffee and raided the kitchen cupboards for something to have with it. Finding a container of chocolate biscuits, Edric took four, after which both he and Robert went outside to enjoy the sunshine, leaving Gwenllian to her call.

*

Later that day, after speaking with Freddi, Gwenllian found Margrethe in her garden, gathering daffodils and enjoying the bright, calm, sunlit afternoon. 'Hello!' she called out, waving to her.

Margrethe unbent, adjusted the bunch of flowers and returned the greeting. 'Gwenllian, dear... How lovely to see you again. What brings you out on this wonderful day?'

'I couldn't resist the walk, and seeing you and your garden in person was much better than simply making a call. I'd like to speak with you about something. May we sit down?'

'Of course, but if you don't mind, I'll just put these daffies in water first. I can't relax if I know they're in need of a drink. Do you want to wait here, or come inside with me?'

'I'll come inside. Where's Harriet today? I can't sense her.' Gwenllian wasn't overly concerned about the cat's absence because if there had been something wrong, Margrethe would hardly be in such a good mood.

'Ah, yes, of course. You'd know my old darling wasn't around. She's having her annual visit to the animal healer for a thorough check-up and to have her teeth cleaned. I don't travel too well these days, so a friend takes her in for me and brings her back once everything's been done that needs doing. I'm sure it will all be fine, although she's no longer young.'

Gwenllian touched Margrethe on the arm and felt the assurance the elderly woman had in every fibre of her being: an acceptance of life's difficulties, as well as its inevitabilities.

'There,' said Margrethe, when she had finished arranging the flowers in a green glass vase. 'Aren't they beautiful!' Indeed they were. White, fancy, multilayered varieties were mixed with palest pink trumpets surrounded by cream petals, together with others in their traditional bright yellow. Some of them even had a delicious scent. 'Now, what is it you wanted to talk to me about? We can go back outside and sit under the apple tree.'

As they sat on the garden seat under branches of the old tree, Gwenllian began by saying, 'Freddi called this morning to ask me to speak with you about someone she and Meng Jarrah have met, and who they think could do with your help – and Harriet's. They wanted my opinion, and I agreed that you might both be perfect for the job. Also, it seems I'm needed in Argentina to help them interview someone in relation to Rhianna's death. At the same time, I can meet with this young woman and find out more about her situation.'

'Who is she, and what has happened to her?'

'Her name is Felicity, she's twenty-three years old, and is the adopted daughter of Michiko Yamada, the former bondmate of Kenjiro Kakura. Have you heard of either of them?' Margrethe shook her head. 'I think I have a great deal to tell you, then.'

Gwenllian related how Rhianna O'Connor first met Kenjiro Kakura while they were both studying at university in Seoul, and how she became and then remained his lover until 2450, despite his existing bond with Michiko Yamada, and later, the birth of his children. Gwenllian went on to describe how Rhianna was recruited in 2447 by the former FSIU Coordinator, Rohan Maerz, to spy on Kakura. This was after having been informed of his criminal activities whilst in his role as director of the private conglomerate, Wyvern Meridian.

Margrethe nodded and said, 'That explains many things. What happened next?'

'Kakura died in 2451. I met Morag MacIain, the current FSIU Coordinator, during the investigation into a series of crimes for which he was a suspect.' Gwenllian decided it wasn't relevant to mention having herself been under suspicion at the time. No need to distract from the main story. 'Freddi and Meng Jarrah also met each other, as well as Morag, during that time. It's how we all came to know one another. Anyway, Rohan Maerz died, and after Morag took over his role, she contacted Rhianna and renegotiated her undercover work, with the aim of keeping a watching brief on Michiko Yamada...for various reasons. We think Michiko may have been responsible for Rhianna's death, either accidentally or intentionally.' Gwenllian privately thought it unlikely the death could have been accidental, yet for the time being was prepared to keep an open mind.

'I see.' Margrethe remembered Rhianna's letters and now understood why the name of the man she was so absorbed with had never been mentioned. 'Do you think this Michiko Yamada found out that Rhianna and Kakura were lovers?'

'Yes, we do. Rhianna was wearing a pair of ear circlets when she was buried, which were a gift from Edric. He had them made to match a necklet she was very fond of, but didn't know it was given to her by Kakura, or that it was originally made by Michiko. She's a well-known and highly talented designer of jewellery and ceremonial silverware, but the necklet, to her knowledge, was destined for Kakura's grandmother. Without warning, it turns up in the ownership of a beautiful young woman who was once a student at the same university Kakura attended. She'd have to be unusually naive not to jump to the obvious conclusion. Unfortunately, though, there are several other possible reasons why Michiko may have chosen to kill Rhianna. One of them relates to why I'm here today, other than to let you know what we've discovered so far. It's an ugly story. I'm sorry.'

'I've heard many ugly stories in my lifetime, my dear. Don't think you need to spare me.'

Gwenllian was sure this was true. The details of Rhianna's life with her mother, Leihana, were ugly enough. 'Alright, I won't,' she said, and went on to tell Margrethe everything Freddi had told her about Felicity and the abuse she had suffered at the hands of her adoptive mother. She told Margrethe about the death of Felicity's first love, Guillermo, and how the inquiry into his death was now re-opened due to the evidence Freddi and Meng Jarrah had collected during their time in Argentina.

'I must admit to being shocked after all, Gwenllian. This is worse than anything I have heard of in this small town, or in the news broadcasts. How do you think we can help this poor young woman?' When Margrethe saw the answer in Gwenllian's face and mind, she immediately said, 'This house is small, yet comfortable. I have no one to look after other than Harriet. A young person would be very welcome, if you believe she would be happy here.'

Gwenllian smiled gently and took Margrethe's hand as they sat together while the shadows began to lengthen and the day drew to a close. They communicated directly, without words, about Rhianna, Felicity...and Robert...until they heard the gate open, and there was Margrethe's friend with Harriet. He waved to them, then removed Harriet's leash, allowing the old cat to waddle over to her companion, purring loudly at being home again and rubbing her head against Margrethe's knee.

'Thank you, John. I appreciate your help, as always. Was everything all right?' Margrethe stroked Harriet's head and had her hand thoroughly licked in return.

'She's fine. Nothing at all wrong other than old age, although one tooth had to come out. Luckily it's at the back, which means she won't have a gap-toothed smile!' John grinned and looked fondly at Harriet, who snuffled and wheezed before getting up and winding herself around his legs, tail in the air.

'Do you want to come in for a cup of tea and a scone? I baked some this morning after you went.'

'No, I won't come in, thanks all the same. I'd better get going... I'm expected at home. I'll see you tomorrow, so if those scones are still on offer, I'll have some then. Is 10:00 still okay for me to cut up that wood for you?'

'Yes, it is, thank you. Have a good evening, won't you, and say hello to Jennifer for me.'

'I will. Goodbye now.' John turned and walked back to his landjet, waved once and then was gone.

'He's such a nice young man,' remarked Margrethe, 'and his daughter, Jennifer, is delightful. She sometimes helps with the heavier gardening.'

Gwenllian laughed. John appeared to be at least sixty, but compared to Margrethe, she supposed he was a "young man".

'Now, on that note, would *you* like some tea and scones before you go home to your Robert?'

'Yes, I'd love some, thanks,' Gwenllian replied, and they went into the house, just as the sun began to set and the birds commenced their evening chorus.

CHAPTER TWENTY-THREE

The airjet landed at Seoul International Airport after a longer than usual flight from Argentina due to turbulent weather and an engine fault, a rare event which Michiko regarded as a personal insult. As a result, her mood was anything other than serene when she met the Curator in an obscure hotel on the outskirts of the city. Quickly discerning the situation, he insisted they have a quiet meal, a glass of fine wine, and a brief walk along the river before discussing the reason for her visit.

Feeling calmer, Michiko turned to him and said, 'I believe I have made a grave mistake, even several. I will quite likely pay the price of these mistakes, and therefore want you to understand that if I can no longer communicate with you directly, you are to continue to care for the collection until my eldest son reaches the age of twenty, at which time, you must contact him and inform him of his inheritance.'

The Curator murmured assent and inclined his head, waiting for more; there would be more.

'Neither he nor my other children may want any part of it. They know nothing of their father's activities, other than what is on public record. If my own mistakes become a matter of public record as well, they will be ashamed of me, although I sincerely hope the shame will not outweigh their love.' Michiko faltered, then, with considerable effort, steadied herself. 'I find I cannot tell you what I have done... I regret it all deeply. However, I will continue to honour my bondmate's wishes and retain the collection for our children, should they desire to keep it.'

'What do you wish done if they refuse?' The Curator was genuinely curious; Michiko's attitude was unexpected.

'I want you to return it all to its rightful owners. It may take a long time and must be done without any suspicion falling on you, Kenjiro or myself. I have transferred a fee to your account, but do not be concerned that it might appear suspicious. I have at least learned that much. The fee is a generous donation towards your museum in Austria and includes an amount for your services as an historian investigating the provenance of my most valuable artwork, currently kept in the vault at my home in Córdoba. I have recently had reason to be troubled as to its authenticity and wish to have it verified. A full description will reach you very soon and you will visit me in Córdoba the day after my return to view the actual item.

You will find that the work is indeed authentic, with no taint of illegality concerning the manner in which it was acquired. Is all this satisfactory?'

'Yes, Madame, it is.' The Curator bowed and the two continued walking until they reached the hotel, where Michiko wished him good night then went to her room. The following morning, her return to Argentina went unremarked, as did the Curator's visit the next day. This was fortunate for them both because that same afternoon, Gwenllian and Robert arrived in Córdoba.

In Stanthorpe, Zarifa 'heard' the practitioner's verdict: theoretically, Edric was now cured of his allergy and should reintroduce himself to, firstly, one cat, and then if no reaction occurred within forty-eight hours, another. Zarifa immediately leapt from the chair where she was taking a well-earned snooze after a long, early morning walk along the river with Stefano and Peri. She projected an urgent request to be allowed outside without her leash, then rushed out the door when a startled Stefano did exactly as asked, before realising he probably shouldn't have and running outside after her. Edric was already there, crouched outside the medcentre, ready to embrace Zarifa as she bounded across the trafficway towards him. To Stefano's enormous relief, he saw Edric gather her into his arms, where she immediately proceeded to rub her face against his, purring loudly. Edric laughed with pleasure, while the practitioner smiled in satisfaction – ready with an antidote, however, should it be required. Also, in Gwenllian's absence, Nyneve stood by to assist with security.

Stefano laughed too, particularly when Zarifa attempted to climb onto Edric's shoulder, nearly knocking him over. Standing up with some difficulty, and clasping Zarifa with both hands to prevent her slipping, Edric grinned at his friend, who patted him on his free shoulder, saying, 'It's great to see you both together again! Peri sends her regards. I can't invite you over to see her, can I? Still one cat at a time, I suppose.'

'Yes, but I guess we shouldn't be out here with Zarifa and no leash. Can you fetch it while I wait?' Zarifa, understanding, nuzzled Edric's ear, tickling him with her whiskers. He shifted one hand to stroke her, hoping the next forty-eight hours would be uneventful as far as his medical condition was concerned.

Stefano returned with the leash. 'Now what?' he said. 'Do we just wait to see what happens?'

'That's right. I'll be staying at the medcentre for the next two days, with Zarifa, and if I don't react, you can bring Peri to see us. If I do react, the treatment will have to begin again, but with Robert and Gwenllian gone, Nyneve here has offered to have me stay with her if that happens. You two haven't met, have you?'

'No, we haven't,' replied Nyneve, stepping forward, with hand outstretched to take Stefano's in a firm grip. He smiled at her, instantly liking the peacekeeper – or was it Zarifa who liked her and was passing on the feeling? Stefano was often unsure whose emotions he was experiencing these days, yet felt certain that, with time, the situation would sort itself out. Zarifa chirruped, immediately reassuring him, her sea-green eyes glinting in the sunlight.

'I'm sorry to have to interrupt,' said the practitioner. 'I need to attend to other patients. So Edric, would you mind coming back inside now? I know you'd prefer to stay out here, but we can't take any chances.'

Sighing, Edric obediently followed – with Stefano not far behind once he'd said goodbye to Nyneve and changed into clothing provided by the medcentre to ensure he was reasonably free of cat hair. They spent the next few hours together, planning what they would do on their return to Brisbane and discussing how best to continue their martial arts training. At first, they could see no solution to their dilemma, until Stefano remembered Nyneve.

'What about the peacekeepers?' he said, his voice eager. 'They have to be trained. Wouldn't they need to be prepared to be struck occasionally? Their training would have to be realistic.'

'True,' said Edric, 'but I'm sure they'd wear protective gear. I doubt if they'd be allowed to train without it. Still, the peacekeepers might train harder than most clubs. Should we ask her? Nyneve, I mean.'

'Why not...' Stefano fished his comlink from his pocket and found her just finishing work for the day and on her way home. 'Hi, Nyneve,' he said, turning up the volume on the comlink so Edric could listen to the conversation. 'We have a question for you, if you have time?' Nyneve agreed, still walking. 'You may already know,' continued Stefano, 'that Edric and I used to take part in the full contact tournaments in Brisbane.' He winced as he said this, feeling odd speaking so openly with a peacekeeper about their illegal activities. Still, nothing risked, nothing gained.

'Yes,' replied Nyneve dryly, with a lopsided half-grimace, half-smile. 'We're assuming you won't be organising any more in the future.'

'No,' said Stefano, blushing, 'but we have a problem. Without opportunities for full contact, or some other form of more advanced training, we won't be able to maintain our skill levels. I myself no longer participated in the tournaments as a contestant because I have enhanced, artificial vision, but Edric has no one of his standard in the country to even spar with. *I* could take on people in a higher weight division and quite likely make do, but for him, it's not good.'

'And how do you think *I* could help?' asked Nyneve, keeping her tone neutral.

'We were wondering how peacekeepers got *their* training. Maybe we could become instructors, or at least useful assistants?' Stefano waited while Nyneve considered what to say. She stopped walking and took a seat by the river, staring at the water.

'I see. Look, it's a hard one, because we have our own instructors already, as you'd realise, but let me put the proposition to the unit headquarters in Brisbane and I'll let you know what they say. It depends upon how happy they are with the current instructors, and whether they need any more. You'll also have to understand that they won't be overly happy at your involvement with the tournaments, although they couldn't argue with your skills, I'm sure. If they do agree, you'd have to undergo testing, and then if you pass, training in our own techniques. Would you want to be employed, or were you thinking of volunteering? It might make a difference if you were prepared to volunteer.'

Stefano glanced at Edric, who nodded. 'We'd volunteer,' Stefano said eagerly. 'If Edric's still okay in four days time, we're going back to Brisbane. Then, if they're interested, we could make an appointment to show what we're capable of, as well as discuss *our* training techniques versus yours. What do you think?'

Nyneve was impressed by his enthusiasm and willingness to adapt. 'Sounds good,' she replied. 'I'll get back to you when I have an answer. In the meantime, take care of yourselves and don't hesitate to call if anything happens to worry you. I'm not far away if you need me, though I expect the cats will make sure you're both safe – assuming, of course, that Zarifa can stay with Edric.'

'Thanks, Nyneve, you're a gem!' Stefano blew her a kiss, then immediately felt like an idiot, blushed, and closed the connection.

'She's at least ten years older than you, Stefano,' said Edric. 'Still, I don't suppose that matters.'

'Don't be silly. I was only fooling around. You know me, I can't resist.' Stefano grinned and shoved Edric's shoulder.

'Well, as long as *she* understands. You're quite an attractive young man, I'm told. If I look hard enough, I can just manage to see it.' Edric laughed as his friend pretended to be offended. 'Seriously, though, I hope the peacekeepers take up our offer. The more I think about it, the more I like the idea. Their approach could be very different from ours, and they may even teach us something we don't already know. Let's hope so.'

'I've heard they use aikido in combination with kung fu, which is interesting, to say the least.'

Edric tried to visualise how the two disciplines could complement each other, and saw no reason why they wouldn't if the practitioners were skilled enough, which the peacekeepers no doubt needed to be. Not that Australia had a great deal of violent crime, but they did need to be prepared at all times to defend themselves and the public.

All this talk of martial arts worried Zarifa. After all, with her around, what was there to defend themselves against? She meowed and sent Edric a query. He immediately reassured the cat, then chortled when both he and Stefano simultaneously bent over to pat her. Zarifa rolled onto her back to present her sand-coloured stomach, purring happily while the two played with her for some time, simply enjoying each other's company. Stefano eventually remembered that Peri was waiting for him and took his leave, waving to them as they watched from the entranceway of the medcentre.

'Come on, Zarifa,' said Edric, 'let's see what they're having for their evening meal here, and then we'll call Agathea to see how she is and whether she's heard from Robert. They should've settled into their hotel by now.'

Zarifa agreed, before heading off to the medcentre dining room, where she 'listened' while Edric read the dining room menu. Her preference was for the potato dumplings with cauliflower and cheese sauce, which she demolished with relish, while Edric ate more sedately, also enjoying his meal.

Being an expert in dealing with bureaucracy, Smithson managed to charm the Secretary to the Speaker of the House of Representatives to such an extent that she actually simpered, despite generally having a rather sour outlook on life.

'Murder, if this is murder, is a rare occurrence in our land, thank goodness,' she said, smoothing her hair, even though it didn't require it, being short and cut in a severe style. 'Anything you can do to solve this case will be greatly appreciated by us all, I'm sure. I'll make it a priority to organise for the Speaker to release the records you require by tomorrow. I happen to know she has a free hour this afternoon and will pass on your request then. Will that be soon enough for you?' She smiled, revealing her sudden need for Smithson's approval.

'Thank you kindly,' he said, with a grin. 'I'm delighted to be dealing with someone as efficient as you. It's been a real pleasure talking today. Perhaps we can catch up again some time, although preferably not over something as serious as this. Anyway, must move, so you have a great day, won't you.'

'I will. You too,' the woman replied, feeling more cheerful than she had all week.

When the promised information arrived promptly the next day, Smithson eagerly pored over it. It appeared that Marietta worked her compulsory twenty-five-hour week as an architect for the Department of Residential and Commercial Infrastructure, and had done for many years, since graduating from Melbourne University in 2437. In her spare time, she freelanced as an interior designer and photographer, highly complementary roles. An examination of her income showed a substantial return from her freelance work that steadily increased over the years. 'A talented young woman,' Smithson said to himself, then read on, this time to see how her expenditure matched her income.

A large proportion of her income was spent on improvements to her home, her wardrobe, travel, the equipment used in her freelance work, and beauty treatment. Did she really need it, he wondered, remembering how attractive Marietta had been and, based on the images now on his screen, still was. Other major expenditures were for wine, fees for the various martial arts clubs she competed with – legitimately, both in Australia and overseas – and, surprisingly, transfers to her parents in France. Smithson quickly checked the family background. They had migrated to Australia in 2428, initially to Sydney, before moving to Stanthorpe when her father accepted a position as the manager of the regional power plant and her mother the management of the largest local winery. Not long after Marietta graduated from university, both parents returned to France, where a severe landjet accident left them both incapable of following their usual occupations. Their everyday needs were well taken care of by the Federation, but luxury items required private income, hence the transfers. Marietta's travel records also showed regular trips to France... 'Well, well,' thought Smithson, 'by all appearances, she's at least a good daughter.'

After taking into account all Marietta's substantial income and expenditure, she was nevertheless frequently left with a monthly debit, which was consistently repaid within the required time limit when one of her private customers made a transfer to her account. 'Ah ha!' Smithson said aloud. 'Fairly unusual, but not unheard of. If she likes spending so much, all the more reason to sell a few drugs. How would it be done, I wonder?'

He had no means of finding out who attended the martial arts tournaments in Brisbane other than to demand Ruth Baillieu hand over her list of invitees – if the Brisbane Peacekeepers hadn't already managed to prise the information from her. Smithson decided to check immediately and was pleased to learn that Ruth had cooperated fully and provided the BPF with the names, although they had preferred to simply close down the tournaments rather than prosecute such a large number of people. 'Sensible,' murmured Smithson, as he closed the connection and began comparing Ruth's list with the individuals who had paid Marietta for, ostensibly, her professional services.

The comparison gave him twenty names in common, all regular customers for the past one and a half to three years. Naturally, if she was distributing Mandrax, her circle of customers might well extend beyond the tournaments – most likely amongst those with whom she came into contact in Melbourne. Therefore, if her additional paying clients from

Melbourne were included, this gave a total of twenty-eight individuals who were worth following up.

Everyone on this list held a highly skilled position and appeared to have sufficient private means to pay well for Marietta's services. Fourteen of them lived in Melbourne and seven were from Brisbane, while the remainder came from various places in Australia, including one from Stanthorpe. Well, he could at least interview *him*. Interviewing the others would require cooperation from other peacekeeping forces. Smithson considered who best to ask for assistance... Morag MacIain, without doubt. He grinned. This should be interesting! Checking his comlink for her whereabouts, on the assumption she would allow this information to be known, Smithson then remembered it was still night-time in Switzerland, so left a message.

Almost three hours later, he was pleasantly surprised to receive a call from the FSIU Coordinator. So soon! He was even more pleasantly surprised to notice that, like him, she was a redhead with a sprinkling of freckles across her nose. 'And a beautiful one at that,' thought Smithson, also noticing how green her eyes were.

'Good work, Smithson,' said Morag, after he'd given her his information. Smiling, she added, 'Freddi mentioned you were efficient. I can suggest someone in Melbourne who could help with the interviews. His name is Chiu Liow Jones. You may have heard of him? He also happens to be Freddi's half-brother and my bondmate. I'm sure you'll get along very well.'

Smithson laughed, loudly. He had indeed heard of Chiu Liow Jones, yet the connection with Morag MacIain and Freddi had somehow been kept private. Morag laughed with him, and said, 'Call in about half an hour. I'll have a quick chat with him first so he has some background to the case. He can follow up the rest with you and with Freddi as he needs to...and don't worry, he won't try to take over; he'll just help with the interviews, unless there's anything else you want from him.'

'Good, and thank you. I can liaise with Brisbane regarding the ones who live there, but what about the remainder? Can you arrange for someone to deal with them as well?'

'I'm sure I can, with Chiu's help. He has lots of contacts all over the place. I'll let you know once I've organised something. Bye for now,' and Morag left to have her breakfast.

Feeling thoroughly pleased with this result, Smithson called his BPF colleagues again. They were intrigued to learn of the FSIU involvement in the case and of the likelihood that Mandrax was being distributed in Australia, or anywhere else for that matter, and promised to complete the seven interviews as soon as possible.

*

The half hour now having passed, Smithson called Chiu Liow Jones, feeling more than a little curious about the man. He was amused to find him still in a bath gown, towelling his hair dry. When Peacekeeper Jones finished drying his hair, rather than combing it, he simply ran a hand through it, giving him an unruly appearance, which contrasted oddly with his formal manner of speaking. Smithson was also somewhat startled by his having the same unusual golden eyes as Freddi, although his skin was nowhere near as dark.

'Good afternoon, Peacekeeper Smithson. Morag has informed me that you require my assistance. I am more than happy to offer it. I understand there are at least fourteen interviews to conduct? May I suggest we keep in close contact as we progress, since some of the people on your list could lead us to others, or give us evidence we can use in our other interviews? May I also assume you will act as the go-between and be the person who reports back to Morag?'

'You can, Peacekeeper Jones, and thank you. I've already spoken with Brisbane, and they're happy to cooperate. I've only one person to interview here in Stanthorpe, and you probably know that Coordinator MacIain needs to organise someone to interview the other six. They're spread out all over the place, so it might take a while. Thank goodness we have comlinks to track them!'

'Yes indeed, Peacekeeper Smithson. I gather you once knew this Marietta Ross. How likely is it she's involved?'

'Fairly. She was always an odd one, with a malicious streak. My impression is that she'd have no conscience whatsoever about turning someone into an addict. By the way, did Coordinator MacIain mention she can be quite dangerous? Marietta is a kung fu adept of the highest order. Within their weight division, only the deceased woman, Rhianna O'Connor, was known to have the ability to defeat her.'

'Well, we shall have to make sure we never corner her, although it would be interesting to see her fight. I am an "adept", as you put it, myself.' Chiu Liow smiled, tilting his head slightly to one side.

Smithson raised an eyebrow. 'Good to hear. Some of the people she deals with could potentially be dangerous as well, particularly the ones who fought in the tournaments. There are three on your list. I've marked them.'

'Thank you; I noticed. Well, please excuse me if I leave you to your work. I have some kookaburras to feed... I can hear them calling me.'

'Kookaburras! Really? How many?' Smithson had noticed them in the background. They were being even louder than usual.

'Seven. I began with one, then a pair, and now three sets of offspring. Wonderful birds, but they eat meat, which I am not overly fond of giving them. However, they don't intend to become vegetarians, so meat they shall have.'

Smithson laughed. 'Alright, thanks again, and I'll look forward to speaking with you soon.'

'Likewise,' said Chiu Liow, then bowed slightly before turning away to feed 'his' birds.

Not one to leave anything undone that could be done immediately, Smithson soon located his Stanthorpe suspect at a nearby winery. The earlier check on the man's occupation showed him to be a horticulturalist and someone the peacekeeper knew only by sight, even in this small town. He had never before come to the notice of the law, although neither had any of the other people on Smithson's list.

When Smithson found him, the horticulturalist was busy putting the finishing touches to his grape vines. A tall, broad-shouldered man, he wore only a light shirt tucked into his work trousers, despite the chilly weather. His fair hair was neatly trimmed, as was his short beard. Bright, friendly grey eyes regarded Smithson with a tolerant air.

'Hello,' he said. 'What brings you out here? You must be Smithson, though I can't say we've ever met before. It's not often I have much to do with peacekeepers, other than at the occasional social gathering.' He put away his secateurs, wiped a hand on his trousers, and held it out to Smithson, who shook it, then winced. The man was exceptionally strong and apparently unaware of his grip – or quite possibly, fully aware.

'Yes, that's right, Smithson's my name. Do you have a few minutes? I need to ask you some questions.'

'Ask away.' Grinning, the horticulturalist leaned against a fence post.

'Thank you. To begin with, do you know a Marietta Ross?'

'Marietta? Oh yes, I certainly do.' He laughed – a pleasant, good-natured laugh. 'Gorgeous woman, but oh my, what a bitch, if you don't mind my saying so.'

'If that's your opinion, at least it's an honest one. How do you know Marietta, and what makes you dislike her?' Smithson leaned against a fence post as well, moving a little to the side to keep the sun from his eyes.

'She cheated me. But to start from the beginning, I employed her to redesign the interior of my Brisbane studio. I'm a photographer too and travel to Brisbane a fair bit for my work, so I knew her professionally and, coming from Stanthorpe originally, thought she'd be ideal for the job. She asked for a deposit, promised to do the work, then reneged. I could've made a complaint, but quite frankly, decided it wasn't worth it. The amount of money wasn't huge.'

'Had you paid her for anything before?' asked Smithson, knowing that he had, but not what for.

'Oh yes, certainly. That's the other reason I decided not to make a complaint. I had hoped we could get together, if you know what I mean, though I'm over that now. I'd never met her in person until she came to see my studio, only over the lattice. Like I said, she's gorgeous, if a bit overwhelming at times. Still, to answer your question, when I was too busy to take on commissions, I'd pay her a fee to do some of the work, rather than refuse outright. I still have a reputation to build, you see. I can show you her contributions if you like?'

'Yes, that would be helpful. Thank you.' Smithson was coming to the conclusion that even if he did attend the illegal tournaments in Brisbane, this young man was not one of their drug addicts and hoped appearances weren't deceptive.

'Good. If you come inside, I'll hook up to my computer at home. I prefer to store it all offline. Call me paranoid if you will, but I don't entirely trust the lattice. Won't take a minute.'

They went into the winery's main office, where Smithson was soon admiring Marietta's superb renderings of interiors from all over the world. There was no doubting her artistic ability. 'They were worth paying for,' he said, looking through the set of images one last time. 'Thanks for your help. If there's anything else later on, I'll let you know, but for now, that's all I need.'

'Right... I'll get back to work, then. Great to meet you, and if you ever catch up with Marietta, *don't* say hello for me!' The horticulturalist laughed and held out his hand to Smithson, who shook it, although this time managed to extract his own hand before that vice-like grip crushed it.

Satisfied with the interview, the peacekeeper went back to his normal duties while he waited for Morag, Chiu Liow and his Brisbane colleagues to contact him.

Rhianna's voice spoke to Morag as she finally broke through the access codes on her comlink. It was heartbreaking to hear her. The FSIU Coordinator had become fond of Rhianna O'Connor over the years, and admired her courage and resolution. Shaking her head, Morag watched the images on her screen and listened – under any other circumstances, she would have enjoyed hearing Rhianna's voice: mellow, confident, with little discernable accent...

"I'm not sure if you'll ever hear this, Morag, and hope you don't, but I've made this recording in case things go very wrong." Rhianna looked down for a moment, then faced the screen again, a wry expression on her face.

Her black hair flowed around her shoulders, and the dark blue eyes were enhanced by a wine-red tunic, close fitting around her long, shapely neck. At forty-two, Rhianna showed little signs of age, other than attractive laughter lines at the sides of her wide mouth. Morag paused the recording to study her, sad that so much beauty was irreversibly gone – beauty of character, not only of appearance. With profound regret, she touched the face on the screen then allowed the recording to continue:

"You warned me long ago, as did Rohan, not to become close to anyone I was investigating – one of the risks of undercover work. The problem is, Morag, Michiko reminds me of Kenjiro, and until recently, I liked her more and more. I think she has also become fond of me. I've needed to keep reminding myself not to allow a real friendship to develop, but I'm afraid it's been difficult not to. To be honest, I've hoped all our suspicions were groundless and that we could actually be friends. As you know, I've found nothing to suggest she's involved with either the theft of artworks from the Federation or the distribution of Mandrax. It doesn't necessarily mean she isn't, only that I haven't found any evidence.

"Unfortunately, something has happened recently that's changed her attitude towards me. It's not anything definite I can pinpoint, but after all these years working for the FSIU, I've learned to trust my gut feelings. Something is definitely wrong. She seems angry with me, although she's trying hard to hide it, and I've come to the conclusion Michiko is taking out her anger on Felicity. I've noticed her behaviour towards Felicity has been a bit odd for some time, but had no real excuse to ask any questions. The hints I've dropped haven't resulted in either of them coming to talk to me about anything, so there's been no good reason to let you know, until now.

"Last night, I accidentally overheard something going on that leads me to suspect Michiko is mistreating Felicity. I've recorded what I heard in an outbuilding Michiko uses for relaxation and as a workshop, and today decided to take a good look around in there, finding things I would much rather not have and which indicate that the sounds I heard were associated with some form of sadomasochism. The images of what I saw in the outbuilding are included with this recording.

"Not having actually seen what was going on, I can't be sure if the activities were mutual, but my feeling is that Felicity is not a willing partner. She is, after all, Michiko's daughter, and whether adopted or otherwise, the power relationship makes the situation unhealthy, to say the least. However, I have to leave tomorrow morning, so can't follow up on all this. I want to think about it a bit longer anyway, but being the cautious type, couldn't rest until I recorded what I suspect. If, when I next return to Argentina, the atmosphere between Felicity and Michiko hasn't improved, or if there's anything at all to suggest abuse is definitely occurring, I'll make a full report to the peacekeepers here, as well as to you."

Rhianna paused, then added, "I've been thinking a lot about Kenjiro lately and how besotted I was with him. I'd hate to think I've made the mistake of transferring those feelings to Michiko. If I have, then I've let you down, for which I'm sorry. The ridiculous thing is that when I compare what I feel for Edric now with what I felt for him, there's no comparison. I truly love, respect and trust Edric, whereas there was never complete trust between Kenjiro and me, even in the early days before I became aware of who he really was. When I think of how long it took me to believe Rohan when he told me Kenjiro was evil, I could kick myself. Still, that's over and done with, and at least my dear Edric never gave up on me. Now, enough of that...I'm being maudlin. I'll shut up and go to bed!" Rhianna grinned, those slightly longer than usual incisors giving her face such an odd appeal.

After having listened to the sounds Rhianna heard as she stood outside Michiko's outbuilding, Morag sat with her hands cradling her face, staring at the screen for some time before looking at the images taken inside. Eventually, sighing and feeling deeply troubled, she sent the material to both Freddi and Meng Jarrah.

Twelve minutes passed without anyone saying a word. Michiko sat as if in meditation, Freddi stood looking out the window, while Meng Jarrah and Gwenllian sipped the tea they had all been provided with at the beginning of the interview. The Witness remained in the background, watching and listening. Shela was located elsewhere, Michiko having flatly refused to cooperate unless the cat was absent. She now lay in a patch of sunshine in a rear courtyard, sulking, her chin resting on folded paws, occupying herself in catching the stray thoughts and feelings of the occasional passer-by. After a while, she became bored and fell into a light doze, one ear still on alert, one golden eye opening occasionally to survey her surroundings.

Meanwhile, the silence within the Reconciliation Centre interview room lengthened, until Michiko decided, at long last, to answer Freddi's question: 'Felicity is, how shall I put it...naive. However, there is no harm in her that I know of. When she was left alone so many years ago, I volunteered to adopt her because the Federation officials experienced some difficulty placing her in a suitable environment. Other children her age seemed to bother her unduly and she was afraid of most adults, withdrawing and sometimes becoming highly agitated. Within our home, where there was peace, routine and a quiet existence, her ability to cope improved. She has no comlink, since we felt that too much interaction with the outside world would cause her to withdraw into herself again. I acknowledge we may have been mistaken, yet hope your giving her one now will not create any issues.'

Freddi turned from the window to carefully study Michiko, then glanced at Gwenllian, who nodded slightly. 'Tell me about Guillermo,' she said.

This time Michiko was startled and her eyes widened. A hand went halfway to her mouth before dropping back into her lap. She took several seconds to compose herself and to consider her answer: 'Guillermo was a beautiful young man who had the misfortune to want both the mother and the daughter. He had the double misfortune of being someone too eager to please and of then regretting his impulses. *I* regret he died, and also regret my own indiscretions. That is all I wish to say.'

'His case is to be re-opened. The Coroner will require you to say a great deal more, unless you prefer to speak now, in relative privacy.'

Michiko shrugged, yet remained silent.

'As you wish,' said Freddi, 'but let me ask you this. Did you kill him?'

'No one killed him, Peacekeeper. He killed himself.' There was scorn in Michiko's voice. 'Ultimately, he was a coward, unable to face his own shortcomings. If I contributed in any way to his death, it was a small contribution, believe me.'

'Tell us why we *should* believe you, Michiko.' Freddi sat down, facing her directly and looking into Michiko's eyes, her own half-closed, a grim expression on her dark face.

'Because I tell you so. It is your choice whether you do or you don't. It makes no difference to me whatsoever.'

Freddi shook her head and tried again, bending the truth somewhat. 'We know you associate with a select circle of people here in Córdoba who enjoy certain exotic forms of sexual expression. In itself, this is no one's business but your own. However, we have evidence that you and Guillermo both knew a certain senior systems technologist who recently had the bad luck to die of food poisoning. We also have evidence that Guillermo was present at one of the venues used for your entertainments, and was in the house of the deceased, too. This case is soon to be more closely investigated by the Coroner. Would you prefer to speak to us now about these remarkable coincidences, or would you prefer to attend the Coroner's Court?'

'I have nothing to say,' stated Michiko, frowning. Judging by her expression, her confidence now seemed far less than when they first entered the room.

'Are you sure?' Freddi did not wish to take her eyes from Michiko's face to look at Gwenllian for guidance. When Gwenllian 'told' her there was no point in further questioning along this line, Freddi went on to the subject of the illegal martial arts tournaments, intending to return to the question of Michiko's relationship with Felicity a little later. 'There is another area of activity we wish to discuss with you,' she said. 'During a previous interview, you told us that you have practiced martial arts since your bondmate, Kenjiro Kakura, died – kendo and kung fu to be specific.'

Michiko agreed that this was true.

'Commendable, particularly kendo. I gather it's exceptionally difficult to master. Your bondmate *was* a master, if I recall.' Freddi recalled only too well how Kakura used his abilities to execute those who failed to follow his commands with sufficient skill or loyalty.

Michiko nodded. 'Yes, I enjoy the training. As I have said before, Rhianna and I practiced kung fu together. She was an exceptional instructor and taught me a great deal. I miss our sessions, as well as the opportunity to occasionally suggest small refinements based on my increasing knowledge of kendo.'

This was the first time Freddi had heard genuine regret in her voice, and began to gain some insight into the enormity of the disappointment Michiko must have felt when she discovered Kakura had given the silver necklet to Rhianna – and the gnawing anger that must have followed at the betrayal.

'Tell me,' said Freddi, a sudden inspiration striking her, 'did you ever speak with Felicity about Rhianna having known your bondmate while they were at university together in Seoul?'

'Why yes, I did...' Although startled by the question, Michiko quickly recovered. 'When I received the order for the ear circlets to match the necklet, you can understand I was upset and needed to discuss it with someone. My daughter has a talent for listening, if not for giving advice.' She smiled briefly. 'Felicity told me Kenjiro was too honest to have given the necklet to Rhianna on anything other than a generous impulse, soon forgotten after they each went their separate ways. I tried to believe her, although I must admit to having my doubts for some time.'

'How did those doubts affect your relationship with Rhianna?'

'I was angry at myself for having doubted my bondmate, not with Rhianna. How could I be? What woman would not accept such a gift from such a man as Kenjiro?' Michiko shifted into a more comfortable position, crossing one elegant leg over the other. 'Rhianna may have felt a romantic attachment to him, and he may even have been attracted to her, but that is of no consequence. We spent every evening together when he was home, which was often enough for me not to feel neglected, and for our children, including Felicity, who adored him, not to feel their father's absence too keenly. We wanted for nothing.' Michiko's lips trembled, but she controlled herself and met Freddi's eyes. At no stage had she so much as glanced at the others in the room.

Freddi leaned forward a little, her elbows resting on the table between them. 'I can readily accept this, but weren't you angry with Rhianna, despite what you say? She didn't tell you about the gift. Don't you think she should have?'

'She may have been embarrassed and did not wish such a small thing to create misunderstanding between us, to damage the trust we felt for each other. After all, the necklet was given to her many years ago.'

'Trust? Yes, you must have trusted each other – given you both attended full contact martial arts tournaments here in Córdoba. You lied to us when we first asked whether you knew of any illegal tournaments in Argentina.'

A quick intake of breath was the only indication of Michiko's reaction to this news. How did they know? Rhianna! Had Rhianna told someone? This Edric – did she tell him and had he in turn told the peacekeepers? What to say? 'Yes, we did attend them from time to time, and yes, I know they are illegal. Does it matter? Where else can dedicated martial artists train properly? How do you train, Peacekeeper, if not without protection, and do you avoid learning the more effective strikes simply because they are dangerous?'

Freddi laughed. The woman was quick, very quick. 'We have better things to do than charge you with unlawful combat, Michiko, which I expect you know perfectly well. No, we'll leave the tournaments to the local authorities to deal with. We're far more interested in what else goes on during them. They're the perfect opportunity for people with connections to distribute goods the Federation frowns upon. Drugs, for example.' Freddi waited for Michiko to react, yet was disappointed. She stood up, walked around to the other side of the table, bent down and whispered in Michiko's ear: 'Drugs produced by Wyvern Meridian, to be precise, and distributed with your help.'

Michiko turned to face her. 'Don't be ridiculous! Why on Earth would I want to involve myself in such a sordid trade! I have more private wealth than anyone else on this planet. What would I do with more?' Her voice had risen in anger, and her hand, now lying on the table, was clenched.

'Indeed, why would you,' replied Freddi, stepping back and quickly taking the opportunity to look at Gwenllian, who raised an eyebrow and sent a prompt for Freddi to continue, which she did: 'I'll tell you, Madame Yamada. Power. You don't need the income, but you do like power, and drugs give people like you the power you crave. Power over the poor fools who become addicts; just like the control you exercise in your little club of sexual fantasists. We know what you do. We've seen the recording one of your playmates kept. We've also seen the instruments you keep in your workshop. Instruments that only by the wildest stretch of the imagination could be used in silversmithing. We also know what you've done to Felicity, and that's what you'll be charged with: the assault and rape of your daughter. That's why she's left your home, never to return. To get away from you!'

Freddi towered over Michiko, her expression fierce, contemptuous. Michiko leapt to her feet and slapped Freddi across the face as hard as she could. Freddi grasped her wrist and held her, silently daring her to try again. Michiko made no attempt to free herself, merely staring at Freddi with hatred in her eyes, her whole face contorted in rage.

'You think you know!' she snarled. 'You know *nothing*!'

Freddi released her wrist and Michiko sat down, refusing to say another word.

CHAPTER TWENTY-FOUR

While Freddi rubbed her face, a guard escorted Michiko from the interview room. The slap had taken her completely unawares and Freddi was angry with herself for not having prevented it. 'I've obviously neglected my training,' she muttered.

Wryly amused at Michiko's effrontery and even slightly impressed, Meng Jarrah patted her sympathetically on the shoulder. 'We'll find you a sparring partner, Freddi. Can't have you being assaulted by your suspects.' She chortled, unable to help herself, while Gwenllian kept discreetly silent.

'You're right,' replied Freddi, with a shamefaced grin. 'I might solve Edric's training problem for him once we're back in Brisbane!' Brightening at the prospect, she added, 'He'd be a good match. I'll put the idea to him next time we speak.'

Meng Jarrah nodded, smiling. 'Great... Now, after we've finished dealing with Madame Yamada, I'll fetch Shela. She must be utterly bored by now.'

At the same time as Michiko Yamada was being charged and an identity chip inserted into her left shoulder, arrangements were made for her to be placed under house arrest. Soon afterwards, Freddi, Meng Jarrah and Gwenllian returned to the interview room, with Shela now settled comfortably on the floor, listening.

'Well?' began Freddi, her arms folded, long legs stretched out before her as she sat in one of the more inviting chairs the room contained.

'Michiko has so many complex emotions and, in general, such excellent control of herself, that she's surprisingly difficult to read,' replied Gwenllian, sitting opposite, her eyes closed as she reviewed her impressions, her voice clear and steady. 'I'm certain the account of their adoption of Felicity is true, as is her belief that Guillermo killed himself.

'This belief is based upon a number of things: his having been dismissed from his employment, which he confessed to her, but not the reason; his behaviour towards Felicity, as well as his eventual confusion over his relationship with them both; and his having taken part in the sex games. Apparently Guillermo even put himself into debt in an attempt to continue the more opulent lifestyle begun in Michiko's company. It seems he eventually developed a strong sense of shame, which counselling was unable to alleviate. However, the most surprising result of the interview is that Michiko doesn't appear to have been aware that the systems technologist has died.'

'Really? In which case, it seems he may have died accidentally after all. What an extraordinary coincidence... Unless Guillermo killed him, of course, though at the moment I'm at a complete loss as to why he'd want to, particularly if they were friends.' Freddi sat forward and drummed her fingers on the arm of her chair, thinking. 'Did anything to do with Sensa enter Michiko's mind when I was questioning her about Rhianna?'

'No, nothing at all, only when you accused her of assaulting Felicity. I'm sorry to say there's no doubt she used it on her, and there's absolutely no doubt the abuse occurred – over a long period of time. I think we have a fairly accurate picture of the overall situation.'

'And what about the Mandrax? Is Michiko the supplier?'

'Oh yes, definitely. The problem is, it may be extremely difficult to find any hard evidence. The operation has been cancelled and everything used in its production has been destroyed, together with all stocks. Unless we obtain admissions from the actual dealers, or something from the users to implicate her, I don't think we can lay charges. Still, when you spoke of Rhianna and the martial arts tournaments, I found out who her dealer in Australia is. Edric and Stefano were right. It's Marietta. Apparently Rhianna's description of her gave Michiko the idea. She sounded like exactly the right type of person to want to become involved. I have the name of the main distributor here in Argentina too, but we can leave the local peacekeepers and the FSIU to follow up on them, can't we?'

'Well, it depends upon whether Michiko had anything to do with Rhianna's death or not, and if she did, why. If the drugs were a reason, we'd need to be involved to some extent, if only to liaise with Morag. So, Gwenllian, did she kill Rhianna?'

'I don't think so, Freddi. She may have buried the death so deeply beneath the layers of her mind in some form of complete denial that I can't reach the memories, but I don't believe so. Despite what she says, it seems to me that her anger was mainly directed at her bondmate, and not at Rhianna, whom she sincerely liked and admired. Michiko definitely felt betrayed by him, yet there was no reason for her to think the relationship between them went any further than their time together at university. Who else would have known otherwise to tell her? No one, presumably.'

'Well, who on Earth *did* put the amanita into Rhianna's jar of Sensa, and why?'

'At this stage, we simply don't know. If a background check can rule out the staff, and for the moment, we assume it wasn't the children, there was only one other person in the house who could have accessed Rhianna's things before she went home: Felicity.'

'If he was able to enter the house secretly, Guillermo had access too,' said Meng Jarrah, handing a cup of coffee to each of them. 'He knew the place well enough. The erasure of the Sensa records would begin to make sense if it was him. But *why* he'd do it is beyond me...unless Felicity put him up to it for some reason, or if he'd discovered something about Rhianna and thought he was protecting Michiko. Though surely, if that was the case, he would have talked to Michiko first.'

'Thanks, and yes, one would think so,' replied Freddi, with a grimace.

As their questions continued, the Director of the National Fine Arts Museum of Argentina sat across the table from his three interviewers, making every effort to appear unconcerned. Although Gwenllian's information alone was not enough to charge him with either distributing Mandrax himself or, if the scale of the operation was large enough, coordinating a ring of drug traffickers, it provided sufficient evidence for him to be held for questioning. An artist in his free time who undertook many commissions, large and small, he had a great deal of explaining to do.

Between the time the peacekeepers received his name and the beginning of the formal interview at the Reconciliation Centre, all relevant personal financial records had been obtained and examined. These records showed that many of the Director's individual customers for his works of art were themselves associated with either museums, the arts, or private dealerships in antiquities. In itself, this was not necessarily surprising. The interesting point was that the prices paid for the Director's artworks were sometimes considerably above market value.

'You admit to knowing Señora Michiko Yamada, then?' said the first interviewer.

'Of course I know Michiko Yamada! Who doesn't in the art world? She is the most prominent patron of the arts here in Córdoba and within Argentina. In her role as Cultural and Artistic Director of Wyvern Meridian, her reputation even goes beyond our borders. Her *own* artworks are exquisite. Have you seen our collection? It is one of our most prized holdings.'

The interviewers declined to answer his question. One of them merely rubbed his nose and glanced at the other two. The second interviewer passed a likeness to the Director. 'Do you know this woman?' he asked.

'No, I do not. I have never seen her, although I confess to wishing I could. She's lovely. What is her name?'

While the image of Marietta Ross was put away, once again, his question went unanswered. 'Have you ever heard of a drug called Mandrax?' asked the third interviewer, a tall, heavyset woman in her mid-fifties.

After a moment's hesitation, and carefully controlling his expression, the Director answered calmly, 'Why, no... What is it?' He ran a hand over his already smooth brown hair.

'We expect you know what it is *and* what it can do to people who become dependent on it. Are you someone who enjoys people becoming addicted to drugs? Tell me, does it give you pleasure to control them in this way?' The third interviewer frowned and placed one large hand, clenched into a fist, onto the table.

'I have no idea at all what you are talking about,' replied the Director, a slight film of sweat on his brow.

He was an unusually handsome man, with a pleasant, mellow voice. Probably highly attractive to women, the third interviewer concluded. 'Well, not to me, you underhanded, lying piece of dirt!' she thought, and crashed her fist onto the tabletop. The Director jumped in his seat. 'Tell me! What do these drugs buy you? Power? No, they pay for your expensive art supplies and sumptuous lifestyle. How else could you afford them? Only the very best for you, being an eminent citizen of our fine country. Or is it because you find Señora Yamada irresistible and would do anything to please her?'

The interviewer stood and walked around to the other side of the table, then leaned over and gazed into his eyes. The Director flinched and looked away. 'Ha!' she thought. 'I think I've got him. He does find her 'compelling'. I wonder if he also plays her little games.' Aloud, she said, 'Have you ever had any fantasies about Señora Yamada? Any fantasies that she perhaps allowed you to act upon? Is this how she buys your cooperation, eh?'

This time, the Director flushed a dark scarlet and stood up, turning to the interviewer, rage contorting his face. 'You insult me and you insult her! I don't understand what you are talking about, but it seems to me your mind is in the gutter! I will not sit here and listen to such disgusting things. Let me out at once!' He marched towards the door, but his way was barred by a guard. Frustrated, the Director faced them all and then returned to sit down again, arms folded, mouth compressed in a determined line, staring defiantly at them. The third interviewer glared back at him, yet was reasonably satisfied sex games were not the reason this man involved himself in Michiko's schemes.

The second interviewer pressed their advantage. 'We have all the names of the people who have bought your work at higher than usual market prices, and intend to speak with them. Trust me, at least one will tell us what we need to know. Why not save us all a great deal of effort and admit you distributed Mandrax obtained from Michiko Yamada? You are wasting your time and ours by denying it. The evidence is already in our hands,' he lied, 'and all we need is your cooperation to ensure the Judge takes this into account at your trial.'

The Director's mouth opened as if to speak, but he changed his mind and simply shook his head. Further questioning obtained nothing more and he was released, told not to attempt to leave the country, and placed under surveillance.

After the interview, the Córdoban peacekeepers systematically worked their way through their list of suspected drug users. To their intense annoyance, they could find nothing to confirm Gwenllian's information. Even a thorough search of each person's premises and their workplaces found nothing. They began to doubt her, but a personal demonstration of her abilities soon reassured them that what she had told them was true. Yet how to confirm it and bring the Director to trial, let alone prove Michiko Yamada was the main supplier? In the meantime, they could at least close down the illegal martial arts tournaments and make sure the word was spread that no one could safely buy or sell Mandrax, or any other illicit drug. This was something, if not enough to satisfy anyone.

The three children stood before their mother, uncertain what they should do or say. At thirteen, the oldest, a boy named Kisho, stood tall for his age, with his father's proud bearing and both his parents' fine features, handsome of face and form. His brother, Yukio, sturdier and of average height, looked up at him, hoping to find an answer, but saw nothing to help overcome his fears. The youngest of the three, Aiko, a girl of eight years, held her brother's hand and tried not to cry. They all knew their mother would not have called the family together in this manner without having something very serious to speak with them about. The expression on Michiko's face showed she was struggling with her own emotions, which made it more difficult for her children to deal with theirs. Only five years had gone by since their father's death, and now Felicity had left, with no warning, no explanation, no farewell. The house seemed empty without her.

'Please, come closer and sit down,' began Michiko, mastering herself. 'We have a great deal to discuss. Life is about to change for us and I need you to understand why. Come here, little one,' and she held out an arm to encircle her daughter. The two boys followed and sat next to them, waiting. Kisho took his brother's hand, holding it tightly.

'I am under suspicion of having mistreated Felicity. It is the reason she has left this house and I am deeply sorry to say that she will not return. At the moment, she is in our medcentre receiving treatment and should recover quite soon. My hope is that one day you will all have the chance to visit her as often as you like, but for the time being it is simply not possible. In the meantime, I cannot leave the house. The peacekeepers want me to stay here until the Judge decides whether the information Felicity has given them is true or not. Please don't worry. This is the only restriction placed on me at present, and you can all go about your lives as usual.'

'What did you do to Felicity, Mother?' said her daughter, lisping slightly.

'I hit her. I was angry and I hit her. It should never have happened, yet it did. I also hurt her in other ways, which was wrong and quite unforgivable.' Michiko stroked the girl's dark hair and held her close for a moment. 'I think that since your father died I have not been myself, and have done things I now regret. It is difficult to explain it all to you now. In time, you will know more and I hope you will all forgive me, even if I cannot forgive myself. Please remember that I love you all very much, and no matter what happens, you will be well looked after. This is your home and always will be.'

'What about Rhianna, Mother?' asked Yukio. 'Will she be coming back? She was such fun.'

'No, Rhianna will never be coming back either. I learned recently that our friend died in an accident. It was no one's fault and I know we will all miss her dreadfully.'

Her son burst into tears, while his brother placed a hand on his shoulder and tried not to follow suit. He had enjoyed Rhianna's visits, their occasional picnics and other outings. Both Rhianna and Felicity gone and their mother under arrest! The world suddenly seemed very bleak indeed.

'Rhianna's never coming back, Mother?' repeated Aiko, confused. 'Why is she dead? How did it happen?'

'You all know how Rhianna and I both practiced kung fu? Well, she was highly skilled and took part in tournaments where no special equipment was worn for protection. During one of these tournaments, Rhianna was struck, and died soon afterwards. The blow connected only because she was already ill, but did not realise just how ill she was. I'm unsure why Rhianna became so ill, but think it may have been something we bought during her last visit here. It somehow became contaminated and made her sick.'

'What does "contaminated" mean?' asked her daughter, her lips trembling, still unable to comprehend why both Rhianna and Felicity were never coming back.

'Sorry, my darling. It means it had something nasty in it...something that shouldn't have been there.'

'Oh. How did that happen?' The girl peered into her mother's face, trying hard to understand.

'We don't yet know. Some peacekeepers are here from Australia to find out. When they do, I expect we'll all be told.'

'How long will you have to remain at home, Mother?' asked Kisho, beginning to realise the situation was even more serious than he first imagined.

'I don't know. It may be for a long time. Still, it won't matter, will it? We'll all be together and are fortunate in having a lovely home. We can picnic in the courtyard garden when the weather is good, and once the Judge makes up its mind what to do, I'll show you my workshop. I think it's time you were allowed in there to be with me when I work. That way, I won't be lonely and neither will you. I might even teach you all how to draw and to make things from silver, if you want. Would you like that?'

Kisho nodded, feeling a shade more optimistic. The other two were unsure how they felt. Never having seen inside the workshop, they had no idea what was in there, so it seemed to have a strange and mysterious air. Their parents had spent a great deal of time in the outbuilding, and then Felicity and Michiko spent time in there after their father died, yet *they* were still forbidden to enter. They looked at their brother for guidance and this time found the reassurance they needed.

'Alright, Mother,' said Yukio, 'you may teach me how to draw. I'd like that.'

'Good!' Michiko hugged her children and they sat together in silence for some time until the housekeeper came in to announce dinner.

After the reintroduction to Peri, and the requisite further forty-eight hours having passed without incident, a greatly relieved Edric was on his way back to Brisbane, together with Stefano and the two cats. Once there, it would be necessary for him to attend the nearest medcentre to have a series of tests to determine whether his immune system was functioning normally. He regarded this as a small price to pay for keeping Zarifa.

Before leaving Stanthorpe, they had all passed a pleasant few hours with Margrethe, catching up on old times. Edric even allowed his lap to become a convenient place for Harriet to have her nap, although the amount of hair she left on his clothing wasn't quite so welcome!

In two days time, both Edric and Stefano were to meet the Brisbane Peacekeeping Force's coordinator of martial arts training. Nyneve had been as good as her word in obtaining agreement to at least explore the idea of their volunteering as instructors. If the meeting went well, it was almost certain they would soon have a busy schedule. However, for the time being, it was simply good to be going home, although Edric was unsure how he would feel once he was alone in Rhianna's apartment. Somehow it was still hers, not his. Well, in truth, he would not be alone; Zarifa would be with him. She quickly reassured him and licked his hand.

The two cats shared a seat on the small airjet, sitting comfortably between their companions and thoroughly enjoying the attention they received from their fellow passengers. Cats were still a novelty on aircraft, even though it was now routine for them to be given seats inside rather than being expected to travel in the cargo hold, as had been the case not too many years ago.

Once back in Brisbane, they went to Stefano's house to check on his plants, and afterwards to Edric's apartment. However, the two friends began to experience a strange sense of unreality. Too much had happened over too short a period of time for them to fully absorb.

'I'd like nothing more than peace and quiet for a while, Stefano,' said Edric, with a small sigh, as they sat in the elegantly furnished lounge room sipping a glass of the vintage port Rhianna laid down several years ago. Somehow it seemed fitting to open it in her memory. Zarifa was contentedly curled up in Rhianna's favourite armchair, and Edric's eyes often returned to her, imagining Rhianna sitting there instead, yet glad the chair was not empty.

'Would you rather we didn't meet with the BPF instructor on Monday after all?' replied Stefano, wondering if it would be best if he stayed the night. He was almost certain Edric was lapsing into melancholy. The life and laughter in Robert's house had kept him buoyant, and the contrast, were he to be left with only Zarifa tonight, might be too much, no matter how good company the cat might be.

'No. We need to keep training, and this seems the best plan either of us have come up with so far. I'll be fine. What about you? How are you managing...really?'

'Surprisingly well. I miss Rhianna and I'll never forget her, but the visit to Stanthorpe did me good. I'm not sure why, it just did, and having Peri with me makes all the difference in the world. I'll be okay. Still, how about I stay here tonight? I could even stay longer, if you want?'

'Thanks, I'd like that, but tonight is probably enough. I should begin going through Rhianna's things and try to get used to being here. It will all belong to me now, which is so strange. I don't know what to do about the consultancy, though. Then again, if it was set up by the FSIU, I suppose they'll take care of it. I wonder if they'll let me keep the landjet? I wouldn't mind having it. Comes in handy at times.' Edric managed a grin and Stefano laughed.

'Good to hear you're thinking about nice everyday things like luxurious private transport! Can I borrow it if you *are* allowed to keep it?' Stefano winked at Edric, who shook his head to tease him, but then said, 'Of course you can. Just don't crash it. Do you even have a licence to drive one?' He poured another glass of port for them both.

'Well, no, I don't. Damn! I'll simply have to get one.'

Edric laughed, and they spent the rest of the evening slowly finishing the bottle, until they were both tired enough to go to bed and sleep. Early the next morning, a somewhat hung-over Stefano took himself off to his own house to spend the rest of the day reading about landjets and how to obtain a licence. Edric rose late, and after breakfast, opened the wardrobe where Rhianna's clothes were kept. He found one of her hand-knitted jumpers and held it to his face. Her scent was still on it. Zarifa wound herself around his legs, sensing his sadness and the depth of his loss, then leapt lightly onto the bed. She knew there was little more she could do, but at least it was better than him being alone. They sat together for some time, Edric's arm around the cat, the garment on his lap, remembering all the life and love he had shared with Rhianna. Eventually, he heaved a sigh and put the jumper away. Now was not the time to go through her things after all. Something practical, like going shopping for food, would be better. He fetched Zarifa's leash and they walked to the market, happy to be outside in the clean, fresh air.

Peace and quiet were the last things on Marietta's mind. Disgusted with how things had turned out, she sat at her greenhouse table to eat her midsun meal, watching the enormous rainbows on the far wall. The rainbows, created by the combination of winter sunlight and the design of the plastiglass, were usually a constant source of delight, but today, everything failed to please, even the food, specially prepared by a chef in celebration of this, her Namingday.

'Alone,' she thought. 'Yes, I am truly alone. Pah! But what does it matter. Rien!' Still, perhaps it was time she paid a visit to Ruth and to Edric, possibly even Stefano. He always made her laugh.

The wine selected to complement the meal was an excellent pinot grigio from the Mornington Peninsula, its light, yet complex, fruit flavours balanced by exactly the right amount of acidity. A wine connoisseur, Marietta spent a significant proportion of her income on travelling to wine estates, sampling their wares and buying judiciously. Her 'cellar' held pride of place in the coolest part of the house and now numbered over five hundred bottles of the best Australian wines she could find. She held the wine glass up to the light to admire the colour of the liquid, as well as the glass itself, part of a beautiful set purchased from the Orrefors factory in Sweden. One last mouthful of food, and then, the wine finished, Marietta picked up her comlink to make a booking for the last afternoon flight to Brisbane.

The departure of her flight coincided with a call from Peacekeeper Chiu Liow Jones, who explained that he had a number of questions to ask her relating to the ongoing inquiry into Rhianna O'Connor's death.

'You are going to Brisbane?' he remarked. 'That is unfortunate. I had looked forward to meeting you sooner rather than later. Still, the questions can wait until you return. That is, if you intend to return before too long. If not, I will simply take a trip to Queensland myself. It is a while since I visited my colleagues in the Brisbane Peacekeeping Force.' Chiu Liow waited, expecting a prompt reply. When he didn't receive one, he added, 'When will you return to Melbourne?'

'Je ne sais pas, Monsieur Jones. It depends upon many things. It is not urgent, is it?' Marietta managed not to glare at him. Peacekeepers were the last people she wanted to talk to, particularly since some of her former 'customers' were beginning to put even more pressure on her. She could easily imagine they might come to the notice of the law if their increasing desperation caused them to act in an 'unbecoming' manner.

'Urgent? Certainly not urgent, but the sooner we speak together, the sooner we can leave you in peace. Otherwise, the questions will simply mount up and we may need to take up a great deal of your time.'

'Very well, I understand, and will return on Wednesday evening. If you wish, we can meet on Thursday morning. Will that suit?' Marietta clearly wanted to maintain control of the situation and Chiu Liow smiled to himself as he noticed.

'Thursday morning will be perfectly suitable. Shall we say 10:00 at the Reconciliation Centre in Hawthorn? That should be convenient for you. A Witness will be present, since this will be a formal interview.'

Marietta frowned, hesitated, then agreed. It appeared there was little choice.

The call over, Chiu Liow regarded his list with satisfaction. Their interviews had so far found two people prepared to exchange information about Marietta in return for immunity from prosecution for having attended the Brisbane tournaments; little did they know that prosecutions were never actually intended. These two were quite enough to have prompted his call to Marietta, and there was every possibility more might be just as forthcoming, given how remarkably unpopular she seemed to be. By Thursday morning, he planned to have worked through the entire list of suspects supplied to him by Smithson.

The Brisbane peacekeepers were also making good progress, as were those of Chiu Liow's colleagues who were chasing down Marietta's remaining contacts. The airports were now on alert for any attempt on her part to leave the country, more for convenience than any other reason, since it would be difficult for her to escape Federation detection, no matter where she went.

Meanwhile, of more immediate concern to Morag MacIain, was the situation of the young woman, Felicity. The recordings of her formal interview and of her counselling session dismayed and puzzled her. How could Michiko, after all those years spent as a dutiful bondmate and loving parent, almost overnight change into a monster who sexually abused her own daughter? Not only that, but the other recording Freddi sent, of the bondage session between the recently deceased Argentinean systems technologist and the unknown woman who bore a remarkable resemblance to Michiko, suggested she had become a sexual predator. If Felicity's information was to be relied upon, the relationship between her mother and the other dead Argentinean, Guillermo, added to this picture. Perhaps the Mandrax was used as an adjunct to Michiko's sex life, associated with her apparent need to control others and as a way of enticing them into even more uninhibited behaviour?

From Morag's understanding of Kenjiro Kakura, there was little in his past relationship with Michiko to explain it all – unless there was something Rohan Maerz failed to detect? True, she definitely behaved in an unusually subservient manner towards her bondmate, behaviour which Rohan had felt to be extremely unhealthy. In addition, their three children were born in defiance of Federation regulations, which, in most instances, limited parents to one child. The rare second-child quota announced by the Federation explained the second son, but the daughter? Morag shook her head. It was unlikely they would ever know why Michiko agreed to break the law in order to bear Kakura a third child, or why she was prepared to remain in a relationship where, according to Rohan, she was treated with condescension, even if also with loving kindness. Still, Kakura had in many respects been a remarkable man, perhaps in some ways even an admirable one: a man whom Rhianna loved deeply for many years, with a love that continued for some time despite the evidence of his corruption presented to her by Rohan. Rhianna eventually had the courage to break free from the relationship. But then, she did not have three children, and Felicity, to consider, and was also someone with unusual strength of will.

Morag stood up to make herself a coffee, then returned to read the latest information provided by Smithson and Freddi. Something Smithson had noticed was that all the people who seemed likely to have purchased Mandrax from Marietta were influential in, or somehow associated with, the arts. Apparently this was also the case for the Director of the Argentinean Museum of Fine Arts. This observation led Morag back to an earlier concern: that of the theft of valuable works of art and historical artefacts from the Federation. What if Mandrax was being supplied to Marietta and the Director in exchange for information? In turn, were they using the drug as a lever – as a tool for blackmail? Once dependency had been established, drug addicts could be manipulated. The problem was that while Marietta and the Director's financial situations could readily be accessed and examined, it was far more difficult to do so in Michiko's case, considering how her wealth was intertwined with Wyvern Meridian's and its myriad subsidiaries. Federation scrutiny of the company was considerable, yet Morag had the unpleasant feeling that with their gradual release of control, the company's web had once again begun to grow and spread.

The magnificent medcentre garden where Gwenllian and Felicity were walking extended down to the river. The building itself towered above the old central city. The creation of both the garden and the new medcentre was a cooperative effort between the architects, artists and engineers of Córdoba, sponsored heavily by Michiko Yamada. A fantasy of complex plastiglass forms, created to change colour as the light varied, with each of its facets showing a different hue, it gave the effect of a three-dimensional rainbow. All its energy requirements were met by the sun, with sufficient left over to provide for those of the older buildings nearby that were too difficult to make self-sufficient. In addition, climate control was enhanced by both the design itself and the use of indoor plants, while internal recycling systems minimised the use of fresh water.

Felicity spoke proudly of the project, completed only four months ago. 'These grounds and the building are an inspiration to us all. It shows what can be done when everyone works together. My mother followed the progress at every stage, and sometimes even discussed the works with me.'

As they neared the riverbank, the two turned to look back. The medcentre seemed almost like a gigantic crystalline structure sprouting directly from the earth, its edges softened by the surrounding trees. Gwenllian could understand the pride Felicity felt, yet in light of what Michiko had done to her, it was surprising she could still speak of her mother in this manner. Then again, perhaps more than a decade of gratitude and love could not be destroyed so easily. Or was this the only way in which Felicity could rationalise and cope with the ill-treatment?

Gwenllian was unable to find the answer, because for the first time since she had fully developed her powers to reach into and understand other people's feelings and thoughts, this woman was able to block her to quite a significant extent. She linked arms with Felicity in a friendly, companionable manner, which helped establish a closer connection with her mind, yet Gwenllian still could not penetrate beyond its surface layers. Nevertheless, from the manner in which the younger woman accepted her touch, she concluded that a considerable degree of healing had already taken place. 'Felicity,' she said, 'we've talked about a possible option if you still want to leave Córdoba. Do you feel well enough to discuss it now if I tell you what it is?'

Felicity stopped walking, gazed into Gwenllian's face, and apparently felt reassured for she smiled, openly and joyfully. 'You have not forgotten! How kind you all are! Thank you, yes. What is it you suggest?'

'Do you want to sit down while we talk? There's a lovely seat here and the sun is so wonderfully warm.' Gwenllian indicated a nearby pergola, overhung with large clusters of scarlet flowers that she had never seen before, but which had a delicate, fresh, almost citrus-like perfume. 'Do you know this plant's name, Felicity?'

'Yes, I do. It has become famous and is a recent variant of *Pyrostegia venusta*, the Flame Vine. It is one of Michiko's favourites.' Felicity cupped some of the flowers in her hand to enjoy the perfume.

'I'm impressed you know its botanical name. Do you like gardening?'

'Yes, I do. I spend a great deal of time caring for the plants at home, both in the house and in the garden. That is, I did.' Felicity looked away for a moment, making an effort to control her feelings. 'There were gardeners, of course, but I enjoyed the work.'

'That's good, because what we would like to suggest could easily include working with plants, although they might not be the same as the ones you're used to. What would you say to leaving Argentina and coming with us to Australia? There's an elderly woman we know, with an elderly cat, who lives alone in a small country town and who would be very happy to have you stay with her. Her house is small, but lovely, and her garden is wonderful. She grows all sorts of different things, like fruit and vegetables, as well as roses and spring bulbs. Have you ever seen daffodils?' Gwenllian could not directly sense what Felicity's reaction was to all this, which was disconcerting.

'No, I have never seen daffodils. What colour are they, and what is the name of this woman?' Felicity's voice held a tremor of doubt. Leaving Argentina was a huge step.

'Daffodils are often yellow, but also come in white, pale pink, a mixture of these colours, and even pale green. They flower in winter and in springtime and some of them have scent. I love them, and Margrethe does too. That's her name...Margrethe. Her cat's name is Harriet, who isn't what I'd call beautiful, but has lots of personality.' Gwenllian almost felt as if she was talking to a child. There was something about Felicity that was not quite what she would expect from someone her age.

'What if she did not like me? What would I do?'

Saddened by the question, which displayed such lack of confidence, Gwenllian took Felicity's hand and said, 'She *will* like you, Felicity. Why shouldn't she? And besides, if something happened and you couldn't stay there, we'd arrange somewhere else for you. We won't forget you, I promise.'

'Could I return to Argentina if I wished? I might want to visit my brothers and sister, perhaps even my mother one day.'

'Of course you could. You are perfectly free to go wherever you like. You *would* be required to work, as you do now, for twenty-five hours a week, but it'd be easy enough to find something you enjoyed. There's always work that needs doing. What would you prefer to do if you could choose?'

Gwenllian had checked how Felicity spent her working hours and found she was a remarkably proficient seamstress, providing fashionable clothing for those who preferred individual designs. Her work was relatively solitary, yet took place in one of the best fashion houses in Córdoba, where she assumed that Felicity's not carrying a comlink until recently went unremarked due to her quiet demeanour and lack of social interaction with her fellow employees.

'I can garden, cook and sew, nothing more. Would that be enough? I can learn other things if I need to.' Felicity's expression became almost eager as she considered the possibilities.

'I'm sure you could learn other things if you wanted to. You're young, and would soon adapt to new surroundings and new ways of doing things. Well, what do you think? Would you like to speak with Margrethe on your new comlink? We'd have to wait until this evening. She'd be in bed at the moment, sleeping.'

'Oh! Yes, I see. There is a time difference. I had not considered that before.' Felicity smiled again. 'Will you help me make the call?'

'Yes, Felicity, I'd be happy to. Let's walk back to the medcentre now, and I'll come back at 20:00, when we can speak with Margrethe. She might even show you Harriet!' Gwenllian laughed at the thought of the old cat's nose sniffing at the screen.

Felicity stood up, holding out her hand to Gwenllian, and they chose the long way back to the medcentre to finish their circuit of the gardens. During their walk, Felicity pointed out the plants she admired the most, giving their botanical names and discussing their merits, surprising Gwenllian with the extent of her knowledge.

CHAPTER TWENTY-FIVE

Restless after her flight from Melbourne, Marietta was unable to settle down to sleep in her expensive hotel room, some two kilometres from the centre of Brisbane. Instead, she put on dark, comfortable clothes and took public transport to Edric's apartment. At first there were no lights on, either in the shopfront or upstairs. 'He's either not at home or must be sleeping,' she thought, wondering whether to approach the door, but deciding against it. The street was deserted at this late hour, so there was no one to notice that for the next ten minutes, Marietta simply leaned against the building opposite and watched, as she had done so many times before over the past two years when martial arts practice sessions had finished for the evening. Her jealous preoccupation with Rhianna hadn't died with her, nor had Marietta's inability to accept the rejection of her earlier attempts at friendship when Rhianna first joined their club. Worst of all, though, had been Rhianna's taking the Australian middleweight championship from her. Marietta's jaw clenched as she remembered the humiliation of being bested at every tournament.

Her angry deliberations were interrupted by a curtain being drawn back and the window opening, followed by the sight of Edric silhouetted against the dim background glow of flickering candlelight. 'Such a romantic,' she murmured to herself, partly in admiration, partly in contempt. He appeared to be doing nothing other than looking at the view, but soon turned away and shut the window, without closing the curtains. After watching for another few minutes, Marietta made up her mind and approached the building, putting her hand to the identification panel.

Surprised by her appearance on his doorstep, particularly at this hour, Edric told the security system to open the door and then went downstairs to meet her. Zarifa poked her head out from beneath the bedcovers, concluded there was nothing to be alarmed about, and went back to sleep.

'Hello, Edric,' said Marietta, presenting her cheek to be kissed. Having returned the kiss, she led the way back upstairs. Edric followed, wondering why on Earth she had chosen to visit at this time of night. As far as he knew, Marietta had never visited before, and knowing of her interest in architecture and interior design, felt the daytime would have been better for taking a good look at everything. After all, both the early-twentieth-century exterior and the beautifully decorated interior were worth seeing, as was the collection of artworks.

Marietta walked around the living room studying the paintings and old photographs on display, saying nothing but occasionally pausing to examine a piece more closely, putting her head to one side as she did.

'May I offer you something, Marietta? A coffee? I have some Darjeeling tea, if you'd prefer. Are you hungry?' Edric was puzzled by her silence and wished he could simply go back to bed and sleep.

Marietta turned to face him. 'Mais oui, a coffee would be agreeable. I am not hungry, although if you have something special to tempt me, that would also be very pleasant. May I sit?' Without waiting for a reply, she chose Rhianna's armchair, somehow sensing it had been hers. Edric, startled to see her sitting there, abruptly turned away to make the coffee, leaving her alone for a few minutes.

While he was gone, Marietta fished around in her shoulder bag for her cosmetics, touched up her appearance, then retrieved a small package and placed it in her pocket, at the same time making sure to arrange herself more attractively. Edric returned with coffee for them both, a dish of sugared almonds, some dried fruit, and a small selection of good cheeses accompanied by thin slices of black rye bread. He set it all carefully on the table next to where Marietta sat, then looked around for some serviettes. They were somewhere in here, he was sure. Ah, there they were...in the sideboard. After fetching them, Edric pulled another armchair closer to the table and picked up his coffee.

'Help yourself,' he said, doing likewise and cutting a piece of cheese.

'Thank you, I will. You entice me after all.' Marietta smiled sweetly, picked up a plate, then contemplated the food and took what she wanted. Elegant in all her movements, her black hair hid her face as she bent over. Settling back into the armchair, she said, 'We miss her, do we not? You more than me, naturally, but yes, I also miss her. It is lonely without Rhianna. Everything has changed for us...and for Ruth and Stefano, n'est pas? How is Stefano? I have not heard from him.'

'He's fine. We're both better than I'd have expected.' Edric had no intention of discussing his feelings, the cats, or Rhianna, with Marietta. He drank his coffee and tried to look as if he didn't wish she would simply leave.

He must have succeeded, because she said, 'That is good, very good. I have been concerned about you and considered it time I paid a little visit. It is late, I know, yet what of that? We are free to sleep when we wish, yes?'

Edric put down his coffee, leaned forward and rested his elbows on his knees, his face in his hands. 'Sleep? Yes, I suppose so, but for some reason, I can't tonight. Too many memories and thoughts rolling around in my head. I can't seem to settle down.' He stood up and added, 'Would you like a glass of port?'

'Why, yes. I am fond of good wine. Perhaps you knew?' Marietta smiled again, her even white teeth almost glinting in the light reflected from an antique mirror hanging on the opposite wall.

'Not really, but I'm glad. Rhianna was too.' Edric wandered out of the room and found a bottle of port that, by its date, appeared to be ready to drink. Entering the living room again, he found Marietta had taken off her shoes and curled up in the large armchair, looking remarkably at home, two port glasses from the sideboard already arranged on the table.

He raised an eyebrow but decided not to comment, instead pouring the wine, then standing back for her to sample it.

'Excellent! You have good taste, or is this one of Rhianna's choosing?' Marietta took another sip, savouring the flavour and putting out a hand for the bottle. Edric gave it to her and she read the label, nodding a few times.

'Rhianna chose it,' Edric replied, when she had finished reading. The bottle sat on the table between them, reminding them both of whose apartment this had been.

'Does it all belong to you now, Edric?' asked Marietta, holding the stem of her glass in both hands, gently turning it around as she watched him.

'Well, yes, once the Will has gone through probate. The consultancy won't, but I'll even own the actual building and I may inherit Rhianna's landjet too.' He seemed faintly bemused, as if unable to come to terms with owning so much all at once. 'It turns out she was quite wealthy.' Edric scratched his chin and poured himself another glass of port, offering one to Marietta as well, which she accepted.

'Très bon. In which case, perhaps you can help *me*.' Marietta laughed when Edric's eyes widened and he gaped in astonishment. 'No, no,' she reassured him. 'I am joking. Me, I have enough and can find more if I wish. Still, there is another way you might want to help. Are you not lonely? I am. Could we not help each other a little?' Marietta stretched out one long, shapely leg to touch Edric on the knee with her bare foot. He flinched and moved away.

'Ah, I see. You do not think I am...interesting. It may be too soon. Well, we can at least be friends, yes?' Marietta was not prepared to give up that easily.

Edric looked at his hands holding the port glass, then looked at her. There was no doubting her beauty, but compared to Rhianna, she was nothing at all to him. Nothing!

His feelings showed in his face, and this time Marietta understood there was no chance of her seducing him – not now, and presumably, not ever. Well, there was more than one way of getting what she wanted. She hid a polite yawn with her hand, then said, 'I should be going. Could we have one more coffee before I leave? You prepare a good coffee.'

Edric nodded, muttered something about it definitely being late, and went into the kitchen, returning before long with the freshly brewed coffee.

He poured some for each of them, accidentally spilled a small amount on the table because he really was becoming dreadfully tired, then went back into the kitchen to fetch something to wipe it up with. While he was out of the room, Marietta quickly took the small package from her pocket and stirred some of its contents into Edric's cup. By the time he returned, she was drinking her own coffee and nibbling on a piece of fruit.

'I'm sorry to be ungracious,' said Edric, as he sat down and picked up his cup. 'I've been in Stanthorpe for the past two weeks and haven't slept well since I came back.' He drank a few mouthfuls of coffee. 'Stefano's been there with me, and we met Robert, Rhianna's cousin. Did you ever meet him?'

'Stanthorpe? Really? I have preferred not to go back. There is nothing there for me... And Robert? Yes, I seem to remember meeting him several times in the town. A handsome man, so like Rhianna. What did you do there?'

Edric did not trust Marietta enough to tell her the truth, so merely spoke about visiting old friends, especially Margrethe and her cat, Harriet. Marietta did not interrupt and gave every appearance of listening. As he talked, Edric began to feel far better than he had since his return to Brisbane, even in comparison to when Stefano was here in the apartment with him. His tiredness slipped away and when Marietta made some humorous comment, he laughed.

'Shall we sit on the couch over there, Edric? It looks to be so much more inviting than these chairs.' Marietta poured both of them another glass of port. 'Is it at all possible you have some chocolate in this house of yours? I feel like chocolate. It goes well with sweet wine.'

'As a matter of fact I do!' replied Edric, jumping up and rummaging around in the sideboard, soon finding an unopened box of pralines. 'Will these do?' He handed the box to Marietta to open. She carried them over to the couch, made herself comfortable and undid the wrapping, holding the chocolates up to her nose to sniff their wonderful perfume. 'Mmm...delicious! Come, sit down and try one.'

Edric sat next to her, chose a chocolate and bit into it. The dark, fine texture of the outer shell and subtle flavour of the filling seemed better than he had ever tasted before. 'These are fantastic!' he exclaimed, reaching out to take another one.

'Here, let me.' Marietta held one up to his mouth, but Edric took it from her and moved away. Refusing to feel slighted, Marietta watched while he ate the sweet, and then stared in horror as Edric suddenly gasped for air and became bright red in the face.

'Mon Dieu! What is the matter with you?' Marietta looked at the chocolates and put a hand to her throat. Surely not! The Mandrax in his coffee? Edric collapsed onto the couch, his head flung back, struggling to breathe, his lips and throat beginning to swell. Standing up, she was just about to use her comlink to call for an ambulance when an enormous, tawny cat hurtled into the room, throwing herself at Marietta, knocking her over and pinning her to the floor by the throat.

Unable to cry out, Marietta struggled with Zarifa, hitting the cat on the head and grasping her by the neck. Zarifa let go and spat, hissing furiously when Marietta began to sit up, staring at this strange animal. Zarifa snarled and stood over her, tail lashing from side to side.

Marietta's years of training paid off as she controlled herself and spoke calmly: 'I must call for help. Edric is ill and may die if I do not. You *must* let me call for help, now!' Zarifa backed off a little. Marietta, leaning on one elbow, pulled her comlink from her pocket and called the nearest medcentre.

By this time, Edric was unconscious. Zarifa, with a warning glance at Marietta, leapt onto the couch and licked his face, then turned and watched, listening as the call was made and hearing the result in the wight's mind. She sent an urgent plea for help to Peri, who immediately woke and answered, reassuring her that she would bring Stefano; they lived relatively close by in Highgate Hill.

Both Peri and Stefano had crossed Victoria Bridge and were running along Adelaide Street towards the apartment in the same time it took for the ambutechs to be on their way. They arrived almost simultaneously, to find Marietta still sitting on the floor, Edric barely breathing, his face and neck swollen, and Zarifa guarding them both, her green eyes huge and glowing in the dim light of the room.

Stefano seized Marietta by the arm. 'What are you doing here?!' he cried. 'What have you done to him?'

Marietta wrenched her arm free and struck him on the side of the head. 'You imbecile! I have done nothing to either of them!' She stood up and faced him, struggling to regain control of the situation, but Stefano gripped her wrist and held on, surprising her by his strength and speed. His face close to hers, he whispered, 'If you've done this, you won't get away with it, believe me!'

Releasing her, he looked around the room and saw the port, the wine glasses and the coffee cups, as well as the open box of chocolates. There were only two possibilities, since he could not picture Edric setting a cosy scene for a midnight seduction. Either Edric's allergy to cats had resurfaced, or Marietta had invited herself here and put something – most likely Mandrax – into either the coffee or the wine, which Edric then reacted to. He received a quick confirmation from Peri, who was sitting close to Zarifa, still crouched by Edric's side while the ambutechs examined him.

'Do either of you know what's happened here?' one of the ambutechs demanded, staring suspiciously at Marietta. 'He's having a reaction to something. We have his medical record and can see he's allergic to cats, but he could be reacting to something else now – unless his treatment didn't work.'

Marietta coloured, but said nothing.

'He's been fine since his treatment, but it could be something he ate or drank, couldn't it?' suggested Stefano. 'Maybe you'd better take all those things on the table with you for testing.'

'Yes, we will,' replied the ambutech, reaching for his bag to find some sample containers. He carefully emptied the coffee into one container, the wine into another, then took the cups and glasses, as well as the box of chocolates, labelled them, and put everything into an evidence box, with his thumbprint on the seal.

Marietta watched, and for the first time began to feel less sure of herself. Satisfied, Zarifa purred softly. This wight would not escape after all...

'I think you'd better come with us to the medcentre, Marietta,' said Stefano in a low voice, making sure she understood he was not giving her a choice. She glared at him, but collected her things and put on her shoes. 'Can you wait while I use the toilet?' she said, glancing up at him, before straightening and hoisting her bag over one shoulder.

Stefano frowned, yet could hardly refuse. When Marietta returned, she seemed much more her usual confident self. 'Well,' she said, 'when are we to leave this place?'

'We can all go now,' replied the second ambutech, who had his hand on the head of the hoverbed, where Edric now lay, breathing more easily, although still unconscious. Zarifa leapt onto the foot of the bed and tucked herself into the smallest shape possible, while Peri moved over to sit at Stefano's feet, sending him a silent query.

'Yes,' he replied, 'you can both come with us. I'm almost certain you're not the problem this time.' Peri wound herself around his legs for a moment, then all three followed the hoverbed out to the waiting ambulance. Once everyone was settled in, it lifted off and a few minutes later landed outside the medcentre. As they alighted, Stefano glared at Marietta, who glared back, unwilling to accept she had anything whatsoever to do with Edric's condition. Peri walked between the two, still filtering Marietta's thoughts and attempting to make sense of them. She sighed and came to the same conclusion Shela arrived at in Argentina: wights were sometimes very strange!

The practitioner who examined Edric soon discovered the cause of the problem: he had Mandrax in his bloodstream and had reacted badly to it. By this time, Zarifa had taken up a position beneath the hoverbed, having been in the way at its foot. She lay at full length, her head resting on her paws, miserable at not having prevented this disaster, at having been asleep when her Wight was attacked! Peri promptly reassured her, but Zarifa continued to blame herself.

'How did he happen to take this drug?' asked the practitioner.

Stefano turned to Marietta, who shrugged her shoulders and said, 'I did not see him take anything, although he did seem a touch less inhibited than usual. He may have taken it after I arrived; I noticed his mood change.'

Zarifa growled and came out from beneath the hoverbed to stare at her. When the cat sent Marietta an image of her stirring the Mandrax into Edric's coffee, she almost jumped in fright. For an instant, her hand went to her mouth, but then, controlling herself, she ignored the cat and pretended not to have noticed anything. This time, Zarifa planted herself at Marietta's feet and gazed up into her face, whiskers erect and dark ears twitching back and forth. Even when Peri focused on her as well, Marietta refused to yield. Instead, she moved over towards Edric and took his hand. It was all Stefano and the cats could do not to pounce on her; they all wanted to shake her until she told the truth!

Oblivious to this undercurrent of tension, the practitioner administered an antidote and Edric soon began to recover, first regaining consciousness, then breathing almost normally. The swelling slowly began to subside and his face lost some of its redness. He opened his eyes, saw Marietta and felt his hand in hers. 'What happened?' he asked, bewildered at being in a medcentre again. 'Am I still reacting to the cats?'

Having no idea what he meant, Marietta simply pressed his hand and looked at Stefano, the smile on her face a silent challenge. He joined her and said, 'No, Edric. It's not the cats this time. You had Mandrax in your bloodstream. Apparently it doesn't agree with you, but you've been given an antidote, which seems to be working.'

Edric snatched his hand away from Marietta's. 'You idiot! Did you think you could get me into bed by giving me drugs? Get her away from me!' He tried to sit up, but fell back, gasping.

Shocked, the practitioner turned to Marietta and then to Stefano. 'Are you telling me this woman gave you the Mandrax?' she asked, pointing at Marietta.

'Yes, I am,' said Edric, in a hoarse whisper, and then coughed, but managed to continue. 'I certainly didn't take it myself. I want her charged!' His colour worsened as he attempted to say something further. The practitioner told him to rest while she called the peacekeepers. The accusation could not be ignored, but sorting this out was their responsibility, not hers.

'I have no intention of staying here to listen to this nonsense,' stated Marietta calmly. 'Edric, how could you accuse *me* of such a thing? You were tired when I arrived, yet soon wanted to enjoy the night in my company. You took it when you made the coffee, yes? Très bien. If you want me to go, I will go. Do *not* try to contact me again. I can live perfectly well without people who turn on their friends to hide their own shortcomings.'

Marietta began to walk towards the main entrance, but Stefano and the two cats blocked her path. Each time she tried to step past them, they moved. If she wanted to leave, she would have to physically force her way out. Even though Marietta seriously considered doing exactly that, her sense of decorum won. Too ridiculous to be seen scrapping in public! Instead, she sat down, crossed her elegant legs, folded her hands, and waited. Before long, the peacekeepers arrived and the practitioner told them what had happened. They spoke with Edric for some time, occasionally glancing at the small group near the entrance before finally approaching them.

'Marietta Ross,' said one the peacekeepers, 'we are placing you under arrest on suspicion of administering Mandrax to Edric without his consent or knowledge. You must accompany us to the Brisbane Detention Centre. Is there anyone you wish to call or to bring with you?'

Casting a contemptuous glance at Stefano, Marietta stood up, shook her head, and without saying a word, went with them. Stefano, his arms folded and his face grim, watched from the entrance as they walked to the waiting airjet. Peri and Zarifa watched as well, until the airjet lifted off and disappeared from sight. By the time they joined Edric again, he was now sitting up and feeling a great deal better.

'Maybe there's an up-side to all this,' joked Stefano. 'At least Marietta is being charged with what she should be charged with, and we can hope they find out more, now they have her in custody.'

Edric frowned. 'I suppose so. Damned woman! Did she honestly think I'd be interested in *her*? Rhianna's hardly been dead a month!'

'What happened? Did she try to lead you astray?' Stefano saw the humour in the situation, and so, all of a sudden, did Edric. He laughed, relieved his symptoms would not be as troublesome as when he reacted to the cats, and because Marietta was totally unaware that he and Stefano were the ones who suggested to the FSIU that she was responsible for distributing Mandrax here in Australia. The irony of her being caught in this way amused them both.

'Mind you,' said Edric, once he'd calmed down, 'I don't know how they're going to prove she gave it to me. If she had any left, she'd have gotten rid of it by now.'

'Down your toilet, I suspect,' said Stefano, no longer laughing. 'She went just before we left. I couldn't exactly tell her not to, could I?'

'No, I suppose not. Still, it's a pity. I wonder whether the peacekeepers will feel like searching for it.' He laughed again, even though it wasn't particularly funny this time. 'I also wonder if I can go home yet,' he added, patting his pocket for his comlink. 'What time is it? 04:12! No wonder I want to go home. I'd love to get some sleep!'

Stefano looked around for someone to ask and soon found the practitioner.

'I'll check him one more time, and if everything has returned to normal, you can take him home. Although make sure you, or someone else, stays with him, will you? It's unlikely anything will happen, but it's best to be certain. I'll give him a light sedative first.'

Stefano nodded, and once Edric was ready to leave, helped him walk to the main entrance since he was still a little unsteady on his feet. The cats followed, voicing their concern with the occasional soft burble. A few patients watched them leave, pointing and smiling, never having seen cats in a medcentre before, and particularly without their leashes: Stefano had completely forgotten to put them on. It was cold outside and he'd also forgotten to bring something warm for Edric to wear, so gave him his own jacket to put over his shoulders. Before long, they reached the callstation and shortly afterwards were back in the apartment, both exhausted and ready for bed.

Chiu Liow Jones was never one to procrastinate. Earlier in the day, he had contacted the Brisbane Peacekeeping Force to let them know Marietta was on her way and that he would be conducting a formal interview with her on her return to Melbourne – *if* she returned to Melbourne. Otherwise, he would come to Brisbane for the interview, so in the meantime, could they please keep an eye open for her and let him know if anything 'unusual' turned up? Consequently, the peacekeepers who arrested Marietta soon contacted Chiu Liow. They told him they would search her, together with wherever she was staying, and agreed that if anything at all suspicious was found, she could be held until Chiu Liow came to Brisbane to conduct his interview. If nothing was found, then all they could do would be to place her under discreet surveillance until she returned to Melbourne. Meanwhile, a search of Edric's apartment would be done a little later, given he needed time to recover from his ordeal.

As a result, an 'interesting' procedure awaited Marietta at the Brisbane Detention Centre. She put up with the indignity of being searched and examined, and of being kept in detention until the peacekeepers returned from her hotel, with nothing to show for their efforts. The search of Edric's apartment failed to turn up anything either. Their only hard evidence was his coffee cup with traces of Mandrax in it. Logically, there was no reason to say he hadn't put it in there himself, despite his vehement denials.

Consequently, Marietta was released during the afternoon, angry, tired, and in no mood for further visits; Ruth would have to wait until another time. What to do instead? Fortunately, she had her camera and equipment with her, so rented a landjet and drove to the Lamington reserve area to spend a relaxing evening and night in the mountains, followed by a full day's photography, and a second evening doing very little other than viewing the results of her work. Feeling a great deal better, she returned to Melbourne as promised and to his amazement met Chiu Liow at the Hawthorn Reconciliation Centre at 10:00 on the Thursday morning.

Marietta held out her hand, which Chiu Liow briefly shook, suggesting they begin the interview at once. He led the way into a small, sunlit room with a wonderful view of the Yarra River and offered her coffee or tea. She accepted the tea, and after Chiu Liow fetched some for himself, he introduced her to the Witness, who inclined her head in acknowledgement. Finally, Chiu Liow indicated Marietta should take all the time she needed to reply to his questions; they had all day if necessary.

'I am not in the habit of playing games,' he began. 'We have interviewed a large number of people with whom you have financial dealings and three are willing to testify to your being a distributor of the drug, Mandrax. We believe a significant number of the remainder also purchased Mandrax from you, although to date we have no evidence to confirm this. Two of those willing to testify are contacts you made via the martial arts tournaments in Brisbane. The other you met when you were employed to design the interior of their new living room...which, I might add, they were extremely pleased with. I am sure you will be glad to hear this... However, all three appear to dislike you intensely, which we will take into account in terms of the veracity of their testimony. Even so, we are convinced they are telling the truth. Now, what have you to say?' Chiu Liow smiled pleasantly and waited.

The silence continued. Marietta watched the small dust motes floating in a beam of sunlight and wondered how it had all come to this. Since the arrest in Brisbane, she was intuitive enough to know the Mandrax issue would almost certainly be followed up, and there was always the possibility that one of the addicts would rat. Such people could usually be counted on to disappoint. Stupid! How could she have been so stupid? There was only one choice, for underestimating this peacekeeper was not something she felt inclined to do. Taking a deep breath to calm herself, she said, 'Before I tell you the whole story, Peacekeeper Jones, I wish to bargain. What have you to offer?' Marietta did her best to be polite, knowing it was in her own interest, yet could barely refrain from snarling at him. Fortunately, she was a good actor.

'I can inform the Judge you cooperated fully, which it will take into account. However, I can make no promises. So far, you will be charged with assault and with distribution of an illegal substance. Anything else you have to tell me may increase the number of charges, or may introduce mitigating circumstances. Either way, it is up to you, but in my opinion, the best idea is to tell me everything and accept the consequences. In that manner, you can move away from what I can only term this 'ugliness' and begin a fresh path. From what I already know about you, there is a great deal that is worthwhile in your life. I am sure you would prefer to lose as little of it as possible.'

For a few moments Marietta once again weighed her options, then calmly related how Michiko Yamada, whom she had never before met, contacted her by comlink to introduce herself as a sponsor of artists and to issue an invitation to attend a gallery opening in Córdoba, all expenses paid. The exhibition consisted of works by the most promising new interior designers in South America and was therefore of particular interest to people in Marietta's field. She didn't hesitate to accept, and enjoyed both the exhibition and the company of the people to whom she was introduced.

After a sumptuous dinner at the gallery, Michiko invited her home for the evening and showed Marietta some of the most valuable artworks in her private collection, kept under high security in a purpose-built, environment-controlled gallery. A tour of the house impressed Marietta with its grandeur, tasteful design and obvious wealth. Even the collection of exotic plants was arranged for maximum effect. She had her camera with her and took several excellent images, later presenting them to Michiko, who was delighted, expressing her gratitude with a small silver armband, decorated with gryphons. Marietta was astounded; the gift far outweighed her own, no matter how well the images were composed. Michiko explained that she herself took great pleasure in designing jewellery and other silver items, so was more than happy that Marietta was pleased with the gift. They parted on excellent terms.

Before long, Michiko contacted Marietta again, this time with a proposal for a series of portraits, where the artists were to pose with one of their own artworks. The series was to be used for an exhibition in its own gallery space, for which Marietta was to be the chosen designer and photographer. The commission was accepted with enthusiasm and the end result caused a sensation within Argentina. Afterwards, Michiko used her influence to bring work to her new protégé. As a result, Marietta's circle of acquaintances widened considerably, which in turn led to further work, both in South America and within Australia.

As the trust between the two women deepened, Michiko shared with Marietta her interest in martial arts and full contact tournaments, together with the fact that Rhianna O'Connor was a mutual acquaintance and personal friend. Knowing of this relationship made Marietta uncomfortable. She was already envious of Rhianna's martial arts prowess and annoyed at the rejection of her own offers of friendship. Nevertheless, Marietta did her best to overcome her feelings and pretended to be interested when Michiko related how Rhianna and she were becoming increasingly close, and how much she and her family enjoyed the Australian's visits. Subsequently, by keeping a close eye on Rhianna's movements and staying abreast of anything Ruth, Edric or Stefano knew of her travels abroad, Marietta made sure her own visits never coincided with those made by Rhianna. Fortunately, Michiko herself never suggested they visit together.

This almost overwhelming feeling of jealousy and the sense of being in competition for Michiko's friendship caused Marietta to be accessible to the skilful approach that eventually led her to begin using her connections within the art world to exchange Mandrax for information: information that could help Michiko obtain worthwhile additions to her collection of artworks and antiquities. To begin with, Marietta thought these additions were legitimate, that Michiko merely wanted to purchase them at the most competitive price and was prepared to go to unusual lengths to ensure she was first in line. However, when Marietta's curiosity finally overcame her need for Michiko's approval, she began to investigate further. She found, initially to her severe discomfort, that the items in question formerly belonged to the Federation and were not originally for sale. Having an acute sense of self-preservation that was already feeling threatened, Marietta refused to have anything further to do with the Mandrax operation.

At this point, Michiko threatened to reveal Marietta's role in distributing the drug, as well as her participation in the Brisbane tournaments. When Marietta replied to the threat with one of her own, Michiko simply stated that if she was to be exposed, then Marietta would become known as her accomplice in the illegal acquisition of valuable Federation property. This was seven months ago.

'You must understand, Peacekeeper Jones, that I had no choice but to continue. What was I to do? I have been stupid, without doubt. Did I truly think this woman was my friend? Yes, I did. I have been undeniably blind and will now pay the price. I ask only that she pays as well...heavily!'

'Thank you, Marietta. Your evidence will help corroborate our other information associated with Michiko Yamada's role in the distribution of an illegal substance. It will also give us a useful foundation for investigating your allegations relating to theft from the Federation. I will discuss the situation with my colleagues in the Federation Special Investigation Unit, since this comes under their jurisdiction. For the time being, you will not be charged as an accomplice, but you are not to leave the country and will be placed under surveillance until such time the matter is fully resolved. Do you understand?'

'Yes,' said Marietta, meeting Chiu Liow's eyes, 'I understand.'

'Good. I expect the case against you for the existing charges will not take long to prepare. You will be asked to attend a hearing, at which time the Judge will deliver its verdict. Are you familiar with this procedure?'

'Yes I am,' she replied, 'although I am quite sure you will tell me everything I need to know.' Marietta gave him a small smile. Somehow, she trusted this man, despite there being very few people she had ever trusted.

'You will certainly be kept fully informed, and in the meantime, will be allocated a Defence Counsel. May I suggest you are completely frank with them and avoid doing anything to compromise your case.' Chiu Liow studied her closely, wanting her to fully understand just how serious her situation was.

'Oh yes, you can be quite certain I will behave myself. There will be no more midnight visits to anyone.'

'Very well. On that promising note, you may leave. I shall escort you outside.' Chiu Liow opened the door for her.

Marietta went home and spent the rest of the day thinking about how best to celebrate her revenge upon the Artistic and Cultural Director of Wyvern Meridian.

'Hello, sweetheart, how did it go?' Morag missed Chiu Liow, having now spent almost seven weeks in Luzern. It was time she returned to Melbourne and felt his arms around her. Comlink calls, no matter how frequent, were no substitute.

'You were right,' answered Chiu Liow. 'Our Madame Yamada *has* been adding to Kakura's collection of stolen Federation art. She used Marietta Ross to obtain information that would lead her to people who could help obtain the pieces she wanted, so I think we can safely assume the Director of the National Fine Arts Gallery in Argentina will have been similarly used. We don't, of course, know whether he was also a dupe, or whether he was a full accomplice. At least we can now ask him the right questions. Do you want me to call the Argentineans, or will you?'

'I'll do it. That way, they can report directly back to me if they manage to get him to confess – or at least give himself or Michiko away. Do you believe Marietta when she says she didn't know what was really going on at the beginning?'

'Yes, oddly enough, I do. She's an arrogant, selfish woman, but is intelligent and has a strong enough sense of self-interest to know when she's in far too deep. Distributing Mandrax is serious, yet the scale of distribution seems to be small, even if the financial returns were fairly substantial. Taking on the Federation is entirely out of her league. Now, when are you coming back?'

'Soon...unless you want to come here?' Morag had retained her beautiful Swiss house on The Rigi, overlooking Luzern.

'I can't just now, even though I wish I could take the next flight this evening and be with you tomorrow... I'll have to dream about you instead.'

'Well, sweet dreams, my darling.' Morag touched a finger to the screen and Chiu Liow did the same. 'Let me know if anything else turns up, though I'm delighted with the witnesses you and the peacekeepers in Brisbane have found. I'll call Freddi once it's morning over there and ask her to interview Michiko again. Hopefully, Gwenllian will be able to learn more when the question of the thefts and the relationship with Marietta is raised. What we need to know is, where's the collection?'

'We certainly do. There'd be some very happy gallery directors throughout the world if everything was returned.'

'We'll look forward to it...but I'd better go. Bye for now.' Morag blew him a kiss and closed the connection.

For a few minutes, Chiu Liow sat quietly contemplating the situation, then set about making the arrangements required to substantiate Marietta's information.

CHAPTER TWENTY-SIX

Michiko Yamada, a Witness, Gwenllian, Freddi and Meng Jarrah were seated facing each other in the guest room of Michiko's home, where she took the lead, inviting them all to choose from the wide variety of beverages available. Her housekeeper offered them a selection of small cakes and dainty open sandwiches. Everyone, including the Witness, helped themselves. Since the day was cold, wet and windy, the open fireplace flickered and glowed, the flames leaping from the wood, which spat and crackled as if in protest at being burnt. All Michiko's 'guests' were fascinated by so rare a sight. For some time, the only sounds came from the fire and from small murmurs of thanks as the housekeeper went from one person to the next with his tray.

After sipping her tea with appreciation and eating one of the smoked salmon sandwiches, Freddi began the formal interview by handing Michiko an image of Marietta Ross. 'We have testimony that suggests you supplied this woman with Mandrax to use as a tool for gathering information from influential people within the art world, which she subsequently passed on to you. You then used this information to obtain a number of rare and valuable items that were stolen from the Federation at various points in time. We believe you used your position within Wyvern Meridian to the same end, adding to a collection your bondmate, Kenjiro Kakura, began many years ago. We intend to pursue this matter until we locate the collection. What have you to say?'

'Why, nothing at all. It is all lies. I have met and know this woman – that much is true. She is a conceited, self-indulgent, spiteful person who contacted me some time ago, no doubt because Rhianna mentioned her friendship with me. Marietta Ross simply saw an opportunity to widen her circle of customers through my patronage. To begin with, I saw her as intelligent, talented and generally hard-working. As a result, I had no objection to recommending her to my contacts for commissions where it seemed appropriate. To my disappointment, as time went by, it appeared she was not entirely reliable and I told her our business relationship was at an end. Marietta reacted badly, even sending a threatening message, after which I had no further contact. I kept the message. Do you want to see it?' Michiko found the entry on her comlink and handed it to Freddi. 'I can give you a copy, if you wish,' she offered.

'Thank you,' said Freddi, reading the message and frowning. 'Why didn't you report this to the peacekeepers? She makes it clear that as far as she's concerned, you're responsible for the supply of Mandrax to Australia.'

'Why would I report something so patently false? What else could she do other than continue to lie, as she has now, in order to exert pressure on me? As I have said, Marietta is a spiteful woman.' Michiko shrugged her elegant shoulders and glanced disapprovingly at the screen when Freddi returned the comlink.

Freddi took care not to show her surprise at Michiko's explanation, which, unfortunately, was plausible – unless Marietta could provide more than her own word as evidence. 'Do you have any reason to think Marietta may have taken Mandrax herself?' she asked.

'No, I honestly cannot say I have noticed any behaviour that might suggest it. In my view, she is not the type to take drugs, yet I suspect she might enjoy exactly what you accused me of: having the power to give and to withhold.'

Since their last interview, Michiko had apparently taken time to think about her situation, now adopting a far more conciliatory and helpful attitude. Their interview was interrupted, however, by a knock at the door, which Michiko turned to answer. Her small daughter came in and approached, standing by her mother's knee, at first shy at being in a room with all these strangers.

'This is my youngest child, Aiko.' Michiko invited her daughter to sit next to her on the settee, then held the girl close, kissing her forehead. Aiko smiled sweetly and kissed her mother's cheek, before carefully studying the others in the room. 'Who are all these people?' she asked, turning back to her mother.

'They are here to ask me some questions. Do you want to know their names?'

'Yes, please,' lisped Aiko.

'This tall woman is named Freddi,' explained Michiko, indicating the peacekeeper. 'Next to her is Meng Jarrah, who helps investigate when people do things that are wrong. Then there is Gwenllian, who also helps, and finally, there is someone whose name we don't know, but who is a Witness – someone who is here to make sure that what we say is recorded accurately so no mistakes can be made later. Do you understand?'

'Yes, Mother, but why do they want to ask questions? Have you done something wrong?' Aiko peered into her mother's face, her own expression trusting and open.

'Yes, you know I have done something wrong. Do you remember when I told you all about how I hurt Felicity? But that is not why they are here today. They want to know if I have done something else wrong.'

'Have you?' the little girl asked, playing with the sleeve of her mother's gown.

'No, my sweet one, not this time. This time, someone has tried to hurt me by saying I have. Now, you go into the kitchen and ask Dorothea for some milk and a banana. It's time for you to have something. You don't want your little stomach to start growling, do you?'

'No, I don't want my stomach to growl.' Aiko giggled and hopped down onto the floor, making her way out of the room and leaving her audience to wonder whether her entrance had been orchestrated for their benefit. Even Gwenllian was unsure.

'Is there anything else you wish to know?' asked Michiko, meeting Freddi's gaze.

'Yes. How much have you told your children about Felicity?'

'I have told them I am under house arrest and their sister has left home. They deserve to know it is my fault and that Felicity may never return. Naturally, I have not told them everything, only that I struck her. I regret what I have done and expect the Judge to hold me to account. It is only a matter of hearing exactly what Felicity has said and then ensuring there are no exaggerations or misleading statements. My Defence Counsel was here this morning and has explained that we will have access to the interview records.'

Freddi was yet again surprised by this woman. It seemed there would be little resistance when it came to making their case against her for the abuse, assault and rape charges already laid. 'Yes, you will,' she replied. 'With your full cooperation, it's unlikely to be long before your trial is held. Still, I'm not entirely happy with your explanation of Marietta's conduct, and we haven't yet dealt with the question of stolen goods to my satisfaction. I've met Marietta, and although I agree with your assessment of her personality, it doesn't fully explain some of her testimony. She's able to provide a great many details...details which show a disconcertingly close relationship with the disappearance of the items I mentioned earlier. I put it to you that it is *you* who are lying, not her.' Freddi sat back, served herself more tea and watched Michiko closely, hoping she had said enough to give Gwenllian some answers. It was doubtful they would get them any other way.

Michiko picked up a small iced cake and ate it, then wiped her fingers on a serviette. 'You are entitled to think whatever you like,' she said eventually. 'I say it is Marietta Ross who lies, not I. Now, you are welcome to stay as long as you like, but I have work to do, and unless you have concrete evidence for me to answer, there is no point in *my* staying.' She stood up and left the room. At this point, without the concrete evidence referred to, there was no justification for preventing her from doing so.

*

The Witness went her own way while the others returned to their hotel, where Shela was waiting impatiently with Robert. Her annoyance at being left behind yet again soon disappeared when Freddi apologised and she was given a cuddle by them all, one after the other. Purring contentedly, she curled up by Robert's feet, thoroughly enjoying the experience of being near someone who had a mind as attuned to cats as his. Shela regarded Gwenllian as a type of grimalkin, but Robert...he was different. Definitely a wight, yet his ability to almost bond with her mind and channel her powers – and even amplify them – was exhilarating. In the process, her own understanding of wights – their feelings, lives and relationships – was expanded until she could almost begin to fully understand them. When Gwenllian was in the room as well, the potential was almost too much to contemplate, so she kept this to herself...for the time being.

Meanwhile, Freddi checked her comlink for messages from Chiu Liow, but was disappointed not to find any. Marietta had given the peacekeepers access to her household computer and surrendered her comlink to allow the items to be examined for any records that had not been permanently deleted and which might confirm her version of Michiko's involvement in the supply of Mandrax. Freddi was waiting to hear the results.

'Did you manage to find out anything, Gwennie?' she said, putting her comlink away. 'I hope so, because we still don't have any real answers.' Freddi made herself comfortable on the deep-crimson couch by the window, with Meng Jarrah curled up next to her. Gwenllian and Robert sat opposite in matching armchairs.

'I'm sorry to say that Michiko is confident we won't be able to prove she's involved with the drugs,' answered Gwenllian. 'Unless there's been a slip-up and Marietta can provide us with something more substantial than she already has, I don't think we'll be able to make a case against her. I suppose the main thing is, it *has* all stopped. That's something to be glad for, isn't it?'

'Yes, I suppose so,' replied Freddi, 'although it's unfortunate that so far no one who's been interviewed in Australia has suggested that Michiko, or Wyvern Meridian, are involved in any way...only Marietta. Anything else?'

'Yes and no, I'm afraid. She really is able to suppress her feelings and memories to an extraordinary extent. What I did manage to see is that there *is* a collection, though not here. I received an image of someone Michiko refers to as 'the Curator': a man, quite elderly, whose real name she doesn't know, strangely enough, and who had a close association with her bondmate before he died. There are also two countries in her mind: Korea and Austria, although I'm not sure whether the collection is kept in one of them, or if this Curator lives there. Still, I think whoever manages the collection must have extensive training in the handling and storage of valuable works of art and antiquities. Not everyone could do it. Would that be somewhere for the FSIU to begin?'

'It might well be,' answered Freddi, feeling more optimistic. 'Based on your information, I'm sure Morag will soon narrow down the field, and at least we may have confirmation that Marietta was telling the truth about the reason for the Mandrax operation. Overall, I'd say we've done fairly well, though we still don't know whether Rhianna died accidentally or was murdered, and if so, by whom. Mind you, it doesn't seem possible that the Sensa she used could have contained amanita by accident. Someone must have put it in the jar on purpose, but whether to kill or not, that's still the question.'

She glanced at Robert, who held Gwenllian's hand as it lay on the arm of her chair. He returned her gaze. 'We *will* find out,' he said, 'one way or another. We have two suspects, one of whom is dead, but Felicity is still alive, so we need to work out how to get around the shield she uses to prevent Gwenllian and Shela from fully entering her mind. I have a proposal, if you're willing to allow me to become involved.'

The three women listened closely while he outlined his plan. After a great deal of discussion, they agreed to it, bizarre as the idea was. Even Shela felt uneasy, but also agreed to participate.

'Are you sure it's wise?' Chiu Liow's golden eyes met Freddi's across the distance separating them.

Freddi grinned, having heard these words many times before, and even more frequently as a child. 'No, but I can't think of anything else to do. I know it's a radical departure from normal procedure, but Guillermo is dead, Gwenllian finds Michiko remarkably hard to read, and apparently Felicity can block her. Even Shela is confused by Felicity, so what else is there left?'

'Not a lot, I must admit. When will you do it?' Chiu Liow raised one eyebrow, imagining the scene that would take place. He suddenly shivered.

'As soon as the Judge gives permission. Has everyone finished entering everything they have on Marietta? We need to be sure the Judge has all the facts before it comes to a decision about this.'

'Yes, Smithson and Morag have both confirmed that all the interviews are done, and all our evidence is as tidy as it will ever be. Now, tell me, Freddi, how good is the security system in Rhianna O'Connor's apartment, and is there any chance Marietta could have killed her intentionally? Edric said she seemed remarkably familiar with the apartment, and despite what she's told you, she certainly had plenty of reasons to want her dead.'

Since Freddi liked sharing her cases with her brother when they were somewhat out of the ordinary, she had filled him in on the details of her first interview with Marietta, held soon after Rhianna's body was discovered. So, although he knew Shela was present during this interview, and had been told that neither Peri nor Zarifa sensed Marietta intended to kill Rhianna, Chiu Liow was nevertheless beginning to wonder whether the cats were as reliable as they had earlier thought.

Freddi frowned. She hated the notion of Shela, or the other cats, being wrong. 'Apparently the security system is state of the art,' she said. 'It seems Rhianna was an expert, and with FSIU funding, unless there's even more to Marietta than we already know, I doubt she could have broken in. Still, it would explain a lot if she did. Obsession makes people do strange things. Rummaging around in the bedroom and finding the Sensa may have given her the idea.'

'She'd need to have an unusually good knowledge of botany, or access to people who do, to come up with something like amanita poisoning. Of course, Kakura died from eating the wrong mushroom, which is on public record, and if Marietta was jealous of Rhianna's relationship with Michiko, she may have done some reading.'

'True... It's the link to Kenjiro Kakura and the coincidence of them both dying from amanita poisoning that started us thinking Michiko might be involved, particularly once we discovered who made Rhianna's silver ear circlets. However, according to both Edric and Stefano, Marietta appeared utterly astounded when Rhianna died. On the other hand, if she did do it, she may only have wanted to harm Rhianna with the poison, not kill her...possibly to keep her from winning the tournament, yet again. Losing all the time must have driven Marietta crazy.'

'It's certainly a worthwhile theory, though didn't you say Felicity has extensive botanical knowledge?'

'Yes, Gwenllian did tell us, and it's one of the reasons we've decided to proceed with our plan.'

'Well, I'll look forward to hearing how it works out. By the way, do you think Marietta was ever in Rhianna's apartment *with* her permission?'

'No, I don't, because I imagine Edric would have known, but perhaps downstairs in the travel consultancy. Being so obsessed with Rhianna, and also being an interior designer, Marietta quite likely couldn't resist taking a look at where she lived. I did a search and found that, being a heritage-listed building, its plans are publicly available on the lattice.'

Chiu Liow nodded thoughtfully, then paused and said, 'Going back to the reason I called, there was only one message left on Marietta's comlink that's of any help in confirming her story. They were both remarkably careful. The last one, sent by Michiko on the twenty-fifth of July, Argentinean time, reads, "Suspend all operations immediately". Now, even though we can easily conclude what Madame Yamada meant by this, it's of little use as actual evidence. Still, it'd be interesting to see how she explains it, so could you ask?'

'Yes, of course, Chiu, though I imagine she'll come up with a plausible explanation and we'll *still* be no further ahead. Wasn't there anything at all on Marietta's household computer we can use?'

'No. She told me she didn't keep any records of their transactions on it. Marietta went to the trouble of using pen and paper to write down anything she wanted to remember, then destroyed the notes once they were finished with. Unusual, to say the least... However, don't be so pessimistic, Freddi. After all, at least the Mandrax is no longer being distributed, and we've closed down the tournaments in Australia and in Argentina. Morag's happy with what you've given her as well, and thinks it may be possible to track down the stolen collection, even if it does take time. She now has access to Michiko's personal financial records too, so can begin reconciling them against expenditures. Something will turn up. She has a way of ferreting out the truth.' Chiu Liow grinned.

'As do you, brother dear! Come to think of it, how's Edric?'

'Ah, yes... I've met both Edric and Stefano since we last spoke. The occasion was most enjoyable and quite fascinating. *You* would have enjoyed yourself immensely, I'm sure.' Chiu Liow paused, teasing Freddi, as he often did these days. Morag had wrought some small changes in him, passing on a little of her own mischievous sense of humour. Freddi, used to him, waited patiently for him to explain: 'It seems that *I* am now the unofficial Australian heavyweight martial arts champion, although I admit to using rather irregular techniques to defeat him.' He laughed, waiting for Freddi's reaction, and was pleased when her expression showed her complete astonishment.

'What on Earth are you talking about?!' she exclaimed.

'I came up to Brisbane yesterday and they were here to speak with the BPF about applying for positions as martial arts instructors, or even assistants, on a voluntary basis. Apparently they discussed the proposal with Nyneve before leaving Stanthorpe. She followed up and arranged the meeting, although they had to postpone because of Edric's run-in with Marietta. It seems this is their way of making up for the absence of their full-contact tournaments. Not that they'll get *quite* the same experience, but I'm sure both sides to the agreement will learn a great deal.' Chiu Liow raised his eyebrows and waggled them at his sister.

'But what happened? How did *you* become involved?' Freddi knew her brother was her superior in the field of martial arts, though mainly because of his being her senior and having many more years experience. Still, to defeat Edric! She studied the screen more closely, trying to see if he was joking. He soon told her the rest of the story.

'Stefano and Edric have one great weakness,' he said. 'Despite it being extremely difficult to bring them down, once down, they're fairly easy to keep that way. They don't know aikido; we do, and if I may say so, I'm really rather good at it.' Chiu Liow grinned and bowed.

'Were you wearing protective gear?' asked Freddi, wondering how far the 'interview' had gone.

'Oh yes, some... Just enough to keep us from serious injury, should an accident occur, but not enough to hinder us. Exhilarating, although somewhat against regulations. Naturally, the event won't be repeated.'

'No, I imagine it won't,' answered Freddi, pulling a face. 'Well, as a matter of fact, it's good news for me. I was intending to speak with Edric about him taking me on as a sparring partner. I'm out of practice.' Freddi was too embarrassed to tell Chiu Liow about Michiko slapping her. The teasing would be more than she could endure, even with her unusually high store of patience.

'We don't see each other often enough, otherwise you wouldn't be. I enjoy our bouts, even if I do nearly always defeat you.'

With a mock grimace, Freddi favoured him with a rude gesture. 'Tell Edric I commiserate and that I look forward to meeting him for some exercise. That should give him some incentive to learn more about *our* methods, besides having been sat on by you!'

'I didn't *sit* on him as such. Still, I suppose being pinned down has the same psychological effect. He took it well, though. He's a good man. I can see why you like him. He and Stefano will make an excellent addition to your team. Now, Freddi, I promised to call Morag, so give my love to Meng Jarrah, will you?'

'Yes, I will, and likewise to Morag. I'll speak with you again soon, I'm sure.'

Freddi rejoined the others and they all listened attentively while she gave them the details of the call, laughing good-naturedly, however, when Edric's plight was described. Robert had yet to meet Chiu Liow, but if the peacekeeper was as impressive as Freddi, there was little doubt Edric had met his match.

As Morag trusted Rohan Maerz's assessment of Kenjiro Kakura's relationship with his bondmate, she felt sure Michiko Yamada had no knowledge of his criminal activities until the Federation intervention into the affairs of Wyvern Meridian. There was every reason to believe more of his deeds became known to her only after his death, and it was therefore conceivable that she was unaware of the existence of the stolen collection. If so, why did Gwenllian find references to it in her thoughts and memories? Was it possible Michiko had something entirely different in mind when interviewed?

Searching through Michiko's financial and other personal records for more information was a complex and time-consuming task, even when so much of the search was automated – there were tendrils reaching out all over the globe. However, using Gwenllian's insights, Morag concentrated on two countries and one area of expertise: Korea and Austria, and anyone Michiko had dealings with who was associated with the conservation of artworks, antiques or historical artefacts.

Recent travel records showed she had taken an overnight trip to Seoul on the thirtieth of July. Shortly before the flight, an amount had been transferred into the account of someone called the 'Curator', as well as into the account of a privately owned museum in Austria for which he or she held overall curatorial responsibility. The museum appeared to have been founded one hundred and twenty-two years ago with the purpose of preserving items of interest specific to the cultural history of Austria, concentrating in particular on ceramics from the nineteenth through to the twenty-second century. To all appearances, the organisation seemed entirely legitimate and of high repute.

A search of Federation records revealed that the Curator, a man, was born in 2374 and that he was also employed by Seoul University as their Conservator of Japanese Archives. This seemed far too great a coincidence. Knowing Kenjiro Kakura usually inspired an almost fanatical loyalty in his employees and followers – and at the cost of their lives if not – it was a reasonable working assumption that whoever helped him care for the collection during his lifetime might still do so.

Upon checking his recent travel records, Morag discovered the Curator had taken a flight from Seoul to Córdoba the day after Michiko's return home. A call to Michiko confirmed he had paid her a visit to view an item in her own private collection and to provide a certificate of authenticity, should its provenance require verification. Michiko had shown Morag the artwork in question, an impressive sixteenth-century still life by a Dutch master, wonderful in its richness of hue and attention to fine detail.

'How long have you known the Curator?' asked Morag, after the vault had once more been securely locked.

'Since Kenjiro's funeral. He introduced himself to me as a former colleague of my bondmate's and wished to give me his condolences. He is a memorable man, which you will understand when you meet him, as I am sure you will. I found him to have an excellent reputation within his field, so have frequently consulted him over the years.' Michiko glanced at her comlink. 'If there is nothing else, will you please excuse me? It is time for my daughter's music lesson.'

'Yes, of course. That's all I wanted to know. Thank you. Perhaps we'll meet in person some day.'

'Yes, no doubt, Coordinator MacIain,' replied Michiko, raising one finely outlined eyebrow and then closing the connection.

*

Fortunately, the Curator was currently in Austria, so Morag's next call was to make an appointment to meet him in person that day. Although surprised by his appearance, she reserved judgement until they met. When they eventually shook hands, she noticed his had a soft, dry, papery texture. He reminded her of a giant fruit bat, only not as appealing. With a polite smile, Morag asked him about the origins of his name.

'I have no other name, Coordinator MacIain. I am known only as the Curator. If I ever owned another name, I have forgotten it.' He bowed, the ribbons on his hat bobbing about in an almost ludicrous fashion.

Morag obviously found his words difficult to accept, and yet the Federation records contained no former name... Odd, very odd indeed. 'I am here in relation to a complex case the Federation Special Investigation Unit has been following for a number of years,' she said. 'In particular, we are interested in tracing the disappearance of certain Federation-owned items, which we felt you might be able to help us with, being a renowned expert in your field. Would you be willing to spend some time now going through the list with me?' Morag smiled winningly, whereupon the Curator showed his uneven teeth in an answering smile, although Morag somehow wished he hadn't.

'Most certainly, Coordinator MacIain. It would be my pleasure. Would you like to come with me to my little office? It is most comfortable.'

'Thank you. This shouldn't take too long, I hope.'

The Curator led the way down numerous corridors, all lined with impressive display cases, which Morag glanced at, promising herself to take a leisurely tour one day. She was sure the collection housed here rivalled anything the Federation could boast. Eventually they came to what was indeed a "little office" in terms of size, but as promised, the room *was* extremely well furnished and comfortable. Somehow the unusual décor suited this man and his unique taste in clothing, with the result that he appeared almost normal in this, his own setting.

Taking the seat indicated, Morag showed him a series of images of the more recently stolen Federation artefacts. The Curator examined each one closely, murmuring to himself and nodding from time to time. At one point, he consulted his computer, made a few notes on his comlink, cast a glance at Morag, then went back to the list without saying anything. Morag raised her eyebrows, relaxed a little further back into her chair, and waited. The silence in the room was punctuated only by the sound of the Curator's low voice and the ticking of an old clock, kept in a cabinet at one end of the room.

'Well,' he said, looking up, 'I hoped to have a lead for you, but it is only a copy, although a remarkably good one. Please accept my sympathy for having lost so many wonderful pieces. The Federation Assembly must be very annoyed. They are clever at having kept their losses secret for this long. If any information comes to my attention, you can rest assured I will let you know. You can also have confidence in my ability to keep this matter to myself.' The Curator inclined his head, his odd-coloured eyes studying Morag, taking in every nuance of her expression.

'Thank you; however we've decided not to keep the losses to ourselves any longer. A full description of the missing works will be circulated to all known museums, galleries and dealers tomorrow, and security measures will be improved to ensure nothing further goes missing. Also, a reward will be posted for the return of any of the missing items, together with an amnesty for anyone providing information leading to their recovery. Do you think this will be sufficient? I am interested in your professional opinion.' Morag studied the Curator in turn, her expression serious.

The Curator understood exactly what Morag had just implied, and folded one hand over the other, holding them close to his chest while he deliberated as to the best words to convey an equally unambiguous reply that, at the same time, gave nothing away. The old clock broke the silence by chiming the hour, a sound Morag had rarely heard before. Startled, she turned to look. When she turned back, the Curator replied to her question:

'Yes, I am sure your measures will give a clear warning to those responsible for the losses, as well as to anyone contemplating such reprehensible actions in the future. Nevertheless, I expect you will need to maintain your vigilance for many years, possibly even forever. Can the Federation manage to do that?'

'Oh yes. Once the Assembly has determined upon a course of action, it is exceptionally good at maintaining its momentum. Now, there's one last favour I would like to ask. Would you be willing to assist us with our list of dealers? There could well be private operators we are unaware of and, from your many years of purchasing and managing collections, you may be in a position to give us some names.'

'It would be a pleasure to assist, Coordinator MacIain. It would also be gratifying to think we could enjoy a much closer professional relationship in future. From time to time, there may be movements in the market that would be useful for you to be aware of. I have many contacts and can easily maintain a watchful eye for the Federation.' He bobbed his head, rubbed his hands together and sighed. 'How pleasant this has been! Is there anything I can offer you before your return to Switzerland?'

'No, thank you. It's such a short flight, I'll be home again in no time.' Morag stood, held out her hand, and was faintly relieved when it was released and she could leave the small room, no matter how cosy and inviting it seemed.

Once she was back in Switzerland, Morag arranged for the Curator to be placed under close surveillance, sure in her own mind that the collection existed and he was its caretaker.

*

'Are you ready, Robert?' asked Gwenllian, staring down at him as he sat, carefully positioned to minimise the eventual distance between them.

'Yes,' he said, his expression as serious as her own. 'Are you?'

'I think so... No, I'm sure I am. We can't afford to make a mistake. This is our only chance.' Bending over, she kissed his forehead and left the room, leaving Shela crouched at Robert's feet, apprehensive, tail and ears twitching, her eyes narrowed.

The interview room was silent, everyone waiting for Gwenllian to enter. Freddi, Meng Jarrah and a Witness were present, as was Felicity. Gwenllian sat down to Felicity's left, out of her immediate field of vision and facing the door to the passageway. Freddi greeted her with a nod and commenced the interview.

'Felicity, I understand from Gwenllian that you and Margrethe had a good talk, and that you even saw Harriet on your comlink screen. We're all glad to hear you got along so well and that you now feel you could make your home with them in Australia.'

Freddi paused, waiting to see if Felicity wanted to comment. The young woman simply smiled, her face happy and relaxed for the first time since Freddi had known her.

'Gwenllian has also told me you have an excellent knowledge of plants and suchlike, as well as a love of gardening. You and Margrethe will have a great deal in common, which we are very pleased to hear. However, I must ask you another question. Do you remember, the last time we spoke together, I asked if you knew how Rhianna died?'

Felicity nodded, so Freddi continued: 'I explained how we found something in her body that shouldn't have been there, and as a result, we were investigating further. I also told you that Rhianna used some Sensa, bought for her by Michiko. Our tests have revealed that it contained a certain type of fungus from the amanita family...an unknown species. Therefore, we are fairly sure she died from the effects of an amatoxin. Do you understand what I mean?'

Felicity's face had become a shade paler than normal and her expression was almost mask-like in its controlled neutrality. Her lips felt stiff when she finally replied. 'Yes, I understand perfectly. It would have been highly unpleasant for Rhianna before she died. I am sorry to hear it.'

'Yes, we think your friend would have begun to feel sick about half a day after using the Sensa, then would have begun to vomit and suffer violent abdominal pain, with diarrhoea. It's difficult to understand why she didn't tell her friends, but she was exceptionally fit and strong, so could have recovered quickly, to feel perfectly well for a few days. If she hadn't been weakened and then accidentally killed at the martial arts tournament, she no doubt would soon have died in agony, because by that time her internal organs would have been damaged beyond repair.'

Felicity's eyes were wide as she listened to Freddi and her breathing had become so shallow that she hardly seemed to breathe at all.

'Mind you, we did have a certain amount of trouble identifying the body,' lied Freddi, gambling that Felicity's knowledge of forensics was limited. 'It had lain in the open for around five days, so was badly decomposed. This means there is always the possibility that we were wrong and it was not Rhianna. You did point out how strange it was that she even considered using Sensa.'

Startled, and thoroughly confused, Felicity's eyes widened even further.

'All this may have been a huge mistake and perhaps Rhianna has simply gone on one of her trips,' explained Freddi.

'How...how could that be? You said she was killed at the martial arts tournament!' Felicity's voice trembled and her hands grasped nervously at her robe.

'We were *told* that the person who was killed was Rhianna, but these tournaments are illegal. For all we know, it was someone else, whose identity the organisers of these events don't want us to find out. It may even be someone *they* wanted dead.'

At that moment, they heard a soft tap at the door and turned to see who it was. The door opened and Rhianna O'Connor walked in, a warm smile on her beautiful face.

CHAPTER TWENTY-SEVEN

'No! No, you are dead! This cannot be! I killed you!' shrieked Felicity, leaping up from her chair and backing away. Rhianna walked towards her, hand outstretched as if to offer comfort. Felicity ran to the corner of the room and crouched there, trembling, her head bowed, hands over her face, hiding from this apparition. When she felt a hand on her shoulder, Felicity screamed in fear, turning to thrust it from her, only to find the hand belonged to Gwenllian. She gasped in horror and stared around the room. Rhianna was nowhere to be seen.

'Felicity, tell me how you killed Rhianna. Her spirit must be laid to rest. It's time you unburdened your conscience and told us everything.' Gwenllian spoke kindly, convincingly, insisting on being listened to and obeyed.

When Felicity searched her face, desperately hoping to find an answer, Gwenllian nodded and said, 'It's time to tell us. You know you want to. Come over here with me. I'll sit next to you, and you can tell me what happened.' Gwenllian took Felicity by the hand and led her to a seat by the window, where they were facing a little away from the others. When Felicity, her face pale and still, finally spoke, her hand trembled in Gwenllian's.

'I wanted to kill myself, so put the amanita in the jar of Sensa I was to take with me next time my mother chose to use me for her entertainment. I wanted her to know it was *she* who made me die! I didn't *want* to die, but where was I to go? *Where was I to go?!* I only wanted her to be my mother again, as we used to be before Kenjiro died...' Felicity's face crumpled in a grimace of loathing, whether for herself or for Michiko, Gwenllian could not tell – perhaps both. 'I went to Rhianna's room to say goodbye. She was to return to Australia the next day, which meant I would never see her again. Then I heard her! I listened to her make the recording for the Federation and heard her say my father had been evil! He was the best man in the world...the best father anyone could want... Rhianna betrayed him! She was his lover and betrayed him to the Federation. It was her fault my mother became lost in grief when he died...*her* fault my mother treated me the way she did!' Felicity grasped Gwenllian's hand even tighter, staring into her face with wild, frightened eyes, her breathing fast, gasping between the sobs.

'What did you do, Felicity?' Gwenllian gently stroked her hair, looking directly into the tear-filled eyes.

Felicity made an effort to calm herself, breathing deeply, shaking her head as if to throw off the guilt. 'I knew Edric was her lover and that Michiko bought some Sensa as a gift. I also saw Rhianna open the jar to look at its contents, so I waited until her things were packed early the next morning, crept silently into the room and put my jar where hers was, then left. I did not think it would be long before she died.' Felicity abruptly turned to where Freddi sat, listening. 'You lied to me!' she shouted, leaping up from the chair, her hair tumbling out from its fastenings and falling down around her shoulders. 'You lied! How did you bring Rhianna back to life? Some trick... She's dead! *I* killed her!' Felicity collapsed onto the floor, weeping hysterically.

Freddi spoke to her comlink. Moments later, Felicity's counsellor entered the room and knelt by her charge, ready to help and to listen. Meng Jarrah rose and went over to Gwenllian, who looked exhausted. 'I think you and I should leave now,' she said softly. 'There's nothing else for us to do here.' Gwenllian nodded, going with her to the door, then a short distance down the corridor to where Robert and Shela waited in the next room, also exhausted by their combined efforts to bring the illusion of Rhianna to life.

Felicity lapsed into a state of complete withdrawal, which lasted for two days. Eventually, she told the counsellor she had confessed to Guillermo, who then took it upon himself to amend the Sensa purchase records. How he had done this, Felicity did not know because Guillermo refused to say, only reassuring her that she was safe. When he died, Felicity was convinced he had been killed because of what he did, refusing to even consider the possibility of suicide. 'There was no reason for Guillermo to kill himself! I loved him and had forgiven everything. We would have been happy together!' At this point, Felicity again withdrew, and nothing the medcentre could do was able to persuade her to tell the counsellor anything further.

'That still leaves us with Guillermo's death as a likely suicide and the death of the systems technologist either a highly coincidental accident or a possible murder at Guillermo's hands,' said Freddi, annoyed at having no further information to give the Coroner. 'I can't see any reason why Michiko would have arranged either death, can you?'

Meng Jarrah and Gwenllian both shook their heads. 'We'll have to leave it to the Córdoban peacekeepers and the Coroner to work out,' replied Meng Jarrah, stroking Shela, who lay between the two women, her dark head on Gwenllian's lap. 'We've solved the case we came here for, and have done our best to give them something to work with for the other two. Also, Freddi, while you were out, Morag called to say she and Chiu Liow are tidying up the last few threads of the Mandrax operation, and that the FSIU are still chasing Michiko for the art thefts. She's fairly sure now there's a collection somewhere and that Michiko continued the work Kakura began, though for what reason, we don't yet know. It's possible, of course, that to begin with the stolen pieces were simply resold for a profit, and when this was no longer necessary, Kakura kept them for his own enjoyment.'

Having been busy all morning speaking with Felicity's counsellor and her medcentre practitioner, as well as entering all their latest evidence into the Judge, Freddi had not been available when Morag called. 'Yes,' she said, 'that would make sense. Where does Morag think the collection is?'

As Freddi spoke, she nudged Shela with her toe, and the cat lazily put out a paw to play with her foot for a while, then curled up and fell asleep, sighing once or twice as she dreamed of their home in Australia. In her opinion, it was time to return.

'Most likely either in Austria or Korea somewhere,' said Meng Jarrah. 'She's tracked down the person called 'the Curator', who *is* a close associate of Michiko's and who literally is a curator, both at the university in Seoul and for one of the better museums in Austria. Apparently he's quite weird, but well respected within his profession. He openly admits to having known Kakura and to undertaking commissions for Michiko...of the legitimate type, obviously.' She paused, then added, 'Morag was impressed with our idea of having Robert and Shela amplify Gwen's powers, so asked if we could do the same with Madame Yamada – not to shock her with any 'ghosts' as such, but something similar.'

Freddi considered the idea for a few moments, then agreed. 'Yes, why not... It can't do any harm, and we wanted to re-interview her anyway. We also need to hear what she says to Felicity's confession. That alone might shock her enough to answer some of our other questions.'

They talked for a while longer about the arrangements for the next interview then met up with Robert to have afternoon tea in the hotel dining room. Shela had by this time become a favourite with the other guests, which meant they were no longer required to occupy a table in a far corner to avoid offending anyone. Instead, the group were given a place overlooking the river, where they could enjoy the view and where the other guests could also admire the cat to their heart's content – although they did so discreetly. She basked in their fascination, occasionally strolling over to playfully rub herself against a guest's leg and to accept any tidbits they chose to give her. As a consequence, she had noticeably put on weight, but ignored Freddi's threats to put her on a diet once they returned home. Shela knew the threat was an empty one, and besides, their regular runs by the river would soon allow her to regain her former trim figure.

Their afternoon tea was briefly interrupted by a call from the Coroner. Based on their evidence and the formal testimony of Michiko Yamada – which revealed little more than she had already given Freddi – the Coroner had come to the conclusion that the death of Guillermo should be recorded as a suicide, while that of the senior systems technologist was to be regarded as accidental. Nevertheless, each case would be flagged as open for reconsideration should the Judge determine it as being necessary once the pending trials of Michiko, Felicity and Marietta were concluded.

'Although it's likely Guillermo knew the systems technologist well and went to him for help after Felicity confessed, yet nevertheless decided to kill his friend in order to protect her, we have no evidence to support this theory,' said the Coroner. 'However, we do have a more complete picture of their circumstances at the time they died. This at least is satisfying, so I would like to thank you for your input. It has been extremely helpful, and I wish you all the best with your own case. Presumably I will hear the outcome in the near future?'

'I think so,' replied Freddi. 'Once we've dealt with some remaining loose ends, we can ask the Judge to set a date for the trial.'

'Good, good. Very well, I will allow you to return to your afternoon tea. The hotel usually keeps a delectable table.' The Coroner smiled, having noticed the background sounds and recognised the setting when Freddi answered her call.

'Thank you, and thank you as well for all your help. We greatly appreciate the level of cooperation we've received here.'

'Well, you may wish to return for a holiday some time soon. There is much to enjoy.'

'Yes, we were actually hoping to take some time to see the mountains while we were here, but I think it's time we went home. There are matters we should see to back in Australia.'

'I understand. On that note, I must leave you. If we do not meet again, please accept my best wishes for your return journey and the remainder of your stay.'

'Thank you,' said Freddi, and the Coroner closed the connection.

'I have no other explanation whatsoever to give you regarding this message. It is merely my final statement to Marietta Ross after deciding to terminate our association. I admit the wording could be misinterpreted, but at the time I was not in the mood to be expansive.'

Michiko sat quietly at ease, apparently unconcerned by the question relating to the message found on Marietta's comlink, which read, "Suspend all operations immediately". Gwenllian, with Robert and Shela's help from the nearby room in the Reconciliation Centre, could readily tell Michiko was lying, yet without further proof, their impressions would be insufficient to lay charges.

'I don't believe you, Michiko,' answered Freddi, standing with arms folded, glaring down at her, although this time keeping well out of striking distance. 'We are quite certain that you did in fact organise the manufacture of Mandrax through your association with Wyvern Meridian. You then used the drug to obtain information from people within the arts world that would allow you and your associate, the Curator, to arrange for the theft of artworks belonging to the Federation, or in other instances, to purchase, illegally, a number of pieces originally stolen from the Federation. Marietta Ross has confessed and given us everything she can recall relating to her role as your Australian distributor. Her memory appears to be exceptionally good and what she has told us has been verified and entered for the Judge to consider.'

Compressing her lips, Michiko looked scornfully at Freddi, but made no comment.

'We also have the person who was your contact for distribution here in Argentina: a prominent member of society who is the Director of the National Fine Arts Museum – or should I say 'was', since he recently resigned. In a similar vein to Marietta Ross, he is a successful artist in his spare time, and many of his individual clients are themselves associated with some aspect of the arts, or with work connected to the handling of valuable artefacts – as are a number of Marietta's clients. Perhaps you can see where I'm heading, Michiko?'

Michiko gazed up at Freddi and said, 'Yes, I can. I would be a fool not to. However, I am not foolish enough to admit to a crime I did not commit.' She looked away.

'Very well, I agree you are no fool, Michiko. Neither Marietta nor the Director are fools either, and did not use the drug themselves. They simply wanted the profits from their sales to help maintain their preferred lifestyles. They are both people with little conscience – as are you, it seems. I think you chose Mandrax as a useful tool because once your victims became dependent on it, the drug could be used as a lever, or for blackmail whether they became dependent or not. It may not be illegal to *use* Mandrax, but it is not necessarily socially acceptable, particularly within the public sphere you and your associates inhabit.'

'Conscience? You speak to me of conscience! What about you, Peacekeeper? You helped destroy my bondmate's work, and in doing so, almost destroyed me and my family. Does this count for nothing?!' For a moment, Michiko lost control, her face dark in its vivid outburst of hate, but she managed to resume her poise, although not quite as readily as before.

Freddi smiled. 'Yes, you are perfectly correct. I met your bondmate and was impressed by him in every respect: other than that he was a fanatic, a murderer, and a man capable of bringing the Federation into disrepute should his plans have succeeded.' She took a small risk and bent down to speak, almost whispering. 'Yes, I have a conscience, and my conscience would not have allowed me to let him continue his work. I would have done anything within my power and within the law to stop him. Fortunately, fate caught up with him and he died – not before time.'

Michiko leapt from her seat and attempted to hit Freddi, but this time the peacekeeper was ready and caught her wrist, holding fast. The two women glared at each other, until Michiko wrenched herself free and sat down, breathing rapidly. Gwenllian glanced meaningfully at Freddi, who pressed her advantage.

'You dare accuse me of having no conscience when it is *you* who drove Guillermo to his death and who almost killed Felicity in the process. Your own daughter! How could you use her the way you did! If you had any conscience at all, you would confess your role in the manufacture and distribution of Mandrax, your accumulation of stolen artworks, and your payment to the Curator for his services. We know it is he who helped your bondmate steal to gain financial benefit for Wyvern Meridian, before he resorted to even worse criminal means. Do you want to know how we came by this information?'

Michiko shook her head and made a small sound of disgust.

'Well, I'll tell you anyway. Do you remember Rohan Maerz, the former coordinator of the Federation Special Investigation Unit? I see you do. Good. He kept a watchful eye on Kenjiro Kakura for many years and pretended to become his friend in order to keep an even more watchful eye on his activities. He was instrumental in bringing your bondmate to justice, and he left a legacy after he died: he also kept an eye on you. Your 'friend', Rhianna O'Connor, was his protégé, an agent for the FSIU.'

'No! Not Rhianna! You are lying... Not Rhianna!' Michiko's beautiful, elegant hand went to her mouth as she stared at Freddi – horrified, shocked, completely at a loss as to what to say.

'Yes, Rhianna. And do you know what else Rhianna was? She was your bondmate's lover. They loved each other, and your friend only gave him up when she, at long last, became convinced of just how truly evil he was. The FSIU asked her to become your friend, and for a long time we were almost sure it was you who killed her.' Michiko bowed her head, close to tears. 'No,' continued Freddi. 'We now know you did not kill her. We *do* know who did. Your daughter, your adopted daughter, Felicity, has confessed.'

If Freddi wanted to drive Michiko Yamada to the point of confessing her own crimes, she underestimated her. Michiko wept openly, her self-control gone to that extent, yet all she said was: 'She *is* my daughter, something I should have remembered well before now. My poor, poor daughter... I have wronged her deeply. Yes, for some time now I have known she killed Rhianna. Felicity confessed to me, wanting to warn me of what she was capable. I rewarded her rebellion with retribution. I admit to hating her that night, hating her for having killed my one true friend. Yes, in spite of everything you have told me about Rhianna, I still believe she was my friend. She may have begun as a spy, an agent of the Federation, but she became my friend. I am *sure* I could not be deceived about this.' Michiko glanced at Freddi, almost as if in appeal, then bowed her head, still ignoring the others in the room, as she had done from the beginning.

'Was that on the twenty-fifth of July, the night before Felicity ran away from you?'

'Yes, it was. I went too far, and my daughter left me. It is possible I will never see her again, and I deserve no less. Please, you *must* understand why she did it.' Michiko raised her face to look at Freddi, one hand raised as well, this time in a plea for understanding. When Freddi nodded, Michiko continued. 'Felicity heard Rhianna speaking to someone on her comlink, the night before she was to leave to return to Australia. She said Rhianna knew what I had done and that if it continued, next time she was here it would be reported to the peacekeepers. Despite my behaviour towards her after my bondmate died, Felicity was terrified of losing me. She even feared I would force her to leave her home if anyone found out, so took her own jar of Sensa, added something she had collected from the forest, then substituted the jar for the one I gave Rhianna... My gift, poisoned... It is too horrible to think about! Tell me, did Rhianna suffer much before she died?'

Freddi hesitated, thinking how, even while Felicity had been distraught and confessing to having killed Rhianna, she did not tell her mother the whole truth. Perhaps the young woman was not quite as naive as they all thought? 'No,' she replied. 'We believe Rhianna was strong enough not to have suffered for long after the substance first made her ill. She even appeared to recover for some days, before finally dying at the tournament. In some respects, it's just as well she was struck and died soon after; it most likely saved her a great deal of suffering.'

'What was it Felicity put into the Sensa? Are you able to tell me?'

'No, we'll leave that to the trial. Michiko, I understand you were trying to protect Felicity by not informing us of what you knew, but she must be charged with Rhianna's murder. The Judge will take into account her state of mind and her past behaviour, as well as your treatment of her. You will have an opportunity to give evidence on her behalf. We can arrange for you to do so this afternoon, if you wish.'

'Yes, I would appreciate it. Thank you.'

'Good. However, we still have the unresolved question of the Mandrax and the activities you have undertaken together with the Curator. Are you absolutely sure you have nothing further to say on these matters? This is your final chance to make a clean break with your past and to begin a new life, free of guilt and the ugliness you have been part of for so long.'

Michiko considered what Freddi had said, even studying the faces of the others in the room for the first time. 'No,' she replied at last, shaking her head, 'I have nothing further to say.'

'In that case,' answered Freddi, 'we would like to show you something that will almost certainly be of interest.' She stood up and walked across the room to a curtain covering the entire length of the wall opposite to where Michiko sat, then drew it back, revealing a securely locked, shatterproof display cabinet.

Michiko's eyes widened and she gasped, then quickly recovered and said, 'How beautiful! May I take a closer look?'

Freddi nodded, and stepped away from the cabinet, waiting while Michiko examined the exquisite evening gown it contained. She turned to Freddi with a puzzled frown. 'I know what this is, but why have you shown it to me?'

'Perhaps we should sit down again, and I'll explain,' replied Freddi. She closed the curtain and, after they returned to their seats, said, 'This gown is one of only three surviving originals, created in the twenty-second century by the Canadian haute couturier Alain André. It was on tour in Quebec when, earlier this year, it disappeared.'

'How tragic!' exclaimed Michiko. 'It would have been a great loss to the Canadian people and the world of fashion had it not been recovered.'

'Indeed,' said Freddi, leaning forward and gazing directly into Michiko's eyes. 'Marietta Ross claims to have provided you with sufficient information to acquire this priceless work of art – without, shall we say, the permission of its owner, the Federation. With her assistance, we have managed to retrieve it, and intend to charge you with its theft.'

'Nonsense! As before, her accusations are nothing but lies. I regret ever having made her my friend and protégé.' The disgust on Michiko's face was real, although Gwenllian knew it was directed not only at Marietta, but also at having apparently lost one of the most treasured additions to her collection.

While Michiko did her best to control her anger and dismay, Gwenllian, Robert and Shela allowed the illusion to fade into nothingness. If Marietta's claims were true, which they tended to believe was the case, the real gown, unfortunately, remained in Michiko's possession. Unless they succeeded in obtaining a confession from her, there it would most likely remain because they still could not 'see' where the collection was housed, or how the theft had been managed, and further questioning failed to break Michiko's resolve. As a result, the threat to lay charges was an empty one.

On the day of the trial, held in Córdoba, the three women whose fate the Judge was to determine sat together, although several metres apart and with a guard seated between them. Their Defence Counsels, the Prosecutor, Consultants and Witnesses were all present, together with everyone who had a direct interest in the case. Chiu Liow and Morag MacIain were seated towards the back of the Court, even now wondering whether there was anything else they could have done to bring things to a more satisfactory conclusion. Much to Morag's disgust, there was insufficient evidence to charge the former director of the Argentinean Fine Arts Museum with anything, and she would have preferred to see Michiko charged with having distributed Mandrax, yet reluctantly accepted that without further proof or an admission of guilt, this was simply not possible.

Smithson and Nyneve had come all the way from Stanthorpe to be here today, as had Margrethe and Harriet. Old Harriet was somewhat bemused by the proceedings, never having had anything to do with legalities such as these before. A few steps ahead of Margrethe, she waddled and wheezed her way through the gathering towards Gwenllian, Robert and Agathea. Although Agathea had nothing to add to the proceedings in terms of evidence, she wanted to be present to support her son.

Edric and Stefano were also in the courtroom, after having spent several days in Córdoba going over their evidence. Much of what they needed to say had already been entered into the Judge by Freddi and Chiu Liow, yet it was important they give their own personal statements, as much to satisfy their sense of justice as to add detail and veracity to the formal version provided by the peacekeepers. However, both men were still unaware of the full story, for the investigators were not permitted to discuss the case with them. They knew only that Felicity had been charged with Rhianna's murder, Michiko Yamada with the assault and rape of her adopted daughter, and Marietta Ross with distribution of Mandrax and the assault upon Edric. Consequently, Edric and Stefano felt both confused and apprehensive.

Although Zarifa and Peri understood their feelings and did their best to soothe their companions, the two cats also wanted to enjoy the novel occasion. The flight from Brisbane intrigued and entertained them both, and they were now fascinated by everything they saw and heard, particularly since Marietta Ross was present and their evidence helped bring her to this point.

Freddi, Meng Jarrah and Shela sat towards the front of the Court, as did the Córdoban peacekeeper responsible for the charges against Michiko. He and Freddi held joint responsibility for the charge against Felicity, she being an Argentinean citizen. Ruth Baillieu sat with them, there being no one else she wished to sit with. Her appearance in the Court had little to do with providing moral support for Marietta. Instead, she had been summoned to be present in case any question of relevance arose in relation to her role in the whole affair.

The murmuring and feet shuffling normal to such an occasion abruptly ceased when the impersonal tones of the Judge called the Court to order. The Prosecutor then identified himself to the Judge, followed by all the other officials. Each of the Accused were required to follow suit, which they did – Michiko and Marietta with heads held high and all the appearance of unconcern, Felicity with a tremor in her voice and her hands clasped tightly together.

'Now that all present have been properly identified,' the Prosecutor began, 'the trial of Felicity, Michiko Yamada and Marietta Ross can commence. We have chosen to try all the Accused together as their cases are interrelated and have a bearing each upon the other. The first case to be heard will be that of Felicity, in relation to the death of the Australian, Rhianna O'Connor.

'Felicity is currently residing at the Córdoban medcentre, and is undergoing counselling. She is charged with the murder of Rhianna O'Connor, whose death resulted from the use of a herbal product by the name of 'Sensa'. The body of the Deceased was discovered on the fifteenth of July 2456, in the Girraween National Park, Queensland, Australia, by a cat named Bella and her two companions, Pietro and Elena, on holiday from Italy. They are pronounced as being clear of any guilt associated with the death.

'Testimony has established that the body of the Deceased was taken from the place where she died – in Brisbane, Australia – by her lover and companion, Edric, with the agreement of her cousin, Robert O'Connor. It is the determination of this Court that no charges be laid against them for their actions, although a formal notation of their breaking the law in this respect will be placed in their Federation records.'

Both Edric and Robert looked startled, then realised it was hardly likely their actions would have gone uncensored. Quickly recovering from their surprise, they concentrated on the Prosecutor's next words:

'All evidence relating to the crime of which Felicity is accused has been entered for the Judge to consider. The Summary of this evidence will now be given to those gathered here today. Anyone wishing to provide or request additional evidence or explanation will then have an opportunity to do so, having previously registered their interest in being present, or having been called by the Defence or the Prosecution. Silence will be maintained while the Summary is read.'

The text of the Summary, as delivered by the Judge, appeared on each person's comlink:

'...Taking into account the elapsed time between the death and the discovery of the Deceased, we are of the opinion that the forensic examination of the body of Rhianna O'Connor was thorough and undertaken in accordance with all due procedure. The subsequent investigation by the Brisbane Peacekeeping Force and the Stanthorpe

Peacekeepers led to the discovery of the method used to kill the Deceased. However, they were initially unable to establish how a poisonous substance was introduced into the herbal product, Sensa.

'With the assistance of Gwenllian, a registered telepath with extensive training by the Werribee Breeding Centre for Cats in Melbourne; Robert O'Connor, also a telepath, but without training or formal recognition; and the cat, Shela, the investigator in charge of the case, Freddi, of the Brisbane Peacekeeping Force, managed to obtain a full confession from the Accused, Felicity. Gwenllian has testified that the confession is genuine, as has the cat, Shela, via an intermediary Witness. In addition, the confession was subsequently corroborated by Felicity's adoptive mother, Michiko Yamada, who eventually informed the peacekeepers that her daughter confessed to her on the twenty-fifth of July 2456. Due to the close family relationship involved, the fact that Michiko Yamada did not immediately report the confession will not incur any charges.

'Initially, and in the presence of the Deceased, a jar of Sensa was purchased in Córdoba as a gift from Michiko Yamada, with whom Rhianna O'Connor had been living as a visitor since the fifth of June 2456. On the morning of the first of July 2456, Argentinean time, this jar was then substituted with a similar one containing a poison. The poison in question was an amatoxin derived from an unidentified species of amanita, which the Accused has admitted to collecting from the forest. She had initially intended to use the poison to cause her own death, but after overhearing Rhianna O'Connor provide certain information to Morag MacIain, the Coordinator of the Federation Special Investigation Unit, the Accused decided to use it instead to kill Rhianna O'Connor. The Deceased used the Sensa upon her return to Australia, and on the tenth of July, at a martial arts tournament, died from its effects.'

Tears ran down Michiko's cheeks as she listened. Felicity, driven to suicide! How *could* she have been so cruel as to have let this happen! She dried her eyes and forced herself to listen to the Judge's next words:

'At the time of her death, the Deceased was engaged in a martial arts contest bout with Marietta Ross. She struck Rhianna O'Connor, who immediately collapsed then died shortly afterwards, despite being given appropriate medical attention. However, the Accused, Marietta Ross, is absolved from having contributed to the death, although her intent in delivering a blow that could nevertheless have had the potential to kill Rhianna O'Connor, even were she not ill at the time, is of grave concern to this Court and will be noted on her Federation record.'

Marietta frowned – not at the notation that would be added to her record, which was of little concern to her, but at the mention of Rhianna having been in communication with the FSIU. She composed her features into their former expression of studied indifference and listened as the Judge continued:

'It is now my initial determination that the Accused, Felicity, is guilty of murder. Before giving a formal verdict, is there anyone who wishes further explanation of this Summary, has additional evidence to enter in the presence of Witnesses, or wishes to challenge this initial determination? The full transcript will be made available to the public after delivery of the final verdict.'

The silence in the Court was broken by Felicity's sobbing. Michiko attempted to push past the guard to reach her, but was firmly, although gently, forced to stay where she was. Margrethe reached out to stroke Harriet, who slowly rubbed her head into the gentle hand. They were faced with a dilemma. Was it truly feasible, or even realistic, to still take Felicity home with them? Was she someone they could live with, learn to trust, help to live a normal life, given she had murdered their Rhianna? There was the other matter to deal with too: the treatment of Felicity by her mother. Clearly, the young woman had her reasons, but murder? Margrethe shook her head, deeply disturbed despite the briefing she received before the trial commenced and the opportunity she was given to withdraw her offer.

Edric and Stefano sat, stunned. The Judge had not divulged the content of the recording overheard by Felicity and had not given the full reasons for her having chosen to kill Rhianna rather than herself. There was obviously a great deal to this case that, for all they knew, might not be made public for quite some time. They only hoped that once the formal verdict was given, they would obtain sufficient details from the public transcript - or from Freddi, if necessary.

Robert and Agathea held hands, comforting each other, while Robert had his arm around Gwenllian's shoulders. Knowing the whole story, they all regarded Felicity with deep sadness and could not find it in their hearts to judge as harshly as they might otherwise have done. Fear and desperation drive people to do things they might not normally even consider. On the other hand, they also knew Felicity was someone who might be difficult to ever fully trust. Could they still bring her back to Australia? Could Margrethe still take the risk of having Felicity in her home? They sincerely hoped the Judge would have the wisdom to see more clearly than they could at the moment...

Eventually the Judge delivered its final verdict, since no one present requested further explanation, or needed to provide additional evidence. It confirmed the earlier finding, then said, 'The question of sentencing has now to be resolved. With the support of Gwenllian, a recommendation has been made by Freddi – as the representative of the Brisbane Peacekeeping Force – that Felicity be allowed to leave this country in order to be given the chance of rehabilitation. She herself has no wish to return to her former home, or even to remain in this city. Margrethe, a former preceptor and an inhabitant of the town of Stanthorpe, in Australia, has offered to give Felicity a home, on condition she undertakes weekly counselling and remains within the grounds of the property until such time the counsellor believes it is safe for her to leave from time to time, under the supervision of a responsible adult. Margrethe, is this offer still current? Please stand and give your answer.'

Margrethe stood and said, 'Yes, it is,' then sat down again, slightly shocked by her own statement. Being in the same room as Felicity had allowed her to 'sense' the young woman's thoughts, the results of which had given her the hope and confidence she needed to make her final decision. By being present in the Court, Harriet had also been given the chance to make up her mind as to whether she felt comfortable with the arrangement, which she did.

'Very well. It is hereby ordered that Felicity shall reside with Margrethe in Stanthorpe until such time I, the Judge, deem she is fit to be reintegrated into society. She is to have an identity chip inserted into her left shoulder, which will be monitored at all times. Formal counselling will continue on a weekly basis then gradually reduce to monthly. These sessions will be recorded and entered into my database. Depending upon the progress made by the Accused, further conditions may or may not be imposed. Moreover, if at any time Margrethe feels she is no longer able to continue with this arrangement, the Stanthorpe Peacekeepers are to be notified immediately. They will in turn apply to me, the Judge, for alternative arrangements to be made. Felicity, do you understand this verdict?'

Felicity, her eyes wide, looked over to where Margrethe sat with Harriet, glanced at Gwenllian, then at Freddi and Meng Jarrah. She did not look at Michiko. 'Yes,' she answered in a subdued voice, 'I understand and accept the conditions.'

'It is thereby determined. You will remain in the Court while the other Summaries are given.' The Judge paused as if to take a breath – which was, of course, impossible, yet everyone in the room could almost imagine it. The bland, hypnotic voice then asked the Prosecutor to read the next charge:

'Michiko Yamada, you are accused of having intentionally, and without provocation, assaulted your adopted daughter, Felicity, on many occasions and in her own home. On the sixth of January 2556 it is alleged that you struck her on the face with your hand, causing her to suffer significant bruising. You continued to slap her on occasions when you felt she had failed to perform one of her household duties to your satisfaction, the last such action being taken on the morning of the twenty-fifth of July this year, and which you admitted to when questioned by Freddi later the same day. However, the Court notes that it does not accept Felicity's failures to be grounds for physical punishment.

'Prior to these incidents, and apparently unrelated to any domestic cause, on the eleventh of October 2455 you are accused of using a whip on many parts of her unclothed body. Then, on the second of December 2455, you used a cane to beat Felicity, which action you repeated on the twenty-ninth of June 2456 when you struck her on the hands and about the legs. The sounds, on this occasion, were overheard by Rhianna O'Connor while living in your home as a guest. She subsequently examined the room where the beating took place, finding various instruments which, in her opinion as an agent with the Federation Special Investigation Unit, could be used for these and other forms of physical punishment. The Deceased's account of her findings was the main subject of the recording referred to earlier and subsequently overheard by Felicity, leading to her decision to commit murder instead of suicide.

'Michiko Yamada, you are also accused of having first whipped and then raped Felicity during the evening of the twenty-fourth of July. You used the handle of the whip to penetrate her vaginally against her will, and while she was bound and unable to defend herself. Having used your power as her adoptive parent to persuade her on many occasions to partake in what is best termed 'bondage', by this act you abused the relationship with your daughter even further.

'Furthermore, during the evening of the twenty-fifth of July 2456, you applied heat to silver circlets you had attached to Felicity's breasts, causing them to blister and burn. Your reason for having taken this course of action is stated as being an overwhelming sense of hatred for her after she confessed to murdering Rhianna O'Connor, a woman you regarded as a close friend, and for whom you state you held a genuine and deep affection. The Court can understand your horror, but cannot accept the revenge you took as being justified.

'As a result of your behaviour, Felicity fled your home on the twenty-sixth of July and sought refuge with the Australians, Freddi and Meng Jarrah, whom she met during the course of their investigation into the death of Rhianna O'Connor. At this point, the Court notes that Meng Jarrah is a forensic specialist working as a consultant with the Brisbane Peacekeeping Force, and that she and Freddi immediately arranged for medical assistance to be provided to Felicity, afterwards escorting her to the Córdoban medcentre, where she has since remained.

'Finally, when confronted by Freddi during a formal interview, you admitted to having exacted your revenge upon your adopted daughter in the manner described and expressed your remorse. The Court notes in your favour that you afterwards voluntarily provided the Judge with further details that elaborated upon and confirmed your having committed the crimes of which you have been accused.'

'Mon Dieu!' thought Marietta, shocked out of her usual self-absorption. 'What a pity she will not answer for everything!' She glared at Michiko, but was ignored, so, after one brief glance at Felicity, Marietta turned her attention back to the Prosecutor, who was giving his final statement:

'All evidence relating to the crimes of which Michiko Yamada is accused has been entered for the Judge to consider. The Summary of this evidence will now be given to those gathered here today. Anyone wishing to provide or request additional evidence or explanation will then have an opportunity to do so, having previously registered their interest in being present, or having been called by the Defence or the Prosecution. Silence will be maintained while the Summary is read.'

As the Prosecutor spoke, many in the courtroom turned to peer at Michiko, but were careful not to gaze for too long at Felicity, who sat with head bowed, tears streaming down her cheeks. Those who did not already know of these events were appalled, unable to understand how anyone, particularly a parent, could have done such things to their daughter, adopted or otherwise. That Felicity had remained in the house and not sought refuge earlier was also difficult to comprehend, given that the Judge did not proceed to provide the other details of her family life in its Summary. It did, however, include the contribution made by Shela in having alerted Freddi and Meng Jarrah to the abuse suffered by Felicity at Michiko's hands.

Once the Summary was finished, Margrethe stood and asked to be allowed to put a question to the Judge. Taking no notice of those who stared at her, Margrethe said, 'If I am to give Felicity a home, I must know even more about her family situation and why these events took place.'

She remained standing while the Judge answered: 'The question was anticipated. A guard will bring you into the Court antechamber, where further information will be provided. Edric, the Court calls upon you to accompany Margrethe. As Rhianna O'Connor's designated next of kin, what you will see and hear will, in all likelihood, be helpful.'

Startled, Edric, accompanied by Zarifa, obeyed, turning back for a moment to look at Stefano, who shrugged his shoulders and shook his head. Once inside the antechamber, the voice of the Judge filled the entire room, without seeming to come from any particular direction. 'Please be seated,' it said, which they did.

Edric and Margrethe watched while the relevant portions of the interviews conducted by Freddi were replayed for them. Deeply saddened by what they saw and heard, they remained silent while the Judge told them that the next recording was an edited version of the one made by Rhianna O'Connor the night before she returned to Australia for the last time. As Edric listened to Rhianna speak, it was almost impossible not to weep, and when she told Morag how much she truly loved him, he could contain himself no longer. Taking a kerchief from his pocket, he wiped his face, only to begin again. Margrethe's own pain upon seeing Rhianna in this manner was deep enough, but with her years, she had learned to accept life's hardships, so put her hand on Edric's, doing her best to comfort him.

Although Zarifa could sense how hurt they both were, she was unsure whether to attempt to help her companion, so 'spoke' to Margrethe instead. When Margrethe suggested she wait, the cat withdrew, patient and with an understanding beyond what might normally be expected. 'Still,' thought Margrethe, 'she *is* a guardian... I do hope they decide to stay together.'

'Edric,' said the Judge, 'this last recording was found on the comlink belonging to the Deceased. The comlink now belongs to you and has had its access codes set to your own. The portion of the recording relating directly to you has not been erased. Please take it, together with my deepest condolences for your loss.'

Astonished the Judge would express such sympathy, Edric watched as a small black tray slid silently out from the wall. In it lay the comlink. Edric picked it up, and together, he and Margrethe left the room, with Zarifa following closely behind.

Once they were settled back into their former seats, the Judge called for silence and delivered its final verdict:

'There being no one to challenge the veracity of the record of events, the accusations made by Felicity, or the admissions made by the Accused, the Court finds Michiko Yamada guilty of seven counts of assault, noting that these are specific instances amongst others that occurred, and which are sufficient to establish an overall pattern of behaviour, as well as the severity of the crimes committed. Michiko Yamada is also found guilty of the rape of Felicity on the evening of the twenty-fourth of July 2456.

'The Sentence of this Court is that Michiko Yamada will be placed under house arrest, with full surveillance, for a period of twelve years. During that time, her access to the lattice will be restricted and she will no longer have the right to earn income from employment or commerce. Her position as the Artistic and Cultural Director of Wyvern Meridian is hereby revoked. In addition, a sum of two-point-four million credits from her private account is to be paid into the newly created account of her adopted daughter, Felicity, who will have access to the sum in five years time, should her own rehabilitation be successful, or at a later date to be determined, if not. Michiko Yamada, do you understand this verdict?'

Michiko stood, and in a clear voice said, 'Yes, I do, and fully accept it,' then sat down, her head held high, her expression composed. Michiko realised that for twelve years she would be unable to sell her silverware or her designs. Well, what did it matter? She was young and twelve years was not long. In time, her work would again find its way onto the world markets for fine jewellery and ornamentation, although under another name and with a completely new style; Michiko doubted whether anyone would wish to buy the articles under her current name. People had remarkably long memories for the types of crime she had committed.

Interrupting her thoughts, a Court Official rose from his place at the front of the room and said, 'Before the next case, the Court will now recess for forty-five minutes. Refreshments will be served in the foyer.'

Freddi, Meng Jarrah and Shela moved through the small crowd to find Edric, Stefano and their two cats. 'How are you coping?' asked Freddi, placing a hand on Edric's shoulder, while Shela stood nose-to-nose with Zarifa, learning for herself exactly how Edric was feeling.

'Relieved... I'm glad I know who killed her and why. The Judge gave me Rhianna's comlink. It still has part of her last recording. Did you know this would happen? It means a lot to me.' Edric showed her the comlink.

'I made the suggestion to the Judge. I'm glad it was accepted.'

'Thank you, Freddi, thank you. When we were in there with the Judge, it almost sounded human, you know. It even said it was sorry for my loss, and the voice was different from the one it uses in the courtroom...deep and mellow.' Edric sighed. He truly did feel a little better, yet could not bring himself to forgive Felicity, in spite of all she herself had suffered. Perhaps one day...

'Let's go outside and have something to eat and drink,' suggested Meng Jarrah. 'We'll all feel much better if we do. There's still Marietta to deal with.'

CHAPTER TWENTY-EIGHT

'Marietta Ross, currently a resident of Melbourne, Australia, you are accused of having distributed the illicit substance Mandrax to former associates within Australia, as well as to customers of your photography and interior design business, commencing during March 2455. You are also accused of having given this substance to your former friend and associate, Edric, without his knowledge or permission, during the early morning of the seventh of August 2456, while visiting him in his apartment in Brisbane, Australia. The substance caused a severe, life-threatening reaction, resulting in Edric being admitted to a medcentre for treatment.

'The records show you have previously come to the notice of the Court, when you were eighteen years of age, for the illegal possession of a weapon, being a sonic rifle, which you used to kill an Australian native bird, a rosella. You also participated regularly in certain martial arts tournaments held in Brisbane, Australia, which involved illegal forms of combat. These tournaments were organised by your associate, Ruth Baillieu, who has since cooperated fully with the Brisbane Peacekeeping Force in providing comprehensive information, which in turn has assisted in developing the case against you. Ruth Baillieu is undergoing counselling and will not be charged with her offence. She is also absolved from having any connection with the charges laid against the Accused.'

Marietta cast a quick glance at Ruth, who had become bright red in the face and could not meet Marietta's eyes.

'The Court takes into account your admission of guilt to the first charge and your full cooperation with both the Brisbane and Melbourne Peacekeeping Forces. It also notes the continuing support you provide to your disabled parents, currently living in France and whom you visit on a regular basis.'

The Prosecutor went on to give an outline of Marietta's academic qualifications, her professional career, and current occupation. This was followed by the usual preamble given before the Judge delivered its summary of the evidence:

'In June 2455, the Coordinator of the Federation Special Investigation Unit, Morag MacIain, received information from Rhianna O'Connor, an undercover agent, that she strongly suspected drugs were being distributed amongst some of the spectators who attended the Brisbane martial arts tournaments. Nevertheless, she was unable to determine what the substance was or how it was being obtained. Some years beforehand, at the request of the FSIU, Rhianna O'Connor had undertaken to join the club associated with the tournaments in order to gather certain information, which we will not detail as it was of a type unrelated to this case.'

'Merde!' Marietta swore under her breath. Her guard glanced at her, then looked away when nothing further seemed to be forthcoming.

'Based on information already in the hands of the FSIU that illicit drugs were in all likelihood being distributed in Argentina and elsewhere, she joined the martial arts club holding similar tournaments in Córdoba. After some time, evidence was obtained indicating that Mandrax was being sold to a select number of people attending these events. The FSIU decided to proceed on the initial working assumption that Mandrax might also be the drug being distributed to persons attending the tournaments in Brisbane. Rhianna O'Connor therefore continued her investigation, yet was still unable to find either the distributors or the manufacturers.'

Marietta raised a hand to her face to hide a satisfied smirk. At least this was one time Rhianna had not beaten her! Well, not until she died...

Ruth shook her head, disgusted at having been the unknowing pawn of her 'friend' Marietta, and sure, in hindsight, that Marietta was guilty of giving the drug to Edric. He would never have taken it voluntarily; of that Ruth was quite certain. And Rhianna...independent to the last!

Michiko took a deep breath. This was something worth knowing! She turned her attention back to the Judge:

'The death of Rhianna O'Connor prompted the FSIU to examine the case more closely and to enlist the help of peacekeepers from Australia and elsewhere. During this process, the social, professional and financial situation of the Accused was examined and it was found that Marietta Ross was well placed to meet and cultivate a wide network of people, many of whom attended the martial arts tournaments in Brisbane. Twenty-eight of her close associates with whom she had financial dealings were interviewed, and three were willing to testify that they bought Mandrax from her on numerous occasions. When Peacekeeper Chiu Liow Jones of Melbourne confronted the Accused with this information, she chose to make a full confession. The Court notes, however, that no Mandrax has been found either on her person or in her dwelling, and that blood tests taken in Brisbane on the morning of the seventh of August were negative.

'Relating to the second charge, on the afternoon of the sixth of August 2456, Marietta Ross chose to take a flight to Brisbane, where she paid a late night visit to Edric, a person she has known since her schooldays in Stanthorpe, Australia, and who was also a participant in the unlawful martial arts tournaments. At this point, the Court notes that no charges will be laid against Edric for this activity.'

Startled to hear the Judge mention his association with the tournaments, Edric was relieved to also hear that he would not be charged. Zarifa, who had a seat to herself, as did Peri, purred and rubbed her head against his shoulder, while Stefano raised his eyebrows and gave his friend a supportive nudge.

'During the visit,' the Judge continued, 'Edric suffered a severe adverse reaction similar to one he experienced earlier when first encountering cats, and for which he had apparently been successfully treated. His own cat, Zarifa, woke to find her companion seriously ill, attempted to apprehend the Accused, and in the process, was assaulted. Zarifa used her telepathic powers to contact Edric's close friend, Stefano Salvarez, as well as his cat, Peri. Living relatively close by, they immediately travelled to the apartment by foot. In the meantime, the Accused called the nearest medcentre to obtain assistance for Edric, an action which the Court notes in her favour.

'Upon his arrival at the apartment, Stefano Salvarez confronted the Accused, believing it was she who had caused Edric to become ill, but the Accused denied having done anything wrong. The ambutechs, who arrived at the scene at almost the same time as Stefano, collected evidence from the apartment: being the remains of the coffee Edric had drunk, the cup, wine, wineglasses, and various foods served during the visit. Later, when the evidence was analysed, Mandrax was found to have been in the coffee Edric consumed.

'Stefano Salvarez, Zarifa, Peri and Marietta Ross accompanied Edric to the medcentre, where the attending practitioner found Mandrax in his bloodstream and confirmed that it had caused the adverse reaction. Appropriate treatment was administered and the symptoms subsided. After his initial recovery, Edric demanded that Marietta Ross be charged with having administered the Mandrax. The Accused denied having given it to him and attempted to leave the medcentre, but was prevented from doing so by Stefano Salvarez and the two cats. The practitioner contacted the Brisbane Peacekeeping Force, two of whose members arrived promptly and arrested the Accused. While under detention, the Accused was searched, as was her hotel room and Edric's apartment. The search yielded no evidence of Mandrax or any other illicit substance. However, the two cats, Zarifa and Peri, have both provided 'statements' to the Court, via a Witness, that in their opinion, Marietta Ross did indeed administer this substance to Edric in his coffee, later disposing of the remainder in the toilet of the apartment before leaving for the medcentre. Stefano has confirmed the Accused did ask to use the toilet at the time in question. The Court accepts this evidence and that of Edric when he stated he did not administer the Mandrax to himself. Therefore, in the context of the Accused admitting to distributing Mandrax, it is the initial verdict of the Court that Marietta Ross is guilty on both counts, as charged.'

The Judge, having finished its Summary and given its usual concluding statement, waited for anyone present to ask questions or make objections. As no one did, the verdict was confirmed and Marietta was sentenced to five years community service as a martial arts instructor to the Melbourne Peacekeeping Force for twelve hours a week. She was also fined twenty thousand credits, to be paid into Edric's account as compensation. Edric and Stefano laughed openly; they simply could not help themselves. Freddi grinned, seeing her brother's sense of humour in this outcome and sure he had made the recommendation to the Judge, no doubt with Morag's support. Meanwhile, Marietta glared at them all as she left the Court in the company of a guard, silently telling Zarifa and Peri exactly what her opinion was of them! They returned the compliment without hesitation, then followed their companions out into the spring sunshine, delighted that their evidence had been accepted.

A beam of sunlight coming in from the window formed a pool of warmth where the three cats lay together, enjoying their temporary truce from play-fighting. Outside, a small flock of tiny wrens twittered loudly as they swooped in and out amongst the branches of a mauve wisteria in full bloom. Although Zarifa was by far the smallest of the three, she was also the fastest and most agile, so when Shela suddenly decided the truce was over and leapt to grasp her by the back of the neck, she twisted aside, bit Shela's tail, then jumped onto the nearby windowsill, where she sat and snickered at her foe. Peri yawned, showing her long sharp teeth, so Shela pounced on her instead. Unperturbed, Peri swatted Shela over the nose, scratching her just enough to leave a tiny mark. Startled, Shela abruptly sat down to rub her face with a paw, never having been scratched before. Peri padded over to her and licked the small wound, following up with a thorough clean of her face. The older cat had had enough for one day!

Stefano, who had been watching Edric and Freddi sparring for almost an hour, came over to scratch Zarifa under the chin for a few moments. Turning back, he saw his two friends finishing their session with the traditional bow, and grinned when Freddi burst out laughing. Edric, having dropped to one knee, with his head bowed, extended an arm in a gesture of defeat, then looked up, saying, 'Don't laugh, Freddi! That's the second time in the past five weeks that I haven't won... First your brother, and now you! It just isn't funny.' Nevertheless, he burst out laughing himself. It *was* funny, and certainly a novelty. A week of daily training with Edric had considerably sharpened Freddi's reflexes, which at first were definitely not up to scratch and it had been Edric's turn to laugh when he easily defeated her.

'Well, Edric,' said Freddi, holding out her hand to help him up – not that he needed it – 'what do you think? Am I up to Chiu Liow's standard yet?'

'Not quite,' replied Edric, grinning, 'but almost. One of his strengths is his ability to combine aikido with kung fu. You do too, it seems, although perhaps not quite as well. I can't help you in that respect, but would you be willing to teach *me*? I'd love to meet him on his own level one day.'

'It's a deal, though I doubt you'll ever defeat him. It takes a long time to master and he's had too many years ahead of you.' Freddi smiled, making it clear she meant no insult to Edric's ability to adapt to a new style.

'Stefano!' Edric called out. 'Freddi's agreed to teach me aikido. Do you want to learn too?'

Stefano ambled over to them. 'Why not... Something new would be good. Do you mind teaching us both, Freddi?'

'No, not at all, but our size difference will eventually make it an unfair competition. We'll have to find someone in your weight division to test your skills against, once you develop some. Still, that's a long way off, so when you're ready to begin, let me know.'

'How about tomorrow?' suggested Stefano, delighted at her easy acceptance, as well as with their new roles as instructors with the BPF.

'Excellent. We can begin after Edric and I have our usual sparring session.' Freddi turned to Edric and said, 'Have you and Zarifa made up your minds yet whether to stay together?' Freddi had become fond of the cat, and also of Peri, and knew Shela had as well, although she needed to tone down her exuberance a degree or two. No doubt the novelty of having two other grimalkins as almost daily companions would wear off, but it was wonderful to see her enjoying herself with them.

Edric's face lit up with quiet joy. 'Yes, we have. I never thought I could love a cat as much as I do Zarifa. I can't even imagine life without her now.'

Stefano patted him on the shoulder, fully understanding how he felt, being in exactly the same position.

'I'm glad,' said Freddi, 'and so is Shela.'

'Marietta, I can see the anger in your eyes, your desire to dominate. You need to break free... *You* are the only one keeping yourself in this cage. When you hurt others, you hurt yourself. It is time to learn humility, and if you succeed, one day you may become a master. If not, you will simply remain what you are now: a slave to your emotions.' Chiu Liow released her, stood back, bowed, then left the room where they had been training together for the past one and a half hours.

*

Everyone who knew Rhianna and who had attended the trial of Michiko, Felicity and Marietta were now present at Rhianna's funeral – even Ruth Baillieu, who was amazed to receive an invitation. The funeral was being held in the greenhouse Robert, Edric and Gwenllian had worked so hard to restore. The fountain sparkled with new life, its waters seeming to laugh in joy at being free to play in the light, the drops forming small rainbows, entrancing to see. Rhianna's presence was almost tangible. Her ashes were held in a bronze urn Robert had cast especially for her in the likeness of a grey cat. All his doubts and misgivings were gone. Robert's memories of his cousin were now of her as a loving child, and as a young woman of courage and great strength of character. Her loss was tragic, yet somehow, almost inevitable...or at least, so it seemed to him.

The soil in the greenhouse was sweet, fertile and moist, Gwenllian's efforts having produced excellent results. Edric stood ready to plant the fruit tree they had found in honour of Rhianna and Sylvie. It was grown from seed obtained from the Global Seed Vault in Svalbard, Norway, a sister institution to the Federation Herbarium in Oslo. Rhianna had loved apples, especially this rare variety, the snow apple. Stefano handed Edric the spade and they all watched as he dug the hole, placed Rhianna's ashes carefully in its centre, then planted the tree.

Agathea stepped forward to water the young sapling. 'May the Sun warm you, my beloved little girl,' she said, and stepped back.

Robert placed his hand on the slender trunk of the tree, saying, 'And may it shine for you every day of your life.' Tears ran down his face, his dark blue eyes closed for a few moments, remembering. Gwenllian took his hand and they stayed there a while longer, until Agathea led them away to speak with their guests.

The Curator bowed and then straightened, wincing as his back twinged painfully. Michiko's son, Kisho, returned the bow and shook the thin hand the Curator held out to him.

'You are here at your mother's behest so I can inform you of your inheritance. Has she mentioned my role in your father's life, or hers?'

'Not really... She just said you were someone who worked with my father, helping him establish his company, and that later on you helped her continue some of his work.'

'Ah... Very well, I understand... I want to show you something. If you come over here, you will be able to see much better.' The Curator beckoned Kisho to look at the screen of his computer. Outside, the weather in Seoul had turned to rain, the wind rising as if to tear the roof from the University building in which they stood.

Kisho stared at the screen, hardly knowing what he was looking at. He turned to the Curator, a question in his eyes.

'This wonderful work of art is part of a substantial collection kept here in Seoul, but not on display. You see, all the pieces were acquired secretly, over a period of many years. Your father was in some respects a ruthless man and not always fussy about how and where he obtained them.'

At Kisho's black expression, the Curator held up his hands and exclaimed, 'No, no, please do not misunderstand me! I admired your father immensely, and his death was a sad loss to us all. However, you must understand, the Federation disapproved of much that he did. The works in this collection once belonged to the Federation, and after his death, when I informed your mother that the collection existed, she considered restoring everything to its rightful owner – if you understand what I mean.'

Kisho gazed at him, not fully comprehending. 'You're saying the collection didn't really belong to Father?'

'It did, and it didn't. He paid a fair price for each piece, but preferred to ignore the fact that the works were acquired without Assembly permission. Do you understand now?'

Kisho frowned, glaring at the Curator and wishing he had never come to Seoul. 'Why didn't Mother return it all immediately?'

'Once your father's company grew to the extent it was financially sound...more than sound...he kept these works as insurance against the future, for his family. Your mother kept them for the same reason, even adding to the collection from time to time out of respect for his wishes. However, she wanted you to have a choice in the matter, being the eldest of her own children. You are of an age now to make a decision. I will carry out your wishes, whatever they are, as I did for your father, and afterwards, for your mother.' The Curator bowed again.

Kisho stared at him, making no effort to hide his distaste. How could his parents have dealt with this man? He was evidently immoral. 'Give it back,' he said, his young voice stern.

'If you are sure?'

'Yes, I am, but may I see the collection first?'

The Curator nodded and said, 'Certainly you can...just this one time.'

EPILOGUE

100 Years Earlier...

At the centre of the little known town of Bunyip Creek, an ancient remnant river redgum grew. Huge and gnarled, its silver trunk measured a full one and a half metres in diameter, and its canopy was so large and heavy it almost touched the pale golden sands below. To the inhabitants, this tree was a sacred meeting place, and today, shelter from the blistering sun. A meeting of elders was being held to discuss the man one of their scouts had noticed that morning: a stranger, whose presence created a dilemma.

'Just north of Lake Tyrrell, you say? Well, that's a bit too close. Now, young Leyla, he was quite thin and not old. What else did you notice?'

Leyla stood completely still and thought very hard about what she had seen in the distance. 'He didn't look at all tasty, if you ask me,' she replied, with a slight smile on her dark features.

'The last one was,' said the oldest resident, cackling and showing her gleaming white teeth in a broad grin.

'Hee hee, that's for sure,' answered the elder sitting next to her, 'very tasty indeed...lovely and plump.' He rubbed his lean jaw, reminiscing.

'Did he seem dangerous, this man?' asked the first elder, her light blue eyes narrowed against a sunbeam breaking in through the canopy.

'No, I don't think so,' replied Leyla, 'but from that distance, I can't be sure. Do you want me to sneak up on him tonight, once he's asleep? By the way he set up camp, it looked as if he intended to stay for a few days.'

'Yes, do that, Leyla. I won't get a good night's sleep myself until I know more about him.' The elder stood and held her by the shoulder in a firm grip. 'Be careful. You know they can't be trusted, no matter how innocent they look.'

'I will be, Auntie; I always am.' Leyla patted the aged hand, its soft skin fine and wrinkled.

'Good. I don't want to lose you as well.' She kissed Leyla's cheek and then stroked it, before turning away and sitting down again to discuss the situation with the others.

Leyla, knowing she had been dismissed, left the meeting and prepared herself for the journey. Her first priority was to check the hunting knife, her constant companion, to make sure its blade was razor sharp.

*

321

At twenty-two years of age, Leyla had never travelled beyond the outer boundaries of Bunyip Creek's territory, although for that matter, neither had any of the other townsfolk. No, it was far too dangerous for any of them to venture further. A thousand years ago, their people were free to roam wherever they wanted, free to hunt whenever they wanted, and to walk along the banks of the mighty Murray River. Leyla knew from the stories passed down from generation to generation that the river was once broad and deep, full of fish and home to many different types of animals and birds: her kinsfolk. All were gone now, the Murray a poor, brown stream, long since dead of all life. Not even algae could live in its poisonous waters.

Pushing the morbid thoughts away, Leyla concentrated on the task at hand. It was a particularly difficult task tonight, with the air tinder dry and the sky completely clear and full of stars. However, this was no time to enjoy the panorama, so dramatic and full of glory that at any other time she would have sat, spellbound, watching for hours instead of sleeping, as she ought. Suppressing a sigh, she focused instead on maintaining her shield, and crept closer and closer, careful not to make the slightest sound, in case the man in the nearby camp woke and noticed her.

Although there was no light in the tent, with her keen eyes, Leyla could make out his form as he lay sleeping. Well, not exactly with her eyes – her mind's eye, to be precise. She giggled. He was dreaming, and the dream was absurd – all about him flying over the land, the sand dunes below forming endless windswept patterns. Even Leyla could not do that, although she often envied the hunting birds their ability to fly, to soar, to swoop down to the earth, and to carry their prey back to their young, safely hidden in a cosy nest.

Drat! She really must be more careful. For a moment her skin had shifted colour, and that simply would not do. There was always the chance the man would wake and come out, shining a torch in her direction, though hopefully she was a good enough scout to avoid being noticed should that happen.

Fortunately, he did not wake, and Leyla had plenty of time to probe his mind. A botanist, hunting for rare species to take back to Bendigo. Hmm...as long as his samples were small, taking them would do no harm.

A tawny frogmouth disturbed her thoughts for a moment as it flew past, its wide mouth open in order to attract insects into and down its bright yellow throat. Leyla sent a quick thought of encouragement to the bird, then smiled when she received a brief reply: 'Yes, hungry!'

Another hour went by and the botanist was still fast asleep, so it seemed safe enough to leave him in his tent until sunrise. As far as Leyla knew, there were no night-flowering plants in this region of the Mallee that could bring him out earlier. She curled herself up to sleep in the sand beneath a stunted old gum, drawing her cloak over her head. To any casual passer-by, she would have been completely invisible.

A bright, cool dawn found Leyla awake and eating her simple breakfast of smoked rabbit and cold water, followed by a piece of freshly picked soursob, a weed growing in these parts where there was shade and a little moisture in the soil. The botanist had begun to wake as well, and she gently probed his mind again to find out what he called himself. "Cameron"... A nice name, she decided, and then, with interest, found he also used a family name: Nguyen, a good old Australian name, originating with people who also knew what suffering was.

Leyla watched as Cameron emerged from his tent, stretching and yawning, then scratching his bare chest. 'Mosquitoes,' she thought, and grinned, being immune to the little monsters. 'He's not at all old, either. In fact, young and quite presentable, for one of his kind. I rather like his golden skin and long, straight hair. His ears are pretty, too: small and neat.'

He turned in her direction and she quickly ducked, even though it was not really necessary – just instinct. Unfortunately, he also chose to walk directly towards her gum tree. 'Damn!' murmured Leyla, and crept on all fours towards the nearest large saltbush, where she could just manage to keep herself well hidden, as long as he didn't walk in that direction as well.

Cameron amused himself for several minutes examining the leaves and young buds of the mallee gum. He peeled off a few strips of bark and examined them as well, before digging a small hole at the base of the tree and poking around its gnarled and bulbous roots. Apparently satisfied, he began whistling tunelessly and wandered back to his campsite, where he made himself a breakfast of billy tea, fried eggs and tomatoes, toasted bread and, finally, a fresh apple. Leyla sniffed the breeze, enjoying the scents and approving his choice of food: nothing nasty, like dead kangaroo or wallaby.

Reminding herself that it was time she returned to her Auntie and the other elders, Leyla again touched Cameron's mind, and immediately put a hand to her mouth in shock. He intended to visit Bunyip Creek! Worse, he was on his way there now, today, after breakfast.

She could not get back to town quickly enough to give the elders sufficient warning, so Leyla needed to send a message. Using all her training and skill, she called silently to her avian kin in the immediate area. Before long, a large black raven settled on the ground beside her, head to one side, silver eyes peering inquisitively into hers. Placing her hand tenderly on the bird's head, Leyla gave the raven her message and it flew off, soaring high into the air and then into the distance. After one last inquiry to learn what the botanist wanted in Bunyip Creek, Leyla crept away and was soon running as swiftly as her long legs could carry her, back to her townsfolk and safety.

Though slender and of only average height, Cameron Nguyen was strong and very fit, used to walking long distances and preferring to do so whenever he could. After checking his precious botanical specimens and packing his few belongings, he strode off towards Bunyip Creek, his small landjet following several metres behind, its sensors ever ready to stop or to slow down the vehicle, should its owner choose to do so.

As far as the he knew, Bunyip Creek was no longer inhabited. The small town was now derelict, the only building still in good order being the travellers hut, maintained by the local ranger. Well, 'hut' was a poor description of the solid stone building, erected centuries ago to withstand both heat and storm. His information gave him to understand there was also a good water supply, a solar heating system for cold winter nights, and even facilities for cooking, bathing and washing clothes. After almost three weeks on his journey, Cameron looked forward to a hot shower using more than just the few litres of water his bush rig allowed.

Walking steadily through the stark, dry landscape, he wondered what it looked like before most of the vegetation was cleared for farming, four hundred years ago, and before much of the topsoil had blown away as a result. The absence of so many of the nocturnal creatures that once, long ago, lived in this region filled him with aching regret.

His research had shown him what the region most probably looked like in its original condition and which species of plants and animals had inhabited the Mallee. However, virtual representations, good as they were, could never substitute for the real experience of walking through pristine bushland, filled with the song and laughter of colourful birds, large and small, living in almost every tree and shrub.

'Well,' he said optimistically, having rather a tendency to talk to himself, 'perhaps our work can bring a few of them back, and maybe one day, even the soils can be fixed.' Whistling, Cameron walked on, expecting to reach Bunyip Creek shortly after midsun.

A heat haze shimmered on the distant horizon by the time Cameron reached his destination, where he thankfully parked his landjet beneath the shade of the single, huge redgum dominating the centre of the town. He sat on the sand and leaned against the smooth bark of the tree, taking out his comlink to contact the ranger. They would want to know of his arrival. To his intense surprise, there was no signal. 'Strange, must be the tree's canopy,' he thought. Cameron stood and walked out into the sunlight. There, he saw someone who could only be the ranger and, startled, swore. She smiled and held out a hand in greeting.

'Hello. I was expecting you to arrive around about now. You're right on time. My name's Leyla, by the way. The hut's ready, so I'll show you the place then let you settle in. Three days you're staying, aren't you?'

'Why, yes, I did intend to stay three days. How did you know?' Cameron released the ranger's hand. Tall, far taller than him, her grip was strong and firm, and she had looked deep into his eyes as they shook hands, as if assessing him. Come to think of it, she was also remarkably attractive, with rich chocolate-brown skin and extraordinary light blue eyes. Black hair, long and curly, cascaded over her shoulders.

'Your university called. There's a storm expected tonight, or early tomorrow morning, so they wanted to make sure you were well looked after.' This was not entirely true, as no one living in Bunyip Creek carried or used a comlink, and certainly did not possess household computers or hand readers.

'Oh, I see... Tell me, what's the transmission signal like around here? I couldn't get one when I was inside the canopy.' Cameron held out his comlink, which still showed no reception.

'It comes and goes, and yes, the tree doesn't seem to like comlinks at all,' she replied, still smiling. 'But don't worry, you won't need one here. You're quite safe, and you'll soon be back within signal range. So, unless you need to call someone urgently, I wouldn't be too worried, if I were you. It doesn't usually bother me too much.' The ranger nodded towards the travellers hut and said, 'Do you want to unpack your things now and take a look around?'

'Thanks, yes, I will. It won't take long. You'd be welcome to stay for a midsun meal, if you like. I have plenty of provisions. It'd be good to have someone to talk to about this place. How long have you worked here?'

'I've been the ranger for about four years.' Leyla turned and led the way back beneath the tree canopy. She studied the landjet with interest, having rarely seen one before, and said, 'Cute model. Handy, if you don't feel like walking.'

Cameron laughed. 'I like walking, particularly in the early morning. The air's so crisp and the light's incredible. I've walked most of the way from Bendigo. The landjet just follows along behind me. Saves having to carry anything, and I can keep my specimens cool and fresh at the same time.'

'Have you managed to collect much?' asked Leyla, picking up one of his packs and tucking it under her arm.

Cameron raised his eyebrows in astonishment. The pack she had taken weighed around twenty kilograms, and she handled it as though it weighed almost nothing. Gathering his wits, he followed her to the hut and listened carefully while she showed him the controls for the various facilities.

'Don't use too much water, Cameron,' said Leyla, showing him the small bathing room. 'If you keep within thirty litres a day, that should be fine. The tank is almost full from the last rains a few months back. Even so, who knows when it'll rain again. The storm might only bring lightning and strong winds.' She paused, then in a lighter tone added, 'Although, apparently there's a fairly good chance it might bring rain as well.' The wistful expression on her face showed clearly just how much the rain was needed.

'We can hope so.' Cameron found himself wishing for the rain as well, even though it would make his work more difficult. 'Where do you live? Is it far from here?'

'I live with my family about ten kilometres away, but I'll check in again in the morning and give you a hand, if you like.' Leyla briefly touched his shoulder as she spoke.

Surprised by her touch, Cameron hesitated, and then agreed, even though he generally preferred to work alone. 'Yes, that'd be great. I usually get up soon after dawn. I want to spend the day sorting through my specimens and surveying the area...depending, of course, upon what the weather decides to do.'

'Good-oh. Well, did you want any help preparing that midsun meal? I'm not a bad cook.' Leyla grinned, and for a moment, Cameron was lost in the depths of those blue eyes.

They spent the next hour preparing a far more elaborate meal than the botanist usually allowed himself on these trips. By the time they had almost finished eating, it was late in the afternoon and both were still absorbed in their discussion of the work they each did to care for the region's natural environment, such as it was. Cameron began thinking of ways to amend his schedule so he could stay longer than the intended three days. Leyla, in turn, wished there was some way he could remain with her, and not for just a short while, either. Sighing inwardly, she knew this was impossible and forced herself to be realistic.

After eating the last fried banana of the dessert Cameron had made, she said, 'The river's the worst, of course. If only we could bring it back to life. We'd be happy for some fresh fish to add to our diet, too.'

'You'd fish?' replied Cameron, surprised.

'Yes, we would. As long as there are plenty, it does no harm, and living here, we'd have the right.'

'You're indigenous, then?' Cameron hadn't been sure, given the blue eyes and long, aquiline nose.

'Yes, we are, though we don't advertise our presence and prefer not to have too many visitors. We like our privacy and keep to the old ways as much as we can.'

'How many of you live here?' He expected her to tell him there were very few, and was astounded to hear there were four hundred and thirty two in her kinship group.

'Yes, it sounds like quite a number, but it's not, considering there were once thousands of us, a long time ago.' Leyla's face lost its smile, and again she looked deep into Cameron's eyes. For an instant, he thought he saw her skin change colour, but realising this was impossible, dismissed it as his imagination – as well as the effects of the half bottle of rice wine they consumed with their meal. However, he did not dismiss the intense feeling of grief he felt as she spoke these last words.

'I *am* sorry, Leyla. I wish your people had never been so hurt...and likewise, the land.' His voice, low and warm, was hesitant, and he turned away as his eyes filled with tears.

For a long moment, Leyla put her hand over his, saying, 'Yes, I know you're sorry, and I also know you care deeply for our land and are doing your best to help it heal...you and your university, and others like you. It's too late for many, but perhaps not for us.'

As she spoke, the first roll of thunder crashed around the small building. They both jumped to their feet and went quickly to the window. Lightning streaked the sky, now dark grey with rain clouds, huge and moving rapidly in from the north-west. The room lights came on as the natural light dimmed. Great sheets of rain swept over the land, bringing the promise of life to the soil and to the dry creek beds. Leyla reached for Cameron's hand. Her scent, of honey myrtle and the sunlight of golden wattle, filled him with a longing so intense he could barely stand. They turned to each other and embraced, gently at first, and then with deep passion.

Leyla rose from their bed. In the moonlight, her skin shone – silver, bright silver. When Cameron awoke to find her gone, he called out to her and she went to his side, but did not resume her shield. He saw her for the first time as she really was: a being he had never imagined could exist. Yet he felt no fear, only awe and rapture at being chosen. Leyla placed her hand against his face: his beautiful face, with its dark brown eyes and golden skin.

'You will soon forget me, my love,' she said. 'When the storm is over, I will be gone, and you will think all this was a dream. You will continue your work, and one day, when you have a child with one of your own kind, as I know you will, she will be one of us. I give you my promise.'

Three days later, when Cameron had completed his survey of the area and left Bunyip Creek, the elders met under the canopy of the redgum tree.

'You let him go,' said the first elder, Leyla's aunt.

'Yes, he is a good man. He will help us and help our land, and through him, another of our kind will walk amongst them. He will remember nothing he shouldn't. I made sure.'

'Good, young Leyla. We are proud of you.'

The children of Bunjil rose and, one by one, left the shelter of the tree, returning to their dwellings, deep beneath the earth where the town of Bunyip Creek once stood.

www.ingramcontent.com/pod-product-compliance
Lightning Source LLC
Chambersburg PA
CBHW060420030726
47495CB00003B/671